Beyond the Dreams We Know

Rachel Neumeier

D1409924

Published by Anara Publishing
2018
Cover Art and Design by WillowRaven
2018

This is a work of fiction. Any resemblance to any real people,
events, or places is entirely coincidental.

CONTENTS

HEART'S DESIRE

This novella takes place a short time after the events of The City in the Lake.

Neill, with his difficult family relationships and strong sense of duty, was always my favorite character in City. *From the first, I knew that any story set in this world would feature Neill.*

-1-

Neill found the great forest unexpectedly looming before him, though he'd gone less than a day's ride from the Lake.

He had come out to ride alone, a rare and treasured opportunity. Ordinarily his days were filled with a continual round of duties and obligations, but the weather had cleared at last after days of rain and mist and more rain. No one had been minded to stay penned up in the damp and chilly Palace when sunlight danced at last across the Lake and the whole Kingdom beckoned. Cassiel had taken one look at the clearing skies and declared a general holiday, riding out with a crowd of companions and attendants and musicians, as well as nearly all the young ladies of the court.

Muriel had gone as well. Neill had seen her among his brother's company. His eye had gone to her as it always did lately, whether he willed it or no. This morning Muriel's amber-gold hair had been braided with green ribbons and coiled in a figure eight at the nape of her neck; her amber-brown skirts looped up and tied with more green ribbons to be out of the way of stirrups and splashing mud. At the moment Neill had glimpsed her, one of her many friends had been handing up a basket, the kind with a woven strap mean to lie across a horse's withers before the saddle so that delicate

1

goods might be carried safely. Muriel had been laughing as she fastened the basket in place and bent to check its contents.

Muriel was always laughing. She was a light-hearted girl; light of heart and easy of temper and quick of tongue, always best pleased when surrounded by friends and merriment. She and all her friends had naturally been delighted with the proposed outing, and why not? A fine spring day, an unplanned holiday, dozens of easy-tempered young men ready to wait on a lady's slightest wish. Not to mention Cassiel himself, free of heart and fancy but certainly intending to marry, and that soon.

Since Cassiel had taken the throne, every father with a marriageable daughter had sought a place for his girl at court; how not? Any family able to bring forward a young lady with looks and breeding and wit and poise had rushed to find her a place. Even among the rest, Muriel stood out for all those qualities. Naturally Cassiel was as much taken with her as anyone—of course he was. Anyone could see it. Neill could hardly mistake it. Especially when his brother had reined his pretty chestnut mare back beside Muriel's bay for one moment and another, delaying the departure of his whole party. Neill had not heard what they said to each other. Commonplaces, no doubt.

Commonplaces were enough to make companionship and then friendship and then courtship, with young people as easy of manner and light of heart as Cassiel and Muriel. Neill knew that very well.

The company had taken hawks and hounds to provide ostensible reason for the outing, but it was hardly a hunting party. No doubt those baskets contained pastries and cream cakes and early strawberries as well as more solid fare, not to mention the pavilions and rugs rolled up and brought along by the servants so that everyone might have a place to lounge in comfort while they enjoyed an early supper. No doubt everyone would have a wonderful time and come trailing home tired and happy through the dusk.

Neill had not been in the least inclined to join his brother's company. He had intended to make use of the day's unexpected quiet to consider one and another of the pressing matters awaiting his attention. There were the accounts from the tinsmiths, which did not seem entirely in accord with Neill's knowledge of the mines; and the chilly, wet spring weather was creating problems for the northern farmers, who sent word that they could hardly get seed in the ground without it rotting. He needed to consider whether to have surplus stores of grain sent from the City to the northern farmers, and if so, which grains. Would they have time to plant and harvest wheat after the weather settled, or would it be better to suggest they put their fields into oats or cowpeas or hay? Or perhaps it would be best to send a broad variety and let each local farmer choose what he would plant according to his knowledge of his own fields and resources.

There were always such urgent matters waiting consideration, and generally a lack of uninterrupted quiet in which to consider them. With so many gone for the day, obviously Neill was presented with an excellent opportunity to complete many important tasks.

But he had stood at the window of his study, which overlooked the Palace's courtyard, and watched his brother's company gather, sweep up seemingly the entire court and all its staff, and ride out with no pomp at all but a great deal of noisy good cheer, Muriel's bay in the fore right along with Cassiel's chestnut. Somehow, even after that clamor had taken itself out of the courtyard and down into the City and away toward the Bridge of Glass, Neill had been unable to bring himself to appreciate the renewed quiet and peace. The tinsmiths' accounts had failed to hold his interest. Even the important questions raised by the conditions facing the northern farmers could not quite capture his attention.

First he tried closing his shutters to shut out the sunlight and the spring breeze and the sparse voices of the much-reduced residents of the Palace. That did not help at all, because he knew that the sunlight and the breeze and all the rest of the world pressed upon his closed shutters. In the end, with an unusual sense of annoyance, he entirely gave up his anticipated day's work, weighted each stack of papers with a fist-sized round stone collected from the shore of the Lake, went down the stairs and through the courtyard, saddled his black mare with his own hands, ignored all cheerful suggestions that he might still catch up with his brother's party, and rode out of the City the other way, toward Tiger Bridge.

The stone tigers that lined the bridge stared unblinking from their plinths into the day and the distance. When Neill drew rein and looked down into the Lake, the reflected tigers wavered gently with the movement of the water so that they seemed to move and breathe and it seemed they might at any moment turn their heads and shrug off their stone and leap from their plinths.

At dusk, perhaps they might. Neill had known it to happen. He had seen stranger things than that.

Tiger Bridge had been decorated with more than tigers. The flowers and leaves once caught in fine relief all along the bridge had blurred with time and weather and the slow encroachment of lichens and mosses. In the reflection of the bridge, of course, all that intricate carving still gleamed as bright and new and delicate as ever. Neill knew exactly what those cleanly carved flowers would feel like under his hands, just as he knew the ghost-sound made by the velvet paws of living tigers.

He looked up deliberately, away from the reflected bridge and the reflected City, and sent his mare forward into an easy swinging canter across the bridge.

Neil had intended...he hardly knew what he had intended. A long slow day's ride with no company but his own, no sound but his own breath and the hoofbeats of his mare, perhaps later a meal at some inn where no one knew him and he knew no one. A word with a farmer here or there, a chance to see for himself how the spring lay on the land.

Certainly Neill had expected to be back before his brother's company. He was not inclined to have Cassiel return to the Palace, ask after him, and discover he was not there. He did not want his brother to think, *Neill went out after all...But not with me?*

Cassiel would not ask him why. But Neill did not wish to see that question lingering unasked in his brother's eyes. Especially when he could hardly frame an answer, even to himself.

Muriel had come to court only this past winter. A girl, hardly a woman; she was not quite twenty—more than ten years younger than Neill; much more of an age with Cassiel. Her father, a wellborn man of the City, had undoubtedly had an eye for the new young King when he had encouraged his daughter to seek a place at court. But it was Muriel's own skills, not her autumn-colored hair nor her dancing eyes, that had won her that place. Her beautiful penmanship and quick wits, her friendly manner and clever turns of phrase had earned her a place among the small army of scribes and secretaries without whom the business of the Palace and the City and the Kingdom would immediately become hopelessly confused.

So it was that Neill had met her, for all that business passed under his eye. All those scribes and secretaries ultimately worked for him, and so it was his duty to become acquainted with them all.

It had been no chore to become acquainted with Muriel. There was no falsity to her; she was genuinely a cheerful, friendly girl, even with Neill, who did not encourage familiarity from any of the staff or the servants or the courtiers.

Of course she had happily joined the company so enthusiastically making plans for the day's pleasure. She was too friendly and warm-natured a girl to hold herself aloof. Neill could perfectly well have joined them himself. He knew that. Remaining solitary today had been his own choice.

He had meant to ride alone. But he had not intended to ride all the way to the edge of the great forest, far less pass into its chancy reaches.

Neill drew rein where the sunlight gave way to the reaching green shadows of the forest. A path began not far away; he marked that at once, without surprise. Of course there was a path. He would hardly have found the forest here before him, less than a day's ride from the Lake, if there were not going to be a path. Though from his vantage here it seemed hardly wider than a fox's track, he knew that if he nudged his mare that way, he would find it wide enough for a horse and rider. More than likely it would widen still further if he went on out of sight of the edge. All ways that led into the forest were easy. Only later, once one had gone farther in, would a man find the way becoming steep and crooked and difficult.

Even if one kept to the true road, obstacles might well wait for a traveler. A little track like that one...obstacles were inevitable, on such a path as that.

His mare, plainly wondering at Neill's irresolution, swiveled an ear toward him and took a step toward the visible path. She checked at his light touch on the rein, but tipped both her ears back in a sharp comment about a rider who did not know his own mind. Neill had to chuckle, though he had not seen much amusing in the day before that moment. His mare had better sense than he did himself, sometimes.

The mare's name was Raven, which suited her as she was as wise as the bird from which she took her name. She was not large, but pretty and well made, with sloping shoulders and straight legs. She was not young, for Neill had picked her out from among the rest many years ago, but she was still swift of foot and sound of wind. She was not precisely good-natured, for she had too much wit and too keen a humor to allow docility. But she had good judgment and good sense, and she never put a foot wrong on broken ground or misjudged a jump.

When she tucked her chin and took another step toward that trail, Neill let her go, though he hardly knew even yet why he was of a mind to humor either the mare or the unpredictable whims of the great forest. Except that he was of no mood to turn and ride away, back to the City and the Palace and the endless round of his waiting duties.

Cassiel would no doubt have forbidden him, if he had been here. He would declare Neill indispensable and bid him keep to the sunlit farmlands. But if Neill were truly indispensable, that would speak ill indeed of his ability to train the many functionaries of the Palace who among them actually saw to all the important daily tasks that had to be overseen.

Among them, various scribes and secretaries. And among that number, of course, one particular woman with hair like autumn leaves and quick humor and a generous nature that won her friends as easily as breathing.

A woman such as Muriel might someday become more nearly essential to the smooth functioning of the staff than Neill himself, for folk obeyed him out of respect and a little fear, but they would listen to Muriel and follow her suggestions because they wished to please her.

Cassiel could do far worse for himself than a girl like that. Muriel would make a fine queen. Neill knew that perfectly well.

On consideration, Neill thought the staff and the court—and his brother most of all—might very well spare his own presence for some little time. Besides, he was his father's son, and so perhaps had less need to be wary of the forest than others might. So he rode forward, hardly considering his reasons or the reasons that might have brought the edge of the forest to this place before him. His heart beat more quickly as he passed into the green shade, but he did not look back.

2

Eliet rode away from her brother's farm in the grey light that came before dawn, along the road, west.

She rode away from her home while the mists still lay silvery and cold over the wide pastures and the owls called from the barn where they nested, and she drew rein at the edge of the great forest just as the first rays of the sun peeked above the horizon behind her.

She had not wanted to leave the farm that was her home. She had been born there; had lived her whole childhood there; had grown into a woman there. She had married there, beneath the big oak that stood in lonely splendor a stone's throw from the brood mares' paddock. They had draped the oak's branches with streamers of sweetly fragrant honeysuckle and mignonette, and Eliet had stood up before everyone, blushing and shy, to trade marriage vows with Chares, second son of the finest town weaver. Eliet had been eighteen, heartlight and happy. She had believed Chares the handsomest man in the Kingdom, and the kindest. She had believed herself blessed by fortune, lucky beyond measure to have been the girl who'd caught his eye, lucky again that Chares loved horses better than wool and was glad to leave his father's house and come to her own family's farm. She liked visiting town well enough—Brewer's Vale was small, but prosperous; there were two dozen shops there, in addition to the market twice a month. But she loved her family's farm better. She lost nothing by marrying and gained everything, and when she thought of the future, she had only imagined it would be as sweet as the past.

Six years later she had stood alone among the crowd of her family and his and watched as Chares had been buried in her family's plot, marked off from farmyard and pasture and garden by its hedge of roses and spirea and lilac. Her mother's headstone stood there, and her father's, and her uncle's, and others. Losing each of them had been a grief to those they left behind, but they had all died old, leaving children behind to mourn them.

Her husband's carved headstone was not the same. His stone had been raised up beside the small stones that belonged to his sons, Eliet's tiny twin sons, that had neither of them lived to draw a hundred breaths, and the one that belonged to their little daughter, who had lived only long enough to give everyone hope she might not die.

On that day, standing silent witness to her husband's burial, Eliet had laid down her heart among those headstones. She had sworn she would never weep again. She would never love again, never look at another man, above all never bear another child in her body. She was done with love, and loss, and mourning.

She smiled wryly now, here at the edge of the great forest, to think of that stone-hearted certainty. From seven years farther on, she could see she had been very nearly as young and foolish at four-and-twenty as she had been at eighteen. She had mistaken grief for insight, but deep grief was no more a font of wisdom than happiness.

No doubt like most women—aye, and most men—she would manage to be one kind of fool or another all her life. If not necessarily young.

Eliet curved a hand across her softly rounded belly and looked as far as she could see along the road that led forward from the ordinary countryside and in among the great trees. She could not see very far, both because bright morning had not yet broken through this misty dawn and because the road curved gently as it entered the forest. But she did not turn to look behind her. She did not want to see the road that led back.

It seemed she had become the sort of fool who would not look back at family and home and all her familiar life, but only forward, along the road that would lead her...she did not know to what place or what fate that road might lead her. But she hoped. For a new life. For her heart's desire: a child that might live. For a daughter or a son who would belong to the future and owe nothing to lost dreams and old sorrows.

Not that she knew how to build that new life for herself, with or without a child. At thirty-and-one, she was surely old enough to know better than to ride away from her old life when she had no idea how to build a new one. Old enough to know that even if she gained her heart's desire, there would be no easy answers and no smooth path into the future.

But she had left her old life behind, and now she was here, and she knew she would go on and not back.

She was that kind of fool.

Besides, though she did not wish to leave her home, even less could she endure to stay.

This was the season of apple blossoms and buzzing bees, the season of gamboling lambs and kid goats and, on her brother's farm, unsteady long-legged foals. They were fine foals this spring: one colt that was bay with two white feet and a filly that was chestnut with a star on her forehead and a second filly that had been born black but would probably turn gray. Eliet's brother, Tomas, had been very pleased that two of the three were fillies, particularly the likely gray because her mother was the best of all his mares. The mare's name was Fly By Night's Mourning Dove, after her mother, Fly By Night, a long-legged black mare who could not be beaten over a half-mile at either the trot or the gallop. Dove was not the equal of her mother for racing, but she was a fine tall mare, the color of winter ice, with a pretty head and smooth gaits.

Eliet's mount was neither so pretty nor so smooth-gaited, though he was also a son of Fly By Night. From his warmblood sire, he had inherited heavy bone and powerful quarters, a thick neck and a plain head. But from that warmblood stallion he had also inherited a kind eye, good sense, and a steady disposition. Like Dove, he was gray, but he was darker: the pewter-gray coloring of a stormy sky, shading to black on his face and feet. His name was Fly By Night's Ponderous Thunderhead, which was a mouthful and a half. Eliet called him Ponder, which suited him much better. He was a sensible beast, willing and good-natured, not likely to spook or shy at anything no matter how astonishing. That was why Eliet had chosen him from all the horses she might have taken, for all he was neither the handsomest nor the swiftest, and far from the youngest. She patted his neck now, while they both peered ahead past the edge of the forest and along the dim and misty road.

Eliet patted the horse's neck again and said aloud, "Good

sense, Ponder. That's what we need now."

The gelding stood foursquare with his ears pricked forward, interested and not in the least nervous. So how could Eliet be so poor-spirited as to turn back? When she spoke to him, he leaned gently against the bit and swiveled an ear back toward her, wondering why she hesitated.

The nearest edge of the great forest always lay near the farm, or almost always. On this misty morning, she had not quite been certain she would find the forest at all. Almost she had thought she would quietly saddle Ponder and quietly lead him out through the yard and quietly mount and ride out the gate and to the track and then at last down the road to the east, and yet find nothing but pastures and ordinary woodlands and perhaps a neighbor's farm, though ordinarily no other farms lay between theirs and the forest. It was a capricious forest, she knew. Everyone knew that.

If she had been forced to turn back in defeat, her return to her brother's farm could never have been so quiet. It she turned back now, having ridden straight up to the forest's edge and then lost her nerve, it would be well into morning before she reached the stable yard. Everyone would be out about their early tasks. Everyone would see her come up the road. They would have missed her. Tomas, if no one else, would have realized she'd taken not only Ponder but also a loaf of bread and a small round of cheese and a bit of salt pork and a generous measure of grain. He might be able to tell she had taken a change of smallclothes and her second-best dress and the stub of a candle. He would know perfectly well what she had tried to do. The only thing he wouldn't have guessed was why.

He would ask her. He would assuredly ask her. She was no longer a shy young girl, but she flinched from imagining how *that* would go.

That was the thought that at last made her lift the reins and click her tongue, signaling Ponder that yes, he might go forward into the mist beneath the great trees. He strode out with a will, finding nothing to fear in the green shade or the drifting mist. He was cheerful by nature, was Ponder: cheerful and willing, pleased enough to take an unfamiliar road. *He* was not afraid of what might lie ahead. The interested way he looked from side to side, fearless and alert, put heart into her.

Mist had drifted over all the pastures and the low-lying meadows alongside the road, and over the pond and the brook which fed it. But the mist that drifted between the ancient trees was heavier, colder, and more secretive. Eliet flinched from it as she might have flinched from cobwebs, wiping her hands across her face. The moisture clung. The very air was different; no breeze came here beneath the trees, and the air smelled damp and shadowy and green, as though even at noon sunlight might never make its way past the high crowns. She could see only a little distance before them, and when she turned uneasily to look behind, less far still. Yet the road ran smooth before them, and Ponder flicked his ears and strode along with his head high, eager to see where this new road might lead, not in the least worried. Slowly Eliet relaxed, comforted by his evident ease and by the failure of anything exciting to appear out of the mist.

Ordinary woodlands stood everywhere, stands of timber along hillsides and across rocky slopes between one farm and the next, between one village and the next. Folk gathered dry wood and herbs in the woods, and berries in their season, and nuts in theirs, and set snares for unwary rabbits. Those woodlands were nothing like this. The great forest had depths no one had ever seen, mysteries no one had ever encountered. Every tale Eliet had ever heard came back to her, especially the frightening ones.

To pass through the forest safely, a traveler must keep to the road. Eliet did not merely desire to pass through, but to gain her heart's desire. But she did not know what that would require. She did not know whether she would have the courage to leave the road, whatever wonders she might glimpse past the boles of the trees.

Wonders aplenty were said to be found in this forest: tall slender towers hiding treasures within, guarded by dragons coiled around their foundations; trees with hundreds of lit lanterns dangling from their branches instead of fruit; bottomless pools that reflected not only the sky or the overhanging trees but also the past and the future.

Eliet had heard many tales. All of them came to mind

now. She had heard that in the forest, a traveler might spy a small homey cottage where he might hope for succor. But instead of finding some kind goodwife or woodsman, he would find a family of bears or wolves living there, who would smile with sharp white teeth to see their supper walk up to their home.

Or a traveler too wise to approach such a cottage might instead glimpse a pearl-colored stag with antlers of gold, that would sing in a beautiful voice and try to lure her into an endless pursuit. Or a boar that spoke in all the tongues of the world and would answer any riddle put to him, always honestly but never helpfully. Or a falcon with feathers of fire, so bright its endless burning could light any darkness.

Eliet did not intend to approach any tower, dragon-guarded or not; nor be tempted by any cottage, however weary she might grow; nor carelessly intrude on any pool or glade or creature she might encounter. She was surely carrying enough trouble with her; enough and more than enough. She didn't wish to offer any other a foothold in her life. Yet at the same time, she hoped she would have the wisdom to recognize what chance might offer, and the courage to pursue it, and then the strength to meet whatever challenge she encountered.

She knew, or at least she had heard and she believed, that the journey along this road's dim reaches might take days or weeks, sometimes even months, for that was part of the forest's caprice. But she hoped that for her, with Ponder's easy company and long stride, the journey would take only a day or two or three, or at least not much longer. It was hard to imagine Ponder stirring himself to pursue a stag of any color, no matter how beautifully it sang; and he would surely know better than to walk carelessly up to a cottage occupied by wolves or bears. For him, perhaps the road too would prove cooperative and easy. Then she might find what she sought and seize it and ride on, through the forest and out the other side, to the City at the heart of the Kingdom, where she might build her new life out of whatever chance and wit and courage put into her way.

But for a long time Eliet had no sense that they were making any progress at all. The great trees stood shadowy and secret to either side, veiled by the mist, unchanging whenever she looked about her. The road curved gently up low hills and down again, and sometimes it led her around a soft curve to the right hand or the left, but always the great trees seemed the same; and the light neither brightened nor changed, and she saw neither wonders nor anything to fear. Indeed, she began to be more bored than anxious, and watched Ponder's gently nodding head and small alert ears rather than the forest which seemed always the same.

Then at last, after a time that might have been hours or even days, without any particular sense of anything changing, she realized that the mist had after all lifted and cleared and that small dapples of sunlight now glimmered on the road and among the trees to either side of the road, and that the air had grown warm. She found she could see much farther into the forest to the left hand and the right. Then of course she could hardly resist looking, first one way and then the other, searching for towers or white stags or any other wonders.

She saw nothing but endless trees.

The trees that pressed close to the road were so large that it would have taken half a dozen men to wrap their arms about their gnarled trunks. Each looked a thousand years old, and probably was. Many were so tall that often the first branches stretched out far above Eliet's head, so she hoped she would have no reason to try to climb one. Even if she stood on Ponder's back, she thought she would be unable to reach even the lowest of those branches. Far above, the mist still drifted here and there.

The leaves in this season were new and soft, green above and silver underneath. In shape the leaves were much like those of oaks. But the leaves of these trees entirely lacked the reddish tint of new oak leaves. The light that filtered past and through them was a pure and delicate green. That light almost made Eliet think of what it might be like to ride beneath the waters of a lake, with silvery fishes overhead instead of birds. Though at first she saw no birds, even when she looked. But once she began to listen, she thought she heard one, not too far off, low to the ground. Its call was a little like that of a towhee, but with a deeper tone and a musical ripple of notes at the end. A little later, as she continued to look up and around, she saw a little bird, an ordinary nuthatch, making its way headfirst down the trunk of one of the great trees. The birds, visible and invisible, made her feel happier, like she rode through a real place and not a dream forest drenched in silence and peril.

In the autumn, the leaves of these trees turned flame orange and gold and burning red, and even now glints of all those colors showed on the earth between the great knobby roots that thrust up. Spring flowers also spangled the forest floor: six-petaled opalescent white flowers smaller than Eliet's thumbnail opened in little clusters above bluish palm-shaped foliage; here and there sky-blue flowers shaped like bells, streaked with pink inside their throats, quivered atop stalks as long as her hand. Colonies of mayapples, familiar and comforting, spread the wide jagged parasols of their leaves above their single white flowers. These too put heart into her. She would not have dared pick even a common mayapple, would not have dared leave the road to gather any flowers, no matter how unusual or lovely, but the flowers, like the birds, made the forest feel more welcoming.

Ponder might have felt the same, or might have responded to Eliet's gradual relaxation. Either way he shifted from his easy trot to a swinging walk, unhurried but more ground-covering than it seemed.

Eliet saw neither bear nor wolf and no cottage where either might lair. She saw neither a white stag nor an ordinary hind, neither a rabbit nor a squirrel nor any common woodland creature. But at least there were the birds. An ordinary-seeming wren called from a twig overhead, and far above she heard the shrill cry of a hawk.

Ponder strode along with a will, tireless on this wide and easy road. Up a long, low slope and down again; high-stepping over the occasional tumbling stream that crossed the road or even more occasional heavy roots that had thrust up across the traveler's path. In an ordinary woodland, there would be fallen trees here and there, including some that had fallen across the road. In an ordinary woodland, travelers had to now and then make a new way around a fallen tree, or waggoneers had to get out axes to clear such obstacles out of the way. Eventually Eliet realized the oddity that here in this forest no trees appeared to have fallen at all, except long ago, for very occasionally she glimpsed a long low shape, moss-covered and gently moldering away. But these were never close to the road.

"The road is *meant* for travelers, of course," she murmured to herself, out loud. One of Ponder's ears swiveled back toward her, in case she meant to say anything useful about apples or chunks of carrot or anything else of interest to a sensible horse.

Then a voice said, near at hand and utterly unexpected, "Certainly many travelers find it more comfortable to think so."

Eliet nearly fell off Ponder's back, which would have been deeply embarrassing as well as awkward and possibly bruising. She grabbed his black mane to steady herself, looking wildly around to find the speaker. Images of boars who spoke in riddles and golden-antlered stags tumbled through her mind, but at first she saw no one, not even an enchanted boar or stag. Ponder had halted when she scrambled for balance, waiting for Eliet to figure out whether she was frightened, or should be. His ears were hard forward with interest, and though he blew lightly through flared nostrils, he seemed more curious than alarmed. He lifted one of his front feet an inch or so and then the other, setting each hoof in turn down exactly in the same place from which he had lifted it, as though he were considering whether he should take alarm and bolt, but thought, on the whole, that there was no need.

Following the direction of her horse's attention, Eliet at last found the one who had so startled her.

It was a large serpent, larger than any rat snake or corn snake she had ever glimpsed in the barns and stables. If it had uncoiled itself, she guessed it would be longer than she was tall—possibly much longer. Its head, broader than her hand, did not have the blocky triangular shape of a viper. It was jet black, with an intricate lacey pattern of gold decorating the scales of its throat and belly. Its eyes were a rich, molten gold, like the light of the sun caught in an autumn leaf, with narrow pupils like slits into night. The serpent was coiled about the branch of a tree beside the road, an unusually low branch but not too near. It was a little above the level of Ponder's head, nearly at eye level for Eliet, but far enough away that it could not possibly strike either of them.

Now that she saw it, she couldn't understand how she hadn't realized it was there long before, for the serpent was by no means camouflaged against the gray bark. She knew of no serpent of such coloring among the common snakes of woodland and field and stable, but then she already knew this serpent was none of the common sorts. Besides, though Ponder would trample a snake if he could, he did not seem alarmed by this one.

She knew at once that it was the serpent that had spoken to her, even though she had never heard any tale of serpents that spoke in human language. She wasn't certain whether she should answer, or whether it might be more prudent to lower her head, fix her gaze on the road, and ride on by as though she had never heard a thing.

Except no tale she could remember, of any of the wonders or terrors of this forest, suggested that it would be better to pretend the wonders and terrors were not *there*. And so far, at least, the serpent did not seem precisely unfriendly. Though there had been nothing friendly or reassuring about what it had said, either.

She managed at last, in a voice only a little too quick and high in pitch, "Is the road then *not* meant for travelers?"

The serpent tilted its broad, flat head, regarding her from unreadable golden eyes. "Is the earth meant to yield a harvest of wheat? Are the summer rains meant to succor the thirsty? Does the sun rise so that those who need light may see?"

Eliet blinked. She thought all those things were true, except that she thought she heard mockery in the serpent's tone, if not malice. This made her wonder. Its voice was sweet and husky, not as she would have imagined the voice of a serpent. Its flickering tongue was long and black, and its delicate fangs, visible as it spoke, as long as a woman's thumb. She said stubbornly, "No one makes the earth or the rain or the sun, but a road is a made thing. It *is* meant for the use of travelers, or there is no reason for it to be made at all."

The serpent asked her, "Is a child born to be a consolation to its mother?"

Eliet stared at it. Ponder dipped his head, mouthing the bit uncomfortably, and she realized she had tightened her grip on the reins. She eased her hold and tried to answer sensibly, and with reasonable courtesy considering to whom she spoke, "A child may be a consolation, but that is not why it is born."

"Just so," said the serpent in its sweet voice. "Yet a child *is* both a burden and a consolation. A grief and a misery; a comfort and a delight. Or so it may be. Even now you carry within you a child aborning, and is this not a burden and a terror and a solace and a plea? I will give you advice if you wish it."

If she had been on her own, on foot, Eliet might have been too afraid to listen. But every word the serpent spoke was true—and she had come into the forest to find her heart's desire. When she had eased her hold on the reins, Ponder had lifted his nose toward the serpent, his attitude all of curiosity and friendly interest. Eliet took courage from that. She set one hand flat on his neck, drawing comfort from his warm strength. She said firmly, "I would be glad to hear your advice, if the price you ask for it is not too dear."

The serpent tilted its narrow head, watching her with its unblinking golden eyes. "Ah, you are sparing of coin. Wise the frugal heart, so long as thrift does not take council of parsimony and become meanness. But I ask nothing for my advice—this time."

Definitely that was mockery. Eliet did not know how to answer it. She said merely, "Coin I might offer, if I knew what manner of coin might be demanded. But as you ask nothing, I would gladly hear your advice."

"Very wise," said the serpent. "Then it is this: Fear may be a useful guide, but it is a poor master. Credulity is dangerous, but self-deception is worse. Kindness is not to be despised even when it costs nothing, but generosity is greater when it bears a cost. It is in giving away your heart's desire that you will receive it back again, twofold."

Eliet blinked. "I will remember," she said, which seemed a safe promise. She nodded her head deeply in respect, "Thank you." Courtesy was always wise; she knew that. Everyone knew it was best to be polite to any person or creature one encountered in the great forest, and everyone knew it was best to be cautious as well. *Tell no lies and make no promises,* that was what Eliet had heard all her life—what all children were taught, but especially those who lived near the forest.

The serpent turned its narrow head, fixing her with one golden eye. "That would be best," it said, sounding somehow amused and kindly and mocking and just a little malicious all at the same time. Before Eliet could think how to answer, it uncoiled itself and slid around its branch, up and around the rough-barked trunk of the tree, into the shifting shadows of the young leaves, and disappeared.

Ponder whuffled through his nose in the way of a horse who isn't certain about something that's just happened but isn't much concerned about it. He tipped his ears back toward Eliet, shifted his weight, sighed, and began to dig a small hole in the packed earth of the road with the tip of one hoof to show her that he would rather go on than stand still.

"Me, too," muttered Eliet, not very forcefully. She continued to stare up into the green heights for another moment, but she could see nothing. Nor could she hear anything. Not even one of the little birds that had comforted her through the morning.

Was it morning still? Or noon? Or later? She was hungry, she realized, but the quality of the light did not seem to have changed and she did not want to stop here in this place anyway. "All right, walk on," she said to Ponder, relaxing the reins and sitting forward a little, and the horse strode forward with a will.

3

The forest in early spring was less forbidding than it might seem later in the summer. The leaves were still small and pale silvery-green, and the shade they cast lay lighter than it would later. Sunlight made its way through the high canopy of twisted branches, stippling the earth and fallen leaves, picking out the occasional clump of mayapple or the tiny four-petaled white flowers of woodruff.

As Neill had expected, the path was wider than a first glance would have suggested, and widened further once his mare turned decisively along the first curve, out of sight of the edge. He did glance back then, but already the broad sunlit farmlands through which he had been riding had fallen away, out of sight. He saw nothing but the gray boles of trees, most too large around for a man or even two to compass; and the shifting shadows and dappled light that came through the branches; and last autumn's leaves scattered over all the ground and over the path as well, muffling the sound of his mare's hooves.

The path turned and turned again, leading around one massive gnarled trunk and another. Then it tumbled abruptly down a series of steep, rocky ledges, crossed a narrow creek, and climbed again on the other side to run along the top of a winding ridge. It was rougher going than any proper road would have offered, and any horse larger or less neat-footed than Raven might have had some difficulty navigating it. But, though the mare laid her ears back and minced sideways several steps in expressive comment when he put her at that course, once she consented to go, she hopped down the ledges as lightly as a deer, jumped the creek, scrambled up the slope on the other side, and finally turned to trot along the ridge. She picked her feet up higher than strictly necessary as she went, because despite her display of irritation, she had enjoyed that slithery course and now looked forward to what else she might find. Certainly she found this path more interesting than any road through farmlands.

The forest was filled with marvels and curiosities and all manner of unpredictable dangers, all of which one was especially likely to encounter if one ventured off the road. Every child knew it. Neill certainly knew it. Drink from the wrong pool and he might turn into a fox with a golden pelt or a swan with the voice of a flute; taste the wrong fruit and he might fall into an enchanted sleep for a year and a day; unwisely offend the wrong creature and he might find a finger missing, the bones worked into a flute whose playing he would hear in his dreams for the rest of his life. Neill had heard tales that began—or ended—in each of those ways. All those tales were true. He was not afraid of what he might encounter...not precisely afraid. Or no more than was wise. He knew what he had done, entering the forest when it had put itself in his way. He was prepared to be cautious. And polite.

Yet for a long time he saw nothing out of the way. No alluring pool with ferns trailing their fronds in its opaque water, no mysterious tower guarded by dragons or griffons, no strange moss-draped statue with unreadable letters carved around its base. Neither beast nor bird; only occasional butterflies and once or twice a rustle in the fallen leaves that might have been a lizard or a mouse or some other such small creature. Neill might have turned back—he considered turning back—except that he felt somehow disinclined to check his mare, who still went forward with quick light steps and an inquisitive air.

Besides, though the path here was wide and easy to follow, he doubted he would find it so cooperative if he turned back.

And besides that...besides that, he had deliberately chosen to ride into the forest, and even though he did not know precisely what had prodded him forward, he did not like to look a fool by turning about before he found that out.

The trees gradually increased in girth and grew more contorted in form. Twisted branches often stretched low over the path so that he had to duck low to pass beneath them, or dismount and lead Raven. One hill supplanted another, so he rode more often up or down than along any level way. Yet the path remained clear. Twice it divided, one branch wandering more uphill and the other tending more downward. Each time

Neill, guided by no impulse he understood, took the way that seemed narrower and less traveled, and each time that track tended downward. The earth became marshy beneath his mare's hooves, and they began to pass shallow pools and sloughs. Streamers and curtains of pale mosses festooned the branches that overhung the path, and knobby roots reached out of the earth so that a less neat-footed horse might have stumbled. Raven stepped delicately, unalarmed by the uneven footing, even when she must splash through one or another pool.

Here the deep quiet of higher ground gave way to a hum of insects, though so far neither flies nor mosquitoes plagued Neill or his mare. Still, it was not a comfortable place. The draperies of moss swayed in a breeze he did not feel and blocked his view, the splash and soft thump of his mare's steps sounded overloud, the contorted shapes of the trees seemed to remind him of half-glimpsed shadows dimly recalled from uneasy dreams.

By this time the light was dimming. Somewhere high above the green canopy, the sun was sinking low. If the shadows in this place had been more distinct, they would have grown long and dark. But here in these damp bottomlands of the forest, the light was not clear enough even to cast shadows. It had simply become twilight, though no doubt for a man outside the forest the day was not yet done.

This was not a good trail for a fast pace, but Raven was walking faster now, responding to Neill's growing tension. He could not quite recollect what impulse might have led him to turn down and down again when he might have climbed instead, perhaps breaking clear of the deeper forest into less close-grown heights. Now every direction seemed the same. The marshy bottomlands stretched out flat and secretive in every direction.

Then Neill realized that the path too had disappeared, and that truly, every direction seemed precisely the same, and none in the least welcoming.

Raven checked as his hand tightened on the rein. But when he gave no further signal—he had not even clearly meant to draw her to a halt—she tossed her head, irritated, and struck forward again, choosing her own way.

Seeing no reason to signal her one way or another, Neill let her go as she would, and found that after all the mare had not lost the path even when he himself had mistaken it. Raven skirted the low branches of one enormous moss-draped tree, and then another, and he saw, as though his gaze focused for the first time, how the lacey foliage of meadowsweet and angelica spread out to either side and the path ran clear between. Though he did not trust this track, the sense of relief was immediate. Neill found himself smiling despite the fading light and the increasingly pressing prospect of a damp and chilly night. The forest might be deceptive, but he trusted Raven to find her way even when he had lost his; and if he had neither candle nor candlelighter, nor bread nor beef, nor soap nor spare shirt, at least he did carry, in his mare's saddlebags, a few handfuls of grain for her and a packet of dried apples they might share. Damp and chilly the night might be, and he no longer so young as to think nothing of a sleepless night, but at thirty-and-four, he was not yet so aged he could not bear with minor privation if an ill-judged whim carried him out of his customary round.

Then the mare suddenly planted her feet, jerking her head up in sharp unease, so that Neill straightened his back and peered ahead, laying a hand to the short knife at his belt—not an effective weapon, but the only one he had—and followed the direction of her gaze.

Not far ahead, a short way off the track, with a narrower path leading to it in a long curve, a door stood open, with lantern light shining through it into the gathering dusk. But this door was set not into any ordinary house or tower, but directly into the massive trunk of a great tree. The tree was even larger than was the general order for the forest; Neill guessed that ten men together could not have stretched their arms around it. Inside, if the whole thing was hollow, it must be larger than any ordinary hut; larger than many well-kept cottages.

Once his mare had drawn his attention to the tree and the door and the shining lantern light, Neill had no idea how he had come so close without noticing. He was surprised, though in this forest, he should know better than to be surprised by anything. Now he had finally seen that doorway, brightly lit in the gloom, he thought nothing had ever looked more welcoming. The chill in the air was sharpening, and as the sun sank lower, all around came the piping of frogs and the whine of insects and the muted, distant splash of some creature larger than either. But the lantern light glowed steady and warm, clear promise of shelter.

Neill knew perfectly well what risk a traveler bore, entering any such place in this forest. But, he thought, he had already accepted this risk. The forest had put itself in his way and offered him a path. When he had permitted his mare to take that path, he had tacitly accepted what would come of that choice. He did not look for safety, or comfort, or ease. But he hoped...he thought perhaps he hoped for wisdom, and for a clearer understanding of...something. Some question he had not framed clearly, even to himself.

When he touched the reins, Raven went forward without hesitation. All around the sloughs stretched out, pools of black standing water as reflective as mirrors. But the mare's hooves struck a more solid beat as she came up an imperceptible rise to drier ground and then to the great tree and the open door. Paving stones had been laid in an arc outside the doorway, butter-yellow in the lamplight; the wood of the doorway was smooth and irregular, as it will grow around the place where a branch has been lost. The door itself, standing open, was smooth as well, but neither painted nor polished.

Neill dismounted and stood for a moment, the reins gripped in his hand. He could see nothing of the interior of the tree. The light that shone out of it was opaque as water.

He had decided already. He had decided the moment he guided his mare into the forest. He stepped forward, into the light, into the tree, leading Raven because he certainly would not leave her behind.

The light opened up as he walked forward, warm and welcoming. Neill had half expected to find that, outward appearances notwithstanding, he had stepped into a great castle or fortress: something much larger and more impressive than any tree could possibly contain. But this was not so. The space was impressive for a hollow tree, but a hollow within a tree it clearly was. There was a single room, unevenly round, walled with the smooth wood of the tree. Behind him still stood the door through which he had entered and, on the other side of the room, a round shuttered window offered the only other apparent means of access. Above, the hollow interior of the tree extended as far as he could see; underfoot, the floor was covered with mats of woven grasses and one simple rag rug of faded blue and red and yellow.

Straight ahead, standing a little before the far wall, stood a small but well-made iron stove. Coals glowed within and the black metal poured out heat. Upon the stove sat a wide pot steaming with savory broth and a smaller one containing something fragrant with honey and some unfamiliar spice, floral and warm. To one side of the stove stood a curved table with a short bench beneath it and a chair at its head; to the other side a wide sideboard held a large enameled bowl of water and a narrow flat cake of soap.

Wooden bowls were stacked upon the table, with wooden spoons laid out beside the bowls; a round loaf of bread and a bowl of butter and a crock of dark red berry preserves had been laid out beside the stack of bowls. A pewter pitcher beaded with moisture sat on the table as well, with several wooden mugs beside it.

Across from the table, on the other side of the tree, a thin gray cord delineated a generous stall spread with hay and wood shavings, with hay hanging in a net and water in a narrow bucket. Raven leaned in that direction, nothing hesitating, laying her ears flat in acerbic comment when Neill hesitated to let her go.

No one else seemed to be present. No one occupied the chair or stirred the pots on the stove. Certainly there was no place in this singular room where anyone might stay out of sight. After a moment, Neill led his mare into the stall, stripped her bridle and saddle off, laid these aside, and gathered up a handful of straw with which to rub her down. After which he spotted a shelf holding everything he needed: brush and curry comb and hoof pick. So he went over Raven with these tools as she lipped the hay out of the net and nudged around in the straw to find stray wisps.

Then he left her, not without a backward glance. But his mare seemed content where she stood. So he washed his hands in the basin and went to examine the pots simmering on the stove.

The broth proved to be a soup of chicken with carrots and parsnips and spring onions. The other pot contained a thick, creamy porridge of oats sweetened generously with honey and flavored with that unfamiliar floral spice. Neill ladled up generous portions of both soup and porridge, sliced half the round loaf of bread—dark and moist, it was studded with raisins and walnuts—and pulled out the bench to sit, wary of claiming the single chair.

The food was good, if simple, and as he was hungry, Neill made a satisfying meal. No one came or went while he ate, but as he spread a second slice of bread with butter and berry preserves, he became aware that the chair was occupied.

At once Neill set down the bread and straightened on his bench, folding his hands on the table. The appearance of his host had startled him, but he was not actually surprised, and after a moment he said steadily, "I thank you, sir, for your hospitality. I hope I have not presumed upon your goodwill in availing myself of the comforts here, which I took to be offered to a weary traveler."

The man had come without notice or warning, but he seemed ordinary enough to a first glance, and a second. This was not an impression Neill trusted in the least. The man appeared old; he was white-haired, with a lean, seamed face. His mouth was thin-lipped, his nose narrow and arched, his eyes deep-set and dark. He seemed in some way half-familiar, which was a second impression Neill did not trust. Whether he was truly a man or some other manner of creature entirely was impossible to know. If he were a man, then whether he was merely old or actually ancient was hard to guess. In either case, whether he was unwelcoming or merely cool-tempered was also difficult to judge. Certainly he did not smile, but regarded Neill from beneath bushy white brows.

But though the man did not smile, he flicked a dismissive hand at Neill's careful speech. "Of course you have presumed, Lord Bastard. From your first step within the bounds of the forest. But you are welcome here, and I ask no price for supper or shelter for yourself or your mare. Yet I doubt you came into the forest intending only to seek a plain supper and simple lodgings."

26

Neill had already framed and discarded several guesses about who this person might be—a mage, no. Neill knew several mages, and this man had something of the manner but nothing of the...the *feel*, for want of a better term. Whatever their other qualities, mages possessed an underlying dispassion. This man...he neither smiled nor frowned, but Neill felt even in so brief a time that dispassion was not his ruling nature.

The white hair...that might be a sign of more than age. But whoever this man might be, Neill did not believe there was even a remote possibility that a man of his mother's people would be found here, in this peculiar home, in the midst of the thickest part of the great forest. No.

A face of the forest itself...that seemed more likely. Yet there was also that feeling of familiarity, of half-recognition.

He said, "I think...I hoped to find the answer to a question I do not know how to ask."

The man lifted white brows. "Indeed, Lord Bastard. Wisdom is not a treasure to be tripped over in the dark, nor a prize to be won. It is born of experience carved from the past and carried into the future. But perhaps you may discover at least the question you wish to ask. Or perhaps you may make yourself in some manner useful. One never knows what task one might discover awaiting one's hand. Awaiting one of your blood in particular, perhaps."

"Indeed, sir?" Perhaps this white-haired strong-featured man owned something of Neill's mother's look after all. Neill laid his hands flat on the table, preparing to get to his feet, collect his mare, and see whether it might yet be possible to retreat from this place. It seemed unlikely, but if he could not find the way out, perhaps Raven might. He did not yet wish he carried a weapon, and hoped that he might not soon wish for one. He asked plainly, "Would it be my father's blood or my mother's that is at question? I very much doubt whether I should feel inclined to draw upon my mother's heritage."

A piercing look from under white brows. "I am glad to hear it, Lord Neill. I doubt you would be called upon to do so. Certainly not within the deep heart of the forest. Least of all by me."

Well. Mage or ordinary man or face of the forest, that

seemed clear enough. Neill thought he heard an edge of mockery to those words, but not deceit. He let himself lean back a little on his bench. "Then I should be curious to discover what task might lie waiting for me. As my father's son, I have no doubt I will be willing to perform some small commission in service to the great forest that lies at the heart of the Kingdom."

"Indeed." The old man regarded Neill with piercing clarity, but added only, "The morning will be time enough to seek such a task. No doubt dawn and day are better suited to pursue a quest."

Neill would rather have discovered the details of this task or quest immediately. But he was weary, and not unwilling to be guided by this man. He answered politely, "No doubt you are correct. I am most grateful for the shelter you have been kind enough to provide, if not the answers you see fit to withhold."

"Impudent," the man judged. "Impudent, yet not without some measure of courtesy. I might answer your questions, but no answer I could give would aid you. You already know any answer I would give." He regarded Neill with impenetrable calm. "Do you know who I am?"

That sense of familiarity niggled, but as yet Neill could not honestly claim any such knowledge. "I...fear not, sir."

"Perhaps you will, in time." The man gestured, and Neill, following the direction of his wave, saw that a simple pallet had been laid out near the iron stove, blankets folded neatly beside the thin mattress. "Rest easy, Lord Neill. Dream peacefully. Nothing will trouble your sleep tonight."

Neill did not entirely accept this assurance, but he bowed nonetheless, turning back toward his host. "And you, sir?"

But the man had gone, between one breath and the next. Neill, who had glanced away only momentarily, nevertheless had felt no sense of movement or breath of intention. But the room was undeniably empty, save for himself and his mare. There was now no suggestion that anyone else had ever been there.

Neill ate the second slice of bread and fed a slice to Raven. Then he stacked the dishes to one side, moved the simmering soup to the back of the stove where the heat was less, took off his boots, and lay down on the pallet to wait for whatever task the dawn and the day might bring.

4

Never leave the road, or you might wander in the forest for much longer than you intended. Everyone knew that. Certainly Eliet knew it. Never leave the road: there is no other way through that leads straight from the start of your journey to its end. Set foot off the road and your path will thenceforth go by fits and starts, or it will turn and turn and turn again until you have no idea which way you're going and can no longer find your way home either.

Stay on the road or who knew where you might come out of the forest—if you found your way out at all. Drink only from streams that cross the road, pick berries only from bushes that encroach on the road, seek shelter only in the lee of a tree that leans into the road.

Everyone knew that.

But sometimes, to find your heart's desire, you had to leave the road. She knew that as well.

Fear and credulity and self-deception. The serpent had warned against all of those. It had also said, *Kindness is not to be despised, but generosity is greater.* Something like that. But there had been more to it...generosity is greater when it bears a *cost.* And something about giving away her heart's desire in order to receive it back again. Twofold.

Eliet could hardly imagine what the serpent might have meant by any of that. Except perhaps that she should not let herself be ruled by her own fears, nor deceived by her own hopes. That seemed good advice whatever its source, but easier to give than take. It had been fear that had driven her to take this road through the forest; but it had also been hope. Maybe it was hard to be afraid unless one also had hope.

Kindness and generosity...she hoped she was kind, generally. But generous? She had so little. She could not imagine what she possessed, that she might give away to anyone else. Certainly her heart's desire was not something she could *give away.*

As had become her habit of late, she spread a hand

across her belly. Barely rounded, as yet. She no longer had the narrow waist of a girl, and showed less now than she had when she had been younger. But she knew. Of course she knew. She had not felt the child quicken. Not yet. Soon she would. She would feel it quicken, and move, and kick. And then she would bear it, as she had borne all the others, too early and too small, and it would die, this child she carried.

It would not even be granted a headstone in her family's plot beneath the shade of the oak. Because this child was not her husband's child and carried no man's name.

Tomas was not unkind. He wasn't *unkind*. But he would very kindly and gently ask her who the father was, and when she refused to tell him, he would very kindly and gently explain that the child must be laid nameless within the earth. And then ever after he would watch Eliet, kindly and gently, to be sure she confined herself decently to the restraint and decorum expected of a widowed woman in general and that he expected particularly of his own sister.

Or if the child were born alive and actually lived, then as Tomas had no child of his own it would be his heir. Then he would demand even more stringently to know the father's name, and though she wouldn't tell him, she knew in that case the father would declare himself, and that would be...not *worse*. Nothing would be worse than the death of her child. But it would be awkward and painful, and after Tomas found out, he would hate her.

Eliet couldn't bear it. Not any of it. And so she had ridden into the great forest.

In tales, men and women who went into the great forest to find their hearts' desires sometimes emerged having paid more dearly than they would have wished, or in some coin they would never have chosen. Eliet was willing to pay in any coin she held, to any power of the forest; or to a mage in the more ordinary sort of coin if she did not find what she sought within the forest.

So she had intended. Now she wondered if her encounter with the serpent portended choices and chances she had not expected.

"Nothing for it but to go on and see what we find," she told Ponder. She meant to speak cheerfully, but her voice came out louder than she had meant, and fell flatter upon the close air of the forest, and she closed her lips tight and said nothing further.

Her horse, undisturbed, tossed his head and moved without her signal into a smooth, reaching trot.

The road became narrower after that, and more twisted and hilly. At the beginning more nearly level and wide enough for three or four horses to travel abreast, now often enough there wouldn't have been room for two and Eliet found herself frequently leaning far forward in the saddle as Ponder climbed a slope, then equally far back as he picked his way down the other side. The trees here were just as tall, but more contorted, with low-set branches that seemed to bar more of the light. Occasionally those branches crossed the road so low that Eliet pressed herself down on her gelding's neck to pass beneath them, and once she had to dismount and lead Ponder under such a branch. Even then twigs scraped the saddle, and she thought for the first time that a smaller horse might have been a wiser choice. Except she would not have wanted any other horse, even discounting the ill turn she'd have done her brother by taking one of the mares.

Ponder was fourteen years old and had been Eliet's particular horse for seven of those years. Tomas had given him to her the week after she had buried her own heart in her husband's grave, beside the little graves of their poor babes. Her brother had been *trying* to be sympathetic—Tomas did not know how to break through the muffling gray grief that had taken her, and for her brother a new horse was the best remedy for any ill. Ponder was plainer-headed than any townsman wanted for a carriage or saddlehorse, so Tomas had not been able to sell the gelding for as much as he was worth. But the gelding was a good, trustworthy animal, suitable for a child too young to look after himself, or a woman wrapped in grief. That was why her brother had given him to Eliet.

Tomas had chosen better than he knew; better than Eliet had guessed herself. She had not cared that the gelding was plain because during those weeks and months she had not cared for anything. But even then she had found it oddly comforting, how Ponder had possessed a peculiarly serious

32

way of looking at anything out of the ordinary, as though he were weighing it up and deciding what he thought about it. He was the sort of horse who declined to spook at fluttering bits of cloth caught on a hedge, who didn't mind a barking dog, and who carried a rider safely home when she forgot to pay attention to the road or mark the turnings between the town and her brother's farm. Gradually Eliet had realized she could trust him to keep her safe even when she fell into one of the blank, black, thoughtless moods that took her in those years, when she might ride halfway to town or back without noticing anything of the road or the weather or the folk she passed.

Ponder was big for her—Eliet was not especially tall, and by that time Ponder had grown into his sire's height and heft. But later, when Tomas offered her a smaller horse, a neat-footed little mare three hands shorter and with a prettier head and a darker eye. Eliet had shaken her head and thanked her brother and refused. In all those years since, she had ridden only Ponder.

Four months ago, she had ridden Ponder up into the woodlands where folk went to look for late-cropping hickory nuts and hazelnuts. The woodlands where she had met Bram. In the honeyed light of late afternoon, with the nut trees golden all around, and all around the fragrance of sun-warmed earth and the ending of summer, Bram had straightened up from his half-filled basket of hickory nuts, the sunlight catching in his black, black hair and kindling in his black eyes, and in that moment it had seemed to Eliet that she had never seen him before in her life.

The sunlight had kindled in her eyes in answer, warmth and life running through her as—she thought later—it had not done for years. At the time she had not thought at all. It had seemed a moment and an afternoon caught out of the daily round, a turning of sense to accompany the turning of the seasons. She had swung out of the saddle with the thoughtless grace of a girl half her age, a girl untouched by time or grief, by life or loss.

A whole chain of bright, shimmering afternoons had stretched out through that autumn. Eliet had never asked Bram what he felt or hoped or intended or expected. At first it had not occurred to her to ask and later she had not wished to find out that his answers differed from hers. And what she had wanted was a bright chain of sweet afternoons, each caught whole and perfect out of time, entirely separate from the ordinary round of days.

Then the autumn had passed away and the chilly winter closed down. She had not minded. Those shining afternoons hardly seemed to have been real after all. For a time, they had seemed to her like a dream.

But nothing of that golden autumn had been a dream. And nothing had been separate from ordinary life.

Eliet's hand curved again across her belly, then closed into a fist. Then, annoyed with herself for giving way to useless wishes, she moved that hand deliberately, rubbed Ponder's dappled neck instead, let the black hairs of his mane run over her fingers.

Tomas would have been shocked and disapproving if he had known Eliet was carrying a child. But he would be far more shocked—worse, he would be terribly hurt—if he knew it was Bram's child.

Bram was near forty now, but he was a fine figure of a man still, with his lively black eyes and his neat black beard and his ready smile. His shoulders were broad and his forearms muscular and his waist trim, and he had a calm way of speaking that pleased a horse or dog or woman or, as far as that went, more often than not a man. He was ready to like anyone and he expected to meet friendship in return, and so he did, except for Tomas.

Bram owned the farm just south and east of Eliet's family's farm, the one just past the woodlot where folk of all these outlying farms went to gather nuts and mushrooms in the fall. He and his forebears had owned that land for even longer than her family had owned theirs. Except his pastures were broader and he had two springs on his land, not only one, and he raised eight or ten or a dozen foals a year, not only three or four. Still, though no doubt it was only natural the two families should be rivals, they had always been friends as well. Bram was generous and Tomas kind, and the two men would never have become enemies in the ordinary way of things. Except for Chane.

Chane had been the girl Tomas had wanted to marry,

long ago when all of them had been young. She had married Bram instead, and four years later died of a winter fever. Tomas had blamed the other man, first for taking Chane—as though it had not been her own choice and neither of theirs, but in this one thing Tomas was not reasonable. When she died, he blamed Bram again for failing to take care of her. Never mind nothing of that was fair either. A man was not reasonable in such matters.

Perhaps Eliet should have spoken up more forcefully, all those years ago. But it was too late now. Unforgivable things had been said on both sides and now bitterness and enmity stood between the two men and there was no mending it.

Tomas would not believe—he wouldn't *want* to believe—that Eliet cared nothing for Bram's prosperous farm or his wide pastures or his fine-blooded horses. That she had hardly thought of Bram at all; that she had thought of sunlight and warmth and golden days and dreams. How could she possibly explain that? No, Tomas would believe Eliet had betrayed him—had deliberately betrayed him—and he would expect her to announce coming nuptials, and worst of all— worst of all—he might even *wish* for the death of this child, her child, rather than let his farm and his horses pass into the hands of Bram's son.

Eliet had known, from the moment she knew she carried a child, that it would be born too young and too small. She knew it would die. But she could not bear to think Tomas might *hope* for that outcome. And she could not bear to stay in that house where they had both been children and happy, where she had been young and newly married, with everything of grief and loss still before her. She could not stay there to endure her brother's anger and hurt, to wait for her child to be born and then die.

She could not bear that. And so she had determined to ride into the great forest and seek a different ending to this child's tale. She had decided that if she did not find what she sought among the trees, she would ride on to the City beyond the forest and look there for aid.

And if nothing could be done and she bore the child and it died, then at least she would have *tried*. At least she would not have to stand with her brother at her shoulder, knowing she had not tried to turn her child's fate, and watch the tiny coffin lowered into the earth.

Ponder halted, startling Eliet from her unhappy thoughts. Looking up from her contemplation of his mane, Eliet found that they had come quite suddenly to an open place in the forest. The trees that had pressed in on both sides of the road now stood back, and then farther back, and the road ran out of the green shadows into a bright, clear meadow about the size of the yearlings' paddock at home. There was no grass beneath the trees, but here the grasses grew lush and thick, dotted here and there with many-petaled yellow flowers and star-shaped white flowers speckled with purple along the edges of their petals, and more of the nodding bell-shaped blue flowers. Broken edges of great slabs of stone pressed out of the grasses here and there, and along one shady edge of the meadow lay the remnants of an enormous fallen giant of a tree, now become a long, low, moss-covered mound.

The road did not quite disappear in this meadow, though its edges became blurred and indistinct. No longer beaten earth, the road led through the meadow as a curving path no wider than Eliet was tall, a path of shorter grasses where few flowers grew and no stones broke through the soil. She had to soften her vision and look at the whole of the meadow at once in order to see the path more clearly, and even then she couldn't quite tell where on the other side it re-entered the forest and became once more the familiar road. If it did. She presumed it must.

Dropping his big head low and leaning gently forward, Ponder let her know that he was more than ready for a rest and a chance to graze. Now that she could see the sky, Eliet could tell from the sun that they had come well into the afternoon. She had not guessed it was so late, but now she took note of the aching of her legs and rear and back...her stomach rumbled as well. She was no longer a girl, to stay in the saddle for ten hours or more and never feel it. At one-and-thirty, she was surely due a brief rest and a bite of bread. Nor was Ponder an energetic three-year-old, happy to charge up hill and down dale all the long day. Besides, though she carried a little grain, the chance to let her gelding graze on all this fine grass seemed too inviting to let pass.

Maybe it was even late enough to consider stopping for the night, in this fine open meadow where one would be able to see the sunset and the stars and the sunrise.

She would not have to leave the road. She could roll herself in her blanket at the far edge of this meadow, after finding the place where the road ran back into the forest. Or she might linger out there in the open, perhaps with her back against one of those slabs of stone. She thought the road ran near enough to one of the largest. That would be more comfortable than having nothing at her back at all. In an ordinary woodland she would have trusted Ponder to notice if anything strange or threatening approached, but in the great forest...she would rather have stone at her back.

Patting her horse's neck, Eliet swung her leg over the cantle and slid to the ground with a little grunt of effort. Truly, she was no longer a girl. Now that she had realized she was tired, she seemed to feel every movement in her bones. She leaned against Ponder's warm shoulder for a moment. Then she sighed, and slipped his bit, and led him out into the meadow.

The sunlight was warm and welcome on her face, the air clean and clear and fragrant with the scent of warm grasses underfoot and with a light, sweet scent Eliet thought came from the white flowers. Bees buzzed amid the flowers, and here and there a small butterfly fluttered, blue wings no wider than her thumbnail. A tiny brook, hardly a hand's width across and scarcely deeper, proved to wander through the meadow. It ran alongside the road for a little way, a swift ripple of crystalline water over shining grit, before crossing the road in a little rush, curving below one of the slabs of stone, and meandering away out of sight.

The brook made the decision about stopping easy. She thought she would lead Ponder to one of the great stones so that she would have someplace to sit that was not directly on the earth, but the horse leaned a different way, preferring an open sweep of grass on the other side of the brook. Eliet saw no difference in the grass on one side of the little stream or the other, but there seemed no reason not to let Ponder choose where he would graze. She did ask him to step high as she led him across the brook, careful of setting muddy hoof-prints in such a clear rivulet. Then she pulled off his saddlebags, loosened his girth, and measured out a double handful of grain for him, and cut bread and cheese for herself. Since she had no cup, she dipped water from the stream with her hands. The water was cool rather than cold. It tasted of earth and shade and secrets.

The first cry, thin as the mew of a newborn kitten, came as she was shaking droplets of water from her hands and wondering whether she might possibly spare an hour to nap here in the sunlit warmth even if she did not stay the night.

When the cry reached her, Eliet lowered her hands slowly to her lap, listening. Ponder, grazing peacefully a few steps away, did not lift his head.

Somewhere not so very far away, perhaps just within the shadows of the trees, the cry came again. Not the mew of a kitten, though the scrap of life that made that sound could hardly be larger. A baby. A small baby, very small. A baby born early and weak, hungry or cold or perhaps just angry at the unfairness of a life almost but not quite within reach.

Eliet knew the sound perfectly.

Whatever perils she had expected from this forest, whatever temptations or enticements, she had not expected this. Wonders, yes. Dangers. But not horrors. The great forest was perilous; everyone knew that. But it was not *inimical*. The serpent had sounded mocking to her ear. But it had not sounded *cruel*.

This...this was cruel.

The cry, reedy and breathless, came a third time. Not far at all, for all its faintness. Eliet looked again, deliberately, at Ponder. Her horse rotated an ear toward her, aware of her attention, as he was always aware of everything. Unimaginable that so wise a beast should hear that cry and pay no heed. It was in fact unbelievable. She did not believe it. Would not believe it.

"It's not real," she said out loud. "It's not real."

Unless perhaps it was real enough, but only meant for her ears. How could she tell?

Fear may be a useful guide, but it is a poor master... if she had courage she would stand up right now and go after that baby. The worst that could happen would be that it died in her arms, and that would be nothing new.

No. The *worst* that could happen would be that she followed a phantom made out of her own longing, lost her way and wandered in this terrible forest until she came to her time, alone and helpless, and her own baby cried like that. Only more briefly. *Credulity is a poor guide, but self-deception is worse,* and was it not self-deception when a woman heard what she most feared and most longed for, and took it for real? Only a fool would believe so specific and intimate a torment could be anything other than a trap and a snare.

Ponder still grazed, half his attention on her but none on the thin crying that came again from so little distance. He did not hear it, or at least did not regard it. And he was the most sensible beast she knew.

Eliet rose to her feet, caught up Ponder's reins, flung the saddlebags over her horse's back, and walked away, her back straight and her steps even, along the road and into the shadowy forest, leaving behind the bright sunlit meadow and the flowers and the little brook. Ponder heaved a sigh and his steps dragged a little, comment on his opinion about leaving good grazing, but he was too well-mannered to set his legs and refuse to move.

The cry followed Eliet, so that at the edge of the woods, she could not forbear to turn and look back just once more, and linger, and listen, and think perhaps she should go back after all and look for the babe she heard.

But, from this distance and this angle and without expecting it or looking for it, suddenly she saw that the slabs of stone dotted through the meadow had not after all been scattered by any random flood or erosion of the soil. She saw now that those stones lay in a wide, uneven semicircle, the edge of one here and the broad side of another there and another over there, and then others past those.

From this angle, she could see the stones might now lie broken and rough, but they had once been dressed and squared and laid out as the foundation of some great tower or keep. She couldn't imagine how she could have failed to see the shape of it before. Except the angle had been deceptive, and she had not been looking for shapes in the tumbled stones.

The road through the meadow curved so as to stay outside that circle of stones. But the crying she heard came from within it. If she had heard crying at all, and not something else that she had let herself hear as the cry of a babe. Because now...now, when that sound came again, thin and reedy and gasping, it sounded less like a tiny infant to her ears. Less like a tiny infant, and far more like the whispering cry of something dark and shadowy. Something that might once have dwelt within the long-fallen tower and hungered now for life it no longer possessed.

A cottage inhabited by bears or wolves would have been perhaps more dangerous, but less frightening. Shuddering, Eliet turned sharply, tightened Ponder's girth, and nearly hurled herself into the saddle. She no longer cared what place they might find to pass the coming night, so long as it was not anywhere near *this* place. And when she kneed her horse around and sent him into the forest, she did not look where they were going, and did not care that they left the road behind them and struck away unguided into the deep forest.

Eliet spent a chilly and uncomfortable night on Ponder's back, riding through the forest because she did not care to stop and because the gelding seemed no more inclined to halt than she felt. It seemed to her that if she stopped listening to the muted thump of Ponder's hooves, she would have to listen for the cry of an abandoned infant, and she was afraid of what she might hear if she listened too closely. It had occurred to her long since that more than chance might have guided her to that meadow—to that meadow in particular, with the tumbled stones of its long-ruined tower and the shadowy malice bound to those stones. She was afraid now of what other fears or desires or hopes or horrors the forest might put in her way.

It seemed better to let Ponder choose their direction. Once, at dusk, she thought she glimpsed the light of a cottage or other such dwelling; she almost thought she could make out the angle of its shingled roof through the trees. But Ponder never flicked an ear or leaned against the reins to suggest they turn that way, so she did not turn him toward it, though she doubted it would have proven tenanted by bears or wolves.

When her horse walked on through the dusk and then into the dark with no apparent idea of halting, Eliet was willing to stay on his back. Her back and seat ached, weariness pressed behind her eyes and weighed down her bones, but somehow she did not mind any of that. She felt as though she rode through a dream; maybe not even her own dream, but Ponder's. He must be tired. Her weight was nothing to a beast his size, but he was not accustomed to go on and on and on, all through the day and then all through the night, even at so gentle a pace. But he did not seem weary.

Of course they went very slowly. Ponder ambled now rather than striding. He walked with his head down, finding his way by whatever means a sensible horse might use in the dark. No other cottage or dwelling made itself known, but a little moonlight made its way down through the leaves, a faint silvery glow, so that it was not absolutely black. Still, Eliet suspected her horse felt his way more than saw it. She never scraped her knees against an unseen trunk; no unsuspected low branch ever knocked her on the head or swept her from Ponder's back. This might have been a kindness on the part of the forest, except that after the haunted meadow she did not expect kindness of the forest.

The ground became damper, even marshy; she could tell from the difference in the sound of Ponder's hooves and from the occasional squelching sounds or outright splashing as he walked through mud and shallow water. Pools of black water caught the faint moonlight and cast it back, so that the blacker boles of trees became faintly visible, and the latticework of branches above. The air, chilly with the early season, carried the scents of mud and moss. But none of this was precisely unpleasant. Perhaps it should have been, but the thought of warmth and sunlight were still tainted, for Eliet, with the imagined sound of a weak, too-small baby's cry.

There were no sounds here other than the splash and squelch and thump of her horse's steps, the quiet creak of the saddle beneath her, the muted jingle of Ponder's bit. Far away, a different splash, as of a fish or muskrat or some such harmless creature.

Eliet supposed there must be harmless creatures here and there in this forest. The small birds she had glimpsed earlier

41

argued so. She believed that little splash had been made by such an animal. She definitely believed that.

And still Ponder strode on. He seemed to know where he wished to go, so she made no move to check him. Gradually the ground sloped upward—she knew this mainly because her own posture canted forward in response, her weight sinking deeper into the saddle. The dark forest seemed to open up a little, and then a little more, until unobstructed moonlight spangled the ground between shadows and the horse lifted his head and lengthened his strides, and then they came out at last upon what must be the crest of a low rounded hill. A single great tree occupied the top of this hill, naked branches stark and black against an indigo sky scattered with stars. A breeze came here, lifting Eliet's hair and riffling through Ponder's mane; very different from the still air beneath the trees. It smelled of the memory of frost, of the coming spring, of the new green of growing things, of the promise of summer's approaching warmth.

Ponder halted beneath this tree. It did not occur to Eliet at first that she might ask him to go on, and once it did occur to her, she could not think why she should. This more-open hilltop seemed welcoming enough compared to the surrounding sloughs. Ponder seemed disinclined to go farther and she could hardly blame him for that.

It was chilly here, certainly, but not cold. She could hear nothing but the breeze. Other lesser trees did not encroach on the one great tree; there was enough light for grass to grow. Ponder had dropped his head to lip at it. She thought in a moment she would find the wakefulness to climb from the saddle and slip his bit so that he might graze more easily. Then perhaps she might sit beneath the great tree and rest a little.

In just a moment, she would do that.

While she recruited her strength for the effort, she tilted her head back and peered upward at the dark sky visible through the latticework of black branches, at the stars and the near-full moon and the scudding clouds that came and went between earth and sky. In all the world there seemed no sounds but the sighing of the wind through the leaves all around this hill, the creak of branches above, the quiet jingle of the bit as Ponder nibbled at the grass, the soft sound of her own breath going in and out. Peaceful sounds, surrounded by an immense quiet. She found she no longer listened for hints of horror. She felt somehow she had come past that, or through it, to a quiet place where she could rest.

She felt as though she had come not merely to the depths of the great forest, but to its center. Not merely to the center of the forest, but to the heart of the Kingdom, and to the very heart of the night as well. She felt as though the whole of the world turned around this one still point. That this hilltop and this tree had waited for her coming, and that now they would all wait together for...something. Dawn, perhaps, and the beginning of a new day.

It seemed a shame to shift at all, but at last Eliet gathered the reins into one hand, swung her leg over her horse's rump, gripped the saddle, and carefully clambered down. In the dark, it seemed a longer way than usual to the ground, but at last she stood beside her horse, leaning wearily on his shoulder. Ponder turned his head and sighed, and she pushed herself upright, loosened his girth and pulled off his saddle, slipped his bit and at last sat down where she was, on the grass beneath the spreading branches of the mostly unseen tree.

Somewhere in the distance, though there was no sign yet of the dawn, a bird began to sing: no bird she knew. A liquid ripple of notes with a soft burring trill at the end, a bit like a song sparrow, but longer and more musical. In all the world there seemed no sound but that and the soft ripping sounds of Ponder grazing. The gelding clearly found nothing amiss here on this hilltop, nothing amiss with the call of the bird or the sigh of the wind in the leaves all around them. The breeze carried a chill, and Eliet had neglected to bring a blanket, or even a cloak. Even so, she tilted her head back against the smooth bole of the great tree, shut her eyes, curled her hands softly over her belly, and drifted away on a soft tide of sleep.

5

Neill did not dream of the old man, as he might have expected; nor of his mother, as he might have dreaded. He dreamed of his father, frowning, but not in dissatisfaction nor discontent. In Neill's dream, his father did not speak, but his scowl was more the expression of a man concentrating upon some important task. It was the mood in which Neill had always felt closest to his father.

He dreamed of his brother. Sunlight surrounded Cassiel, who rode through what seemed a charmed landscape of fields and woodlands, at the forefront of a company of young beautiful companions. Neill dreamed Muriel rode beside his brother, her head tilted toward Cassiel's and his toward her. But in the dream he felt neither bitterness nor thwarted desire at the sight.

He dreamed of a tree, old and gnarled, bark thick and dark with age, leaves dry at the edges, curling and falling; and of a single black husk splitting open to show one ripe kernel within. He did dream of the old man then: the old man with white hair and black eyes and a half-familiar face, reaching to pluck that seed. In the dream, he knew that man's name, and took a breath to speak it, and the name on his tongue was his own name.

He woke wrapped in a blanket, upon a pallet, surrounded by the chill of open air, surrounded by the silvery dawn. There was no sign of the comfortable home fashioned within the hollow tree. The tree was there, or a tree very like it, of vast girth. It stood near at hand, its great branches spreading overhead in an echo of shelter. But there was no door set into its hollow trunk, if indeed its trunk was hollow at all. No iron stove, no table, no bench, no old man. Only the immense tree and, all around, other trees of nearly equal size, their leaves silver in the dim predawn.

But there were wisps of straw caught in Raven's mane. The mare stood hipshot and comfortable, as though she had spent the night in her own stall. She was lipping without much interest at tidbits of hay scattered around her feet. Her saddle rested at the foot of Neill's pallet, her bridle lying across it. The pallet itself was just as Neill recalled it from the previous evening, save for lying now beneath the shivering leaves of spreading branches rather than within the warmth of the home inside the hollow tree. There was no sign of danger anywhere, and no sense of urgency.

Yet somehow Neill felt there was somewhere he should be. Something he needed to do. Someone...someone, perhaps, whom he ought to meet.

Sitting up, Neill pulled on his boots—they stood waiting beside his pallet—and rose to his feet. There was no basin of warm water, but a hand-sized spring welled up nearby, the source of a rivulet that meandered away toward the surrounding sloughs. Its water was absolutely clear and bitingly cold. It tasted of ice and earth and the memory of the dark places from which it came forth.

The stove might have disappeared, and the table, but the half-loaf of bread left from supper rested on the foot of the pallet, wrapped in oiled paper. Neill took that as a welcome sign of continued hospitality despite the loss of the crock of berry preserves. He shared the bread with his mare before saddling her.

He rode away from the spreading branches of the tree, down the slight hill, and into the embrace of the forest just as the edge of the rising sun came above the crowns of the trees and laid its warm light across the world. He felt surprisingly well-rested...more than that: he felt clear-headed and clear-sighted, as though he might have been riding through fog all the previous day, though there had been no fog. The feeling made no sense, yet it persisted. Once again he tried to recall the old man's face, to fit it to someone known; someone he felt was surely not an enemy, though perhaps not a friend. The face and the eyes and even something of the manner persisted in reminding him of his mother, yet he was certain that was not the one he should recall. He felt he had dreamed of some answer he had now forgotten. This was an uneasy feeling, and yet it did not trouble him. He felt that the answers he sought would come to him again when he needed them.

If Raven had dreamed, she plainly felt no concern for it.

The mare strode out with a high-stepping gait, as though she felt light and energetic as a three-year-old. She moved as she might when her mane and tail were braided with ribbons and silver chains, her hooves polished, her bridle studded with silver— as she might when she carried Neill at the head of a holiday parade.

She had always been vain as a cat, had his Raven. Her mother, a polished gray mare with a lovely head and a wicked temper, had been the same way. Ride her about ordinary affairs and she would give you endless trouble. But braid ribbons in her mane and ride her in a parade where she might collect admiring glances, and she purred like a kitten. She had been a great favorite of the King, Neill's father.

A little more than a year since his father's death and Neill could think of him without grief; with only a bittersweet regret that the King had not lived to grow old, had not lived to bestow approval and respect on the man Neill had become. He suffered little doubt now that his father would have learned to do so, eventually.

That was Cassiel's doing, that solid confidence. That was a year and more of his brother's public approval and respect. Neill knew that as well, and had long since given up resentment of the knowledge.

... And why think now of his father, of the fraught relationship between them; of his brother and the far more secure relationship between them? Scattered dreams came back to Neill, fragments of vision. His father, his brother...a tree, massive but dead, naked branches against the sky...

Raven gave a little bounce and lifted into a neat-footed trot, and Neill, catching at the cantle of the saddle and looking up in surprise, found that exact tree rising against the sky before them.

6

Dawn came silvery and fair, waking Eliet from uneasy dreams she barely remembered. She rested at the base of the tree, her limbs drawn in to seek warmth, both hands folded across the rise of her belly. She was shivering, but neither as cold nor as stiff as she might have expected; she was hungry, but not pinched with hunger as she might also have expected. She felt clear-headed and peaceful, not anxious or fearful, as she would most definitely have expected.

She felt she had come to a dawn of a new day—more than an ordinary dawn, rising on a more than ordinary day. And somehow she felt as though she had arrived somewhere. As though she had come to the place she had sought; as though she need not hurry to be somewhere else.

She didn't understand this feeling. But Ponder grazed nearby, lazily. Perhaps his calm explained why Eliet felt no sense of urgency or worry; even in her sleep, she must have sensed her horse's placidity.

Stretching, she clambered to her feet and looked around, and up.

The tree that had sheltered her was dead, its branches naked of leaves; its bark mostly peeled away to reveal the smooth dry wood beneath. Eliet saw this with a faint feeling of surprise, though she had no idea why she should feel surprised. Even in the great forest, trees must die sometimes. Even giants like this one. She had seen, dimly, the shapes of those naked branches even by moonlight, she had heard branches creak without the whisper of the breeze through new leaves; she simply hadn't thought of what she saw, of what it meant.

Though it was not quite dead. One branch, high up, bore a handful of small leaves and a single small black husk. But all the branches low to the ground were certainly dead. And no other trees stood very near. Perhaps the forest might not mind if she gathered a few of the dry twigs from one of those low branches and made a fire...a little fire, a tiny fire, just to heat a palmful of water. Eliet thought she might dare so much. A hot tisane would be very welcome on this chilly morning, when all she had left to break her fast was a heel of somewhat stale bread and a small piece of cheese. And a little packet of dried angelica, with raspberry leaf and rosehips. Raspberry leaf was good for a woman in her condition, and rosehips were said to bring good luck. Besides, she liked the taste.

Surely here on this clear hilltop, with dead wood so ready to hand, a small fire might not offend? There was no serpent to ask; no sign of any creature. She would have asked, if any creature of the forest had been near. But somehow she felt a small fire would be all right. She felt it would not offend: not this morning, not on this hilltop, not if hers was the hand that made it.

The twigs snapped easily when Eliet reached up to break them from a branch, and the small flames kindled easily when she struck a spark with her candlelighter. She fed twigs gently into the tiny blaze and then broke a slightly larger branch into pieces and laid them around the edge to hold her tiny pot over the fire. A cupful of water, a small handful of dried herbs, crushed to release their fragrance...Ponder wandered over and leaned his big head over her shoulder, hopeful for bread. Eliet gave him half of what was left and wondered, but not with any sense of urgency, whether she might find more food sometime during this coming day.

Then Ponder raised his head and pricked his ears, whickering a greeting.

Eliet rose quickly, not precisely alarmed because there was no alarm in Ponder's manner, but nonetheless wishing to be standing when she met whomever—or whatever—approached.

A man on a black horse rode toward them. His hair, long and clipped back at the base of his neck, was white, striking against the dark blue of his cloak and the black of his mare. At first Eliet thought he was old, but as he came closer, she saw that no matter the color of his hair, he could not be more than a few years older than she was herself. His face was stern, stark, powerful—but not old. His eyes were dark, as powerful as the lines of his face.

His mare was a good one. Eliet would have known this

was someone important without the mare, but she was very fine. Tomas would have been more than pleased to add a mare like that to his stable. She could almost hear her brother's admiring comments—he would like the set-on of that mare's neck and her fine sloping shoulders even better than her pretty head.

The white-haired man drew his mare up just beyond the farthest extent of the dead branches. He was frowning. Eliet did not much care for the frown, but she did like the way he set one hand on his mare's neck when she slanted her ears back at Ponder and danced a threatening step closer. The man's light touch on the rein was authoritative, but the automatic caress of his other hand showed how he cherished the mare's bold, assertive air.

The man looked Eliet over quickly, one swift assessing glance; and Ponder, who showed himself ready to make friends with the mare, notwithstanding the wicked glint in her eye; and the small fire, with her handful of herbs simmering in her tiny pot. Last of all he tipped his head back and considered the tree, his eyes narrowing as he discovered the one living twig high overhead.

Then he brought his dark considering gaze back to Eliet.

No doubt he instantly parsed her clothing and manner and the quality of her horse and realized she was a woman from some outlying farm or village, of modestly prosperous family. She had certainly already come to certain conclusions about him. She gave him a little nod of greeting, not quite a bow. "There is tisane, if you would like to share it, my lord."

For a moment longer the man regarded her. Then he returned a thoughtful nod, twisted his reins about the cantle, and swung down from his mare. Eliet liked the way he slipped the mare's bit before he came forward, the way he left her loose without a second thought, clearly trusting that she would stay near, as Eliet trusted Ponder.

The man waited gravely for her to strain and pour out the tisane—she had only one cup, but he produced one of his own from a saddlebag. Then he knelt down by the fire and sipped, his eyes on her face. Eliet sipped as well. The sweetness of the angelica and sharpness of the raspberry leaf cut through the weariness of a night spent half in the saddle, and the warmth spread through her body. The white-haired lord looked as though he also found the tisane welcome.

At last the man set his cup down on the ground, leaned forward a trifle, and said to her, "My name is Neill, and I am told a task awaits me here. How came you to this place, good woman, and for what reason? What is your name and where lies your home?" His tone was courteous, but it was the tone of a man used to having his questions answered and his orders obeyed.

Eliet wondered what he meant about a waiting task; she had never heard of such a thing. A task waiting in the great forest? Who would have told this lord of such a task, and why would he have listened? But she could see no reason not to give him her name, especially as he had offered her his without even being asked. Neill...it was an uncommon name, but not so uncommon that she hadn't met one or two townsmen called so. Lord Neill...there was a familiarity to the sound of that. But she saw no urgent need for her to tell this man, whatever his name and whomever he might be, that she had come into the forest to seek her heart's desire. Far less explain what that was.

She said, "My name is Eliet, sister of Tomas. Brewer's Vale is the closest town to our family's farm, but it isn't so large or fine a town that you would have heard of it."

Lord Neill frowned at her. "Certainly I have heard of it. Brewer's Vale lies generally less than three day's ride from the western edge of the great forest. It's good land around there for barley and hops, as one would expect from the name. Better land for sheep than cattle, though the farms around there raise both. It's good land for horses as well." He glanced at Ponder, acknowledging the gelding's quality. "It's a prosperous town, and the magistrates there are responsible people. Seldom does anyone of Brewer's Vale find need to venture the forest, travel to the City, and petition the King. Still less often, I would think, would anyone leave the road and find themselves here in this place. This is the heart of the forest, or one of its hearts; whatever a traveler may seek, the forest seldom directs any chance traveler here."

Everything in this speech was surprising in one way or another. Eliet hardly knew what answer to make, and so

50

sipped her tisane in silence.

Lord Neill sipped his as well. Then his eyebrows rose, and he examined Eliet again, his glance sharp and knowing. "Raspberry. And rosehips. You are bearing? Forgive my impertinence to ask so personal a question, good woman," he added, at Eliet's astonished blink. "I believe it may have some bearing on your presence here."

Eliet could not imagine how. Except she could. Because she had come into the forest seeking her heart's desire, and the forest plainly knew the shape of that desire. And now she was here, in this place where the forest seldom brought travelers. Or so Lord Neill said. But she did not doubt him.

Constraint tightened her throat. But the very neutrality of the lord's expression drew her. She found herself answering. "Yes, my lord. Only it will die. Or it would have died, if I had stayed at home. I—they are born too early, my babies. And...there were other reasons I could not stay. But that is the heart of it. I thought, if the forest could not show me a way to bear a living child, then perhaps in the City, a mage..." she faltered and fell silent, stopped by the intensity of hope and fear that rose up in her heart as she gave voice at last to her desire.

"Yes," said the lord. He stood up, and then paused, regarding Eliet with a closed, thoughtful expression. She sat still, her cup cradled in her hands, gazing up at him. She could see that he knew something, or felt something, or guessed something. The workings of this forest were familiar to this man in a way they weren't to her, or to any common person. She didn't understand this. But she knew it was true.

Then at last she remembered where she had heard his name before, and she did understand after all. She stood up in astonishment, hardly knowing whether she should bow, or kneel, or call him Your Highness, or apologize for not recognizing him at once. She had never spoken to a prince before. Not even a bastard prince.

What she said, in a voice that, though low, surprised her with its matter-of-fact tone, was, "The City is the heart of the Kingdom. The King is the heart of the City..."

"I'm the King's brother. Yes," said Lord Neill, but absently, as though nearly all his attention was engaged with some other much more important consideration. "This forest is also the heart of the Kingdom. There is more than one layer to the Kingdom; in one form or another, this forest lies at the heart of them all. As the King stands, in some sense, at the heart of them all. A task awaits one of my father's blood, or so I have been told. And now I am standing in the heart of the forest." He looked up at the stark branches of the dying tree, deliberately. Then he returned his gaze to Eliet. "The tree is dying. It is all but dead. It carries one seed, but clearly it no longer has the ability to engender life. You are bearing. And now here you are, with me, in the heart of the forest."

The lord's meaning was clear. Or some of it was clear. Or clear enough. Eliet pressed a protective hand to her belly. And felt, for the first time, the child stir. She felt it quicken, as though in answer to her touch, or her sudden fear, or her stuttering hope. She said, "I won't give up my child's life to engender that seed. Not even if the whole forest withers for want of it. Not even if my baby would die anyway. Not even then." Her words came out flat and hard. She did not recognize her own voice. But she meant every word.

Lord Neill shook his head quickly. Vehemently. "No, and I should hardly ask any mother to make such a choice. I don't believe—I don't see that death could possibly engender life. It's the life of your child that can grant life to that seed. Life for life, flowing in both directions. It's your heart's desire, and the desire of the forest itself. Or so I think it must be." He met her eyes and added gently, "I see that you are frightened. I cannot say that fear is ill-advised. You are the one engendering life. I am, I believe, merely to serve as the channel between the Kingdom and the life that burgeons within you. But the forest is not kind, though it can be generous. There is always a cost to its gifts. If I'm wrong, I think you will be the one to pay that cost, not I."

Eliet stood very still, looking back at him. She was afraid. But she remembered the serpent's advice: *Fear may be a useful guide, but it is a poor master....It is in giving away your heart's desire that you will receive it back again, twofold.*

The serpent had been a creature of the forest. Yet for all its elliptical riddling, she did not think it had lied to her. In all the tales of the forest, though the desire of your heart might not turn out to be what you expected, it always did prove your truest desire. And though the cost you paid to gain your heart's desire might be greater than you wished, it was never *unjust*.

She looked up at the few struggling leaves. At the one black, withered husk, split to reveal a single kernel. She said, "My child will live."

Lord Neill did not murmur kind assurances. He said, "I think it will. But I could be wrong. I think if it lives, it will be bound to the Kingdom and to the forest. I would not venture to guess what might come of that bond."

Eliet brought her gaze down to him, to his ungentle features, to the intensity of his black eyes. "*You* are bound to the Kingdom and the forest. All those of your blood are so bound. You are certainly so bound—that's why you are here."

"Yes," Lord Neill acknowledged.

"Swear you will protect and guide and care for my child, and I will do whatever you ask." Eliet was aware that he need swear nothing of the sort. If sharing her child's life with that seed and with the forest meant her baby would live, she would accept whatever bond that established between them, and willingly endure whatever came of that bond in later years. But she straightened her shoulders and lifted her head and tried to look as though she were capable of mounting her horse and riding away.

One white eyebrow rose. He wasn't fooled. She could tell he knew exactly what she was thinking. But he said merely, "I shall gladly swear that oath. I do swear it."

"Then I'll do whatever you ask," Eliet promised, and waited without flinching.

Lord Neill put out one hand as though he had no doubt in the world what he was about. High above there was a sudden sharp crack, and the husk broke away from its twig and plummeted. The King's brother caught it without even appearing to look. He did flinch slightly when the sharp edges of the dry husk sliced his palm, but only murmured, "Blood, of course. That is life as well." He raised his voice slightly. "Take what you need; I freely give it." Then he carefully separated the kernel within from the husk. It was reddish-brown, about the size and shape of a hazelnut, smooth as though it had been waxed. It did not look magical in the least, even when Lord Neill dabbed it with his blood.

Then he held the bloodied kernel out to Eliet. When she hesitated, he commanded, "Take it." He sounded utterly assured.

Eliet put her own hand out, hesitantly, and let him tip the kernel into her palm. She studied it. Still there seemed nothing magical about it. Only she thought it grew plumper as she held it; she thought its color surely darkened. She could almost feel the life within it, striving to burst out and grow. But it was not ripe. It had not been able to ripen. The dying tree had not been able to bring its dormant promise to fruition.

That she could do so seemed impossible. Yet at the same time nothing in the world seemed more likely. Lord Neill had been right. She carried life already. Fragile, yes. But strong as well. Enough life to share, surely, with something so small.

Eliet knelt to plant the seed in the warm soil beside her fire. She watered it, after a brief hesitation, with the remains of her tisane. The scent of angelica and raspberries and roses filled the air, far more intensely than seemed likely.

Then she pressed one hand against the damp soil and the other against her rounded belly, and said to both seed and child within, "Live. Live. Live and grow."

She felt it happen. She felt the life within her divide and separate and strengthen, and braid together, and grow. It was a most peculiar feeling, but neither her child nor the seed took harm of it—she felt that too. When she lifted her hand away from the earth, a seedling rose up below her fingers as though she drew it forth from the soil by that gesture: a smooth shoot that lengthened and unfurled one leaf and then another and then a third, until a tiny seedling tree stood there beside the remains of her fire. It was taller than the length of her hand already, and though Eliet was not accustomed to examining young trees, it seemed sturdy and strong. Its leaves were pale green above and silvery below, and already there were buds that promised more to come.

"Well done," Lord Neill commended her, but she did not need his praise to know the little tree would live. Nor to know her child would live. Her little son or daughter stirred within

54

her belly, and moved again, more strongly yet. She folded her hands over her stomach and smiled at the small tree and thought perhaps she would someday return, when her baby was grown into a sturdy child, and see what it had become. The thought was a good one.

-7-

Neill gazed down on the tiny tree and the woman kneeling beside it. A surge of protectiveness surprised him— he was not fond by nature, and knew he was not. But what he felt now was certainly something like fondness, for both woman and tree. Very like, indeed, though the tree would surely grow into an impersonal aspect of the great forest and he did not even know the woman: only that she was a woman near his own age and not a girl; handsome rather than pretty; and determined enough to dare the great forest to find her heart's desire.

Though he knew something of her character. Brave as well as determined, this Eliet. A woman who plainly understood loss and grief, and whose purpose had been so unwavering as to bring her not merely into the forest, but here to this place. Whose strength of will had been enough to bring her here. Certainly she had not hesitated to seize the chance the forest had offered her.

Another woman might not have understood the possible cost, though he had laid it out for her as clearly as he could. But this woman unquestionably understood what she had done, using her child's life to bolster the life of that young tree. If she had not understood, she would not have demanded that oath of him, to protect and guide the child. A burden, that oath. An obligation that would last so long as that child lived—and he saw no reason that child should not live long, bound as it was to the forest and the Kingdom.

But he did not regret it in the least. The protectiveness he felt now was not directed merely to tree and woman, but to the child as well. The child most of all. That was a surprise as well.

Neill had no children of his own body. But he gazed down at the woman now kneeling beside that tiny tree and

55

knew the child she bore would be his as much as hers. A son or a daughter of his own body could not belong to him more surely.

He cleared his throat.

The woman had been focused on the seedling tree. But she looked up now, blinking as though her thoughts had been far away and he had recalled her to this moment. When he offered his hand to help her rise, she took it with only the slightest hesitation.

He lifted her to her feet. "Eliet," he said. Though he hardly knew her, he thought the name suited her. It was not a soft name, but crisp on the tongue and a little sharp. He said, "You must come to the City with me. I will make a place for you within my own household. For you and for your child."

When she did not answer at once, a thought struck him. He might have flushed: a trace of heat crept up his face. "I do not mean to suggest anything improper, and only if you are willing and your husband does not object, of course. But if I am to safeguard your child...would your husband be willing to come to the City?" Neill was not at all accustomed to forgetting or disregarding such obvious matters.

But the woman shook her head. "My husband...Chares...he lies these years with my mother and father and with all my family's grief." She added in a lower tone, "With our little sons, and our little daughter. I thought I had buried my heart there as well." Her hands, folded now over the rise of her belly, made it clear that she had recovered her heart from that hallowed ground. Her attention was turned inward now. She wore a listening expression. Neill could see that nearly all her attention had been captured by the movement of the quickening child within her womb.

She knew enough of grief, clearly. Neill forbore to ask her the obvious question. He resolved in that moment that no one would be permitted to plague this woman with comments or observations or questions concerning her years-departed husband and her new-caught child. He said merely, "I am sorry for it. But then there is no barrier. You must come to the City with me. You will come? At least for the present? I would not see you cut off from your family, Eliet." The familiarity came easily to his tongue, so that it took him a second to add, "May I call you by your name?"

She was paying a little more attention to him now, and answered with a faint smile, "I think you may indeed, Lord Neill. I think we may count ourselves as introduced."

"Neill," he told her. "I have said I will bring you into my household, and so I will. It will be yours, this babe, but it will also be mine. Whether a son or a daughter, I will cherish this child. I have never engendered an heir of my body. Whether or not I should do so, still this child will be my heir."

Neill was faintly astonished to hear himself say this. But he meant it. If Cassiel objected—but he would not object. Not once he saw that Neill was determined, certainly not once he understood the child was linked to the Kingdom as surely – perhaps more surely – than if it had been born of Neill's blood. And if his brother approved, Neill did not care for anyone else's opinion.

The woman blinked, recalled to the vow she had made him swear. And to what this vow must necessarily entail; he thought she might not have realized the implications until this moment. Her shoulders straightened, and her chin firmed. "That is a great deal to promise, my lord. My baby's father is a good man; I think he is a worthy man; but he is not wellborn or nobly-born. And you don't know, none of us can know, what sort of man a child of mine would become."

She did not say *My child will be a bastard.* This was obviously true. But she had equally obviously already drawn the correct conclusion that Neill of all people was not likely to reject a child on such grounds.

He said drily, "No man can know what sort of adult any child will become, save that any man can guide a child as best he is able. Your babe will not carry my blood, but it will carry a bond to the Kingdom. For my heir, that will do. Do you wish to return to the father of your child? Do you wish to make the babe known to him and ask him to accept it? Do you wish to marry him—if he is free to marry?"

Eliet answered at once, decisively, "I wish to go to the City, Lord Neill. I will write my brother and...and my child's father, but I...I don't wish to go home. They will quarrel, and if I were there, my presence would enflame the tempers of both men. Only..." her eyes met his with commendable resolution. "I won't be a burden on you, on your household. I won't be an encumbrance upon you, my lord. I have few skills, but—" her eyes went to his mare. "I do know horses."

Her gelding was not a handsome animal, but he was a quality beast; any man who knew horses at all could see that. Neill did not assure Eliet that she need not make herself useful; that he would be glad to support her. Of course she would wish to be useful. Of course she would not wish to be supported. He liked this woman better and better. He liked the idea of bringing her into his household; of coming to know her; of guiding her into a life that owed less to the griefs of the past and more to the joys of the future.

He was more and more certain he would be glad to make her child his heir, if it gained determination and forthrightness and courage as its birthright from its mother.

"We shall find you some task suitable to your hand," he promised her. "But you must call me Neill—" he paused. His mare and Eliet's gelding had both suddenly pricked up their ears and turned their heads, and he saw that the black serpent that was a face of the forest had come. Its slender length draped over a low branch of the dying tree, directly over the new sapling.

Then he saw one leaf drift down from high above, and another, and realized the great tree was no longer merely dying. It was dead. Even as he looked up, the last living branch withered and cracked along its whole length.

Eliet too had turned, but her gaze had gone from the serpent to the sapling, which had grown another hand higher and unfurled another leaf—two more—in the brief time they had been speaking.

The serpent said, to her rather than to Neill, "Thus one layer of the Kingdom is supported. It's always better to prevent any of the great trees perishing without issue."

She nodded, but not as though she cared about such great matters. She might not have understood, though for once the serpent spoke plainly rather than in riddles. But Eliet said instead, her hands folded protectively over her belly, "My child will live. It will be healthy. It won't be harmed by what I did—by what you brought me here to do." Nothing of this was a question. Her tone was fierce, as though she meant to compel the serpent to answer as she wished. As though she meant to compel the world to be as she needed. Neill caught himself smiling, almost believing she could do it.

The serpent tilted its flat head, regarding her from its unfathomable golden eyes. "She will be mine as well as yours. Her name will be Elinor, for she will be a child of the forest as well as the City. She will freely come and go through all the layers of the Kingdom, and she will speak to me in each."

It was not an ordinary or safe fate, this that the serpent described. Neill forbore to say so. He said instead, swiftly, before it could say anything even more fraught, "Was it you to whom I spoke, last evening? Or was that *my* face, years hence?"

The serpent swayed, coiling and re-coiling in order to regard him. It did not laugh, but there was mockery in the tilt of its head. "It was a face you would regard. Was it more than that? Do you wish an answer to that question?"

Neill discovered that he did not. He inclined his head in acknowledgment of this truth.

"An heir and more than an heir you have gained this day," the serpent said to him.

Neill inclined his head again, this time in a gesture that was almost a bow. He was wary. But he said, "I didn't know what I sought, but I am glad I followed the path I found before me."

"So you should be," agreed the serpent. Its slender tongue flickered, and it raised itself up onto the branch, resting its broad head on its gold-enlaced black coils. "Your road lies before you," it said to both of them, and turned its head to indicate the place where the road indeed ran away from this low hill into the sloughs of the forest bottomlands. Neill hadn't seen it until that moment, but the road was plain enough now: framed by massive high-crowned trees, the new growth of their branches spangled with clusters of tiny golden flowers. The trees had not been flowering yesterday, Neill was almost certain. He had not even noticed swollen buds. But all around them now the forest bloomed.

Eliet gazed about as well, her eyes wide, caught by the beauty of the spring morning, a smile lightening her serious mien for the first time since Neill had met her. A short distance away, her big grey gelding whickered, and Raven tossed her head and danced a step, impatient to be on their way.

Neill turned to say something to the serpent, he did not clearly know what, but it was gone. This did not displease him. Turning back, he offered his arm to Eliet, wordlessly. She looked at him for a moment, still smiling, and then gravely laid her hand upon the crook of his elbow and let him lead her toward the horses.

She would not need his assistance to mount. Or to make a place for herself in the City. But he would assist her both now and in the future, and he already knew she would be gracious enough to allow it.

Neill looked forward to introducing her to the City, and to all the folk of the Palace, and most of all to Cassiel. But more than any of that, he looked forward to coming to know her himself—and her child, which would also be his.

A WALK ON THE BEACH

This short story takes place in a world that's not connected to any of my novels. I've always liked superhero stories, so I wrote this in response to a prompt for stories about the everyday lives of superheroes. Who knows, maybe someday I'll write a book set in this world of strongmen and speedsters.

On Monday morning, Scott Rush's fastsight led him to rescue an old man who'd been trapped on the second floor of his house by a fire, a woman who had driven into water too deep for her small car when a creek flooded over a low water bridge, and a kitten that had strayed into a busy road.

The kitten was actually just a coincidence. A good many speedsters had some kind of clairvoyance, just as most strongmen had some degree of invulnerability and nearly all tekes had at least a basic talent for telepathy. Rush's own clairvoyance was good for small-scale problems, but not that small scale. Just as well, or even fast as he was, he'd never get any sleep between snatching kittens out of traffic and rabbits out of foxes' jaws.

Rush didn't bother to put on his suit for any of that, since except for the kitten he didn't slow down enough for anyone to get a decent look at him. On the Nuisance Scale, he rated the old man about a two, the woman definitely a seven— honest to God, people should know better. Besides, even solid-built as he was, Rush nearly threw his back out heaving her out of her car.

He rated the kitten a zero, of course. Kittens were by definition not a nuisance. Even when a kitten's tiny claws left pinpricks of blood across the meat of Rush's thumb. Careless. Rush, a big guy himself, was more used to hefty dogs than little kittens.

He took the kitten along to Emma's vet appointment, for which he was four and a half minutes late. Speed was all very well, but even Rush had to take a car when Emma was with him, and there was nothing he could do to hurry traffic or make lights turn green. Emma didn't mind. She enjoyed car rides. She sat upright and dignified in the passenger seat, ignoring the occasional squirrel but always ready to thump her tail at the smile of any friendly passerby.

Cindy was at the front desk this morning, which was good. Of Dr. McMahon's three receptionists, Cindy was the one who always had patients' charts pulled ahead of time, and an extra biscuit for Emma. Every dog who came through the door got one biscuit. Emma got two: the first a tiny little Milkbone biscuit that was probably too small for her to taste and the other, today, from a special stash of sizable peanut-butter biscuits, shaped like pumpkins because it was nearly Halloween.

"You're right on time, just like always," Cindy said cheerfully. She leaned over the desk. "Good morning, Emma! How's the old lady today?"

Emma accepted the biscuits with a polite wave of her heavy tail; one biscuit and then the other disappeared at a bite. Then Emma whuffled along Cindy's arm to make sure she hadn't missed a hidden treat, sighed heavily, and sat, regal and patient, watching Rush for a cue about what they might do next.

Cindy straightened, wiped her hands on a tissue, and said to Rush, "We've got pumpkin cookies too, if you want one. People cookies. Another client brought them." She set the plate up on the counter and nudged it toward Rush. "You might as well have one; Dr. McMahon's running a little late. Sorry. We had a hit-by-car first thing this morning. You've decided Emma needs a pet?" She nodded at the kitten, currently tucked mostly out of sight under Rush's jacket. It was a pale handful of gray fluff with a white chin and enormous greenish eyes. But it was a bold little thing. When Rush extracted it from its hiding place and set it on the counter, it strolled a few steps with its tail up in the air and then paused to bat at one of the pens lying nearby.

Rush took a pumpkin cookie and broke it neatly in half. "You nearly had two hit-by-cars. Though I don't expect there'd have been much left of this little guy. How's the..." Rush tilted his head, raising his eyebrows inquisitively as he handed Emma her half of the cookie.

"Beagle. Sweet little girl. Poor thing followed her nose a little too far and got lost, I suppose. The driver *almost* stopped in time. Lacerations, bruises, but nothing seems to be broken and Dr. McMahon doesn't think there're any internal injuries. She'll be all right." Cindy shook her head. "The driver who hit her brought her in, but she says she can't keep a dog. You know what my daughters'll say if they hear the story. We'll see if anybody turns up looking for her, but you know, I've always liked beagles."

Beagles weren't Rush's personal favorite breed—too small, too vocal—but he nodded. "No tags?"

"Nope. People're careless." Cindy ran a fingertip down the kitten's back, stroked along its jaw, peeked under its tail, and added comfortably, "Cute little guy. A little young to leave his mother, but he sure looks like he thinks the world's his oyster, doesn't he?" She smiled at Rush. "He's lucky a good Samaritan spotted him. Sure you don't want to keep him? Well, maybe the beagle's owner will turn up and be in desperate need of a kitten to keep his dog company." She scooped the kitten up just before he could jump off the counter and headed for the back of the hospital via the staff door, adding over her shoulder, "Dr. McMahon will be ready in just a minute, if you want to get a weight on Emma."

Rush looked down at Emma. She was wistfully watching Cindy carry the kitten away, but, feeling his eyes on her, she turned her head and gazed into his face. Her ears pricked forward inquiringly: *Are we going to do something fun? Are there more biscuits?* Emma was always hopeful, even at the vet. Perhaps especially at the vet, most especially on beautiful fall mornings. She'd long since understood that arriving at the vet often meant meeting friendly people and, in nice weather, always meant biscuits and a detour by the beach on the way home: overall a combination of all her favorite things in life.

Rush tried not to notice how much gray grizzled her black muzzle or how her blocky head had become bonier over the past year. Her wide-set eyes were just as trusting, her ears just as alert, her broad head just as silky as ever when he rested his hand on it. But he didn't have to ask her to sit on the scale to know that Emma had lost weight since spring—maybe just since midsummer.

He started to turn toward the scale, paused, tilted his head, murmured, "Stay," reinforced the command with a palm-out gesture, and took not quite five and a quarter seconds to catch up with and stop a driverless car that someone had forgotten to put in park. On the way back he prevented a Pokémon Go player from walking right in front of a truck—on the Nuisance Scale, a nine: you'd think people would have more brains than kittens but somehow they didn't seem to. Then he stepped back into his place beside Emma, straightened his jacket, ran a hand down her neck—possibly just a little thinner under her thick coat than it had been—and smiled at Cindy, who, now kitten-less, was just coming back into the front of the veterinary hospital.

"Haven't got her weight yet?"

"Just about to." Rush beckoned for Emma to step onto the scale, lifted a finger to suggest a sit, and frowned at the number that appeared.

"Seventy-eight," Cindy said, scribbling the number in Emma's chart. "Down five, almost six pounds since July."

Rush nodded silently. Cindy's tone was cheerfully neutral, but he didn't need anyone to tell him that a dog Emma's age shouldn't lose too much weight. He'd been trying different kinds of food, but Emma didn't seem to have much appetite lately.

Cindy slipped Emma another peanut-butter biscuit and nodded toward the far end of the room. "Exam room one, and the doctor will be right with you."

Exam room one had a picture of a canine skeleton on one wall and a lot of client photos on another. Emma was up there, nearly in the middle, a big eight-by-ten photo in a narrow black frame. Rush had taken that picture eight years ago, a month or so after a frantic episode involving a swallowed sock and emergency surgery. In the picture, a much younger Emma was standing solid and four-square on the beach, the lacey foam of a retreating wave pearl-white against her massive paws, her black coat shining almost blue in the brilliant light. Her head was up, her ears alert, her gaze fixed on something out of sight. Swimmers, probably. Just in case someone needed rescue. She looked ready to leap into the sea, ready to haul any weight any distance—she looked like she'd be delighted to try to rescue a whole shipload of distressed sailors, one at a time or all together.

Not the biggest Newfoundland ever born; no one ever mistook Emma for a bear. Or hardly anyone. But no one ever mistook her for a Labrador, either. She looked like exactly what she was: the powerful kind of dog who would fearlessly challenge storm waves to rescue drowning swimmers. Serious, intent, alert, waiting for a word: *Give me the go and I'll get that guy swimming way out there right back to shore.*

She would, too. No one had ever had to teach her to haul swimmers to shore. The hard part had been teaching her to wait for permission before bringing them in.

Even these days, Rush had to hold her back on the beach, or she'd go after any splashing kid. Never mind that Rush himself could rescue a drowning swimmer faster and more easily than even Emma. Run straight across the surface of the water, circle the drowning victim, scoop him up and back to shore so fast no one saw anything but a blur across the water.

Come to think of it, the one drowning kid Rush had ever pulled out of a riptide, he'd have missed if not for Emma. Drowning victims didn't scream and flail; they didn't have the breath to scream. They drowned paddling in frantic but quiet desperation.

He hadn't even known that, then. Emma had known it. She'd been born knowing it, apparently. She'd been the one to spot a little girl drowning not a dozen feet from her family, when Rush had been watching blindly, with no idea what he was seeing. His stupidity hadn't mattered. Even if he hadn't been there, the girl would still have been fine. Emma wasn't fast enough to run across the surface of the sea and scoop up a little girl and get back again without ever getting her toes wet, but she'd have done the job. Nobody could drown with Emma on lifeguard duty.

A hero dog. Emma didn't need special powers to be a hero: not superspeed and not the clairvoyance Rush called fastsight. She just needed to be a Newfoundland, and a good dog.

She was that. A good dog. A great dog. Rush ruffled his fingers through the fur behind Emma's ears. She sighed and leaned heavily against him.

Dr. McMahon's voice was audible, the words not distinguishable yet, but approaching. The doctor's voice was deep and unhurried, the kind of voice that calmed skittish dogs and suspicious cats and worried owners. His unseen hand fell on the doorknob, which rattled and began to turn.

Rush blinked, turning his head, his attention snagged by something not too far away... something...his fastsight resolved, and he sighed. Before the sigh was finished, he'd dug his suit out from the trunk of his car, changed, run a couple miles nearly to the limit of his fastsight, and snagged the pistol out of the hand of the kid who'd pulled it on the convenience store attendant at the Shell station. Rush laid the gun on the counter, handcuffed the kid, and said sternly, scowling, "I have important things to do. I'm a busy man, you understand? Don't make me come back here." He didn't let himself speak too fast. That had been about the most difficult thing he'd ever had to learn: how to see fast and move fast and yet remember to speak slooooowly. It took time to get those words out: nearly four seconds.

The kid gaped. The store attendant grinned and started to say something, but Rush didn't stay to listen. He whipped back to the animal hospital and changed out of his suit—a nuisance, but it was his rule to wear it when stopping a crime. Wear it and make sure he was seen. Everyday rescue work was one thing; for that it didn't matter whether he was recognized. But visible costumes might help deter minor crime. That was one theory, anyway. So Rush always wore his suit when he interfered with a mugging or robbery or whatever, and tried to remember to slow down enough to be visible. Even when it was inconvenient.

He was back in the exam room, leaning against the wall out of immediate line of sight from the door, pretending to look at his phone, just as Dr. McMahon entered the room and glanced around for him.

"Ah, yes," said Dr. McMahon, blinking and rubbing his eyes. "Yes, good morning." He refocused on Emma. "And a good morning to you, Emma, my girl. And how are you this fine day?" Bending—he didn't have to bend far—he patted Emma firmly on the shoulder, ran a hand down the length of her body, and frowned at Rush. "Lost a little weight, I see."

"Her appetite hasn't been great, lately. I've been adding treats to her meal..."

"Have you, then?"

"Chicken, tuna, a little sprinkle of Parmesan..."

"Hmm. Yes. That all sounds tasty, I must say. Yes. That's what brought you in? How does she seem otherwise? A little grayer, a little slower, a little stiff getting up and down, I expect, but not much change from July, I hope?" Rather absently, Dr. McMahon began checking Emma over. A casual glance at her mouth, a firm touch down her spine, a light pressure at her hocks. She bent her head around curiously and nudged his ear, and the doctor chuckled and heaved himself back to his feet.

Always short, pudgy, and balding; and now, like Emma, Dr. McMahon was just a little grayer, a little slower, and a little more stiff getting up and down than he once had been. He had given Emma her first puppy shots and, later, a stern injunction against eating socks. Later, he'd heard the story about Emma's spotting the drowning girl with approval but without surprise. "Good breeding, sound instincts, and sensible as they come," he'd agreed. "Her father was just the same. A Landseer Newf. Handsome fellow. Impossible for anyone to drown with that dog on duty. He saved a man once, too. A friend of his owner's son. The young man was too drunk to realize he should stay out of the pool...dogs do have more sense than people, sometimes. His owner sent me a picture."

Rush had found it on the wall, unframed, up at the top. A casual snapshot, yellowing a bit around the edges: a heavy-boned black-and-white Newfoundland, the front half of his body draped across a man's lap. The man was grinning, one arm resting across the dog's shoulders. Even half hidden as the man was, his pride in and love for his dog was clear. Judging from that photo, that dog had probably weighed half again what Emma did. Or what she *should* weigh.

"No, not much change from this summer," he answered now. "But she's lost a few pounds. I just thought...I didn't like to let it go on without checking. She's always been an easy keeper. Never missed a meal, but now lately, sometimes I have to feed her every bite out of my hand."

"Hmm."

"She likes the tuna, though."

"I should think so. Very suitable." The doctor removed his glasses, folded them, and tapped them lightly against his palm. "All good ideas. Keep it up. I'll give you a recipe for liver brownies, if you like."

Rush tilted his head. "I thought you didn't approve of people food for dogs."

"They're medicinal, of course," Dr. McMahon explained with a perfectly straight face. "I'll type the recipe out on a prescription label for you. Chicken livers, wheat flour, barley flour, potato flakes, a couple eggs, a dash of garlic powder. Puree and bake. Some of the most finicky older dogs love them. I had a sick Papillon eat nothing but liver brownies for a month once. We added crushed calcium to his, though. Those little guys, every bite matters." He paused. "I'll also take just a tube or two of blood, if you don't mind. Check this and that..."

"Kidneys, liver..."

"Just a precaution." Dr. McMahon unfolded his glasses and put them back on.

Rush held off the vein himself. A tech could have done it, but Emma was so easy to handle it didn't seem worth the bother of calling a tech.

"Nothing more cooperative than a Newf," Dr. McMahon observed, patting Emma approvingly on the shoulder and heaving himself slowly back to his feet, purple-topped tubes of blood in one hand and the syringe in the other. "Veins like hoses and never nervous about anything. At least not a grand lady like Emma."

Rush nodded. "Results...what, tomorrow?"

"Or the next day. Likely enough everything'll come back normal. Or as normal as we can expect, at Emma's age." Dr.

McMahon took off his glasses again and tapped them gently against his hip. He didn't look at Rush, keeping his slightly myopic gaze on Emma instead. "Listen..."

"I know," Rush said, to stop him.

"These big dogs..."

"I know," Rush said again.

"She's a fine lady," the doctor said gently. Bending, he ran his hand down Emma's neck and along her sturdy back, his attention absorbed. "As fine as they come. A touch of arthritis—well, that comes to most of us. Tuna's fine. Better than fine. Try those liver brownies. Whatever she likes. We'll see if we can't get a few pounds back on her, shall we? Parmesan's got a lot of salt in it. A dog this size, though, a sprinkle of Parmesan isn't going to hurt her."

"That's what I figured." Rush paused. He took a breath...and waved a hand irritably, his fastsight presenting him, inescapably, with the kind of problem a speedster just had to handle. Down on Lower Washburn where the road had flooded, a school bus, a curve where the fast-moving flooded creek had worn away the shoulder—the bus was already tipping—only a few kids on it and no doubt they'd be fine, the drop wasn't far and even flooded that wasn't much of a creek. But still. Any number of strongmen who could shove buses around with one hand, without straining a muscle, and where were they? Brick, Samson, even that oaf Hercules, but not one of them anywhere handy. Naturally.

Rush knew his annoyance wasn't quite fair. Strongmen rarely had any kind of clairvoyance. That's why strongmen mostly did best as team players. Knowing this didn't stop him from being annoyed.

This time Rush was in a hurry. He made it to the bus well before it finished its fall, barely a quarter second after he first spotted it. He had all seven kids and the driver—a heavyset guy, even for Rush not the easiest burden to lug around—off the bus and up the hill on the other side of the road half a second after that. He was back in the exam room less than two and three-eighths seconds after he'd left.

Emma woofed at him, gently, and he touched her head.

Dr. McMahon blinked, rubbed his eyes, put his glasses back on, and straightened with a grunt, rubbing his back.

"Listen, Scott," he said, rare use of a client's first name.

"I know," Rush said, with some force.

"I know you do. So do what you can to make sure she enjoys this fall. As you always have, to be sure. Gentle walking. Swimming is fine, if she wants to. Nothing better, really. Try not to look too far ahead, if you want my advice. This is as pleasant an October as I can recall. *Enjoy* it. That's my official medical advice. Make sure Emma enjoys it. And I'll let you know about that bloodwork in a day or two. Right?"

"...right." Rush met Emma's dark eyes. That was too hard. He looked up instead, but his gaze snagged once more on the framed photograph of the younger Emma, Emma in the spring sunshine with the white foam washing around her feet and the joy of life in every line of her body. That was worse.

"She still loves life," Dr. McMahon said gently. "Taking her to the beach this morning, are you? Good. Go on, then, and try not to worry."

"I never worry," Rush lied. "Bad for the digestion."

"Get a pumpkin cookie on your way out," the doctor prescribed gravely. "Good for the digestion. Medicinal. Give her one. Why hold back? Give her two."

The beach wasn't crowded in October. The water was too cold for swimming, the concessions shut up for the season, the no-lifeguard-on-duty signs prominently displayed. A few other dog owners were out, though. A young woman threw a stick into the waves for her beautiful Golden to bring joyfully back, which the dog did, over and over, with flair and speed and utter delight. Rush couldn't help but watch. He tried not to resent the Golden's obvious youth and vigor. In a few short years, that dog too would be old.

He kicked at the sand and looked away from the Golden Retriever. Emma ambled across the damp sand, moving slowly and deliberately. Her head was up, though, and her tail waving gently. She wasn't watching the Golden or the young dog's owner. She was gazing out across the waves. Just in case someone might be out there after all. Just in case someone might be in trouble. She moved always at that same deliberate pace, and always watched for the distant head of anyone in the water.

And Rush walked slowly beside her. As long as Emma wanted to amble down this beach, at any pace she found comfortable, Rush would walk beside her, and adjust his speed to hers.

FIRE AND EARTH

*This story takes place several years after the events of the
Griffin Mage trilogy.*

*My biggest regret in that trilogy was never finding a way to
give Bertaud a Happily Ever After—I kept trying, and the stories kept
going in other directions. The Griffin Mage trilogy is all about how
choices have consequences, but Bertaud's overall story wound up a
little closer to tragic than I would have preferred. In fact, that's true
of several characters' stories in this trilogy.*

*This story offers Bertaud, and several others, a chance to build
Happily Ever Afters. The rest of their lives will be up to them, but I
wish them all the best of luck.*

Bertaud stood in the solar of the great house, by the
largest of the west-facing windows, several of which he
had opened to let in the damp and heavy air. He was
gazing out at the rain-soaked gardens and the rain-
darkened town and the pewter sky, but without really
seeing any of them. If anyone had challenged him, he
might have said he was lost in his thoughts, though this
afternoon his thoughts seemed even to himself to move
as slowly and sluggishly as the humid air. There was no
real wind, but the soporific breeze that rolled in through
those open windows was fragrant with damp earth and
cut grass and with the honeysuckle and jasmine that
grew up the trellises that lined the stonework outside the
solar.

The many-windowed solar was almost the highest point within the great house, which meant it might be nearly the highest point in all the flat Delta. The house sprawled across a wide, low hill; the only hill for half a day's travel in any direction. The house itself was built wide and low; only one wing rose as much as two stories high, and a single round tower was four stories tall. The tower was red brick, though most of the great house was gray stone or wet-resistant cypress wood. But the room at the top of the tower was windowless. Bertaud much preferred the solar. From its many wide windows, on a clear day, one might be able to see all the way north to the emerald marshes and all the way south to the mudflats where the Sierhanan River flowed out into the sea.

Today it was impossible to see any farther than the gardens and the nearer districts of the town of Tiefenauer. The slate rooftops and cobbles of the town gleamed dully in the wet. The whitewashed homes and shops seemed grey in the overcast, and even the scarlet or spring green or buttercup yellow of the painted shutters and doors seemed dull rather than bright. Nearly every home had vines with purple or crimson or orange flowers tumbling from its balcony, but the flowers hung heavily in the wet.

The rain continued to fall, more than a drizzle but less than a storm, as it had all day and all the night before and all the previous day and most of the previous week. Early summer could be like that in the Delta. So could late summer, except then it would be so hot anyone would be glad of days and weeks of clouds and rain. In this season, warm though it was, one grew weary of the damp.

The town ran down to the river, but today the river was lost in the mist, though from time to time Bertaud caught a glimpse of the high, arched bridge that led from his own more-or-less independent Delta to Linularinum, which had sometimes claimed the Delta and sometimes lost it but certainly did not rule it now. He had intended to cross that bridge today, visit the Linularinan town of Desamion, see what new wares might have made their way this far south...mostly he had wanted to walk through a town that wasn't his responsibility, bargain with shopkeepers who might know who he was but who had less reason to care than his own people.

He could still do that. But such an expedition had less appeal on such a damp afternoon.Bertaud missed his cousin Mienthe. He always missed her when she traveled, but seldom so keenly as today. If Mienthe had been here, she wouldn't have been put off by a little rain—though she might have been more likely to walk the other way, out of town and into the marshy woods. Mienthe was not afraid of snakes or poisonous frogs, and she could imitate the little birds of the woodlands well enough to coax them down from the dripping branches. Especially because she often carried a handful of cracked wheat to tempt them.

Mienthe had been absent from the great house and from Tiefenauer and from the Delta for several months, and if things went well, she would probably be absent for several months longer. Iaor Daveien Behanad Safiad, King of Feierabiand and also King, more or less, of the Delta, had asked Bertaud's cousin to escort his little daughters—not quite so little now—to Casmantium, to the court of the Arobern. Mienthe had met Brechen Glansent Arobern and she knew his son, Prince Erichstaben of Casmantium, quite well, and so both kings had made that request.

Erich had lived at Iaor's court when the girls had been little; a hostage against his father but a companion and almost a foster-brother to the little princesses. A foster-brother was not what either King Iaor or the

Arobern of Casmantium had in mind now, as everyone knew, even the girls. Everyone knew the importance of settling the tension between Casmantium and Feierabiand for another generation or two, if possible. Everyone knew that the best chance to make that happen lay with the children of the two kings. The question that had to be settled now was not whether one of the little princesses would become affianced to the Casmantian prince, but which girl it would be.

Of course Mienthe had agreed to accompany the girls. Bertaud would not have tried to persuade her otherwise. His cousin had a knack for seeing into the hearts of men and women, and of understanding many kinds of truth. She'd be the one most concerned to make sure everyone wound up *happy*. That was important when everyone else would be thinking more about politics and less about people. Bertaud could hardly begrudge her absence, however empty the house felt without her.

Personally, he thought the elder of the two princesses would likely be the one chosen to wed Prince Erichstaben. Karianes was pretty and patient and kind-hearted, with a knack for soothing tempestuous arguments and a very powerful affinity for mice. Both gifts would be very useful to a future queen, because though mice weren't flashy or impressive, they were everywhere. A gift for keeping mice out of grain stores would be a good deal more worthwhile than an affinity for, say, hawks or horses or some other more impressive beast.

Far more worthwhile than Bertaud's own peculiar and dangerous affinity, which he would never use again nor even admit to possessing.

Without question, a simple affinity for mice was far preferable.

The littler princess was Anlin, ten months younger

than her sister. She possessed an adventurous nature and a great deal of charm, along with a stubborn temper that was proving to be, somewhat to Bertaud's amusement, more than a match for that of her father. If she possessed any gift for calling an animal, it had not yet come out in her. She was the sort of child who would be disappointed with any affinity less flashy and impressive than hawks or horses; that child liked spectacle and would delight in a gift that let her call eagles out of the sky or something of that sort. That was all very well, but before leaving, Anlin had taken to declaring loudly that she was going to marry Erich and Karienes could find someone else to marry. Quiet, gentle Karienes hadn't argued. She didn't. But she'd had a stubborn look in her eye. In her own way she could be even more tenacious than her little sister.

Bertaud had no doubt the hardest part, with the girls so young, would be sorting out which would actually turn out to be the better match for Erich once they had grown into women. That and preventing jealousy between the princesses. Mienthe would handle it all with calm, graceful composure. He didn't doubt that either.

But despite the general clatter of busy life going on all around him, the great house seemed empty without his cousin. Lonely, somehow.

The rain didn't help. It dampened sound and closed out the distance and made Bertaud feel more isolated than ever. He never felt lonely...or he was too accustomed to loneliness to be bothered...but today solitude seemed more a burden than he usually felt it.

He turned almost gratefully at a tap on the solar's door. This proved to be Tenned, a brawny young lieutenant in Bertaud's house guard, who offered the sort of shallow bow that made it clear he did not expect his lord to like the message he brought. That dampened Bertaud's gratitude at the interruption, but nevertheless

76

he nodded permission to speak.

"My lord," Tenned said, his tone absolutely neutral. "Your cousin Terre son of Talenes asks whether you might have a moment. He wishes to ask your advice regarding a problem that has come up regarding his inheritance."

"My cousin Terre," Bertaud repeated. Despite himself, his tone on the name was not quite as neutral as the guardsman's. "I gather he doesn't care to wait a few weeks in order to present this problem to me at the end of the month?" The Lord of the Delta customarily made time to hear any of his people regarding problems and petitions during the last four days of every month. Plainly Terre, son of Bertaud's least favorite and most recently deceased uncle, hoped to trade on his cousinly relationship to the Lord of the Delta so that he would not have to wait. That kind of presumption was certainly a good way to put Bertaud out of temper before his interview. Bertaud was actually surprised. Terre, unlike his father, had never shown that sort of presumption before.

"Apparently the matter is urgent, my lord. I've put him in the smaller anteroom of the east wing, my lord, and sent a boy to bring him chilled wine."

"Of course you have." This was not the sort of interruption Bertaud would have welcomed at the best of times. Today his restlessness had transmuted instantly to irritation. He tried not to let it show. He was tempted to tell the guardsman to send Terre son of Talenes away, to say that he was too busy to speak to his cousin today and direct him to append his name to the petitioners who would see their lord at the end of the month.

On the other hand, there would be no point to anything of the kind. He knew very well he wouldn't much care to see Terre son of Talenes later, either. So he sighed and nodded and headed for the smaller anteroom of the east wing of the great house.

The anteroom was in fact not very small; it was only smaller than the larger anteroom. Its furnishings were somewhat shabby and a little behind the current style, which was well enough as anyone asked to wait in that room was supposed to realize that the Lord of the Delta was not especially pleased to see him. In general the guardsmen and servants were quite good at sorting out which visitors to take to the smaller anteroom and which to other, better favored locations within the house.

Terre son of Talenes had inherited his father's property when Talenes had died of a lingering fever early this past spring. Bertaud had sent a note, but he had not otherwise paid much attention. Terre had sent an equally brief and stilted acknowledgment, but he had not otherwise pressed himself on Bertaud's attention. In fact, if Bertaud had met Terre at any point in the past ten years, he could not recall the occasion.

Terre must be...twenty-four or -five now. Always surprising to realize how much time had passed when one had not been paying attention.

Bertaud was also slightly surprised to find that his cousin was not an ill-favored young man. True, he had much the look of his father, but then Bertaud had much the look of his, so that wasn't something he could reasonably hold against his cousin. He could not recollect hearing anything much of Terre one way or the other. He had wed a few years past, Bertaud did recall that much. He had married a townswoman of reasonably good family, a woman whose family's commercial interests were fairly well aligned with his own. Bertaud had not attended the ceremony, though he had sent a note on that occasion as well.

Talenes had once intended to force Mienthe to marry Terre in order to get control of her inheritance...it had all been rather sordid. Bertaud had put a knife firmly through that idea when he'd come back to the Delta and taken Mienthe into his own household. Mienthe had never once mentioned their cousin Terre by name to Bertaud after that; she had never talked much about her years as their uncle Talenes' ward. A few years ago she had made a far more complicated match, with a man a great deal less respectable than Terre; a man who had no significant family and did not care in the least about Mienthe's inheritance. Bertaud had not entirely approved of that match either, but at least he knew her husband loved her and would try his best to make her happy and would never ask her to leave the Delta. She *was* happy, and generally, when she wasn't traveling to the Casmantian court, Bertaud could see that she was. He had no need to concern himself now about her unhappy childhood.

But Bertaud had not forgotten that Terre had been willing to go along with his father's plans. Probably it was wrong to blame a boy of fifteen, maybe sixteen, for that thoughtless disregard for a girl cousin he hardly knew, that casual intention to take advantage of her unfortunate circumstances. Many boys of fifteen or sixteen were careless, selfish, self-absorbed louts. But Bertaud had certainly blamed Talenes, and so he had never made any effort to learn whether Terre son of Talenes might have grown into a different sort of man.

Now he saw at once that, at some time in the past years, Terre must have come to understand the lingering dislike Bertaud held for his father and his family; perhaps not the reason for that dislike, but at least the fact of it. The young man had been sitting in one of the anteroom's less comfortable chairs, a roll of papers lying alongside the glass of wine on a table beside the chair. But he rose with alacrity at Bertaud's entrance and stood straight, with his hands clasped together, not quite the attitude of a supplicant but not far from it. He did not speak, certainly did not say *Cousin,* but waited respectfully for Bertaud to speak first.

That would not have been his father's manner, Bertaud was fairly certain. None of Bertaud's uncles had ever been entirely reconciled to Bertaud taking his own father's place as Lord of the Delta, Talenes perhaps least of all. But Terre seemed altogether less arrogant, or at least if he harbored the same feeling of aggrieved entitlement, he had the sense to hide it better.

Bertaud was annoyed that the young man gave him no immediate cause for offense. This was not an attitude he liked much in himself, so he said, if not entirely graciously, then with studied neutrality, "Cousin. You have encountered some difficulty with your late father's estate or holdings? I gather the problem could not wait until the end of the month?"

Terre lifted his chin, a slight movement that might have suggested pride but in fact made it clear that he was nervous and trying to hide it. "Yes, my lord." Not *Cousin,* for all Bertaud had implicitly granted permission for that familiarity by using it himself. Terre picked up the roll of papers, hesitated, and set it down again. "It's a Linularinan contract, my lord. And papers pertaining to it. I apologize for troubling you, but the terms were written with regard to midsummer."

Which fell two days from now. Well. This annoyed Bertaud again, as he had to acknowledge that his cousin had after all had good reason to approach him before the end of the month. He nodded curtly. Then he was slightly ashamed of his own brusque manner, so he said, "I see that you had to bring it to me now, then." He could imagine how this had happened. Of course any contract written by a Linularinan legist was certain to be dense, complicated, quite likely deceptive, and definitely not something a man could just skim lightly across to get the sense of it. He asked, "Can you briefly explain the difficulty?"

"My lord, it requires the repayment of a considerable debt no later than midsummer, or else the Linularinan establishment with which my father drew up this contract will be able to foreclose on our house. My father—you understand, his health seemed good. I doubt it occurred to anyone that he might not be able to settle our family's affairs to better advantage, or at least not with such a loss implicit in the terms. But in the confusion of his death, I fear some of the contract terms were let slip. I didn't realize—but then I got this letter, it's in the roll with the other papers. I think—I don't think there's a way around that clause. I've had the best legist in Tiefenauer look it over. Her opinion is appended as well. So I've come to ask—" Terre hesitated, darting a quick look at Bertaud's face. Bertaud did not allow his expression to change, although it was clear enough where the young man was headed.

After that slight pause, Terre went on. "I've come to request your assistance in settling this debt, my lord, so that my mother, and my wife and I, and my heirs to come, won't lose our home."

That must have been painful. Bertaud could see from his cousin's taut expression that it had been. This was not a young man who enjoyed asking for favors. It actually spoke somewhat well of him that he knew he was asking for a favor and not for something to which he was entitled.

Bertaud kept his tone mild. "I see. So you ask, as my cousin, that I take on some portion of this debt?"

But Terre shook his head. "No, my lord. I've brought this to you because you're the Lord of the Delta. It wouldn't benefit the Delta to have a Linularinan establishment take my father's estate. I ask for a loan, not a gift. I think it would take five or six years for me to pay back a loan at ordinary interest, my lord. I've worked out the repayment schedule—that's included at the end."

Bertaud sighed. It must be a considerable sum indeed if it would take so long to pay off. Terre probably hoped he would ask the much lighter interest customary for a loan within a family. But the young man had not asked for that consideration. He *was* proud. Bertaud was reluctantly aware he might have liked Terre for that, if he hadn't been Talenes' son.

He held out his hand, and after a second Terre picked up the roll of papers and handed it to him, a little reluctantly. No doubt he did not much look forward to having his cousin look over the evidence of his father's carelessness. Bertaud would not have to say *Your father was too arrogant to take proper care.* That much was obvious from the mere fact of the debt. Of course Talenes had not expected that fever, nor the sudden failure of his heart that had followed—but it was a man's responsibility to be sure such accidents, however unlikely, did not leave his family and heirs vulnerable.

"I'll have my own legist look this over," he said. "I'll speak to you again...I trust tomorrow morning will be convenient?"

"It certainly would be, my lord. Thank you for considering my request."

Terre's tone was stilted on that last, and his manner was stiff as he bowed. Bertaud knew his cousin must realize that Bertaud might feel disinclined to be helpful. Hence his careful manners and his request for a loan, not a gift—and his explicit mention of a loan offered on ordinary rather than family terms. Terre was doing everything he could to get Bertaud to agree.

Bertaud was tempted to crush the papers in his hand, drop them on the floor, say *I don't recall you offered any great generosity to your little cousin when she needed a friend more than anything,* and walk out.

That would be worse than unkind; it would be unjust. But he still wanted to do it.

He made himself say instead, his tone level, "Tomorrow morning, then, Cousin. An hour after dawn, let us say. I will instruct my people to expect you."

Terre bowed once more. "Thank you, my lord."

Bertaud wanted to snap at him, *Don't thank me yet.* He closed his teeth on the words, nodded shortly, and walked out.

Nothing about this had improved his mood. He ought to look at Terre's papers, but he hated wading through Linularinan contracts; he thought if he forced himself to study this one at this moment, he would just refuse assistance to his cousin out of sheer annoyance. He knew the legist Terre must have consulted: a subtle, skilled lady with a powerful gift for contract law. He would read her summary, never mind the rest. If necessary he would ask her to an early breakfast tomorrow and see what suggestions she might have.

At the moment, his dark mood and restlessness were too strong to stay pent up indoors, with nothing to do but examine exasperating, troublesome documents that would no doubt require him to exert himself on behalf of a cousin he did not even like. Let it wait. Let it all wait for a morning that might bring better weather and a more generous mood.

Handing the papers to a startled maidservant, Bertaud told her to take them to his office and himself turned to stride for the door and the rain-soaked gardens.

The rain had stopped. He had not realized that. The skies were still overcast, but here and there the sun was trying to break through. Mienthe wasn't here with her pocketful of wheat and her cheerful manners. If she had been, she would certainly have wanted to go out. Bertaud didn't want the company of anyone other than Mienthe. But he hardly cared to stay indoors. He walked through the gardens that surrounded the great house and on into the town.

Tiefenauer, at least near the sprawling great house, in the neighborhoods where the prosperous folk lived, was a town of broad streets and ancient cypresses and swamp oaks. Wooden boardwalks lay beside all the important streets, allowing passers-by to keep out of the winter muck. Deep drainage channels ran underneath the boardwalks, so that only the greatest storms of spring and fall would flood the town. Even the past week had not filled those channels, only flushed them clean, so the town smelled mostly of wet cobbles and flowers and only a little of horses and sewers.

As Bertaud made his way along one street and another, the afternoon sun came lancing through heavy, broken clouds, and with the sun, heat so that the cobbles steamed. What little breeze had wandered into the high solar of the great house could not be felt at ground level; here the air was hot and still. Fat black bees and purple-backed hummingbirds appeared almost as soon as the rain stopped, making their way from one long, dripping flower to another, all along the balconies where everyone grew great pots of flowering vines. Sapphire-winged flycatchers came out too, and the smaller black ones, all very welcome as mosquitoes whined in the shade.

Bertaud passed the many-layered fountain that stood in the middle of town, all its green copper fish leaping and splashing beneath the great oak that was the symbol and sign of the Delta. Moss draped the wide-spreading branches of the oak, with yellow-throated warblers nesting in the living clumps.

It was not so very far from the fountain to the edge of Tiefenauer, at least not if one headed north, to where the marshy woodlands came closest the edge of town. The land here was too wet for fields or pasture and so it was all left to woodlands, the trees carefully cut and managed so that townsfolk would not run short of good seasoned wood and charcoal for cooking and for the chilly winters. Though at the moment it was hard to imagine any weather but hot and close and humid.

Outside of town, the road wound along the drier bits toward the higher ground where better farmland could be found. With the rain so recently stopped, few folk were as yet out on the road, but Bertaud did not particularly welcome even such scant company. Before long he turned off onto a woodcutters' path that led back down toward the riverside sloughs. Thick-boled trees crowded close along each side of the path, water-oaks and cypresses and such, festooned with great masses of silvery moss and with flowering vines. The air hung still, dense with humidity. Not a leaf stirred, though drops of water pattered from higher in the canopy, and temporary streams ran across tumbled rocks beside the muddy path. Mosquitoes whined, but as long as Bertaud strode along briskly, they were not too much bother. His steps made almost no sound on the damp earth and soggy leaves underfoot. The angle of the light changed subtly as the afternoon moved on toward dusk, but this time of year sunset came late and he had no great urge to turn back. As long as he came to the road before full dark, he should have little trouble making his way back to town.

He did not know how far he had come nor how late it had grown until, all around him, water running beside the path and pooling in low places and dripping from leaves turned suddenly to steam and then evaporated. The muggy heat gave way all at once to a drier, more furious kind of heat, a withering fiery furnace-heat that tasted of hot metal and sand. Near at hand, the moss festooning the lower branches of one great oak suddenly dried into a brittle, silvery lace and then crumbled to dust. The leaves on those branches curled, charring at the edges.

Bertaud stood very still.

Finally he saw the griffin. She was hard to see amid the shadows and the narrow dapples of sunlight that came through the leaves, for she was darker in color than most of her kind. Neither gold nor bronze nor burnished coppery red; this griffin was a rich dark brown from her feathered crest to the tip of her leonine tail. The longest primary feathers of her great wings were lightly barred with gold, but other than that she was dark. Among her larger kin she might have been overlooked, for in addition to her dark coloring, she was small and slim— for a griffin, which still put her head at a level with his. But she was not a danger, or probably not a danger. Not to ordinary men with ordinary gifts, and certainly not to Bertaud.

Her name was Opailikiita. Opailikiita Sehanaka Kiistaike. She knew that he was accustomed to griffins and was in some measure a friend to the people of fire and air. That was all she knew. She did not know, could not know, his secret. Only two people besides himself knew of his unique affinity, neither of whom would ever speak of it. No more than he would himself. He knew Kes had never told Opailikiita, though she and the griffin were friends, or the griffin equivalent of friends. If she knew, she would never have come like this, openly, to find him without trying to strike him down from behind.

If the griffins knew that a man existed who could command them as other men commanded mice or hawks or horses, there would instantly be a war between fire and earth that would utterly destroy one or the other.

Kes, who had been born human and was now a creature of fire, who had been born to an ordinary family and lived now among the griffins in their desert, knew this secret. She might have killed him when she'd learned of his affinity. She had chosen not to, or more correctly she had been prevented and then later had chosen not to try again lest she precipitate the very disaster she tried to prevent. Certainly she would never so much as whisper the truth she knew to the wind. And Jos, who was both her friend and Bertaud's and also knew the secret, was better able to keep his own council than any other man Bertaud had ever met.

No one else would ever learn of Bertaud's gift, not from Bertaud and not from anyone else. Certainly not Opailikiita. That couldn't be why the griffin had come to find him. Something else had brought her.

Bowing his head in polite greeting, he said, "Opailikiita Sehanaka Kiistaike. What urgent need brings you to me here? This cannot be a comfortable place for you."

It is very damp, the griffin agreed, with a little shiver of her feathers in distaste. *But I have found something that belongs to earth and not to fire, and I thought of you.* Then she folded her wings, revealing...a woman.

Yes. A woman, lying crumpled in the now crisp and dry leaf litter below the oak. Bertaud exclaimed, starting forward but then hesitating to touch her in case he hurt her.

The woman lay on her face, and the jerkin and trousers she wore were those of a man, but the curves of her back and rear were not the curves of a man. Her arms were red and blistered with sun, though her hair, thick and dark, had protected her neck to some extent. Her breathing—he could hear it, shallow and quick and with a disturbing rattle.

She had come deep into our desert, Opailikiita told him. *I do not know how she came so far into the realm of fire, and what she sought so stubbornly I cannot guess, but what she found was death. Only she had not yet captured her death in her hands. It did not seem a day for death, so I waited for the winds to become still so that I might step from the heart of fire to the lands of earth. Then, as she had not yet taken in her death, I brought her to you, man. You will decide whether she should capture death or life.*

A scattering of water droplets pattered down around them, half of them turning to steam as they fell and the other half making tiny round spots of damp soil in the cracked and dry earth underfoot. The griffin made a small noise of disgust and her feathers rippled again, little sparks of fire sifting from her wings. She said, *If she lives, teach her to stay to the country of earth.* Bertaud couldn't tell whether Opailikiita meant this as kind advice or an imperative command or something else, but he guessed the woman's trespass must not have seriously offended the griffin. Opailikiita might have dumped her anywhere in the lands of men, most easily just on the human side of the Wall between the country of fire and the country of earth, and left her to die.

Instead she had brought her here.

Before Bertaud could ask the griffin anything else, Opailikiita was gone, blurring into wind and fire. A light dusting of red sand scattered across the earth where she had stood.

He could have called the griffin back. He clenched his teeth on the self-indulgent impulse to call her and instead bent over the woman, turning her as gently as he could.

It was hard to tell much about her, so badly blistered was her face. Her face was broader and rounder than common to the people of the Delta; Bertaud guessed she might be a woman of Casmantium. She was not old, but not a child. Other than that, he couldn't tell. Her eyes were closed. Just as well she was unconscious, as even her eyelids were blistered. Her lips were cracked, but not bleeding. She was too dehydrated to bleed from such small wounds, probably.

Dehydration was seldom a concern in the Delta, though heatstroke was not uncommon. The heavy, humid air had closed in again upon the griffin's departure, and it was easy to cup his hands full of water from one of the many temporary streams hardly ten steps away. Bertaud bathed the woman's face and let a little water run into her mouth. Not too much. He picked her up, an arm beneath her back and one beneath her knees, like a child. It was not the easiest way to carry someone, but even though she was unconscious, he hesitated to put her over his shoulder in case he hurt her. Anyway, she was lighter than he'd expected. Though he doubted he would still think so in half an hour.

Bertaud had not kept careful track of his direction or his distance. He hadn't cared. But now he hesitated. He could go back the way he'd come. But, burdened with the woman, he probably wouldn't make it all the way to the main road before full dark. He could try, but he was fairly certain he'd come too far. Carrying a woman through the marshy woods in the dark would not be easy, and there might be snakes, coming out in the relative cool of dusk. He might even find quicksand if he lost the path. He knew well enough how to get out of quicksand; any child of the Delta learned such things. But he hardly cared to try while burdened with this poor woman.

The path had been leading him down toward the river. A well-traveled path like this one must go somewhere, but all the way to the river? Maybe, maybe not; but he could well imagine woodcutters and charcoal-burners might rather take their wood and charcoal out of the woods by boat than by carrying it on their backs. A path that made its way to the river, a boat tethered waiting, both seemed reasonably likely. If he could find a boat, that would be a far easier and safer and faster means of getting this woman back to Tiefenauer and to the great house and to a mage who specialized in healing.

If there wasn't a boat, he would mostly likely have to try to care for this woman in whatever shelter he could find or make. In the dark, and the rain, and with no means to make a fire or keep the mosquitoes away. He could just imagine the poor woman dying sometime during the night...it was an ugly idea.

Next time he chose to go for a walk, he would change his mind and go for a ride instead. With a couple of sturdy guardsmen to provide escort and carry unexpected burdens.

After another moment, Bertaud began to make his way down the path the way he had been going. Half an hour. He would give this direction half an hour, after which, if he hadn't come to the riverside, he'd have to consider what kind of shelter he might be able to make.

It had started raining again, slow fat drops that made their way past the leaves overhead and fell on his hair and shoulders and on the woman's face.

At least it was still warm. Perhaps the rain would even help her a little.

Bertaud didn't find the river in half an hour. By then the dusk was well along; what occasional glimpses he got of the sky showed clouds that had gone a strange leaden gold, a color that strongly suggested heavier rains to come. Soon it would be full dark. Bertaud was seriously tempted to call Opailikiita back to him and ask her to shift both him and the woman directly to the great house, something he wished fervently he'd thought of much sooner, before the griffin had fled the damp for the desert.

He could not, of course, *actually* summon the griffin. She would come. Of course she would come. She would acquiesce to anything he asked of her. That was why he couldn't call her, no matter how his arms and back ached and no matter how he feared for the woman he carried. She was still unconscious, though every now and then her poor burned eyelids fluttered.

As he had expected, she no longer seemed especially light. He still carried her in his arms rather than over his shoulder, but that was a decision he might well have to revisit soon. He should stop and look for shelter, but he went on. Just a little farther. The path hadn't worsened, and neither had the woman's condition; he'd stopped several times to collect soursop—soursop tea was good for burns, as everyone who grew up in the Delta knew—and to moisten her lips and bathe her face. She hadn't woken. But her breathing seemed a little better; not so shallow. The moisture in the air might be helping her. Unless the shock of the change from fiery and dry to heavy and humid gave her pleurisy. Bertaud, no healer, wouldn't have laid odds one way or the other, except that her breathing did seem easier. He thought it did.

Five minutes later, he still hadn't found the river, and by then it was quite dark under the trees—so dark he nearly missed the woodcutters' lean-to he found instead. It was a good one, large, made with a frame of cypress and the rest woven of willow. Some of the willow shoots had taken root, as they tended to do, and leafed out, so the lean-to was fairly well protected from the elements. It was not cool inside, nor dry. But it was cooler and drier than the marshy woods.

A cot of willow lay along the back wall of the lean-to, with a blanket of well-oiled wool tucked up out of the wet that could be lain over the withes of the cot. A small pot hung on a broken twig and a single fat candle—the kind that was scented to drive away mosquitoes and gnats—stood on a little shelf of woven willow. Dry, or at least dryish, wood was arranged in a ring of stones on the earthen floor, beneath the blanket, where it was best protected from harder rains that might come through the woven willow.

Bertaud blessed the woodcutters and charcoal burners who had made and furnished this lean-to, which at the moment seemed to offer nearly as much luxury as his own house. He lit the candle and set it on the damp packed earth next to the cot; folded the blanket over the withes that made the mattress and resettled the woman; filled the pot with water from a nearby stream that, in the dark, he found largely by the sound of the gurgling water; made tea with the plentiful willow bark and with soursop leaves and spent several moments coaxing the unconscious woman to drink just a little at a time. It was bitter and he had no honey, but she was so dehydrated that she would drink anything, bitter or not. The rest of the soursop made a poultice for her burned skin. She needed a healer-mage, not rough treatment with wild-grown herbs, but tea and poultices were the best he could do.

She did not wake, though now she was opening her mouth when he dripped tea on her lips. Bertaud hesitated to leave her. But after a moment he took up a stick of wood, lit it from the fire, and went out to see whether the river might lie just a little farther on. He could tell the ground was more sloped here; that might mean the river was nearby. If he'd been a woodcutter, he would have built his lean-to near the river, surely.

In the end, he discovered the river by practically tripping over the edge of the narrow dock, which was surrounded by cypress knees and tangled reeds but led out to clear water. Unfortunately, there was no boat tied up to the little dock. Bertaud uttered a few well-chosen words, but half-heartedly because he knew he'd been lucky enough when he'd found the lean-to.

The makeshift torch blew out before he'd made the return journey up the path, which led to a slow and unpleasant struggle to find his way back to the lean-to rather than lose the path, plunge off into the woods, and no doubt fall into the muddy sloughs or quicksand before he found drier ground. Long before he made it back, it started to rain in earnest, so that the steeper parts of the pathway became a series of waterfalls. Bertaud was soaked through and well coated with mud by the time he came out in the little clearing where the lean-to stood. By then he was far beyond cursing.

But when he ducked under the willow roof, he found the woman awake, up on one elbow, her expression dazed and frightened, so that he instantly forgot his own discomfort.

The candle shed a little light beneath the lean-to's roof. What the woman made of her rude surroundings, as far removed as anyone could conceive from the desert where Opailikiita had found her, Bertaud could hardly guess. What she would make of him, dripping and muddy, was much easier to imagine. He knelt down on the damp earth to make himself seem less threatening.

Then he saw she wasn't afraid after all. Confused, surely; but not afraid, or not of Bertaud. Pushing herself up, she tried to speak—urgently, judging by her attitude. She couldn't manage to form recognizable words; her lips and tongue were still too swollen. But she tried, though it must have hurt her. The effort made her cough, which must have hurt her worse. She touched her lips with a hand that trembled, but from the anger in her expression, from the way she straightened her back— with an effort that plainly cost her—he could see she trembled with weakness, not with fear. Some urgent resolve drove her to ignore pain and weakness and bewilderment and try to speak again.

"Hush!" Bertaud told her. "Don't distress yourself.

You're safe. I fear the night will be bad, but in the morning I'll get you to a healer and see you're cared for." He hesitated, looking at her, and then repeated this assurance in Prechen. Yes. That was better. He could tell she understood him now. She was certainly a Casmantian woman, and if she understood Terheien at all, it was only a little. But though she had clearly understood him the second time, she shook her head emphatically, hit the cot in frustration when she could not speak, shook her head again, and made a hoarse croaking sound of anger and fear.

Bertaud did not know how to reassure her, especially since it was beginning to be clear to him that reassurance on her own behalf wasn't what this woman wanted. A terrible surmise dawned. He said slowly, "Was there someone else with you? Someone else who went into the desert?"

At once he saw that he'd guessed right. She glared from her burned face and tried to stand up.

Jumping to his feet, Bertaud caught her when she would have fallen and eased her back down. He said gently, "The one who brought you to me didn't speak of anyone else. If anyone else living had been found with you, she would surely have brought that person to me as well. Or at least she would have told me there was someone else." He was certain of that much. Even he sometimes found it hard to predict how a griffin might react, but he couldn't believe Opailikiita would have failed to tell him she'd found someone else along with this woman.

Despite his certainty, the urge to call the griffin back to him was now stronger than he'd felt it for years. He set his jaw against the desire. He was sorry for the woman's helpless anger and distress, he was very sorry for it, but he could not call Opailikiita, nor any griffin. Not even for something like this. Most certainly when he was certain there was no one living to save.

He said as gently as he could, "My people will be looking for me. If they don't find me tonight, I'll go for help at dawn. The nights are short this time of year. Try to rest. I'll try to find out about your friend—your husband?"

The woman shook her head and hit the cot again, hard enough to hurt her hand.

Bertaud caught her hand to stop her when she tried to do that again. "A friend? A relative?" He paused, realizing. "A child."

The woman closed her eyes in despair. This time she nodded.

"I'm so sorry." Even with her features obscured by blisters and burns, he could tell she wasn't old enough to have a child older than, at most, early teens. A child young enough to wander into the country of fire...probably such a child would have been much younger.

He could hardly imagine.

The Wall should have stopped any such tragedy. He didn't understand how any child could have gotten into the country of fire. But this woman must have been sure. And she had obviously been able to follow her child, so there must be a way through. The Wall stretched for hundreds of miles, after all. No doubt there were occasional gaps.

There would be no way to ask about any of that until she could talk. "I know people I can ask," Bertaud said at last. "People who can search in the desert. Perhaps your child only went a little way and then came back out into the country of earth. I'll try to arrange for people to search on both sides of the Wall..."

The woman was shaking her head. She thought this hopeful scenario unlikely, apparently.

Bertaud could think of no possible comfort to offer,

except to repeat, "I think I can arrange for a search of the desert. I'll try as soon as possible. But that probably won't be until morning. I'm sorry that I have no food, but you might not be able to eat anything yet anyway. There is, believe me, no shortage of water. The tea is good for fever. It's bitter, I know, but drink more. Not too fast. The poultice is the best I can do for burns. A healer will do much better." He was, he realized, babbling—more upset by the woman's obvious distress than he had realized. He closed his mouth and stood up. "I'll make more tea."

The woman took a breath—that probably hurt her too, but Bertaud was cautiously pleased at the depth of it. Perhaps she would escape pleurisy and pneumonia and all such ailments after all. She looked away from him, around the lean-to. Drops of water were making their way slowly through the woven willow, along the long green leaves, to fall at last to the floor of the lean-to. She looked at those drops of falling water. Then she looked back at Bertaud, raising her eyebrows.

"You're in the Delta," he told her, realizing she couldn't have any idea. "You know where I mean? In the far south of Feierabiand, the southwest, with Linularinum across the river. A...friend of mine found you and brought you to me." He hesitated. Then he said, "I am Bertaud son of Boudan. I'm the Lord of the Delta. So you see, I may be able to help you. I shall certainly try."

The woman shook her head, but he thought not in denial or even disbelief so much as astonishment. She opened her mouth, winced, and closed it again without trying to speak. Bertaud gave her more tea.

Then, as her gaze went past his shoulder and widened, he turned.

To his considerable relief, an owl crouched at the open side of the lean-to, its rounded wings half-spread and its round golden eyes glaring and ferocious, much like the eyes of a griffin. It was a barred owl, the most common sort in the Delta, behaving most uncharacteristically. Bertaud couldn't remember anyone of his staff or guardsmen who had an affinity for owls, but obviously someone did. And had somehow managed to make the birds understand to search for people in the woods...probably not for him specifically; an owl could hardly be expected to recognize the Lord of the Delta from a woodcutter; but some basic *Search for someone out of place.* Or more likely, *Look into every shelter and see whom you find there.*

Crouching low, he pulled a coin out of his pocket; a coin that showed the Oak of the Delta on one side and the profile of his great-grandfather on the other. He wrapped this in a bit of cloth he cut from his shirt, knotted the cloth, and laid this on the ground at the owl's feet. It glared at him from fierce round eyes, snatched up the parcel, sprang into the air, and vanished into the night with a heavy downbeat of silent wings.

"There," Bertaud told the woman, who had watched all this with her head tilted to one side and her eyes wide. "I expect someone will arrive before long. There's a dock down below. I hope the person who sent the owls out looking will be able to figure out the river's a faster route to this place than any sort of straight line through the woods." Hard to guess how an owl would communicate direction and distance. If his people did try to come through the woods, it might be practically dawn before they found him—if they found him rather than falling into ditches and quagmires, or getting bitten by snakes, or whatever other accidents might befall someone in the marshy woods at night. Hopefully the captain of his guardsmen would have better sense than to attempt any such cross-country rescue mission.

He didn't say any of this. The woman, unacquainted

with the Delta, wouldn't have understood him—and anyway, her gaze was as fierce as that of the owl. He hoped for her sake that someone would come up with a better idea than following the bird in a straight line.

It started to rain harder again, but after some time the downpour slackened and finally ceased altogether. The overcast finally began to break up and moonlight slanted down between the trees, so that at last it was possible for Bertaud to see the moon through the trees, nearly full and perhaps two hands' breadth from the horizon. From its height and position in the sky, he guessed that no more than two hours, perhaps two and a half, had passed since sundown.

It seemed like it had been longer.

The woman had finally been persuaded to lie down. She might have dozed a little, but every time Bertaud looked at her, she was looking at him or at the sloping roof of the lean-to or out at the darkness beyond its open side. The pain of her burns might have kept her from resting. He thought it was more likely the horror and anxiety of having lost her child, the anger at her inability to leap up right now and search, the impatience engendered by being forced to wait, to depend on the goodwill and competence of a stranger. A stranger who claimed to be Lord of the Delta, but who, for all this woman knew, might actually be a madman who lived in this mean shelter. How could she tell?

Except there had been the owl. The people of Casmantium did not commonly have that gift, to call and coax an animal. They had gifts of their own...if a Casmantian maker had built this lean-to, doubtless it would be a good deal more snug. The woven roof actually watertight, the candle far more effective at repelling mosquitoes, and the mattress springier and more comfortable.

Then the owl reappeared, or another arrived, and Bertaud decided he was glad enough that the gifts of Feierabiand were the kind that best led to timely rescue.

Captain Geroen had come himself, it transpired. Captain Geroen and eight of his guardsmen, and his wife, the healer-mage Iriene, in two boats. One of the boats was larger, with space for an injured person to rest; the other smaller and narrower, better suited for swift travel in case that had turned out to be more important. Geroen was very much a man who liked to be prepared for anything.

There was also a girl of twelve or so, whose presence was immediately explained by the owl that floated out of the darkness and settled on her slender shoulder. She wore a heavy vest, Bertaud saw, and leather wristguards to keep dangerous talons from piercing her skin.

"My sister's daughter," Captain Geroen said gruffly when he saw Bertaud looking at the girl. "Birds run in our family. Owls aren't as clever as my crows, but they've got their uses."

"Well done," Bertaud told him, including the girl with a nod. She nodded back, commendably matter-of-fact, smoothing the owl's breast feathers with the back of one finger. Bertaud was impressed, and made a mental note to be sure and find out her name and see, once she was older, if she might like to take employment as a courier. Girls often did take such employment in Feierabiand and the Delta, and one as level-headed as this and with an affinity for owls besides should do well in that employment. He would have to suggest it to Geroen.

Iriene, not distracted by rain or mud or owls or anything else, had gone at once to examine the Casmantian woman, and very quickly guardsmen whisked the woman down to the dock and settled her as comfortably as possible in the larger boat. "The poultice was the best thing you could have done for her," Iriene said to Bertaud. "You gave her willow-bark tea, I presume? Good. I should be able to make her more comfortable by the time we've gotten back to town. The burns aren't serious, just unpleasant, but it may take some time for her to recover completely from this very severe dehydration. I don't usually see such a condition, so it's a bit difficult for me to estimate her recovery. Still, I'm fairly confident she'll recover in a day or two, perhaps three. Shall I plan on treating her at my town clinic or at the great house?"

"The house." It had not occurred to Bertaud that he might send the woman anywhere else. "She'll want to speak to me as soon as she's able. Don't try to persuade her to wait, just send for me, whatever the hour. And I'll want to speak to Jos," he added to Geroen. "As soon as we're back in town, please send somebody with my apologies for waking him. And an extra apology to his wife for sending a summons on such an unpleasant night."

Bertaud's foot skidded on the slick dock as he got into the smaller boat and Geroen caught his elbow to steady him. "Certainly, my lord," the captain agreed, and didn't ask a single question about a Casmantian woman who'd somehow wound up blistered and dehydrated in the muggy Delta, nor comment about Bertaud sending for Jos, whom everyone knew had friends among the people of fire.

Or not *friends*, precisely. The concept was not quite the same among the people of fire as among the people of earth. But it was enough like, enough of the time. Especially for Jos.

The river did not run straight. It turned and turned again, lazy and broad in the flatlands of the Delta; it divided and came back together and never seemed to run in a single direction for longer than a quarter-mile. Though the river was still the best way into and out of the sloughs and woods, it took perhaps an hour for the boats to travel from the muggy cypress-lined curves of the river into the still warm but freer air where it finally came out into open marshes.

But as soon as the woodlands fell away behind the boat, one could see the edges of Tiefenauer. Lanterns and lamps glowed here and there amid the dark, blocky buildings despite the hour. The main docks were well downriver, past the bridge, but there were smaller docks just inside the city that were more convenient to the great house. The guardsmen rowing the boats pulled for those docks without a word from their captain, and very soon after that Bertaud saw the woman settled as comfortably as possible in a guestroom of the great house, in Iriene's capable hands, with staff scattering to bring clean water and burn ointments.

His own staff appeared—his steward Dessand and a scattering of servants bearing hot tea and chilled wine. Someone had run ahead to explain the situation—or the girl might have sent an owl—because his rooms had been provided not just with a basin of cool water but with a tub of hot as well, and Bertaud's servant Daued had laid out both Bertaud's favorite robe and a complete change of clothing.

The robe and the turned-down bed were inviting. Bertaud was no longer so young that he enjoyed staying up from one sunset to the next sunrise, and by this time the sunrise was not so very distant. But after bathing Bertaud dressed. Without thinking too much about his reasons, he sent the first, plain, shirt back for one with oak leaves embroidered on the collar. Finally he went back out into the hallway and down toward the wing where his guest rested. Or more likely refused to rest.

His guess had been correct; the woman was far from asleep. She had been put to bed, but obviously under some duress. A taut urgency stretched over her exhaustion, and when Bertaud came in, she was trying to get up out of the bed. Plainly she meant to *make* someone—him—deal with her urgent concern before she would consent to rest.

"Please, rest," Bertaud told her forcefully, striding forward. Though the woman did look a good deal better now that she was clean and properly tended, even if she managed to get out of the bed, Bertaud was not entirely certain she would be able to keep her feet and he didn't care to see her collapse.

Certainly Iriene was a gifted healer: she could piece broken bones together and help them knit, coax a gaping wound closed with hardly a scar, and wake a concussed boy who'd fallen from the roof. Shallow burns were not a challenge for her, heatstroke was something she dealt with all the time, and already the woman's blisters had faded to blotchy red patches. But not even Iriene could cure in an hour all the effects of such an ordeal as the woman had suffered. Bertaud stepped past the healer-mage, took the woman's hand, looked into her face, and repeated, this time in Prechen, "Rest."

For a moment he thought the woman would refuse to obey. But after a moment of stiff resistance, she let out a breath and settled back against the pillows.

Definitely a woman of Casmantium, if Bertaud hadn't already guessed as much. With the burns minimized and healing, her features had become much more discernable. Her eyes were blue-grey, a color far more common in Casmantium than Feierabiand or Linularinum. Her face was round, those eyes wide-set beneath a broad forehead. Her bones were strong; too strong for any shallow prettiness, but plainly she would be a handsome woman when she had recovered. She was striking right now, in fact. Her urgency and intensity made her all the more so.

She was not a small woman. He guessed when she stood up she would be tall, perhaps almost as tall as he was himself. He suspected she would be even more arrestingly handsome on her feet, not only because of her clean, strong bones; her whole figure was generous, with big breasts and wide hips.

One of Iriene's girls edged forward, trying to spread some salve or unguent on the woman's arms. The woman shoved the salve aside, ignoring the girl's exclamation of dismay, but one of Geroen's young guardsmen stepped smartly forward to rescue the pot of unguent and steady the girl. Bertaud himself set a hand under the Casmantian woman's elbow when she swayed, off balance with exhaustion and stress. He admired her determination, but he guided her, firmly, to lean once more back against the pillows, lest she should manage to get to her feet, lose her precarious balance and fall.

"She's upset," Iriene said unnecessarily, waving her young assistant back. "She doesn't appear to speak Terheien, but I believe she's worried for someone else, perhaps a—"

"My son," the woman said, her tone level but intense. She spoke in Prechen, of course, but she knew Bertaud understood her. She gripped his arms hard, gave him a little shake, staring urgently into his face. "My son. Cashen. He's only eight. He's been lost...I don't know how long. I don't—two days, maybe three, I don't know, I don't know how long I searched. He's only eight—" her voice, still hoarse, failed her, and she coughed and then couldn't stop coughing.

Bertaud took the cup Iriene wordlessly handed him and gave it to the Casmantian woman. She glared furiously—not furious at him, he understood that. Furious with tragedy and terror, and with her own bodily weakness. She sipped, grimaced, sipped again. Her hand shook. Bertaud closed his fingers around hers so that she wouldn't spill the medicine, which was oily and green and smelled of bitter herbs. She had big hands for a woman. He had always appreciated small, neat hands and feet on a woman, but there was elegance as well as strength to this woman's hands. And Bertaud admired the way she forced her grip to steady and stilled their trembling through sheer force of will.

No doubt she had a husband to go with her son. He drew his hand back, ready to catch the cup if it tipped, but not touching her fingers.

He said in his most impersonally authoritative tone, "Rest. Let my people help you. I've sent for someone who may be able to help find your son. He should be here momentarily. You must have been very certain your son went into the lands of fire, to go so far into the burning sands yourself. You're equally certain you didn't miss each other in the desert, so that he's at your home now worrying for you?"

The Casmantian woman shook her head. She tried to speak, coughed, and sipped the herbal decoction instead.

Bertaud could hardly keep thinking of her as *the Casmantian woman.* "You know my name," he said to her, and rapidly introduced Iriene and the girl—who was the healer-mage's niece and whose name was Miere—and to Captain Geroen, who was too wary to leave his wife unattended as she cared for this angry stranger. Geroen regarded their guest with a glower that wasn't the least bit welcoming, his arms crossed over his chest. He was suspicious by nature, was Geroen, and he could see as well as anyone that this woman was Casmantian and hadn't arrived in the Delta by any ordinary means. But he was kinder than his manner made him seem, for all he was also suspicious enough to linger in this room and keep a man of his here for good measure, just in case.

The woman throttled her obvious impatience. "Gairran Temneichtan," she said of herself. "I am from Tashen...not really Tashen. It is a village near Tashen, only most of our neighbors moved away when the desert came close. The Wall keeps back the sand, most of the sand, but where the hills are steep there are gaps. The blocks are so big, and they're cut straight, so where the ground is broken, sometimes there's a gap."

Bertaud nodded to show he understood.

The woman—Gairran—nodded in return. "When the wind comes from the desert, it carries the scents of sand and fire. People don't like it. But Cashen loves it— loved it—loves it! He won't leave it alone." She stopped, drank some of the oily herbal decoction, and grimaced. "It does help," she said, now with the anger and fear better hidden beneath hard-held courtesy. "Please thank the honored healer for me. And I must thank you as well, Lord Bertaud, though I don't understand..." she looked around, made a sharp gesture. *"Any* of this."

"One of the mages among the griffins is an acquaintance of mine. She found you and brought you to me," Bertaud told her. "She didn't mention a child. You didn't find your son."

"I know he went into the desert." Gairran was plainly too distracted and upset to care whether Bertaud had a hundred acquaintances among the griffins. She looked at Bertaud, but her vision was focused inwardly, on fear and the memory of fear. Her voice shook with more than the roughness of fever and injury. "Cashen would lie on the ground and look through the gaps into the country of fire. He'd crawl underneath to touch the sand. He'd tell me what he saw...golden deer with black horns curved and edged like swords, with fire in their eyes and fire blooming from the sand where their hooves struck the sand. Birds whose wings trailed fire when they flew." Her eyes sought Bertaud's, urgent with the need for him to understand.

He swung a chair around and sat down, not to loom over her. He wanted to take her hand in both of his. He restrained himself, resting his hands on his own knees. "It's beautiful, that country," he said. "Foreign and beautiful. Of course a boy would want to look."

Gairran shook her head angrily, not disagreeing, but in urgent rejection of the whole situation. "It should have been safe!" she said fiercely, and began to cough, but strangled the cough with her urgency to persuade Bertaud—to persuade herself. *"It should have been safe!* Cashen would crawl through partway, but just to look! He'd come back after dusk, with a handful of red sand in his pockets and the memory of fire in his eyes. I should have realized, I should have sold everything and taken him away, moved to Tashen, or Metichteran, or all the way to Pamnarichtan—so far that there would never be any haze of red dust over the sun, so far Cashen would have had to forget the desert..."

"It really ought to have been safe," Bertaud said gently. "It's foreign to us, that country, but no longer inimical."

"I should have moved! But my family's owned that land for a hundred years. We raise bees for honey and sheep for wool...I have five tenant families. There was, is, a man who offered to buy when my husband died, and offered again just last year, but he's the sort of townsman who's too proud to take advice, and his sons are no better. Townsmen ought to let their tenants run a place like that; they're the ones who know the land. But that man would have let the sheep overgraze the pastures and taken too much honey right before winter; he'd have ruined all that beautiful land and everyone would have had to move, and where would they have gone? It's not easy for tenant families to find new places with a good living." Gairran hit the bed, a short, hard blow of anger and despair. "But I should have sold it to him! What good are bees and sheep to me *now?*"

Iriene handed the Casmantian woman another cup, this one filled with a clear, faintly golden liquid. Gairran glared at her, realized she was glaring at a healer offering succor, and dropped her eyes in angry embarrassment. She started to take the cup, but her hand was trembling again. Bertaud steadied it for her, wordlessly. He hadn't been able to help noticing, in that furious tumble of words, that she was a widow. Obviously there was no reason for a civilized man to notice such a detail, under the circumstances. Even so, this time, he wasn't quite so careful not to touch her hand. Only for long enough to steady the cup, which he took back and set aside as soon as she turned her head aside, refusing more.

Just then, in the doorway, Jos cleared his throat.

Jos was a big man, big-boned and broad-shouldered, with powerful, scarred hands and coarse features. No longer young, but certainly not old. A plain man—or so anyone would think. He had married a plain woman two years since; or at least a woman whom anyone would think plain. Like Gairran, Jos' wife had her share of determination. Her life had held one or two serious complications that might have left her in a difficult position, her first husband dead suddenly and under questionable circumstances, and with no family to take in her two growing sons if they had also lost their mother. Except Jos had made sure Bertaud had judged her case himself.

Not long afterward, Jos had married her. Not even Bertaud knew, or would have dreamed of asking, whether he had done so out of simple kindness or some deeper feeling. However complex the situation between Jos and their mother had been or was, the boys adored Jos; that much anyone would instantly realize the moment he met them. Bertaud thought that was ample reason to assume the rest was no one's business.

From top to bottom, all through his life, Jos had been a man who held secrets, his own and those of other people, as securely as though they had been whispered to stone. No one except Bertaud and one or two others—and who knew, possibly his wife—would have guessed any of the thoughts hidden behind eyes that seemed candid and a face that seemed guileless.

A stranger might have taken Jos for simple. He *was* simple, in a way; at least, his loyalty and friendship were steady and unyielding as stone. But he stood at the center of a web of friendship and loyalty that was complex and, even today, sometimes dangerous.

Bertaud nodded to him. He said in Prechen, without preamble, "Jos, this is Gairran Temneichtan. Her eight-year-old son seems to have gone into the country of fire...two days ago, maybe three. Gairran went into the desert after him. Opailikiita found her there and brought her to me, as it did not seem a day for death. But she didn't mention a boy."

Jos listened to this without any sign of surprise. His history was as complicated as his manner was plain, and very little surprised him. Though Casmantium was not stamped in his bones and face as obviously as in the bones and face of Gairran Temneichtan, he had been Casmantian once. So he answered easily in the same language, "I'm sure Opailikiita would have brought the boy if she'd found him, if she'd brought his mother. You had no chance to ask her, my lord?"

"Unfortunately, I had no idea what questions I ought to ask until she had gone. Once I knew, I had no way to call her to return. So I thought of you." Bertaud produced this little speech in his blandest, most matter-of-fact tone, as though every word of it was the exact truth.

Jos received it the same way, without the slightest flicker of surprise. "Of course, my lord. I can ask Kes to come and likely she will. I can ask her now, but it's easier at dawn when the wind dies, as you know, my lord."

He didn't say *An hour more won't make any difference to a boy lost in the desert for two days—or three.* He didn't need to say it. Nevertheless, aware of Gairran's distress, Bertaud asked, "Do you think she's likely to come now, if you call her?"

Never the sort to make any hasty answer, Jos paused. He said eventually, "She might come. But she might not be pleased if I called her like it was an emergency and she came, and it turned out not to be so urgent. Dawn's not far off now. If it were up to me, my lord, I'd wait for dawn."

This wasn't quite a refusal to try early. But no one knew Kes better than Jos—at least, no one human. Bertaud met Gairran's eyes and spread his hands, asking for patience. "The moment the sun edges above the horizon. I promise you. Less than an hour, I think. Take the time to rest. Drink the rest of this. It will help." He gave her back the cup of pale gold liquid.

The woman wanted to argue. That was obvious in the set of her mouth. She said instead, "This Kes, she will be able to help? She is a mage?"

Bertaud couldn't help but glance at Jos. He said after a moment, "A fire mage."

A Feierabianden woman almost certainly wouldn't have looked half as appalled as Gairran Temneichtan. Plainly Gairran, who after all had lived so near the country of fire, understood more about fire than most people of the Delta. She said, making very little effort to conceal her disbelief and anger, "This Kes is a *griffin?* And you would call her for *help?"*

Bertaud exchanged a second glance with Jos, who shrugged, meaning—quite justly—that this woman's reaction wasn't his problem.

After a moment, Bertaud explained carefully, "Not a griffin, no. Kes was born human, but she...isn't, exactly, anymore. Her true name now is Keskainiane Raikaisipiike. She isn't precisely a friend—at least, she isn't my friend."

Every now and then, he still found it hard to believe she wasn't his dedicated enemy. She knew—she *trusted*—that Bertaud would not summon Opailikiita and compel her to do anything. Nor any other griffin. But the knowledge that he *could* was always a constraint between them. Kes never came near him, ordinarily...just to be sure that he never felt he had to summon any of the griffins to protect himself against her. It was a wise caution. Bertaud knew better than anyone else in the world just how dangerous Kes might be.

He could hardly explain any of that. He said instead, with the same care, "She has generally been a friend to Jos, however. There's every reason to think she'll help if he asks her."

Gairran Temneichtan had flushed; aware, Bertaud guessed, that she had been less than polite in openly doubting the intentions, or maybe the judgment, of people who were trying to help her. He hardly blamed her, but couldn't think of any courteous way to say so.

"It's nearly dawn now," Jos said. He had gone across to put back the curtains and open the window. The rain had stopped for the moment, and stars glimmered here and there in a sky that was indigo rather than true black. The windowless tower that was the tallest part of the sprawling but generally low house speared up against the sky, or the gradually lightening of the pre-dawn sky might not yet have been perceptible.

Iriene came forward to tap the woman's hand and indicate she should drink the rest of the straw-colored decoction. "She should rest," she said to Bertaud. "But I'm guessing she doesn't plan to. Should I give her something that will make her sleep?"

And Captain Geroen, who was not a stupid nor an imperceptive man, demanded gruffly, "Somebody after her? She's got some powerful enemy; that how she wound up burned half to a crisp in the middle of a rainy night? What should I tell my men?"

Bertaud had all but forgotten that he and Gairran Temneichtan and Jos had all been speaking Prechen rather than Terheien. He shook his head. "No enemies. Bad luck, I think—and then very good luck, that a griffin who knows me and knows how to step from the country of fire to the country of earth and back again happened to find her. You can pass that word around." Bertaud couldn't think of any reason the basic outline of what had happened should be secret, especially since his guest was certain to be the subject of a good deal of fascinated gossip no matter what either he or Captain Geroen said.

"Huh," Geroen said, more than a little skeptically. He did not like anything out of the ordinary, and most particularly he did not like griffins, though he knew perfectly well that every now and then Bertaud was called upon by his own king or by the Arobern of Casmantium to sort out some minor disagreement or misunderstanding between the people of fire and the people of earth. Geroen also knew that rather more frequently, Kes visited Jos—and he probably liked that even less.

All this was contained in that single grunted syllable. A man of few words, was Captain Geroen. Bertaud nodded to him, but he said to the healer instead, "Esteemed Iriene, I'm sure Gairran needs to rest, but her little son is missing and I think it would be cruel to try to make her sleep until we make an attempt to find him." Then he added to his captain, "In just a moment, Jos will ask his friend Kes to step into this house. We hope she'll be able to help search for the boy. There should be no danger at all, so let's be polite, shall we?"

A healer knew, better than anyone, the devastation brought by a child's loss. Iriene was a very good healer, but she couldn't save every boy who was bitten by the wrong kind of snake or every toddler who fell into the wrong kind of pond. She gave Gairran Temneichtan a stricken look, plainly wishing she had better comfort to offer her than soothing drinks and unguents.

Captain Geroen grunted again, but he also put an arm around his wife and patted her hand, though he wasn't a man ordinarily much give to such gestures, at least not in public. "Lost little boy, is it? Lost in the desert, eh? Then I'll wish you good luck, my lord, and I'll have all my people and my wife out of this room, if it's all the same to you, before you go inviting that fire mage to step in." And he gave Iriene a firm little shove toward the door, sparing an even firmer nod for her young assistant and his almost equally young guardsman.

Bertaud nodded approval and didn't suggest the captain also withdraw. Geroen was a stubborn man, especially when it came to questions of duty and responsibility. The captain went with his wife to the doorway and stood there a moment, speaking to her in a low voice—it might be some endearment, but from the no-nonsense way Geroen next beckoned to his young guardsman and sent him running with a word in his ear, it was probably brisk orders for this and that in the event of disaster. Probably well-thought-out orders, too, knowing Geroen.

"It's almost sunrise," Jos said quietly from the

window, in Prechen. He repeated it in Terheien, then switched back to the Casmantian language and went on, "I think the wind has stilled, my lord. I'll call her now, by your leave."

The sky was still dark, but clouds low against the horizon hid the dawn. When Bertaud looked more closely, he saw that there was, possibly, a sliver of paler color along the clouds to the east. And it was true that the damp breeze had died. The gauzy curtains hung limp in the heavy air. Nevertheless, he made an effort and stopped himself from saying, *Yes, now.* Instead he said, keeping his tone neutral rather than impatient, "I'll defer to your judgment of the moment, Jos."

The big man turned his head and met Bertaud's eyes. "A few minutes one way or the other, I don't expect that'll matter to the boy, probably," he said bluntly in Terheien. "But you never know. And I don't think it'll make much difference to Kes either."

"Then by all means, if you think the moment will do," Bertaud told him. He glanced around, making sure everyone besides himself and Geroen was out of the room. Of course they were; his captain would hardly have been careless about that.

Jos didn't pay any attention. He had a short knife at his belt, the kind anyone might carry for any random task that might require a knife. He drew it now and used it to nick the ball of his left thumb. The pale scars on his left hand were serious enough to limit the range of motion of the fingers and thumb, but his right hand was less scarred and he had no difficulty handling the knife, or taking down one of the lamps hanging at the head of the bed. Carefully he let a single drop of blood fall into the lamp's small flame.

"I thought you might need to use the eternal fire Kes set by Kairaithin's gravestone," Bertaud commented.

"That one, she'll always answer," Jos said absently, most of his attention on the sky outside the window. "This one, maybe she will and maybe she won't, but it's better to be as polite as possible when we want to ask for a favor." He raised his voice slightly. "Kes. Keskainiane Raikaisipiike. If you have a moment."

She came. She wasn't there and then she was, stepping softly out of the motionless air of the dawn, bringing with her a clean, dry, burning breeze that carried the scent of hot metal and stone.

Even at first glance, Kes did not look human. She was more or less human in her form, but she seemed to have been carved from alabaster or poured out of burning white gold. Her skin glowed from within as though fire rather than blood filled her veins, which was probably the literal truth. Her hair, near-white and soft when she had been human, rose in a soft aureole of white fire now. Fire glowed in her eyes, pale gold and utterly inhuman.

But nothing in the room caught fire: not the rugs underfoot, nor the gauzy curtains that stirred now in response to the warm breeze Kes had brought with her, nor any other furnishings. These days, she always remembered to be careful. "Jos!" she said happily. "I'm so glad you called me! Something wonderful has happened!"

Her voice was high and light and timbreless; it was not a human voice at all. She was smiling, filled with a delight that was free and joyful and passionate. A griffin had made Kes into a creature of fire, but she was not a griffin. She was wilder than a griffin and more capricious; no more gentle but often generous, never tender but sometimes kind. Now she stepped lightly across the floor, so careful with the fire that filled her that she did not even leave scorch marks on the rugs. She took Jos's hands, smiling up at him.

She had burned him once with a touch like that, and then burned him worse when she had forgotten he was not a creature of fire, or had forgotten to care. She had been first heedless and then cruel. Later, Bertaud thought, she had been ashamed of that heedlessness and that cruelty. He did not entirely understand her and he couldn't always predict what she would do, but these days he trusted her to remember to take care.

Jos closed his scarred fingers around her small hands without fear, smiling down at her lively, delicate beauty. Whatever he felt for his wife—Bertaud would never have presumed to guess whether that might be affection or friendship or love—Jos had loved Kes first, when she was human. Later, as her humanity gradually burned away, he had loved her still. And whatever she felt for the humanity she had lost or for the griffins who had become her people, Kes was still a friend to Jos.

"You must tell me all about it, of course!" Jos said to her now. "I would have called you just to hear this wonderful news, if I'd known."

Kes laughed, a sweet wild inhuman laugh, filled with fierce joy. "But of course you did not know! I will tell you, I will be glad to tell you, but why did you call me?" She did not let go of his hands, but she turned, examining her surroundings for the first time. She gave Bertaud a tiny nod, recognition and salute, as to an enemy whom she met but would not fight. Kes was not a friend to Bertaud, but she even graced him with a smile, so happy with the news that filled her that she forgave him—for this moment—for the affinity she knew he held.

Captain Geroen she ignored entirely, but she seemed mildly interested in Gairran Temneichtan. Gairran had struggled to her feet when Kes had arrived, very understandably, but swayed a little, hardly able to stay upright. Bertaud almost stepped over to offer her his arm, but restrained the impulse at the last second in case such a gesture from him inclined Kes against the woman. He glanced impatiently at Geroen, but the captain had already moved, supporting the Casmantian woman with an unassuming stolid calm that did not draw attention.

If Kes noticed the captain at all, she showed no sign of it. "You have recently ventured into the country of fire," she observed, regarding Gairran with her unsettling golden eyes. "The scent of the desert clings to you still."

Kes spoke Terheien, which was the language of her childhood. Gairran was gazing at her in astonishment not unmixed with alarm, as well she might. Kes was alarming, and not someone whom the Casmantian woman could have expected, though Bertaud realized now he should probably have tried to explain her a little better.

He cleared his throat. "Kes—Keskainiane. Out of her own generosity and remembering the amicability between our peoples, Opailikiita Sehanaka Kiistaike brought this human woman to me. She is Casmantian. She believes her son, a child of eight, crept beneath the Wall and went into the desert. This woman followed to seek him, and Opailikiita found her and brought her to me, for which I'm grateful. I hoped—I would be twice grateful for your assistance to seek this child, whether he is..." Bertaud hesitated, not wanting to say *dead or alive* even in Terheien, which the boy's mother couldn't understand. She would probably understand that much just from his tone.

"You did not summon Opailikiita to ask her?" Kes asked. Her tone was light and inexpressive, but she met Bertaud's eyes as though drawing a weapon.

He bowed his head, declining the challenge and pretending not to notice the possible threat. "Opailikiita Sehanaa Kiistaike was generous to bring the woman to me, but she is not my *iskarianere,* to ask her for favors."

Iskarianere was a word that meant something like *friend* and something like *ally.* It did not express a human concept and Bertaud did not entirely understand it, but he used the word deliberately, to remind Kes that the griffin mage was *her iskarianere.* He meant that if Opailikiita had been generous, it would be wrong for Kes to treat that generosity as worthless.

Kes smiled at him, not a kind expression. She knew what he meant, and she did not like that he, he in particular, dared remind her of griffin courtesy. But Jos coughed, and she glanced his way, allowing him to break the moment. Though her smile did not gentle, it became indefinably sweeter. She said, "Opailikiita did not find this human boy. But, unless two such children have recently ventured into the desert, Ashairiikiu did. I will take you to see this boy—if you will trust me to take you into the country of fire."

Despite the language difference, Gairran understood this—maybe because she caught a word or two, or maybe from Bertaud's expression, or maybe because of a mother's instinct. One way or another she certainly understood, starting forward eagerly with outstretched hand. Geroen wisely held her back. She tried to shake free of him, but mostly as though she had forgotten he was there. "Cashen?" she asked Kes urgently. She turned to Bertaud. "She knows where my son is?"

"We'll all come," Bertaud told Kes. "If you'll permit the intrusion, Keskainiane." He gestured Captain Geroen back, so forcefully that the man actually obeyed.

And with very little sense of motion or movement or travel, he and Jos and Gairran Temneichtan were all of them suddenly elsewhere.

The sun, well above the horizon here, poured down with ruthless clarity upon red sand and red rock and great twisted red spires and plateaus. The heat was already ferocious, hammering down from above and up from the red sands underfoot; even so early, the desert light was thick as honey and heavy as gold. The wind here hissed with sand and flickered with fire.

That staggering heat was the first thing Bertaud always noticed about the desert because it forced itself so powerfully upon any man's attention.

The second thing was the griffins.

They had come down from the red spires that were their halls and their homes, twenty or more griffins, each large enough to tear a man in half with their great talons or bite his head off with their knife-edged beaks. They lounged all around on the fiery sands, unfathomable and savage, but, at least for the moment, apparently not hostile. They turned their fierce eagle heads to look at Kes out of fiery golden eyes, but pretended not to notice Bertaud or Gairran. They made no such pretense with Jos. Him, they recognized as the friend or *iskarianere* of their Lady of the Changing Winds—the greatest of their fire mages—Keskainiane. Kes.

Jos nodded to one of them and then another. He did not seem afraid of them. Of course it was dangerous to show fear before the griffins, who were merciless predators—but Jos came sometimes into the country of fire. He knew those griffins, or Bertaud assumed he did. And he trusted Kes, which was more than Bertaud could say.

Except Bertaud had trusted her enough to let her bring him—and Gairran—into this desert. And she trusted him enough to bring him here among the people of fire. They both were willing to take risks today, it seemed.

The griffins were magnificent. Their feathers did not look like the feathers of ordinary eagles, or like the feathers of any ordinary bird; they looked much more as though they had been beaten out of gold and bronze and copper, or poured out of sunlight. Every separate hair on their lion haunches looked like it had been spun out of gold. Bertaud did not see Opailikiita at once. Then he did: a small, slim, dark form that slid down from the metallic sky on a rising wind and settled to the sand a dozen paces away.

Closer at hand a griffin of dark bronze, wings barred with flickers of blazing copper-red, opened his beak and snapped it shut again. This produced a savage little sound that might have been a threat but that somehow, from the tilt of the griffin's head, seemed possibly amused. The small feathers of his head and throat ruffled in a dry hot wind that smelled of hot brass and molten stone and fire, each bronze delicately traced with gold.

Bertaud knew this griffin, though not well. His name was Ashairiikiu Ruuanse Tekainiike. He was a mage, like Opailikiita and like Kes herself. Not as powerful a mage as either, but powerful enough in a world where few griffin mages had survived the short, brutal war with Casmantian cold mages only a handful of years ago.

Ashairiikiu was not one of the griffins Bertaud more or less trusted. But the bronze griffin did not seem offended by the presence of human people in the desert. Indeed, at the moment, he seemed possibly pleased and possibly amused and not irritated at all.

Then Ashairiikiu lifted and tilted his immense wings, and Bertaud finally saw that, in the shadow of those half-spread wings, a little boy played with a handful of fire-opals and carnelians, and with the flickers of fire from which those fiery jewels condensed.

Gairran Temneichtan cried out and started forward, and the little boy looked up, shouted, leaped to his feet, and ran to meet her. Opailikiita bounded forward, half leaping and half gliding, flames scattering from the feathers of her wings, but Ashairiikiu did not try to stop the boy or prevent Cashen's mother from coming to her son. The bronze griffin settled back, calling out to Opailikiita in their own language, and the smaller griffin cupped her polished brown wings and settled, making her way forward much less urgently, with the delicacy of a cat.

Bertaud had begun to reach out to prevent Gairran from touching her son, an abortive gesture as he saw that Kes did not seem at all concerned. He didn't necessarily trust Kes to remember how easily a human woman might be burned—but he did trust Jos. And Jos also seemed unconcerned. He stood with his scarred hands hooked in his belt and an attentive look on his face, but he did not appear worried. So Bertaud drew back his hand, and Gairran flung herself to her knees and wrapped her son in a hard embrace, oblivious of the staggering light and heat, and, so far as Bertaud could tell, of all the griffins and the two human men as well.

She was murmuring, her voice too low for him to make out the words. Tears welled in her eyes; he saw that. It seemed intrusive to watch her at such a moment. Bertaud shifted toward Kes instead and said, trying—not, he thought, entirely successfully—to keep anger out of his voice, "You've made that child into a creature of fire?"

He could believe Kes would have done such a thing. He could believe she had forgotten how it had felt, years ago, when the great griffin mage Anasakuse Sipiike Kairaithin had done that to her. She had probably forgotten the confusion and distress, as she had lost nearly everything of the shy human girl she had once been.

To be fair, he could most easily believe she might have done it if she had found that boy dying of heat and

120

desiccation in the desert.

But Jos stepped between them and said in a definite tone, "She didn't." He added with an edge of reluctance to his voice, "Ashairiikiu Ruuanse Tekainiike might have."

Not I, Ashairiikiu said. His voice was heavy and dangerous when he spoke in the way griffins spoke. He did not like Jos, had never liked Jos, but his manner when he tilted his head to study Gairran's son was amused and even...indulgent. He said, *This child plays with fire and is not afraid. No constraint could have made him. He follows his own nature.*

Opailikiita put in, her voice light and quick and a little reproachful, *If I had known the woman of earth sought her child, I would have looked for the child myself, not brought her to you yet left her wondering.*

Bertaud believed her. Of all the griffins, Opailikiita was...not the kindest, exactly. But perhaps the most likely to try to understand what moved a human woman, and the most inclined to go out of her way to meet a human woman's needs. It was hardly coincidence that Opailikiita had been the one to bring Gairran Temneichtan to Bertaud when she felt an intrusion of earth into fire and came across the woman dying in the desert. Very few griffins would have bothered. They would probably have said *It is a day for death* and gone on their way.

"You see?" Kes said to Bertaud. "Not Ashairiikiu, and not Opailikiita, and not I." She lifted fine eyebrows of white flame in a scornful expression, looking at Bertaud. "Ashairiikiu would not have troubled himself over a child of earth. I—*I* would have brought him back to the country of earth. Except that when Ashairiikiu discovered him, he was already at home in our desert and when I came to see, I found him as he is."

Bertaud found all this difficult to believe, but he

didn't actually think anyone was lying. He started to apologize. But it wasn't necessary. Jos said indulgently, "Of course you would have brought him to us," and patted her hand.

"Of course I would!" agreed Kes, laughing—it seemed a joke between them, for she sounded indulgent herself, not a tone that Bertaud would have expected from her. She was plainly willing to be mollified. Sweeping her hands up toward the sky, she laughed, neither a human gesture nor a human laugh, but expansively joyful. She said happily, "Look at him, Jos! Look again, Bertaud! This child was *born* to fire, and also to earth. Both at once! He is like me, but he is more like himself."

Astonished, Bertaud followed her advice and studied the boy more closely. He had not imagined any such thing. He would not have believed it could be possible, however amicable the relationship had become between the people of fire and the people of earth. But now that Kes made that claim, he thought he could see it. Fire flickered in that boy's eyes and sprang up where he stepped, but his mother's tears obviously didn't bother him and she plainly wasn't flinching from his touch. Cashen was showing his mother a handful of carnelians and one bright dancing flame that clung to his palm, but the flame turned into a flake of fine gold when he put it into her hand. Gairran held it, and held her son, and laughed shakily but with no apparent doubt of him.

"Fire and earth, both," Bertaud said wonderingly. "How is this possible?"

"Fire and earth are foreign to one another," Kes said, still happily, but now with a touch of impatience. "But not inimical. Not anymore. You know that." She slanted a sideways look at him and, with one fingertip, drew a spiral of flame in the air that lingered for several long seconds. "You remember, Lord of the Delta. It was your house. You were there."

It was true. The enmity between fire and earth had died when Kes and Bertaud's cousin Mienthe had made a chance for the law of the world to be rewritten. Bertaud had indeed been there. Many unexpected, confusing, peculiar magical gifts had emerged since, none quite the same as any other. He knew that too.

But this...this was different. He wasn't at all certain he was comfortable with this.

Jos did not appear to have any such doubts. When Kes smiled up at him, he gripped her shoulder with one strong scarred hand and gave her a little shake. "Just so long as you don't try to lure him into your desert just yet. Boy that age needs his mother."

Kes tilted her head, an oddly birdlike gesture, unmistakably predatory. "I will not permit that he should be turned away from fire—" she began.

Gairran Temneichtan stood up, her son held close to her side. Turning to Kes, Gairran said firmly, "Lord Bertaud, please tell your—your acquaintance that I see fire has become a friend to my son. If this is her doing, then I think she saved his life by it and I am very grateful. This is a wonderful thing. But tell her that he is far too young to leave me, however kind the country of fire is to him. Tell her that I will take him home now, but that I will—will welcome any visitor who comes as a friend to my son."

This was startlingly perceptive, as the rest of them had been speaking Terheien, the language Kes knew better. Gairran could not have followed more than a word or two, but she had arrived at nearly every important conclusion anyway.

That was impressive enough, but Bertaud admired even more the diplomatic phrasing Gairran had managed, especially after the night she had suffered, and the days she had endured before that. She had to be worried, even frightened, but no one could have told as much from her manner.

Bertaud had actually *been* an envoy from one king to another. And represented the human people of earth to the griffins of fire, and the other way around, more than once, and under terrifying circumstances. Even so, he could hardly imagine putting that all together if he'd been in her place. Certainly not so tactfully.

When the boy was a little older, Cashen might play a role similar to Bertaud's—if he got the right training, and especially if he became accustomed to dealing with powerful people. With a mother like this, the boy would surely prove bright and brave, quick-witted even in difficult moments.

It was that thought—though not that thought alone—that made Bertaud realize what compromise he obviously needed to persuade everyone to accept. That this particular compromise would inevitably require a much closer acquaintance between himself and Gairran Temneichtan was...certainly not the point. But equally certainly, he did not mind that thought at all.

He cleared his throat. "Kes. Keskainiane. If I may suggest a solution that might satisfy us all. Jos is correct. The boy is too young to leave his mother. But you're also right that this gift, this waking into fire as well as earth, is a wonderful thing. It's a gift that should be nurtured by fire as well as earth, and allowed to grow in safety. So—" he paused, cleared his throat, and switched to Prechen. "Honored lady," he said formally to Gairran Temneichtan, "This gift your son holds, of fire as well as earth, will surely present many challenges as well as many advantages as he grows to adulthood. A home in Casmantium, especially in the north where the people of earth have often been at odds with the people of fire, may not be entirely comfortable for a son born allied to both fire and earth. Allow me to offer you and your son refuge against any who might misunderstand your son's gift. In the Delta, the folk neither know nor fear the red desert."

Gairran recoiled slightly, though Bertaud thought her reaction one more of surprise than horror at the idea. Pretending not to notice her response, he turned instead to Kes and went on in Terheien. "In the garden of my home, an eternal flame already recalls the alliance between fire and earth—a gift you gave in remembrance of one we both honor. In my home, the people of fire are always welcome—as you know; you and Opailikiita Sehanaka Kiistaike. We have seen just now how freely a mage of fire may come and go between my home and the desert. I would most willingly host Cashen Temneichtan and his mother in the Delta until such time as the boy is of age to make his own choices and his own way in the world. I hope that if such an arrangement pleases you, it may also satisfy Tastairiane."

Taipiikiu Tastairiane Apailika was the Lord of Fire and Air, the king of the griffins. He was utterly beautiful: pure white, like alabaster and white gold, with fiery blue eyes. He was also the most pitiless, unforgiving griffin Bertaud had ever met. What he meant now was to remind Kes that she might not feel entirely secure introducing a human boy to Tastairiane, however dual that boy's nature might be.

Kes studied him, fire swimming in her narrowed eyes. Pretending this time not to notice her annoyance, Bertaud said to Gairran, "If you take your son to your home in the north of Casmantium where the desert meets the gentler earth, people will surely notice his gift. He'll certainly show signs of it, nor should he be taught to conceal his nature or be ashamed of it. I can offer your son a home where the folk don't fear griffins or fire. Word of Cashen's dual nature is certain to run through all the countries, but I can guarantee that both King Iaor of Feierabiand and the Arobern of Casmantium will find your son's residence in the Delta satisfactory—and the griffins should also find it tolerable."

She looked at him wordlessly, her eyebrows rising—at the whole idea or at Bertaud trying to take hold of the situation, he couldn't tell. He was certain he could get Iaor and the Arobern to agree, exactly as he'd claimed; and moderately certain he could persuade Kes and the griffins. He found himself less confident Gairran Temneichtan would consider his suggestion. She had tremendous determination; he would never be able to *make* her agree to anything, certainly not with any attempt to overpower her own will with his.

He said as persuasively as he could, "There will be no need to sell the land your family cherishes. Let your tenants live there and manage the land for you. You would be able to come and go when and as you please, especially if your son makes a friend of Ashairiikiu Ruuanse Tekainiike." A quick glance at the bronze-dark griffin confirmed that Ashairiikiu was paying attention mainly to the boy. The griffin's mane of feathers was fluffed out, the gold flecks and bars on the feathers particularly evident. Brilliant sunlight gleamed from every feather and slid along the smooth edges of his polished predator's beak.

Cashen clearly was not at all afraid of the griffin. He pulled a little away from his mother toward Ashairiikiu.

That was an attraction that might very well terrify a human woman. Except that Bertaud already knew that Gairran Temneichtan was not at all easy to terrify. She looked down at her son and then—with a courage that astounded Bertaud—let him go and just watched as he scooted over to Ashairiikiu and fearlessly ruffled his fingers through the feathers of the griffin's throat. "Make me some more carnelians," he ordered the griffin. "I'll string them for my mother and then she'll like you better. I'll string more for you, Ash, except it'll take a lot."

"Griffin'd burn right through a string," commented Jos. "A chain'd do better, I expect. A gold chain, of course. Gold would fit a griffin's beauty."

The flattery was deliberate, Bertaud realized, seeing the bronze-and-gold feathers settle as the griffin preened, arching his neck. Jos knew griffins better than anyone in the world, especially the ones closest to Kes; he had known not just that he'd better intervene but exactly how to do it. Kes understood too. Probably not the Prechen words, but exactly what Jos had done. She leaned against the man's side, smiling up at him.

Jos kept one eye on Ashairiikiu, wary of possible offense at the idea that a griffin might wear anything made by any human, even this child. But he grinned briefly down at Kes and added in Terheien, "I'd give *you* a gold chain, with or without carnelians. I've got this nice bit of fire obsidian, picked it up from a Linularinan merchant. Probably paid too much for it, but I bet you'd like it."

Completely missing all the subtext, Cashen looked at his mother. "Could I have a gold chain to string carnelians for Ash?"

Gairran shook her head, but that was probably disbelief rather than refusal because she also said, "Maybe you can. A thin one. If a griffin wants such a thing."

Ashairiikiu declared with haughty assurance, *I do not need adornment. But perhaps such a gift from a brave little fire-kitten would please me.* He bent his deadly beak over the boy's head and nudged him lightly, which made Cashen stagger but also laugh. That might be the fire in him, but Bertaud rather suspected the boy had inherited a good part of his fearlessness from his mother.

"A gold chain would be a political expense, so I expect Iaor would pay for it," Bertaud said in a low voice to Gairran. "There's no need to decide at once," he added, cautious of pushing her too hard in case she stiffened against the solution he had offered—was trying to offer. But he felt uncomfortably that there might not actually be much time to sort this out. Here was the moment when all the pieces were ready to fall into place, but he couldn't *force* them into position. Every piece had to decide to take the place where it best fit. But right now everyone was in a good humor, willing to make allowances for foreign notions. Bertaud suspected this might not last very long. He thought they had all better decide on a suitable plan very soon. Preferably *his* plan.

He couldn't think of anything else he could say to persuade any of them. Odd how he had never noticed before how passionately he hated moments when he could say nothing, do nothing, and had to simply wait to see whether he'd done *enough*—or whether he'd failed.

This moment certainly wasn't the most important in recent years. If Gairran chose to go back to her own Casmantian home, something else would surely be worked out. He could explain all this to the Arobern himself...somehow. No, better, he could explain it to Beguchren Teshrichten, the Arobern's advisor who had once been a cold mage. Beguchren was subtle and clever and above all dedicated to making absolutely certain that fire and earth never again came so close to mutual disaster as in those terrifying days before Mienthe and Kes and the rest of them had managed to avert unrelenting war. If any man could work out some reasonable alternative plan, Beguchren Teshrichten certainly could.

Somehow...somehow, even though he absolutely did believe this, Bertaud could not quite make himself accept that any alternate plan could possibly be as solid and prudent, or half as desirable, as his own.

Kes looked the Casmantian woman up and down. Bertaud couldn't read her expression. But then she walked over to Ashairiikiu and the boy and crouched to look Cashen in the eye. "Fire is your friend," she said to him, but in Terheien, which the boy did not understand. Seeing his confusion, Kes shook her head and said in the silent manner of the griffins which did not depend on any human language and which anyone could understand, *Fire is your friend, but earth is your friend too.*

"Yes," Cashen said—in Prechen, of course.

Would you like to live with fire, or with earth?

The boy stared at her, surprised. "Both!" he said, and then looked at his mother to see if that was all right.

"I think..." said Gairran slowly. "I think I am too tired to think right now." She turned to Bertaud. "I think my son and I would be glad of a place to rest and a chance to...to talk to each other and...and sort everything out. Except I don't want to impose...." She squinted, realizing that she had moved on to considerations that were perhaps of lesser importance.

"No imposition in the world," Bertaud told her firmly. "Just think how we'll all be put to far more trouble in the end if your son's residence isn't considered satisfactory by the kings of men and the lords of griffins. I promise you, honored Gairran, I would never have offered if I had the least doubt of the arrangement."

The woman shook her head. "I hardly know...this is not what I expected!" That last was a bit plaintive, but she added quickly to Kes, "Though it's much better, it's *so* much better than I was afraid I'd find!" Then she remembered that Kes didn't understand Prechen and drew back in confusion.

Bertaud obligingly translated. "Not many of my people in the Delta speak Prechen," he went on apologetically. "But there must be some who do. I shall find someone to help you—or we'll hire someone from Casmantium—"

"We'll learn Terheien," Gairran said firmly, her hand on her son's shoulder. "That would plainly be best, no matter what other arrangements we come to."

Bertaud almost laughed in sheer relief, seeing that Gairran seemed to have moved past questioning the basic plan to figuring out how to make it work. He managed to check the impulse and turned to Kes instead, saying in a carefully sober tone, "If you are satisfied to try this arrangement, Keskainiane; and if Opailikiita Sehanaka Kiistaike and Ashairiikiu Ruuanse Tekainiike are satisfied; and if you believe the Lord of Fire and Air may find the arrangement acceptable, then may I ask you to return us all to my house? The desert is beautiful, but it is hard for creatures of earth to endure it for long."

"I think we would all do well to rest and to think," Kes said, her tone light and whimsical. But her quick glance up at Jos carried a question, and even when Jos nodded, she lifted a warning eyebrow at Bertaud. "I— and Ashairiikiu, and no doubt Tastairiane Apailika— shall expect this child of fire and earth to visit our desert often. To learn fire as well as earth. He must not be hidden away among the people of earth."

"By no means," Bertaud promised immediately. He had no difficulty with that promise. Obviously nothing of that kind could work...and besides, he looked forward very much to seeing how the boy's gifts developed.

He was almost certain Gairran Temneichtan would learn to look forward to that too. Possibly with just a little help from people who already loved fire as well as earth.

"I think all of us here would like to see a closer

friendship between earth and fire," he told Kes. "You know very well I would like that."

Kes bent a long, considering look on him...but then she smiled. "I know you would," she agreed, and swept up her hands.

After the hammering furnace of the desert, the moist, clinging warmth of the Delta was...not precisely comfortable, but familiar and welcome. Kes had brought them—all the human people, not any of the griffins—straight into the guestroom where she'd found them. Their arrival sent staff running in all directions, with Captain Geroen and the healer Iriene and Dessand, Bertaud's steward, all arriving almost simultaneously.

The captain divided a glower between Kes and Bertaud, Kes because he had a healthy respect for her power and Bertaud for letting the fire mage take anyone for whom he, Geroen, was responsible out from under his eye.

For her part, Kes ignored Geroen. She said silently to Cashen in her sweet, light, inhuman voice, *Call me when the day comes that you wish to visit the country of fire. That day should not be far removed from this, so I will expect your call. Jos will show you how to call me. Do not call Ashairiikiu Ruuanse Tekainiike. Ash will be your* iskarianere, *but he will never be comfortable in the country of earth. Remember that you should not call him to you here.*

The boy nodded quickly. "I'll remember! Can you teach me to talk that way, in shining knives that come into your mind? Can Ash teach me?" He caught himself, glanced at his mother, and said much more collectedly, "Thank you, honored lady, and thank the honored griffin for me, for his hospit—hostpit—"

It was a difficult word, in Prechen. "For his hospitality," prompted Gairran, stepping in with an approving smile for her son and a deep inclination of her head for Kes. "I thank you also, honored mage, and the—the people of fire."

Jos translated, quietly. Bertaud left it to him, staying to the background.

Kes nodded to Gairran, smiled at Cashen, patted Jos on the arm, and finally slanted a sideways glance at Bertaud. Her smile tightened, but she said only, *It will never be a day for death, when this young one steps into the desert.*

She might have meant this as a promise or prediction, or she might have meant it as some strange kind of observation of something she just perceived as true. Whatever she meant, Bertaud was happy to hear it. And happier still when she vanished.He let out a slow breath, and with it tension he had hardly noticed until it eased.

"She's all right, my lord," Jos told him, as Gairran sank into the nearest chair to recoup her strength and recover her nerve, and Iriene hurried forward to examine Gairran and her son. "She's too pleased with the boy to remember how much she dislikes you."

This hadn't been Bertaud's impression, but he nodded politely.

Jos went on, "Think what it'll mean to her, to have someone almost like her—someone born human and then gifted with fire. That boy's not quite the same, of course he's not, but he's closer than anyone else ever will be. Even me."

Bertaud had thought of that, of course. He raised his eyebrows, a silent query that he more than half expected the other man to ignore.

But Jos shook his head. "I might be jealous. A little jealous," he said in Prechen, in a low voice to keep his words private even from Gairran, though she probably wasn't listening and wouldn't care anyway. Jos went on,

"But I'm human, after all, my lord. My wife's human. My sons are as human as they come, and I'm grateful for that. Kes...I'd have to be a mean sort of man to grudge her a friend, maybe someday more than a friend, who's part fire as well as part earth."

Bertaud gripped his arm briefly. "I'm deeply thankful she's had a man like you to help her remember she used to be human. If you were less generous, I think she would be as well." Then he let go and stepped back before the moment could become mawkish. He said in a louder voice, "And I'm thankful for your help this morning, of course! Please think of some favor I could do for you or your family. It won't be enough, but I'll be glad to do it."

"Ah, well," Jos said, amused. "I don't figure it quite that way, my lord, but my sons are about that age." He nodded to Cashen. "They're good boys, and he'll need human friends, I expect. If they get along, maybe that'll lead to something for my boys a few years along. They'll earn what they get, my lord, but a chance to earn it would come welcome."

"An excellent idea. I can't think of another man I'd rather have guiding boys into adulthood," Bertaud told him.

Jos said easily, "Ah, well, same here, my lord, and I figure you'll likely be staying close to young Cashen yourself—one way or another." He strolled out, whistling, before Bertaud could find a response.

Dessand immediately seized his own chance, coming forward a step and bowing. The steward's expression was politely reproachful; there was nothing he hated more than having his carefully designed schedules disrupted. Whatever Bertaud had been supposed to do this morning, he had completely forgotten about it. "Yes, Dessand?" he said, resigned to being sternly reminded. Most of his attention was still on

Gairran, who, now that she actually believed her son was safe, had plainly been struck by the enormity of what had happened to him, and to her, and by the profound and unknowable changes that had struck down everything she had expected to matter in his life and hers.

Even facing all this, flung into a foreign country, exhausted to the bone, her skin still reddened and now flaking from the healing burns she had suffered, her hair coming out of its neat braid, she managed a remarkable self-possession.

What an admirable woman. Striking looks, surely, but that bone-deep composure went well beyond looks. Bertaud thought he would feed her a huge breakfast and put her to bed for twelve hours—breakfast and bed sounded like a wonderful idea for himself as well. Probably it was wrong of him to imagine, even briefly, that it would be more wonderful still to share that bed with Gairran.

If he weren't so tired, no doubt it would have been easier to put the idea firmly out of his mind.

"Dessand?" he repeated, but he wasn't paying much attention to his steward. He was much more interested in framing words of welcome that would unfailingly persuade Gairran Temneichtan to accept that he was glad to have her here, without making her feel uneasy or pressured in any way. It was a demanding sort of speech. More difficult in Prechen than in Terheien...

Dessand said reprovingly, "My lord, your cousin has been waiting for you nearly half an hour. In the smaller anteroom, my lord."

"My cousin?" Bertaud thought first of Mienthe, though of course she was away in Casmantium and would hardly have been waiting for him in the small anteroom anyway. It took a startlingly long moment before he remembered Terre.

Shamefully, it took Bertaud an even longer moment to suppress the urge to order Dessand to get rid of his unwelcome cousin. Pulling his thoughts away from Gairran Temneichtan to Terre son of Talenes was almost painful. But nothing that had happened was Terre's fault—not that mess with his father's contract nor Bertaud's own failure to sort through that contract. He rubbed his eyes, let a breath out, and said in an almost normal tone, "Has my cousin had a chance to eat breakfast? Never mind, I don't care. Have a breakfast for three served in half an hour in...my personal chambers." That would make it clear to Terre that this delay was not intended as a backhanded insult. "Invite my cousin to join me there in half an hour."

That would give Gairran and Bertaud time to clean up and change clothing; it would allow Iriene to make sure both Gairran and her son were well enough, barring total exhaustion in at least Gairran's case...the boy was obviously fading as well, now that the excitement was over. His mother had already settled him in the bed, murmuring. She probably wanted to crawl into bed with her son and sleep for days, but she was patting her hair into shape and casting longing looks at the basin of cool water on a side table, so plainly she was determined to sort things out with Bertaud first. Of course she was. She wouldn't be dissuaded either; he knew that. Hence the breakfast. Both of them would certainly be able to think better after food and rest.

Bertaud said, "Captain Geroen, please detail one of your men to stay with the boy for the day. Just to reassure his mother that he is definitely safe."

"Yes, my lord," Geroen acknowledged. "Anything I ought to know, my lord?"

Bertaud rubbed his eyes again. "Probably. Ask me again this afternoon once I've had a chance to think. Late this afternoon. I'll need to write to Iaor—" he stopped, took a breath, and let it out. His first reflexive decision to put everything off was correct. Everything that required thought was going to have to wait until he could string two coherent thoughts together. "Breakfast," he said, and made the effort to switch to Prechen. "Honored Gairran, if you would care to join me for breakfast in half an hour. Iriene will help you. I have asked my captain to assign a man to stay with your son, so you needn't be concerned he'll wake and be confused or frightened."

"Cashen isn't easily frightened," Gairran said, but she smiled despite her weariness and the lingering reaction to everything that had happened. "Breakfast would be very welcome, Lord Bertaud. Thank you."

The private dining chamber in Bertaud's suite was small, appointed for no more than half a dozen people at most. The table stood by the wide window, which was open, the draperies tied back with linen cords to keep them from blowing into the dishes. Rain slanted down beyond the wide overhanging eaves, turning the entire world beyond into a long sweep of vague silvery mist-blurred shapes.

The table itself was not spacious enough for serving dishes, which instead occupied a sideboard. The kitchen had supplied ham and sausages, poached eggs on toast, porridge with honey and cream, and slices of the earliest melons, their green flesh sweeter than the honey.

Bertaud seated Gairran so that she could admire the view—silvery and vague as it was. The rain was pleasant after an hour in the desert. He nodded to Daued to serve her without waiting and turned to face his cousin as Terre came in.

Terre's expression was carefully blank. He had most likely initially taken Bertaud's delay this morning as a deliberate insult, one which he had no choice but to swallow; and then he had probably worried that Bertaud's continued absence might be a sign that his cousin had changed his mind and wouldn't help him at all. Then this breakfast invitation had surely confused him further.

He had plainly not been warned that Bertaud had a newly arrived guest or that this guest was a woman or that she would be joining them for breakfast; his gaze went to Gairran for an instant of bafflement, no doubt exacerbated by the visible remnants of her sunburn. But he only nodded to her with polite reserve before he focused his attention on Bertaud.

"Cousin," Bertaud said. "My apologies for the delay. I fear I've had a complicated night and an unexpectedly busy morning. My esteemed guest is Gairran Temneichtan." He took the necessary second to collect his thoughts and shift languages—tired as he was, the effort required more like five or ten seconds— and added to Gairran, "Honored Gairran, this man is my cousin, Terre son of Talenes, whose concerns I have shamefully neglected."

"I have no notion what might have occasioned such neglect," she said, the first signs of humor emerging now that she was beginning to accept that her ordeal was over. She nodded to Terre.

Who took Bertaud completely by surprise by saying in slightly awkward but quite passable Prechen, "Honored lady, I hope you will enjoy your visit to the Delta, though the weather is not good lately." He smiled faintly at Bertaud's expression, the first time he had smiled. It made him look younger. He went on, still in Prechen but now directing his comments to Bertaud, "I have some business interests to the east as well as to the west, my lord. I could see, anyone could see you were on good terms with Casmantium, and the new bridge makes trade more easy and more profitable. I have find ...I have found that it is easier, better? I have found it is more safe to trust a Casmantian handshake than a Linularinan contract." He paused and then said with studied care, "I think I am not clever enough to read Linularinan contracts."

Bertaud gestured for him to sit down and to Daued to serve them all. He took a bite of sausage to make it clear his guests were permitted to begin, chased it with a poached egg and toast, and managed to stop himself from outright gluttony long enough to say, "Yes, regarding your difficulty, I haven't had time to do more than look at the legist's summary." He had barely done even that, in the few minutes snatched before breakfast. He left that part out, merely saying, "Assuming her opinion is accurate—which I am willing to assume—I'm sure we can work something out. I would like to hear more about these business interests of yours, Terre. But I'm impressed you've extended your interests eastward and more impressed that you've learned Prechen to do it." He added, following a half-understood impulse, "Provided your accounting seems sound, I believe I'll be willing to offer a loan on family terms."

Terre's startled glance showed that he had not expected this. He answered with controlled calm, "I would be grateful for that consideration, my lord. My books are at your disposal, of course." Then, plainly steeling himself, he added, "I think you will consider that my business interests are not on so solid a—a foot as you might approve. But I hope and intend to improve this situation over the next some years."

"I don't doubt that you'll give me an honest accounting of the foundation of your business interests and of your ability to repay a loan over the next few years." Bertaud barely stressed the words *foundation* and *few,* where his cousin had stumbled. He did not stress the word *honest.* He actually did not doubt that Terre would give him an honest account of his financial situation—any problems with which could probably be laid at Talenes' feet, not Terre's. Not that Terre had said so. That showed a decent reticence, and perhaps pride that would not let the young man make excuses. So far, Bertaud was far better pleased with his cousin than he would ever have expected he would be with a son of Talenes.

"I won't be able to discuss this with you this morning—which I do regret," Bertaud added, not wanting his cousin to take the delay as a gesture of petty dislike. "I know midsummer is nearly upon us. If it would be convenient, I would like to ride out to your house this afternoon—late this afternoon—to discuss these matters in more detail and settle the arrangement. I assure you, the matter will be settled before noon tomorrow."

"Any hour this afternoon would be perfectly convenient, my lord. Thank you." Terre took a deep breath and let it out. He leaned back in his chair and slowly ate a piece of melon while Bertaud inhaled sausage, eggs, toast, and porridge.

Gairran's appetite was just as good, and for even better reason. She had waited politely until Bertaud settled the business with his cousin, but now she paused in her dedicated attempt to make up for several days of terror and deprivation, put her fork down, and said, "Lord Bertaud, I am very grateful for your offer to take myself and my son into your household, and I think I understand the reasons for your offer. But you must see it's not possible for me to stay in your house. Iriene tells me you are not married. Perhaps you can recommend an inn, at least for now, and then in a few days we can consider what other arrangements may be better. I could buy a house here, if...if we all still feel that my son should live here in the Delta—"

Bertaud held up a hand, checking her before she could talk herself into not liking that idea. "Yes, I understand." He hadn't thought at all of appearances, of the respectability of a young widow staying in his home as his guest, with or without a young son. He was having more difficulty than he ought, sorting through possible solutions now. He knew he couldn't allow Gairran to sell land and a home she obviously cherished just to support herself in an exile she hadn't even chosen...but he had been *right* when he'd said that the Delta was the perfect place for her son. The Delta truly *was* the only place Iaor and the Arobern and Kes and the griffins would all agree to, as a home for Gairran's son. He was still convinced of that.

He was also adamantly unwilling to let Gairran herself slip through his hands. Though he retained just enough sense not to say that part out loud.

It occurred to him that Gairran had asked Iriene whether he was married. That was...surely that inquiry had not been prompted *solely* by a concern about propriety. He tamped out a smile in favor of carefully serious attention to the problem, though with some difficulty.

He said after a moment, "I can't see how you're to manage an establishment of your own without staff who even speak Prechen. It will take time to find appropriate people. As for today and the next few days..." He didn't much care for the idea of her son surrounded by random travelers at a public inn. He was fairly certain Kes wouldn't approve of that at all. Maybe he could ask Iriene and Geroen to host Gairran and her son, just for a day or two. Or, no, neither of them spoke Prechen...Jos and his wife, except he knew their small house was hardly big enough for their own family... he squinted, trying to think.

"My lord," Terre said quietly. "... Cousin."

Bertaud looked at him in surprise. He really *was* tired; he had almost forgotten the young man was present. And he was doubly surprised Terre had finally chosen to address him familiarly.

Terre's manner remained formal despite his choice of address. He said, "Forgive me if I speak out of turn, my lord. But my wife and I would be happy to offer hospitality to the esteemed lady and her son for as long as they wished to stay with us. No one would think it inappropriate for your cousin to offer shelter and protection to your guest." He paused, swallowed, set his jaw, met Bertaud's eyes, and said steadily, in Terheien, "I think I can promise you that we would make your guest and her son welcome, and that my mother would not make either of them feel otherwise."

Bertaud had not expected this at all. Especially not that last part. He stared wordlessly at Terre.

His cousin flushed under Bertaud's regard. But he did not drop his gaze. "It took me a long time to understand why you disliked my father and mother so much," he said. He got the words out with obvious effort, but even then he didn't drop his gaze. "I didn't actually understand it until—until my wife explained it to me. I don't know why I—" he cut that off and said instead, "I think you would like my wife, my lord. I promise you, you can trust her to make the esteemed lady feel welcome in our home, even if...even if you aren't sure I would."

Bertaud leaned back in his chair. He said finally, "You were only, what, fifteen?"

"Sixteen, my lord, the year you took Mienthe away from my family. Old enough that I should have realized how unhappy she was, and why."

"Sixteen-year-old boys are often fairly self-absorbed."

"Yes, my lord, but still old enough to know better."

141

Terre was tense and steady, his lips pressed thin, his back very straight. He rested his hands on his knees in a pose that was probably meant to look relaxed. He looked anything but relaxed. "If I were going to apologize, it should be to Mienthe, not to you. I wouldn't have brought it up, except I didn't want it to look—I didn't want it to look as if—"

"As if you were following your father's example: offering a false and grudging hospitality in order to gain a financial advantage. In your case, by coaxing advantageous terms from me for your loan," Bertaud said. He wanted to laugh. That would have been unforgivable, so he kept his expression completely sober. "I don't suspect you of insincerity, Terre." He truly didn't. He was confident that no one in the world was that good an actor. Except maybe in Linularinum. No wonder Terre found it easier to do business with Casmantian merchants. He didn't say this. Aloud, he said, "Very well, I accept your hospitality on behalf of my guest and her son. It's a complicated situation. I hope you won't regret your offer. The boy will need a guard—he's peculiarly gifted—but there again, your estate's relative isolation would be an added advantage. I'll explain this afternoon, when I escort the honored lady and her son to your estate. After you understand the situation, if you prefer, other arrangements can be made." But already he hoped that wouldn't be necessary. He could see perfectly plainly all the advantages Terre's suggestion offered.

Terre had relaxed minutely. "Thank you, my lord. I'm sure I won't regret offering the lady hospitality."

Bertaud was careful not to smile. "You need not be so formal, Terre. I do intend to offer you generous terms on that loan. You needn't be concerned that I'll feel later that you manipulated me into it. At this point I can hardly imagine anything from you but the most exacting honesty." He didn't add that he was amazed Terre had managed to develop such a quality. Perhaps it could be laid to the influence of his wife—whom Bertaud now looked forward to meeting.

A deep breath. Then Terre got to his feet and bowed. "Thank you again, Cousin. If I've your leave, I'll go now to—to explain to my wife, and make sure we're ready to receive the honored lady. And her son. May I ask how old—" he cut that off, turned to Gairran, and switched back to Prechen. "My cousin has agreed that my wife and I may have the honor of offering you and your son—" he couldn't find the word he wanted, probably *hospitality,* which truly was a difficult word in Prechen. He said instead, "of accommodating you and your son. May I ask how old the boy is?"

"Eight," Gairran said, after a brief glance at Bertaud. She couldn't have missed the tension between Bertaud and his cousin, but she asked no questions. She told Terre, "Cashen is eight. I hope he will be no trouble to your household. I'm grateful for your hospitality." She pronounced the word with just a little more precision than necessary.

Terre smiled, much more easily now. "I'm sure my household will manage. It had better be capable of such hospitality." This time he managed the word quite creditably. "My wife is expecting our first. She will be delighted to make you welcome, honored lady. She speaks only a little Prechen, but we will all be glad to learn."

"My son and I will be glad to learn Terheien," Gairran assured him. "Please thank your lady wife for me." She rose politely, as a guest would in Casmantium, while Terre took his leave from Bertaud. It was not the Feierabianden custom for a woman to rise when a male guest came or went, but Terre did not show the slightest surprise. He only bowed once more, neatly, and

143

withdrew.

"He seems a kind young man," Gairran ventured after Terre had gone. "He has been in some difficulty with you?"

At last Bertaud let himself laugh. Of course she had realized. He said, "Not him! I doubt that young man could manage to get himself in any difficulty with me even if he tried. I disliked his father. But then, I disliked my own father far more, so perhaps it's time to let that go." Rising, he walked around the table and took Gairran's hands in his, drawing her to her feet. She allowed it, which she probably would not if she had been officially a guest under his roof. So there was that advantage to her regard for propriety and to Terre's solution to the problem. Really, Bertaud felt in better humor with his cousin all the time. Perhaps he would make him that loan at no interest at all. Or forgive it entirely, if Terre made this woman so much at home in the Delta that she was happy to stay.

He said, "If you'll agree that a few hours under my roof may not be utterly unacceptable, we'll both get some rest. You can share your son's bed; that should do—and I'll have Iriene stay with you as well. A late lunch, and then I'll escort you to Terre's estate. It's outside town, but not so very far. I've a little business to conclude with him, and then..." Then, they could both begin to sort out the rest of their lives.

Bertaud would need to write to Iaor very soon. And to the Arobern of Casmantium, with couriers dispatched to both in the same hour; no need to insult either king by implying he was less important. A separate note to Mienthe. She would be very interested in this boy whose gift was almost as peculiar as her own.

No doubt Gairran also had urgent letters to write. To her tenants, if no one else. He said, not quite questioning, "No doubt you'll need to write various people. If you have family who will be concerned for you, I'll include a note, with your permission, assuring them of your safety here. I think I can reliably promise that you and your son *will* be safe here. I hope—" he hesitated, and then said, "I hope you will be happy here as well as safe. The Delta is beautiful. Especially in summer." He had not released her hands, and now turned with her toward the window. "It doesn't *always* rain here, I promise you. I will...I hope you will allow me to show you that there's more to the Delta than the mud and rain and mosquitoes you've already encountered."

Gairran actually laughed at this. "I was glad enough of the rain, as I recollect." She drew her hands free, but not with any urgency. Then she held one hand out the window. Even with the wide eaves, there was enough of a breeze to bring raindrops to fall into her palm.

"There can't be a land anywhere in the world more unlike the desert," she said softly. "And the people here seem kind. And sensible. And brave." She didn't look at him with any of that, but the flush that rose up her throat had nothing to do with sunburn. It wasn't shyness, but it might have been uncertainty of a different kind. She said, still not looking at him, "I think...I think I may learn to like your Delta. I think I may look forward to your showing it to me."

Bertaud wanted to pour all the Delta's flowers into her lap immediately. He contented himself with leaning out the window to pluck a single flower of jasmine. Rain had beaded on the waxy petals, but if anything the damp air brought out its fragrance even more strongly than usual, until the scent seemed to fill the room. Bertaud set a finger under Gairran's chin, turned her head just to the right angle, and threaded the flower into her hair. She allowed this familiarity, and after he dropped his hand, lifted her own to touch the petals.

Then she turned her head to meet his eyes. She

wasn't smiling. But there was something in her eyes that was like a smile. "A kind gesture. But you hardly see me at my best, Lord Bertaud."

Though he tried, Bertaud could not quite keep a smile from curving his own lips. "Oh, I think I have very nearly seen you at your best, honored Gairran. From start to finish of the past few remarkable hours. Let me escort you back to your room. Please join me for lunch when you're ready...any hour will do; sleep until you wake. This afternoon I'll escort you to my cousin's house and see you established there in complete respectability. I hope you'll allow me to call on you. Tomorrow. Or, I don't wish to press you...perhaps the day after."

"I think...the day after tomorrow seems perfectly appropriate for a call."

"It will probably be raining."

"I shall look forward to the occasion no matter the weather, Lord Bertaud."

Bertaud made no effort, now, to prevent a smile. "Good. Because I certainly will." He set his hand beneath her elbow to escort her back to her room, deliberately formal. The fragrance of jasmine surrounded them both, and the scent of the rain, and Bertaud thought he had never felt more at home in this house in his life.

VIGILANTE

I wrote this short story a long time ago, in connection with a novel I started but never finished. The world is one that would probably be considered Urban Fantasy these days, though I'm not sure the subgenre was recognized at the time I started building this world.

I may well come back to that novel, eventually, though probably not to these characters.

I don't know about you, but personally I'd be just as happy if that postmodern mirrored-steel look had never been invented for tall office buildings. What's wrong with plain stone or brick or wood? Yeah, all right—stone has its own disadvantages, can't deny that. There's a reason all those old stone cathedrals build in so many roosts for gargoyles. Nothing like gargoyles for keeping down stoneslithers. Rats, too. Keeping gargoyles happy is worth losing the occasional cat.

But brick, now. Brick is almost always safe, and not nearly as flammable as wood. Sure, you can only build so high using brick. Nine, ten stories and I guess you're about as high as most architects want to go. You want real skyscrapers, you need steel. But you'll never convince me giving your downtown a postmodern look is worth giving unicorns a way into the world.

Fortune 400 CEOs and politicians and all that sort

don't need to worry about unicorns, of course. Armed guards and armored cars and their own private Wiccan practitioners on staff; of course they don't have to worry. They all live in gated communities too, I expect, or in their own private compounds, and you can bet the walls surrounding their homes are good and high. And made of brick. They don't care a fig for the rest of us having to live with the consequences of their fancy glass and steel buildings. If those people had to actually *live* with the unicorns their office buildings let through, I bet things would change in a hurry.

I actually saw this particular unicorn emerge from the McMillan Tower. The mirrored steel bowed outwards and sort of stretched, and the unicorn strode out of the side of the building into the moonlight like it had been poured, liquid and living, out of the steel. Or not exactly *living*, I guess. Creatures of the night aren't exactly alive. I read that somewhere. They sure aren't flesh and blood; if they were, they'd be a lot easier to put down. They seem plenty alive enough if you're the guy who has to deal with them, though.

It's wrong what they say about unicorns, you know. Unicorns don't look like they're made of silver. Silver isn't that shiny, no matter how you polish it. My mother had a bunch of silver teaspoons; I did my share of polishing those when I was a kid, and I can tell you, silver only gets so shiny. Unicorns look like they've been molded out of living mirrors or poured out of absolutely still water. They look liquid, and they move kind of like liquid too. Like the rising tide: They're so smooth and fluid you hardly can tell they're moving at all until they're right on top of you.

Hardly anything is more beautiful than a unicorn. I've seen my share, and I know just how vicious they are, but I still get a shiver down my spine when I see one. Not that I'd recommend going out of your way to see one, or especially not stopping still to look at one. Except guys in my line of work, that's kind of what we do. So when this unicorn came out of the McMillan Tower, I braked gently, then put my Chevy in neutral and gunned it good and loud, figuring to draw the unicorn if I could. They're not real interested in guys like me, but make yourself an obvious target and sometimes you can get one to come take a look. Get a unicorn close enough, you don't need a rocket launcher to take it down; an ordinary AR-15 will do just fine. Can't use rocket launchers downtown, so getting this unicorn in close had to be part of the plan.

This one saw me just about as soon as I saw it. Its eyes were white as chips off the moon, without pupil or iris. It's also wrong, what you'll hear about unicorn eyes. You can't see malevolence in them. You can't see anything in an eye like that—like a chip of glowing white stone. No. The malevolence is just something you know is there, behind the opaque white gleam, like a candle flame behind porcelain.

The problem is, unicorns know what they like. An experienced unicorn isn't going to waste its time with a guy in an armored car. It knows it can't get through the armor, and grown men aren't what unicorns want anyway. This one must have been experienced, cause once it got my scent, it tossed its head and cast about this way and that for something it liked better. Moonlight slid down its gleaming neck and flank and shone through its translucent mane—all right, yeah, they're beautiful creatures all right.

Then the unicorn lifted its head and I saw its nostrils flare and knew it'd caught the scent of virgin innocence on the night breeze. When it turned and cantered down Grand towards Potomac, moving fast, like it had a destination in mind, I wasn't a bit surprised.

It was poetry in motion, if you like Satanic verses.

Really, there just isn't anything in the world more beautiful than a unicorn. My own daughter tried to climb down to one from her bedroom window when she was little. Well, that's why we bar the windows, of course, for just that sort of thing. Now she thinks she's all grown up, and you know, I miss the kid who wanted to climb out windows and run after beauty. What is it that happens to teenagers that turns them into sullen strangers who throw away their stuffed bears and paint their rooms black and treat beautiful things with contempt?

Never mind, never mind, time to focus on the moment. If that unicorn had picked up the kind of scent it wanted, I definitely needed to make sure I got in on the action myself. Of course, I couldn't follow right on its tail. If I pressed it too hard, it'd leave the road and cut across alleys, and I'd be stuck. Not good. So I let the unicorn get out in front of me, and while I was waiting I opened my glove compartment and took out a little alabaster pebble and a disk made of elm wood, dyed blue and carved with the rune *gyfu*. I set the pebble on the disk and the disk on the passenger seat. Nicking my wrist with a little silver knife, I let a single drop of blood fall onto the disk, and said, *"Ades dum. Age dum. Eia age."*

It's not like I'm a real practitioner, but everybody out after dark needs to know a little Latin.

Now, it's not true, what a lot of people think, that white pebbles *turn into* blood fey. But, like unicorns come into the night through mirrored steel, blood fey can come into the night through white pebbles. Some kinds of pebbles are more likely than others, which is why I carry alabaster. This time I got lucky: almost immediately a fey unfolded itself from the pebble like a white butterfly out of a chrysalis and licked the blood off the disk of wood.

It looked, like fey usually do, like a tiny human with butterfly wings. That was until you looked more closely and saw its skeletal gauntness, its elongated hands and feet, its tiny fangs, its opalescent eyes. Blood fey are malicious, but not in a bad way, if you know what I mean. You can deal with them, if you need to and know how. In fact, a blood fey—any sanguine fey, but especially the little ones that unfold out of pebbles—is probably a thousand times easier to deal with than a seventeen-year-old daughter, just to take one random example. "Unicorn," I told this one. "Follow. Blood to follow. I catch it, you get blood." You've got to keep the vocabulary simple, but blood fey can usually understand simple directions if you offer appropriate incentives.

The fey tilted its head a little and looked through the windshield into the night. The unicorn was no longer in sight. This didn't bother the fey, which pointed ahead with one attenuated hand and hissed. I put the car in gear.

The action turned out to be a kid in a car, at the corner of First and Magnolia. I couldn't see her, but I knew it was a kid. A virgin, or at least basically innocent. What else would a unicorn head for like a homing pigeon? Damn car was a civilian model—a sporty little coupe with no more armor than a motorcycle. What anybody thought they were doing out after dark in a car like that, I could not imagine. Kids of a certain age sometimes think they're specially proof against danger. Turn any parent's hair white, they will, scooting out to raves and what-all and staying out all night—at least, you hope they're not actually *out,* but *in,* even at a rave, no matter how heavy the drug scene gets. And here this little fool was, out in the wee hours in daddy's daytime car.

Well, this is why there are vigilantes, I guess—not anything like enough cops on the night beat, and somebody's got to make sure silly kids get a chance to grow up. Guys like me can do that...and sometimes, I hear, our families actually understand why we need to.

This particular kid was a girl, or at least had long hair: I got enough of a look for that. I was pretty sure she was a girl. The unicorn had caught her stopped at a streetlight—that right there tells you she was a civ, because pros don't stop at lights after nightfall. Certainly not in a car like that, where speed's your only defense. The unicorn had already sliced up her tires and broken out her front windshield. It had most of its horn thrust through the windshield when I got there, and it was snapping its long fangs in anticipation. The girl was in the back seat. I couldn't see her clearly, but I could see movement. She had a gun. I heard shots—quiet ones, it wasn't much of a gun, and even at point-blank range it wasn't making the unicorn back off.

My gun, now—my gun made it back off. Besides the AR-15, I had an Accuracy International AS50 mounted on my car. Loaded with Glaser Blue safety rounds filled with silver nitrate. A direct hit from one of those babies will turn any unicorn ever made into lots of little tiny chips of steel and glass scattered all over the landscape. I put a round into the pavement in front of the car, and the unicorn pulled about a yard of shining steel horn out of the interior and stared at me. Malice crept through the night between us, like the moonlight itself had been infected by ill-will. The blood fey crouched down, hiding behind the dash, and I didn't blame it a bit. I eased my car forward a little and re-targeted the gun, this time for the unicorn's back end. If I shot it, there was a pretty good chance the girl in the car would be cut up by flying bits of steel. I could see her whole torso and head through the windows of her car; she hadn't the sense—or experience—to duck under the seats. On the other hand, if the unicorn didn't quit trying to climb into the car after her, getting sliced up a little was not likely to be her biggest problem.

Luckily, the unicorn apparently didn't want to get shattered. That'll ruin your whole night, I guess. It backed away, ears laid flat against its elegant head. I put another round into the road at its feet, and it turned and ran, fast and quiet. The blood fey uncurled, hopped back up on the dash, and hissed after it. I nicked my wrist again—never cut a fingertip, by the way, no matter what you read in adventure stories. Cut fingers hurt, and they distract you every single time you try to use your hand. A little cut on the wrist or the back of the hand is a lot better. I let the fey cling to my left hand and lick blood off my wrist as I got out of my car.

Most vigilantes work with partners, which, can't argue with that, is definitely safer. But I don't have a partner, haven't for years. That meant I was leaving my main gun behind when I got out of the car. I could of grabbed the rifle, but if it gets up close and personal, the handgun I like best for stopping power and accuracy is the Colt Anaconda. Its long barrel means it's tough to conceal, and if I was in a crowd of civilians that might matter. But at night, you want everything that sees you to know damned well you're armed. I had the gun in my hand before I had the door open.

The night was quiet, now. The unicorn was gone, as far as I could tell. The blood fey didn't seem to think it was around. I shook it off my hand and let it flutter into the air as I went to the girl's car.

Yep, a girl. Of course, I'd half expected it to be Cyndi—when there's a girl in trouble and you can't see who she is, what father wouldn't sort of think it might be his kid, even when he knows it can't be? But of course it wasn't. This was a girl maybe a few years older than my daughter. At the moment she was all eyes and nerves, looking no tougher than a kitten. I knew better, believe me. Girls that age are tough—tougher than boys, mostly.

The girl stared at me from the back seat, both hands wrapped around a little tiny Baby Browning with about as much stopping power as a mosquito. You could just about stop blood fey with a gun like that. Great against misbehaving ex-boyfriends, but nothing you'd want to use against a unicorn. As she'd found out. Her mouth was trembling. In fact, she was trembling all over.

"Your dad is going to be pretty upset about his car," I observed. "Come on out of there and I'll give you a lift back home. You little idiot, what in blazes are you doing out after dark?"

As I'd expected, a scolding settled the girl's nerves. "It's *my* car," she told me. She looked even younger when she was trying to be angry, but I guessed she was probably sixteen or so. No way she was over twenty. She had a soft little voice, but it only shook a little. She reloaded her tiny little gun and put it away. I approved; never leave a gun unloaded, not even a silly little gun like that one. An unloaded gun might as well be a rock for all the good it'll do you. Then she squirmed into the front seat and let me open the door for her.

"Then it's your insurance company which is going to be upset, isn't it? What's your policy say about damage incurred on the street at night? Never mind. My car. Unless you'd rather stand out here in the cool night breeze?"

She didn't like that idea at all—in fact, she flinched from the blood fey when it fluttered near—and let me escort her to my car. I held the door for her, then got back in on my side and locked the car up tight again. "Where do you live?"

"Twelve twenty-four East Viburnum."

I stopped and looked at her. "Oh, come on."

The girl gazed away, out the windshield. She didn't look anything like Cyndi. This girl was very fair. That fine straight hair hid her face when she turned her head away. She had delicate features and a weak chin—she was pretty, but she was also the sort of girl who has 'victim' written in letters of fire on her forehead. The sort of girl who gets whistled out after dark by her psycho boyfriend, in fact, and thinks it proves her love for him if she risks it all to go to him. My Cyndi has more sense than that. God, I hope Cyndi has more sense than that.

That little rosebud mouth wasn't trembling now, though. It was set. "It's where I'm going."

"Look," I said patiently, "haven't you had enough of wandering about at night? The clubs on Viburnum will all be locked up for the night. You're going home. If you were going to meet someone, he'll understand when you call him and explain that a unicorn wrecked your car."

The girl twitched.

"He won't understand? Then dump his butt and get yourself a boyfriend who doesn't ask you to go out in the streets at night."

"It's...it's none your business where I go," the girl said. Then she looked suddenly shy, and glanced at me sideways. I couldn't tell what color her eyes were. Something light, blue or gray or green. "Or...thank you for rescuing me, and I would be grateful if you would take me to that—that address I gave you—and I will call an escort service when I need to go home, all right?"

"You *need* to go home right now. And I'm right here to take you."

"No," said the girl, with more intensity. God, things are so important to the young! No time will do but right now, and everything's the end of the world.

She bit her lip, looking at me. Then that delicate chin firmed more than I'd thought possible. "If you take me home, I'll just have to sneak out again." She hesitated, and then said in a rush, "My sister—my sister is there. My little sister. So I have to go. You have to understand. She's—she's not— I have to get her out."

Well, now. That was something else again. It was my turn to hesitate. "You know, the clubs really will be locked down. Your sister's likely safer wherever she is than out on the streets. Even with me."

"She is *not* safer where she is!" The girl said fiercely. "It doesn't matter if it's locked up. I have a key."

I raised my eyebrows at her and she looked down, blushing. Maybe she wasn't quite as innocent and young as she looked. Though the unicorn had seemed to like her just fine.

Either way, I was starting to have a bad feeling about what the sister might have gotten into. "I'll take you," I said, and turned the key. "I'll take you there, and go in with you to get your sister. And then you're *both* going home. You got that?"

"Yes," she whispered. "Thank you."

The blood fey came and clung to the windshield, so I unrolled the window just for a moment, just enough for it to slip through. Having been paid in blood once to come to a summons and again to provide guidance, it likely wanted a third bargain: magic works best in threes and doesn't care for twos.

We hardly passed any traffic on our way, naturally. A few risk-takers who'd decided there was someplace they really needed to be and then had the sense, unlike this girl, to call an escort service. Also one heavily-armored limousine, owned by somebody wealthy enough he didn't need an escort. Probably the sort of very important person who built a skyscraper of mirrored steel and then refused to tear it down or face it with stone after the unicorns started to use it as a doorway into our world.

Nobody stopped at lights. A quick glance left and right and you were through each intersection without even slowing down. Driving at night does have its little pleasures.

The club the girl wanted to stop at was a small one, in an old brick building that had once been a private home. The grace of those earlier times was still visible through the gilt and sham of club décor. Oddly, it was dark.

"Nobody home," I said.

"Oh, yes," the girl said, glancing at me quickly. "He's here."

She sounded distracted, and very young. And it was her *little* sister in that dark shabby club. How old could the sister be, fifteen? Fourteen? Younger? I got out of the car and held the door for my passenger. The blood fey fluttered upward into the night, coming to rest at last clinging to the tip of the antenna of my car. Nothing else unchancy seemed anywhere near about.

The girl wasn't paying attention to the streets at all. All her attention was on the club. A dangerously tight focus. She wasn't fit to be out on her own. But she had the key in her hand already, and the door open a second later. She bit her lip and looked at me quickly. "You— you don't have to come in."

"Don't be silly."

She ducked her head and held the door for me.

The club was dark inside. Nightlights glowed dimly in the low ceiling—low, to give an intimate feel. Without real lights and music and a crowd in a party mood, the low ceiling just made the place seem claustrophobic. Chairs were upended on little round tables. The outsized bar loomed to one side. The ceiling lights were covered with domes of blood porcelain, the bar and tables and chairs all stained red. I guess the idea was to look edgy, daring, dark. With the club shut down and the lights off, it just looked like a cheap imitation of *daring* and *edgy*.

The girl didn't look at the bar, at the room, at anything, really. She wove between the tables, making for another door in the back of the room. Light showed under it, faintly. But she didn't open it right away. She stopped with her hand on the knob and looked back at me. It was obvious she was scared. Afraid of whoever was behind that door. I admit it made me angry, seeing her scared like that. I didn't wait for her to ask me. I was right behind her as she opened the door and let herself in.

The room wasn't much of a love nest. It was, in fact, just an office, and not a very posh kind of office at that. It had a cheap desk and a cheap table—all the décor ideas had been used up in the public areas of the club, I guess. It had a window, which didn't even have silver screen—just an iron grill. Well, it was a small window. Not much could get through it anyway.

The guy behind the desk looked as cheap and sleazy as the club. Not young. Tired, with an edge of seedy depression. I didn't like him. I didn't like his buzzed flattop hair, a style twenty years too young for him; I didn't like his heavy face or thick hands or his world-weary attitude. Most especially I didn't like the way he looked at the girl with pretended surprise, and at me with real surprise and anger. It was plain he'd expected her. He was alone.

No sister anywhere in sight. I thought, *Huh, she lied after all.* I was even surprised. I don't know why. Everybody lies—I know that. After nightfall especially.

"Claudette," the guy said. "An escort is fine, but you hardly need him *here*." His voice was smoother than I'd expected. It wasn't a voice that went with that face, those broad thug's hands; hearing him over the phone, you'd have thought he was an upstanding kind of guy.

The girl—Claudette—was shaking again. She *was* scared. She said, "No. I did need him here." Then she shot the man in the chest twice with that little bitty gun. He looked shocked—that was what I thought, at the time: shocked but not scared. He didn't believe she'd shot him. He didn't believe it even with his blood pumping out over his lap. He opened his mouth and tried to say something, but nothing came out of his mouth except a liquidy kind of sound and more blood.

I'd like to say I managed the situation in some way that was clever, or at least competent. I've been a vigilante for fourteen years. But damn, I guess you never really see it all, do you? I have to admit the girl took me so much by surprise that she had her little gun pointed at my face before I had mine halfway aimed, even if I'd been willing to shoot her, which I guess I still wasn't.

"Lord God," I said involuntarily. She looked just awful, pale and tight-drawn. I don't know what I looked like. Probably as stunned as the dead guy. "Look, kid—"

"I'm sorry," said the girl. "I am really, really sorry. But you'll tell everybody what—what happened—and then there'll be a trial, and prison, and—and Daddy—he mustn't know, it would just kill him—"

"Well, not literally," I pointed out. "Unlike some of us."

"Don't!" she said. Her hands were shaking, but not enough to get that gun out of line.

I concentrated on trying to look harmless. That might be a baby gun, but she was only a few steps away, and even a teeny bullet can kill you if it hits you right. And the girl had already shown she had decent aim.

I set my Anaconda down on the corner of the desk and spread my hands out, clearly empty. "Look, now. You probably had a good reason to shoot that guy. I'm sure you did. He looked like a jerk. But it's not very nice to shoot me, especially after I already saved your life.

Let's just—"

"Shut up, shut up, shut up!" The girl was still trembling, but her hands were steady now and the gun was still pointed right at me. Impressive, really, for a virgin killer. Surely she hadn't made a habit of shooting men previously, or that unicorn wouldn't have gone for her so fast. She was starting out pretty good, though. I shut up and wondered if she'd actually squeeze the trigger. It could be easier for her the second time—or it might be harder. It's tough to judge how it'll hit any new killer.

"Why?" I asked her, stalling for time, knowing I sounded like a B-grade movie. "At least tell me what all this is about. It's plain there's no sister. Come on, Claudette! If you're going to shoot a guy who saved your life, the least you can do is explain why!"

"He—he set me up," she stammered. Her teeth were actually chattering, like she was cold. Maybe she was. "There was—there was a party, and I—I thought it would be fun—but I didn't—didn't *know*—"

"Yeah," I said. "Look, kid, nobody could blame you. I swear I don't."

"He—he showed me pictures. He said he would—he would send them to Daddy, if I—if I went to—to the police—he can't know—it would *kill* him."

"Blackmailers deserve whatever they get. I won't tell anyone."

"You would!"

"I promise I won't—"

"You would!" And she shot me. I don't think she actually meant to; I mean, I don't think she decided to do it and aimed and deliberately squeezed the trigger. I think she just tensed up and it kind of happened. Either way, though, she sure shot me. Luckily she'd changed her aim, so she shot me in the chest, not the face.

I gasped and staggered and went down and

wondered if she would notice there was no blood. I heard Claudette go out and started to get up, but then I heard her coming back, so I lay back down and pretended hard to be dead.

Glass broke, and there was the sharp smell of alcohol. Something strong. And sweet. Damn. Peaches. The girl was going to burn the place down with peach brandy. It made me want to laugh. If I laughed she'd probably shoot me again, and this time she might aim for the head. I didn't laugh. Really, she was a businesslike little thing. She was throwing brandy over everything— desk, floor, dead guy. I bet I was next. Damn. Go for my gun and I'd definitely have to shoot her. Or maybe I'd get shot again myself, except worse. But if I just lay still, I'd get soaked down with peach brandy and set on fire. Nice choice there. I whispered between my teeth, *"Eia age! Revenire!"*

The girl spun around and stood still, trying to decide if she'd heard something. I hadn't thought she would. Damn, but kids that age have good ears.

So do blood fey. My little friend fluttered outside the window. Claudette didn't see it. It clung to the grill and peered in. Under the circumstances I could hardly explain to it what I needed. But fey aren't really stupid—and they like summonings that work by threes. And there was blood all over the dead guy. It must have been a pretty inviting scene, to a blood fey. The little creature tucked its wings in tight and crawled through the bars of the iron grill.

If I'd been able to give instructions, I'd have told it to fly at the girl's face and keep her eyes off me for a second. Instead, it flew, of course, to the dead man's blood. That worked almost as well, because Claudette picked up its flight out of the corner of her eyes and jerked around with a gasp. It gave me time to get to my hideout gun, and by the time she turned around I was sitting up with my wrist supported on my knee and the gun pointed steadily between her breasts. "I bet *you're* not wearing armor," I said.

She'd been under a lot of strain. If I'd been taking bets, I'd have bet on her to burst into tears. I also thought she might try to shoot me again, and if she had I was prepared to try to shoot her first, in some non-lethal spot, which would be a hell of a lot easier with the hideout gun than it would of been with the Anaconda. But shooting people so's just to disarm them is a hell of a lot harder in real life than it looks in the movies, so I hoped she wouldn't reach for her gun.

And she didn't. She didn't burst into tears, either. She made a little sound like a startled kitten, dropped her gun, and clasped her hands together in front of her chest, just as girls are always doing in Gothic movies. I'd had no idea girls ever really did that, but she did. Then she said, *"Oh*—I'm *glad* I didn't kill you!" and took a small step toward me.

"Me, too," I assured her. "Stop right there."

She stopped. She might have been faking remorse, except she definitely wasn't faking anything, I could tell by her blank matter-of-factness when she took a lighter out of her pocket. "I'm going to burn it," she explained to me. "I'm going to burn it all, and burn myself too, so it's all gone—so everything's gone and *over*."

She looked perfectly sane. It was quite an illusion.

"Don't," I said. "It'd kill your father."

But she did. She flicked the lighter open and got a little flame that danced like the malice in a unicorn's heart. Then she dropped it.

What was I supposed to do, shoot her? Let her burn to death in a skuzzy cheap club? I got an arm around her on my way to the door and the next time I looked around we were outside, with the night air clean around us and the club going up like a torch at our backs.

Then she cried. I patted her on the back and told her she was fine, and then I took her home. What was I supposed to do? I'm not a cop. Arresting criminals is not my business. Besides, I'd promised I wouldn't tell.

"You should, though," I told her, as gently as I could. "If not your father, then somebody. Your confessor. Your shrink. Somebody."

"I can't," she answered. "Daddy might find out." Her eyes were open wide, but blank—blind to the night, seeing blood and fire. She was trembling still. She sat tucked into the extreme edge of the passenger seat, as far away from me as she could get. I don't think she was scared of me. I think she was ashamed she'd tried to kill me. I hoped she was ashamed.

He'd understand, I wanted to say, but I couldn't. Because what did I know about her daddy, and what he would or wouldn't understand? What I saw in this girl's eyes made me think of Cyndi, of what dark things my daughter might be keeping behind her eyes. What might Cyndi think would kill me, if I found it out?

What might Cyndi do, to make sure I wouldn't find it out?

"Tell your confessor," I repeated, gently, I hope. I stopped the car and looked at her, waiting until she looked back at me. Until I thought she saw me. "Promise me you will. You shot that guy. Maybe he deserved it and maybe he didn't, but you also tried to shoot me, Claudette. You think I want that burden on your soul? You owe me. Don't you? So promise me."

She bit her lip and nodded. "Okay," she whispered.

I gave her a card before I let her out. I doubted she'd ever call my number, or need to. But I thought she'd keep it.

Then I turned toward home myself. I hoped Cyndi would be home. One truth had lit up for me like a fire in the dark: I didn't care what kind of silence she wanted to keep between us. If my daughter ever got into trouble—real trouble—I wanted her to know that there would be nothing—nothing—it would kill me to hear.

AUDITION

-1-

There was to be a special audition for the kajuraihi. Nescana's youngest brother, Eonii, was the first one to tell her about it.

Normally the kajuraihi only held one audition every three or four or five years, but even though there'd been an audition just this past spring, there was going to be another one now. In just ten days.

For ordinary auditions, the kajuraihi gave notice at least ten senneri in advance so people could make arrangements and put forward petitions. Boys from twelve to eighteen came forward—normally their male relatives petitioned for them, swearing to their good character and intelligence and general fitness to join the ranks of the kajuraihi. Only on rare occasions would a boy petition on his own behalf because he had no one to do it for him. Such a boy was generally regarded as over-proud, but Nescana knew of one boy who'd done it and not only been accepted for the audition but actually

165

succeeded. Nescana's oldest brother, Genrai, had become a kajurai just this past spring, and she had been so proud of him, but then she knew Genrai was anything but over-proud.

Genrai had worried for the whole ten senneri, knowing how hard it would be for his brothers and sisters once he left them for the kajuraihi. Nescana herself had made him put forward the petition...in fact, she'd dictated most of it herself, and paid the scribe with her own coins, and bought a proper wax seal for the parchment. She'd argued and reassured and laid out their finances down to the last quarter-copper, showing Genrai that while the next year might be hard, it wouldn't be *too* hard.

He'd done it. He'd worked himself nearly to death during those last few senneri, building up a small store of coin so his brothers and sister would be secure for a little while. In the end he'd brought forward his own petition and gone into the kajurai tower for his own audition, and he'd made it. He hadn't come back.

Nescana had never seen him fly, not for sure—not yet. Kajurai novices weren't allowed out of the novitiate for their whole first year, like a very intense apprenticeship with no half days off. But someday. Someday, her big brother's shadow would fall across their doorway, huge wings and all, and he would tell her all about it. All about the sky and the wind and the dragons and the joy of flight.

He wouldn't have to tell her. She was certain she'd captured it all in her own imagination. Or she had been certain, until now, when she finally knew she almost, maybe, had a chance to live that dream herself, for real.

Because the truly special thing about this audition wasn't the timing, or the way you didn't need to petition for a place. No.

The truly astonishing thing was that this audition

was for girls.

No girl in the whole history of the Floating Islands had ever become a kajurai. That was obviously going to change. Or at least, it might change. If any girls could succeed in the audition, it would change, but no one knew for sure whether girls *could* be kajuraihi. It wasn't the senior kajuraihi who chose their novices from among the applicants; it was the dragons themselves. Everyone said so, anyway. Who knew what dragons might look for, in the people to whom they granted some small portion of their magic? Maybe they only wanted boys. Maybe that was why kajuraihi had always been male.

On the other hand, mages were always male too, except now there was a girl in the Hidden School. Everyone knew that. So if girls could be mages, why not kajuraihi?

Nescana thought probably that was the argument that had led to this special audition. The Islands needed more kajurai just as they needed more mages; if girls could come into magery, maybe girls could take up dragon magic. Somebody wanted to find out. That was the way she guessed that decision had been made.

Eonii had heard about the audition as soon as the notice went up in the market, where he went every morning to pluck and clean chickens for Lotanei and his sons. Lotanei would first brine the birds and then roast them with lemon and pepper. Bronze and crisp-skinned, Lotanei's roast chickens were very popular, both with people shopping and with stall-keepers all around that part of the market. A farmer sold Lotanei fifty or seventy or, in the right season, as many as a hundred young birds every day, which was why besides Eonii he had two other boys who also worked for him, doing the messy work of cleaning the chickens for the brine.

Eonii earned five copper coins for a morning's

work, plus half a roasted chicken and all the feathers he could carry away. Another boy took the long wing feathers; Eonii gathered up only the small, downy feathers, a big sack of them every day. He sold them to a woman who made pillows. He earned one more coin that way. Six copper coins for one morning's work was very good wages for a boy of thirteen, and he'd found the job himself, persistently asking in the market until Lotanei decided to try him. Nescana had been very proud of him. Also relieved. Six more coins every day made a lot of difference.

Half a roasted chicken every day was also welcome. Along with his news, Eonii always brought his half-chicken home to share with everyone, just as Nekei always brought home some day-old rolls or broken pastries from the bakery where he swept the floors and washed the heavy mixing bowls. Besides the bread, Nekei earned three copper coins a day, plus two lessons a senneri on pastry-making or cream sweets—plus he could watch the real bakers, if he had time. It wasn't a real apprenticeship, but the next best thing, and a promising start for a Third City boy. Nekei was fourteen now. By the time he was fifteen, or at least sixteen, Nescana was sure he would be able to try for a better place at that bakery or another. She was pretty sure he would get a good place eventually. He always brought them the pastries he made himself, which weren't good enough for the bakery to sell. Nescana wasn't as picky as some and didn't pretend to be able to tell a great pastry from one that was just halfway good, but even she could tell her brother's pastries were getting better.

Nekei had also heard the news, so he was the second person who told Nescana about it, half a bell after she'd heard about it from Eonii. This time, prepared, she only rolled her eyes and said blandly, "I know, Nekei. Everyone knows about the audition."

Nekei gave his brother a disgusted look and a shove. "I wanted to be the one to tell her!"

"Should've been quicker," Eonii said smugly.

"Neither of you had to tell me," Nescana lied in her most matter-of-fact tone. "I found a Quei feather this morning, a long flight feather, only it was red as the feathers in the kajurai's wing, so of course I figured it out without anybody telling me a word."

"Liar! You did not!" Eonii nudged Nekei. "She did not. You should've seen her. Eyes like this." He held up his hands to mime wide, round eyes.

"Not me," Nescana declared. "I haven't been surprised by a single thing since I was half your height, and I got tall when I was nine, so that's been a while. No, I happened to look up while I was fetching water and this long red Quei feather floated right down out of the sky and into my hands." She sketched looking up and holding up her hands to catch a long feather. "Couldn't ask for a clearer omen than that. Eonii just surprised me when *he* knew about it."

None of this was true, not even the part about being tall by the time she'd turned nine, though Nescana *was* tall for a girl—at fifteen, still a little bit taller than her younger brothers. They'd get their height soon; everyone in their family was tall; but at the moment Nescana could still look down her nose at Eonii and Nekei. She did now, putting on a superior look.

"Yeah?" Nekei said skeptically. "Where's this red Quei feather, then?"

"I took it to the temple, obviously, and made it an offering to the First God, since it's Gods' Day." Nescana laid out on the table the lamb and lentil pastries she'd bought, next to Eonii's roast chicken and Nekei's cream-filled pastries.

Nescana always bought lamb pastries for the noon meal, or mutton stew with greens and dumplings, or pork simmered to melting tenderness in spicy coconut milk. Meat was expensive, but the boys needed a solid meal in the middle of the day before going to their afternoon work, both of them together, for a business that carved down into the red stone of Milendri to make lower rooms for Second City homes or passageways between First City towers. That was hard work; hard enough that no reputable employer would take on boys their age for more than half days. Breaking up the stone was the hardest part; that was a job for grown men, but even just dragging out the baskets and carts of broken rock was hard enough.

It was work that paid well, or relatively well: eight copper coins, nearly half a silver, for an afternoon's work. But boys her brothers' age were much better off finding lighter work for half the day if they could.

"You made it an offering to the Gods," Nekei repeated. "Of course you did."

"*Nescana* made an offering to the Gods?" Kanbii, sixteen, brushed the curtain out of the doorway and came in, ducking his head to clear the low lintel of the doorway because he'd lately grown into himself and was a lot taller than Nescana. He carried a bag of sausages and rounds of cumin bread, which he set on the table before turning to raise his eyebrows at his sister. "Did you really? Because you heard about the special audition?"

Gods' Day was Kanbii's half-day, and he always stopped to buy spicy sausages as he came home from the glassblower's shop where he was apprenticed. He was sixteen, and this was his second year of apprenticeship, so unless things went very wrong, he'd earn his place as a junior glassblower before this time next summer. Immediately the whole household would shift from their precarious day-to-day existence to a life that was almost secure. The younger boys could stop hauling broken rock and find lighter, easier work for their afternoons; or maybe they could afford to buy Nekei into a real apprenticeship of his own. Eonii wouldn't want to settle to any one trade, but he was clever—cleverer than any of the rest of them, Nescana thought. Give him a few spare coins to rub together and a senneri to think what to do with them, and he'd sort out a dozen different ways to make a living.

But until Kanbii earned rank, they needed every coin any of them could bring in. Genrai's earnings, meant to keep them all the way through Kanbii's apprentice years, had melted away much faster than anybody had guessed possible.

It hadn't been anybody's fault. The boys were careful with their coins. Nescana knew how careful they were. No one could have guessed how bad the summer illness would be; how hard it would hit or how long it would keep someone from working.

They'd been so lucky. None of them had caught the illness until later in the summer, after the physicians knew how bad it was and how aggressively they had to treat it. Nearly everyone who caught it that late lived. But even though none of them had died, Eonii and Nekei and Nescana had all caught it, one after another. Not Kanbii, whom Nescana had made stay away, at the glassblowers. She'd insisted they could manage, they would all get better, Kanbii mustn't risk catching the illness, what if he got ill and lost his apprenticeship? She didn't trust the glassblowers to be generous to an apprentice who couldn't work. She hadn't even let Kanbii in the door when he'd tried to help.

She'd been right. They had managed. Eonii had started getting better before Nescana was too sick to take care of her brothers, and she hadn't gotten as sick as the others. They'd all recovered. But slowly. Too slowly. The illness had swallowed up whole senneri, and then senneri had turned to more than a whole month with no coin at all coming in, and not much for another month after that.

All Genrai's hard work, all their store of coins, gone. Every coin counted now. They needed every copper any of them could earn. Including Nescana.

Auditioning was out of the question. She knew that. She should put the whole idea right out of her head.

"Of course she didn't *really* make an offering," Eonii was telling their older brother. "She's making that up. She didn't know a thing till *I* told her. Go on, Nescana! No one's going to believe you found a red Quei feather."

"I'd believe a red Quei feather before I'd believe you bothered to make an offering to the Gods," Kanbii told Nescana. "But I'd've believed either of those before I'd've guessed the kajuraihi would hold an audition for girls. But I guess they are. It's the only thing anybody's talked about since the notice went up. News-sellers are passing the word free because it's an official announcement." He paused, measuring Nescana with a discerning eye. *"Are* you going to try for it?"

No. No, of course not. No, of course she wasn't. She couldn't. It was impossible.

Somehow Nescana couldn't make herself say so.

Neither of their younger brothers had asked that question, but Nescana knew they'd both been wondering the same thing. Eonii paused with a round of cumin bread in one hand, a chicken thigh in the other. Nekei had been pouring cups of water from the jug in the corner, but he half turned, his eyes jumping to Nescana's face so that he poured half a cup of water on his foot, jumped, cursed, and nearly knocked over the jug.

In that moment of brief confusion, Nescana tried once more to frame a clear, definite *No.* She opened her mouth and set her tongue to the word. *No, of course not.* It was a very brief phrase.

She couldn't say it.

What she finally said, once Kanbii had firmly taken the water jug away from Nekei, was, "Maybe I am and maybe I'm not, but I won't if we can't sort out a way for me to do it right."

That was...that was the truth. Or she thought it was the truth. Or she hoped it was the truth. Unless she let herself be a terrible, selfish person, it would be the truth.

Kanbii definitely couldn't withdraw from his apprenticeship; not now, not when he was so close to earning rank. The younger boys definitely couldn't be forced to work themselves to exhaustion and injury hauling rock and gravel twelve bells a day.

There was no possible way to build up a store of coin in a mere ten days. There was just no possible way for Nescana to audition. She knew that.

But she still couldn't make herself say *No,* straight out, the way she knew she ought to.

Nescana had been so proud of her brother when he'd passed his audition. She'd been so happy for Genrai, and only a little, tiny bit resentful because he'd left the rest of them—her three brothers and herself.

It wasn't at all fair to resent Genrai's success. He'd wanted to audition when he was thirteen, which was a better age for it. Instead he'd waited for the next audition, which had turned out to be this spring, when he was seventeen, almost eighteen. Waiting had meant his chances were much worse and it had meant he'd only have one chance at most. The kajuraihi liked younger boys better. Seventeen was old for it, and for anyone over twenty, there was no chance at all.

But Genrai had already had good employment at thirteen, and the others needed the coins he brought home; needed his support too much for him to even think of leaving. Their mother had died years before, worn out from bearing nine living children in as many years, especially worn from suffering the loss of the two oldest from mischance and the two youngest from fever, all at nearly the same time. That had been a terrible time. Nescana didn't remember much about it; she'd been only nine. What she remembered was mostly the repeated blows of grief and loss, so that the whole year seemed to disappear into a wave of darkness and mourning. She remembered her mother sobbing and then, eventually, tossing with the same fever that had carried away the two youngest. And then lying still.

She never thought of that time anymore. Not ever. Not if she could help it. Only sometimes at night, if she woke up too suddenly from the wrong kind of dream.

Their father, who had labored too hard for too many years starting from too young an age, had aged fast and hard after the loss of his wife. His hands had knotted, his knees cracked, his back bent, his eyes failed, and he had spent the final years of his life sitting in a chair by the one window, listening to the bustle and life of a city he could no longer see.

That was how Nescana remembered him best: as a bent old man sitting quietly in that chair, listening to his children come and go and quarrel and laugh, listening to the neighbors and the city outside. He had been the one to tell Genrai, *Don't work hard labor all day, don't let your brothers work that hard, not till you're all old enough to bear it. Live on less and you'll be glad later.* He'd been the one to say, *If all of you work for it, one of you can get through an apprenticeship.* Even then his attention had been on Kanbii, who even at twelve obviously possessed the determination to learn a craft from front to back and top to bottom and the steadiness to work his way through a two-year apprenticeship.

Their father had been the one to teach his children to save their coins, set them aside, tuck them out of sight. *Any coin put by is a choice you've bought for the future.* Nescana had taken over that task, keeping track of every coin that came in and every coin that anyone spent, when she was ten. Now it was just something she did without having to think about it. But she had learned that careful attention from their father.

He had died when Nescana was eleven. She had been shocked at how deeply she had missed him. For a man who had taken up so little space at the end, he had left behind a very big emptiness in their home.

He had understood the sky-madness...not as one who had felt it himself, but as a man who had felt passion enough in his life. As a man who had given up dreams and the hope of dreams. He had made Genrai promise to try, whether he had to find or make or beg or borrow a chance.

He hadn't known he should give his daughter the same advice. But Nescana was sure he would have, if he'd ever expected the kajuraihi to permit girls to audition. Not much for worrying about tradition, or about what other people thought. He would have told her to try—if she could find a way that wouldn't ruin her brothers. She was sure he would have told her she had to at least *try* to find a way.

Almost sure.

When he'd been thirteen, Genrai had stayed home and let the audition pass. He'd avoided even looking at the sky all that year. Nescana knew—probably she was the only one who truly knew—how much it had hurt him to let that chance pass. For years, even as children, the two of them together had gone up on the rooftops to watch the kajuraihi—they'd shirk chores, risking punishment or missed meals or both so they could make their way through Second City and climb up on the rooftops near First City, where they'd have a better view of the kajurai towers and could watch the kajuraihi come and go. Crimson wings against blue or grey or monsoon-heavy skies, winged men riding the winds as easily as gulls or Quei.

Sky-mad, wind-mad, that's what people called children who lost their hearts to the sky and longed for nothing more than wings. Hard enough on a boy, the sky-madness; hard enough for a boy who couldn't leave his younger siblings. Worse for a girl. Nescana had thought, madly, of disguising herself as a boy and just seeing what the kajuraihi would do if she made it, if she came out of her audition with crystalline eyes and a tinge of dragon magic. What *would* they do, if she proved she was strong enough, smart enough, good enough, as good as the boys? They'd have to let her be a kajurai—wouldn't they?

It had been a crazy idea, but she'd thought of it all the time that year, when Genrai was thirteen and she was eleven and the chance was falling through both their fingers, impossible to catch or hold.

Nescana's brother had waited four long years, praying that the next audition would come while he was still young enough to seize the chance. And that chance had come. Kanbii was settled in an apprenticeship, the younger boys were old enough to work, Nescana was fifteen and old enough to marry. Then, when the audition had been announced, at the last moment he'd almost been too afraid to try after all. Nescana had dictated his petition and showed him the count she'd worked out for their expenses and told him they'd be fine. She'd made him believe it.

And he'd made it. He'd succeeded. He was a kajurai now, a novice, but a kajurai. Nescana always knew, when she looked up at a crimson-winged kajurai overhead, that it might be Genrai.

She always waved, in case it was.

After the summer illness, she'd dictated a letter, doling out words as carefully as coins, because Genrai wasn't allowed to leave the novitiate and she knew he would need to know they were all well, that no one had died. He wasn't allowed to send or receive letters either, but the kajurai wingmaster couldn't be so very strict, because they'd gotten a letter back, a short one, but filled with relief and gratitude.

Nescana hadn't told her older brother how hard it was, how all their reserve was gone, how every coin melted away as soon as it came in. She hadn't admitted adding and re-adding coins week by week, always afraid that this would be the week she would have to tell Nekei that he had to give up the bakery and haul rock all day; that it was a choice between that and asking Kanbii to give up his apprenticeship. She hadn't admitted that she'd stopped eating a meal at midday, that she only pretended. Her brothers needed that food much more than she did; *she* wasn't the one hauling broken rock and gravel.

She hadn't told Genrai that she'd found an afternoon job of her own, an intensely boring job cleaning and carding endless quantities of wool for a dyer's cooperative. She earned four coins for an afternoon's work, plus a small portion of the wool, which she gave to a neighbor. The neighbor—a widow with a young son—spun the wool Nescana gave her, made it into thread, and used it in her own piece-work. She returned the favor by repairing the boys' clothing when they ripped a knee and re-hemming Nescana's dresses when they needed lengthening, which were tasks for which Nescana no longer had time.

She hadn't told Genrai that she'd given up the thought of marrying, that her four daily coins made the difference between lamb pastries for her brothers and nothing. She hadn't told her younger brothers that either. She had offers, or she could have coaxed an offer from one young man or another. There was a metalworker's apprentice, Feraii, she liked him well enough and she knew he liked her. They had used to climb up on the rooftops to watch handball games that erupted between neighborhood boys, cheering whichever players seemed fiercest and most determined. Feraii was big and calm and placid. He would be kind. Plus in less than a year he'd earn his place and be able to stamp his work with the metalworker's seal and sell it for a lot more money.

Nescana could have come to an understanding with Feraii. Genrai had expected her to. But she had put that off, and put it off again, and now Feraii had an understanding with Eonaf. Which was *fine*. Nescana didn't want to be a metalworker's wife anyway, not even Feraii's wife. She wanted to fly.

If she could think of a way to make that possible.

It was a long walk from the westernmost alleys of Third City to the kajurai towers at the easternmost cliffs of First City. That walk gave a girl too much time to think. Nescana wondered how Genrai had felt making his way through Canpra on this same journey. He'd had to do it twice: first to petition for a place and then for the audition itself.

She might have to do it twice, too. If she had enough luck and the blessings of the Gods. Quei flew overhead, but no long feathers fell into Nescana's hands. She would have welcomed a beautiful long emerald-green plume, never mind a special red one dropped into her hands like a word spoken by one of the Gods.

She was nervous almost from her first step. Had Genrai been this nervous? She wondered for the first time how close her brother might have come to turning back.

He had gone on, and he had succeeded. He could put on wings now, and fall into the sky, and fly for hundreds of miles. His work was important, even though he was still just a novice. She'd heard stories about the brief, frightening war with Tolounn; about the kajuraihi novices who flew to Tolounn and blew up their magical engines and made them change their minds about conquering the Islands. Her brother! She had believed it. Genrai was smart and brave and responsible. He would have done something like that.

Prince Ceirfei was a kajurai novice. Nescana knew that—everyone knew that; it had been almost a scandal, but the young prince had somehow persuaded his parents and his uncle to let him audition. Nescana's own brother had met a prince, had lived in the same hall, eaten the same food, learned to fly from the same masters. Nescana assumed the prince had led the other novices on that crazy, brave raid against Tolounn. Genrai had saved them all—she knew it, because whatever the novices had done, she was sure her brother had been the companion on whom Prince Ceirfei depended most. She knew he must have been. Genrai was always the one on whom anybody could depend.

If he knew what Nescana was trying to do now, maybe he would decide she was not very dependable. He might be sorry he'd ever trusted her to take care of their brothers.

Third City was crowded, busy, familiar—narrow streets of tightly crowded small shops, yellow brick mostly, with homes above the shops and upper balconies that often reached right out over the streets until they closed off the sky. Those balconies and the leaning rooftops kept off the sun on hot summer days and protected people from the monsoon rains, but they also closed the streets into shadow. Nescana was glad now

179

and then to break into a public square, each with its wide cistern in the middle and market stalls packed around the edges. The stalls were owned by craftspeople and noodle vendors and herbalists not prosperous enough to afford a real shop. Nescana would have liked to buy a pastry or a bowl of noodles—she hadn't eaten anything this morning, partly from nervousness and partly to save the coin. Now that she was out in the streets and moving, she was hungry, but she still didn't want to spend the coin a pastry would cost.

Second City was very different. Here the streets were wider and more evenly laid out, in concentric arcs cut through by long straight avenues. Every curving street was lined with big trees for shade and smaller, more graceful flameberry trees, with flowers like puffs of red dandelion silk, for beauty. Covered porticos offered further protection from sun and rain. There weren't any stalls, only permanent shops, mostly for things like cloth and finished clothing and brasswork, furniture and spices and fancy confections, expensive white candles and jars of glazed ceramics filled with honey or syrup of pomegranates or other things too expensive for Third City vendors to offer. Shops that stood along those streets were graceful, each with its own separate balconies and rooftops. In Second City, usually only employees lived above the shops—the merchants themselves, and respected craftspeople and all that kind of folk, lived in separate houses on different streets that ran along behind the shopping districts.

The straight avenues cut through the curved streets, offering quick and easy access from one arc of shops to the next, and from the shops to the homes where Second City merchants lived, and as one moved inward toward First City, the larger homes where ministers lived with their families.

In Second City, everything was expensive,

handsome red brick, with here and there black stone or white marble for accents. Balconies didn't block the sun, but welcomed it with tumbles of flowers from pots and planters; nearly every balcony Nescana saw held a lemon or calamondin tree in an ornate pot. No one offered pastries for sale out of a cart, but fancy bakeries offered little tables under canopies so that passersby could sit and enjoy fine weather. She would never have been able to afford a pastry from any of those bakeries. Unconcerned about the price of the crumbs they chased, sapphire-winged birds with orange breasts and gold streaks above their eyes darted beneath and around those tables, and marmosets ran along the rooftops and leaped from one flowering tree to the next.

Nescana did not exactly wish she belonged to Second City—girls here didn't have to clean or card wool for a few coppers a day, but they never climbed on rooftops to shout encouragement as a sudden, violent handball game erupted, or watched actors practicing their lines in the alley behind a theater, or had neighbors crowd in for a spontaneous party because someone finished his apprenticeship or safely birthed her child. Second City seemed so...quiet. And a little boring.

All right, more than a little.

On the other hand, if Nescana had been born to a family here, she wouldn't have to worry that auditioning for the kajuraihi might leave her brothers in desperate circumstances. Girls here might have to get permission from their fathers before they could even walk down the street, but Nescana would have wagered that not a single girl in Second City had to choose between a noon meal for herself or for her brothers.

Coins put by are choices stored up for the future. That was true. It was just completely true.

The question was whether future coins might be turned into choices right now. That was what Nescana needed to find out.

Canpra's First City was all slender white towers and white marble and white limestone and white plaster—always freshly touched up and brightened, not dingy in the summers and streaked with mold after the monsoons, as was always the case for plaster in Third City. The slender white towers glowed like opal and pearl in the morning light.

Though there were white towers and white-paved streets everywhere, Canpra's First City didn't lack color. Vines with violet flowers, or crimson, or orange, cascaded from large pots set on windowsills and balconies and on some of the paving stones of the aerial walkways. More flowers filled planters at the corners where one street crossed another: red and gold and orange and a deep blue that was almost purple. Nescana wondered how many people were employed just to water all those flowers through the hot dry summer, and whether all those stone planters were covered or brought inside during the heavy rains of the monsoons.

This was the part of the city where nobles lived, and where the ministries were housed, and where the palace itself stood. Here and there, high on the towers, Nescana could make out subtle suggestions of carving: a dragon's long, elegant head or slender curving neck or a long feathered wing. All the carving was stylized, so that you might stand for some time wondering whether a dragon's eye might be gazing down at you from a ripple in the stonework high above. Canpra's First City was meant to be more imposing the longer you looked at it, Nescana had always thought.

Aerial walkways and floating staircases led from one tower to another, their big square paving stones set neatly one after another in the empty air. Nescana and her brothers had found those floating pathways and stairways irresistible on their rare visits to First City;

children always did. They'd dared one another to run up and down and through that maze of floating stones, pretending they risked a fall—of course the protective magic that surrounded all those aerial pathways guarded against any such accidents.

Little children were chasing one another over those walkways now, not far from where Nescana paused to watch them. They were quieter than Third City children, and she told herself they weren't quite as daring or as confident. But the truth was, those children looked very much at home on those pathways, in light, gauzy, jewel-toned clothing. Fabrics like that were blatantly impractical; such clothing wouldn't have lasted through an hour of wear at any Third City job.

Those children made Nescana feel out of place. A couple of them might be nearly her age. But they seemed so much younger. They made her feel older, and experienced, and worldly. When she went on, she walked more slowly.

White gulls and black gulls and emerald-feathered Quei flew between the towers and beneath the walkways. The brilliant green wings and heads and long trailing tails of the Quei were vivid against the white stone and blue sky. Nescana hoped one would fly down to her or drop a feather into her hands, but they all stayed high and no feathers floated out of the sky.

The kajuraihi lived in three white towers that stood right on the cliff edges. Like any First City towers, those would have many chambers and galleries tucked out of sight, underground. But this close to the edge of the Island, many of those underground chambers no doubt had wide windows that overlooked the long drop and the empty air and the sea.

Windows like that must have made it much easier to carve out those chambers. No need for boys like her brothers to haul out the broken rock basketful by painful basketful; no need for pulleys and winches; just tip the dross right out into the air and let it fall on the heads of surprised fishes.

Nescana had no idea where in those three towers she might find the wingmaster of Milendri's kajuraihi. No one went in or out while she watched, except that overhead a kajurai swept in toward the nearest tower, backwinged at the last moment, and disappeared through a window at least a hundred feet above street level. His wings were bright saffron gold, not the crimson of Milendri's kajuraihi; he was from Candara. Carrying some important message or maybe just visiting; she couldn't guess.

This tower had wide doors that were standing open, at the top of a short flight of broad, curved stairs. The lintel of the doorway was carved with the merest suggestion of feathers. The sheer breadth of the doorway was intimidating; but that the doors were standing open seemed an invitation.

Nescana looked at that open doorway, biting her lip gently and trying to gather her nerve. What was the worst that could happen? Surely the very worst thing would be if someone told Nescana she had to leave. She would be embarrassed, but what was a little bit of embarrassment? Especially since she hadn't done anything the least bit wrong. She wouldn't be breaking any rules by going into that tower. She was fairly sure she wouldn't be breaking any rules. She ought not care—her brothers would laugh at her if she said she was worried about breaking rules. Eonii and Nekei would laugh.

Kanbii wouldn't laugh. He would offer to come with her. But his next half-day was too long to wait, and she wouldn't let him pretend to his master that he was too sick to work. Kanbii's master was not a patient man.

But Nescana had to admit, she would have been

much happier if a whole lot of ordinary people had been going in and out of this tower, so she could just be one more among a crowd.

In the end, the sheer length of the walk from her home to this tower made Nescana go on up those stairs. She couldn't come so far and then not go on, and so she did, up the stairs and through that doorway, passing beneath the dragon's wing into the kajurai tower.

It was cool and dim and quiet within the tower. The entryway gave immediately onto a wide high-ceilinged antechamber, all white stone unsoftened by rugs or cloth hangings or any kind of furnishing. A stairway curved up on the right and on the left, and straight ahead another stairway led straight down into whatever underground chambers lay under this tower. Sunlight came through many high, narrow windows, but the windows were screened with fine latticework meant to break the strength of the sun; probably also to keep out gulls and smaller birds. Quei were welcome to come and go anywhere, but other birds would not be so welcome in a clean, polished place like this.

No one was here. Nescana nearly turned around right then and left, but if she went out of this tower, she didn't think she'd have the courage to come into it again, nor to go into one of the other ones. She thought of sitting down quietly against a wall and waiting for someone to appear—a servant maybe, someone she wouldn't be afraid to speak to. Her feet hurt from the long walk. But if she sat down, she was afraid her courage would ebb away into the cool stone. So she went up the nearest stairway, which was the one to the right. Her footsteps sounded over-loud in the hush, as she listened for voices or someone else's footsteps.

She went up two long curving flights and opened three narrow doors before she heard voices. They didn't sound friendly. Two or maybe three men were arguing in the polite way First City people always argued; their voices weren't loud, but they sounded vehement. Nescana thought of going the other way, down a hallway, or maybe back down the stairs. Before she could decide, a door slammed—at least, maybe it didn't actually slam, but it definitely closed with some force—and a moment later, one of the men who had been arguing stomped out into the hall where Nescana hovered, indecisive, on the landing.

This was an older man not very much taller than Nescana herself. Though he wasn't tall, he was intimidating. He had a thick, powerful build; a square, stubborn face; a mouth set with anger and disapproval, and crystalline kajurai eyes. He wore unrelieved black, so she knew he was a master kajurai; and the steel rank markers at his wrists and his throat showed he had some rank beyond that, but she couldn't read them. A single red feather was braided into his iron-gray hair.

This man stopped dead when he saw Nescana and glared at her. "Well?" he demanded. Curt though this demand was, at least the man seemed to expect an answer. Simple seemed best when speaking to an angry master kajurai. Nescana nodded, trying to look respectful rather than scared. "I'm looking for the wingmaster, sir, if he has a moment, or for someone who could tell me how to make an appointment to see him."

She half expected the kajurai to say something like *The wingmaster doesn't talk to Third City girls, be off!* At best, she expected him to inform her brusquely that she was in the wrong place and tell her where to go.

Instead he looked her up and down and said, "Looking for the wingmaster, are you? What's it about?"

This was harder to answer than Nescana had expected. She almost wanted to say *Never mind* and slink away. Except her brothers would be so disappointed. And she would never, ever forgive herself.

Clearing her throat she tried to speak firmly. "About the audition, sir, the one set for next Gods' Day."

The man snorted. "Of course about the audition." He looked her up and down once more, more carefully this time, but not seeming actually hostile. "Got it in mind to audition yourself, girl? You're tall enough, Gods know. How old are you?"

He asked like he had every right and reason to question her. Nescana found herself answering. "Fifteen, sir."

"Huh. Good age for it. Third City, are you? No need to see the wingmaster if that's what worries you; I can tell you myself that you have as much right to audition as any other girl. That your concern?"

"No, sir."

"Problems with your family? That's not too common with Third City boys, but a girl might have more trouble than a boy, eh?"

"No, sir. If I could just speak to the wingmaster—"

"The wingmaster, is it?" The man glowered at her. "I'm Anerii Pencara. Milendri's novice-master. Bring off your audition, girl, and I'll be *your* master the moment you wake up with kajurai eyes. You want to explain your problem to me?"

If it was possible to make a bigger or stupider mistake than to insult the novice-master himself before she even knew if she could audition, Nescana couldn't at the moment imagine what it might be. It hadn't occurred to her for a second that she might lay her problem and propose her solution to anyone but the wingmaster himself, if she could only get in to see him. But the novice-master...maybe he was the one she should talk to. She wasn't sure. She managed after a second, "I don't know, sir. I'm not a novice yet...I don't know who makes decisions about who can audition..."

The novice-master's frown deepened. "Anybody

can audition. Any unmarried girl. No need for your father to petition on your behalf. That's how the announcement was supposed to read. That what you heard, that any girl's allowed to audition?"

"Yes, sir, but..."

"But that's not your problem? Got something more complicated twisting you in knots, do you? The wingmaster or no one, is that it? Well, I expect he can spare one moment. I'm going that way, so you may as well come along. Step sharp, now, I don't have all day, and I don't suppose Wingmaster Taimenai does either." The novice-master strode off

Nescana hurried to catch up. Brusque as he was, she decided Novice-master Anerii was actually not unkind. She was glad of that, for Genrai's sake if not—yet—for her own.

Wingmaster Taimenai Cenfenisai was taller than Novice-master Anerii. His hair was darker, just lightly streaked with gray, and his face not as deeply lined, but he did not look young. The metal studs at wrists and throat were different; there were three in a triangle rather than three in a line. The feather braided into his hair was black instead of red. He had a lean, strong-boned face; a thin, austere mouth; and, at least just now, an air of somewhat harassed impatience. But he nodded with brisk courtesy when the novice-master introduced Nescana with a brief, uninformative, "Girl's got a problem about the audition."

The wingmaster's office was smaller than Nescana had expected, furnished with only a wide but cluttered desk, a narrow chair, and a collection of maps pinned to the walls and spread out on a side table. To one side, a broad window looked out over the endless sea. It wasn't often anybody from Third City had so fine and shining a view of the sea. A gull flew past the window, white wings flashing in the sunlight, and she couldn't help but follow the path of its flight across the bright sky and up, and out.

Not so very far away, the small Island of Kotipa was clearly visible. Mist wreathed the tips of its high mountains, while its underside trailed off to jagged red cliffs. Milendri, where Canpra stood, must look a lot like that, if someone got way out away from it and looked back. Kajuraihi must see Milendri like that all the time. Except with the white towers rising along the edge of the Island, the neat red-brick neighborhoods of Second City and the tangled alleys of Third City stretching out inland. How strange and beautiful, to see all of Canpra laid out below as though the whole city encompassed no more space than the palm of your hand!

Far below, a white-sailed ship carved a slow path toward Milendri. That was wonderful too. It might have come from anywhere, from Tolounn maybe, from some harbor a thousand miles from the Islands; it might sail away to anywhere in the whole world. Cen Periven, maybe. Even Yngul. Nescana wondered what cargo it might be bringing, and from where, and what might be loaded into its cargo hold in return.

But mostly she looked up and out, toward Kotipa. It was called the Island of Dragons, she knew. The Island of the Test. Some of the streamers of cloud that slid past its mountains looked almost like the long coils of dragons, and the mist might look almost like trailing feathers...

Novice-master Anerii cleared his throat, and Nescana jumped and turned quickly, abruptly recalled to *this* office and *this* moment. She had drifted toward the window without even noticing, caught by the sky and the unexpected view of the Island of Dragons. Now she flushed hotly, embarrassed. But she also already planned to climb up on some aerial walkway that would let her fill her eyes with the view before she went home.

The wingmaster was considering Nescana with a deeply ironic look in his hooded eyes. He wasn't frowning—yet—but the lines at the corners of his mouth had deepened. He said drily, "Sky-mad, are you?"

That was kinder than asking whether she might be stupid, or so distractible she'd just forgotten why she'd come all the way here from Third City. Nescana said quickly, "Sir, yes, from the first time I saw kajuraihi in the air when I was just little. My brother and I—Genrai. I'm Genrai's sister..." she hesitated, but the wingmaster raised his eyebrows and gave her a brief nod of acknowledgement or recognition, maybe even encouragement.

"We used to climb up on rooftops to watch the sky," she said in a rush. "I was so jealous of Genrai because he could audition and I couldn't. I was so proud, we were all so proud when he passed his audition. We were all...then this audition, this new one, we didn't expect, I never thought I'd have a chance. Only I don't, I don't have a chance, because—" she stopped. It was hard to say straight out. Harder still to say it to this important, stern wingmaster. She was sure he'd been born to the First City himself. He had that look somehow.

"Go on, girl!" Novice-master Anerii ordered.

She took a breath. She was grateful now for his presence. She was pretty sure *he* had come out of the Third City. She *thought* he had. She thought he might understand—and she thought he *was* kind, no matter his curt manner. She looked at him to answer, because it was easier than looking at Wingmaster Taimenai.

She said, "I—Genrai and I—we have three more brothers. Kanbii, he's apprenticed to the glassblowers, he's got another year and more to go before he'll earn rank. Our other brothers are fourteen and thirteen, but they can't look for apprenticeships because we haven't the coin, we can only afford to pay for Kanbii. Genrai—we were happy, we were so happy when he passed his audition, but it's hard. We had enough set by. Genrai worked so hard to be sure we'd have enough set by. And we did, we had plenty, enough for the whole next year if we were careful, enough for Nekei to think about starting an apprenticeship of his own once Kanbii earned his out. But the summer illness—"

"That Gods-cursed illness!" Master Anerii interjected. "No one died?"

"No, sir. We all got it, but we were lucky. We got it later, after the physicians figured out how to treat it. But it took all our savings. It was three senneri before anybody could go back to work. A whole year's savings, gone in less than two months! But we're all right. We're getting by. Except there's no margin, none at all, so there's no way I can audition, unless I can keep earning somehow—"

"We don't pay novices, girl," Novice-master Anerii told her, curt but not without sympathy. "No more than a craftsmaster pays his apprentices."

Nescana nodded. "I know, sir. Only we thought, that is, we hoped, maybe we, maybe I could borrow from my future earnings—if I succeed in the audition. I don't know how much kajuraihi earn, but I'm sure it would be plenty and to spare. My brothers just need enough to keep them until Kanbii earns his place in the craft. They can work, they do work, but we, I mean Kanbii and I, we can't let the younger boys work too hard. *You* know," she appealed to the novice-master.

"I do know," he said gruffly. "Go on, then."

"Yes, sir. It won't be so long till Kanbii earns rank—not so *very* long. Hardly a year. I thought, we thought, if I passed my audition, I could send some of the coin I'd earn later to my brothers now? And then just not have that coin later. Wouldn't that be fair?" Eonii had thought of it, but they had all thought it would be fair.

"The kajuraihi are hardly moneylenders," Wingmaster Taimenai said drily.

Nescana looked him in the face. "No, sir. Of course not. We wouldn't ever have thought of going to a moneylender; we couldn't afford to pay a loan back, not for a year's worth of wages—even short wages. But we thought maybe you, that is, the kajuraihi, might be willing to make some kind of arrangement for a much lower return. I mean, you must really *want* girl novices or you wouldn't have a special audition at all, would you? We thought, since I'm Genrai's sister, maybe that means I'd have a good chance to succeed—maybe better than most. Maybe you'll have a lot of girls who want to try and maybe they'll all pass, but it's never too many boys, and never all of them, is it? More like one in five, isn't it?" Eonii had found that out for her. Nescana wouldn't have known the numbers, but her youngest brother knew how to figure out things like that.

"If I fail, then it doesn't matter anyway," she added. "But if I don't try, then you'll never know if I might have succeeded. What if all the girls who audition fail, don't you think you'd be sorry you didn't make a way for me to try?"

Maybe she hadn't put that exactly right, because Wingmaster Taimenai frowned at her. But Novicemaster Anerii's eyes crinkled. He put up a hand to rub his mouth.

Nescana said quickly, before she lost track of her argument, "And if I succeed, it wouldn't be *much* to pay out, would it, just part of one low-ranking kajurai's wages?"

"A many-pronged argument," the wingmaster said drily. "However, the occupation of moneylender is not one that suits the dignity of our position. I fear I must—"

Novice-master Anerii leaned forward to tap the wingmaster's desk. "The girl doesn't want a moneylender," he said brusquely. "What she wants is a sponsor. If her brother were a couple years older and had earned his own rank, there'd be no trouble about it. He'd stand for her himself. Here, girl," he said to Nescana. "You say it's a year till that other brother of yours earns out his apprenticeship. How much do you figure these brothers of yours'll need to keep themselves in order for that year?"

It took a moment for Nescana to find her voice. Then she managed, prudently adding a cushion to the four coppers a day she'd been earning herself, "Half a silver, Master Anerii. Half a silver a day would be plenty."

The novice-master raised his eyebrows at her. "Unless there's another illness goes through the city, or some fool boy falls off a roof cheering handball, or breaks an arm playing himself! Thirteen and fourteen, you said your brothers are? I know how it is with boys that age. Call it a silver a day. You said you'd saved up enough to get by for a year; was that you or them? Your brothers have the sense to put by the extra without you there counting up the coppers for them?"

"Yes, sir," Nescana promised him. "They're good boys—not careless, I swear—"

"That's fine, then." Master Anerii nodded to Wingmaster Taimenai. "I'll let the girl's family have a dozen silver the senneri, always supposing she passes her audition."

The wingmaster steepled his hands upon his desk and gazed at the novice-master over his fingertips. "I admire your dedication, Master Anerii. However, the occupation of moneylending does not suit the dignity of your position either."

The novice-master snorted. "It's not moneylending. I said, I'll stand for her as a sponsor. The girl won't be paying me back."

"But—" began Nescana.

"Don't argue, girl! I don't *want* you to pay it back—never mind moneylending isn't dignified enough for a kajurai, though come to that, it's not. Wingmaster Taimenai's right about that. What I want in return, I want you to pay it on to some other bright youngster, hear? When you're my age and some Third City girl—or boy, as it may be—has the same sort of problem. I'll expect you to keep an eye out for that, mind."

"I will!" Nescana promised. She faced the wingmaster again. "I would do that," she told him. "I wouldn't forget. I promise."

Wingmaster Taimenai leaned back in his chair and sighed. He considered her for a long moment, then directed an acerbic frown at the novice master. Then he turned back to Nescana with a brisk air of decision and told her, "As wingmaster of Milendri's kajuraihi, I see no reason to take official notice of suitably dignified, suitably private financial arrangements. It's the official position of the kajuraihi that any unmarried girl may audition. Unofficially, I prefer girls who take careful thought to leave their family obligations in good order. A solid sense of responsibility is an excellent trait in a kajurai. The audition begins promptly at the first bell of the morning next God's Day. I look forward to seeing you on the day, and I wish you good fortune in your audition, Nescana."

The walk was such a long one, and Nescana was so uneasy at the thought of not knowing where to go, of being late—first bell was hardly after dawn—she actually walked all the way to the kajuraihi towers the evening of Moon's Day, with her two younger brothers for company. They found a good place to spend the night, an unobtrusive gap between the stairway entrance of one tower and the buttressed flank of the next.

It was a spot right at the edge of Milendri. A balcony not far away had been built out into the air, with no railing or balustrade to block the view of the sky and sea beyond. A few white gulls and one black one winged their way through the sunset, making one last foray for their supper before seeking their roosts for the night. Their sharp cries echoed off the stone of the towers, but other than that the evening was quiet. The foot of these towers was obviously not a place where many people lingered after sunset.

Third City was never so quiet. Nescana was grateful Eonii and Nekei had come with her. They had brought a supper of spicy lamb pastries and boiled eggs and honey cakes, and Eonii had had the foresight to bring a stoppered jug of clean water, which was good because if there was a public cistern or fountain anywhere near the kajuraihi towers, none of them had any idea where it might be.

The shaded white stone was cool even in the evening heat. A warm breeze gusted, carrying the scents of hot stone and salt instead of cooking oil and spices and cooking food and people.

Nekei broke a pastry in half and gave Nescana one portion. "Better eat it now," he told her. "I bet you won't want anything right before the audition. You'll pass. Genrai did. Why shouldn't you?"

"They want you to pass," Eonii agreed, sharing out a handful of dates for dessert. "That novice-master definitely wants you to pass."

Nescana didn't argue. She didn't say that none of that mattered or point out that no one knew why the dragon magic found one person acceptable and not another. Eonii was right. It did help, to know that Genrai had succeeded and that the novice-master did want her to succeed. But all she said was, "Look—a ship!" In the sunset light, the ship's white sails had turned a pale luminescent gold. Then, as the ship passed into Kotipa's shadow, the sails first took on a ruddier color and then turned white again, a purer white than before. Then they shaded rapidly to twilight gray and finally, as the ship came out of the island's shadow, turned back to gold.

The whole beautiful progression took less than a tenth-bell. Nescana and her brothers watched in silence, until the ship curved away from the shadow of Kotipa and dwindled into the east. Nescana felt the sight was an omen, even though she knew such moments must be commonplace, that those who lived on the edge of Milendri must see such things all the time.

The kajuraihi lived at the edge of the Island. Maybe that was why she felt the sight meant something.

She didn't try to put her feelings into words. Maybe her brothers would have understood, but if they didn't, trying to explain how the gold sails had made her feel wouldn't help.

She said instead, "You'd better go. I'm glad you came this far and waited with me this long, but first bell comes early and you don't want to be late for your jobs in the morning."

Nekei might have argued, but Eonii didn't. Her youngest brother scrambled to his feet, kicked Nekei to make him stand up, and said, "We'd wish you luck, but you won't need it. After all, you found a red Quei feather, right?"

Nescana pretended to smack at him. "Irritating child. Don't get lost in the dark on your way home."

It was what a parent said to a much younger child than Eonii. He grinned at her and said, "We won't see you tomorrow—but I bet the novice-master'll let you send us a letter with the first silver coin."

And Nekei added, "Tell Genrai we miss him, but we're glad he's not there taking up nearly the whole bed with his long legs!"

Then both her younger brothers were gone, running away into the sunset, leaving Nescana behind to wait. She sat down again slowly after they were gone, and turned to gaze out over the sea for as long as the last light of evening lasted.

Barely after dawn, before the sun was more than a hand's breadth above the distant horizon, Nescana stood up stiffly, shook out her skirt, washed her face and hands with the last of the water from the jug, and made her way alone around the tower to see if she could figure out where she should go. She had been afraid she wouldn't find the right place, but actually the correct doorway was obvious. She'd waited at the base of the wrong tower, but the right one had its doors wide open and someone— a kajurai, or maybe a servant—was just reaching up to hook a string of feathers over the doors.

All the feathers had been dyed red. They tossed and fluttered in the stiffening morning breeze. The only thing that could possibly have been more clear was a personal message hand-delivered by the wingmaster himself.

Nescana climbed up the long curving stairway toward those doors, one step at a time, not hurrying. It seemed wrong to rush. She thought of the dignity due kajuraihi and went slowly, one wide stair at a time. Even when she reached the doorway, she looked up at the wind-blown feathers and then took a moment to turn and look back the way she'd come—not just down the stairs, but west, inland, back toward Third City and her home.

Her brothers would be off for their morning jobs before the sun was a finger higher in the sky. All of them would be thinking about her. She wished the day were over, the audition past; she wished she were either back home with her brothers, disappointed but home; or looking around for the first time at the kajurai novitiate that would become almost like another home. With Genrai to welcome her. So she would have at least one brother near her even if everything else changed. That was a good thought.

Before Nescana could quite decide to go into the tower, two other girls came into sight, making their way toward this doorway.

These were First City girls. That was obvious. Instead of the undyed linen of Nescana's best dress, cinched up with a plain cord at the waist, one of these girls wore a dress dyed in expensive dark blue with a gold sash and thin gold bangles over one wrist; the other wore a dress in even more expensive and surely impractical white, embroidered in green all around the wide hem and square collar. A thin emerald-green silken cord wrapped three times around her slender waist and then crossed between her breasts and disappeared beneath her hair, which was braided back in a complicated style and had, Nescana saw as they approached, a slender Quei feather braided into it. In fact, the other girl had a Quei feather too, only twisted thin and wound around one of her bangles; Nescana only realized what it was because of the iridescent emerald color. Not even dyed silk could take a color like that.

Nescana wished *she* had a Quei feather. That was just one more advantage First City girls had: fathers wealthy enough to afford to give them Quei feathers for their auditions.

The one girl's coloring was unusual; the one wearing white. Her hair and skin were both almost the color of honey—very dark honey, but still. And as they came to the foot of the stairway, Nescana saw that this girl's large, almond-shaped eyes weren't Islander dark, but an almost greenish brown. She might have Tolounese blood. Nescana thought she remembered that some Tolounese people were said to have lighter hair and skin and eyes than most Islanders.

The other girl wouldn't have stood out next to the first except she was very pretty; much prettier than the honey-haired girl. Nescana was surprised she wasn't married, especially since both girls looked a little older, sixteen or seventeen or maybe even eighteen. They walked hand-in-hand like sisters even though they didn't look a bit alike.

Nescana hesitated, not sure whether she should wait by the door for those girls or go on herself. First City girls weren't likely to be very friendly...except they were all sky-mad together, all here to audition, the first girls ever permitted to try to become kajuraihi. That was important too. Or Nescana thought it was important. If they succeeded, they would all be novices together and it wouldn't matter whether they'd been Third City or First...that was what people said. That was how it was in plays about the kajuraihi. You weren't supposed to think about your family's place or position once you were a kajurai. It wasn't supposed to matter where in the city you'd been born, or even if you'd been born on some sheep farm way out in the country.

It seemed unfriendly to turn her back and walk into the tower alone, so in the end Nescana waited. She didn't quite have the courage to speak to the other girls, but when the one in white nodded to her, she nodded back.

Two other girls appeared before the first pair had quite come up to the doorway. Not together like the first two, but one and then the other. By unspoken accord, Nescana and both the First City girls waited for them as well. Somehow it just seemed better that they should all go into the tower together.

One of these latest arrivals was almost certainly older than any of the others. Nescana seldom found herself having to look up at another girl, but this young woman was nearly a head taller than she was—head and shoulders taller than any of the others. She was wide-hipped and big-breasted, heavy-boned and solid so that it was very hard to imagine her in flight. Not that her size could possibly matter—if grown men could fly, certainly a girl could, even a heavyset girl like that one. She wasn't especially pretty but not plain either. Her expression was solemn, but she didn't look bad-tempered or unfriendly, just serious. She was probably Second City, but from a particularly wealthy family, judging from the style of her dress and from the pendant she wore. A silver dragon glittered on that chain, showing beautifully against her dark green dress. Nescana wished she had a dragon to wear, to bring luck. Though a Quei feather would have been even better.

A young man had escorted this young woman. A brother who hoped she would succeed, or maybe, from his stiff expression and completely different looks, a lover who hoped she would not. Either way, she left him at the foot of the stairs and came up alone, without looking back. She nodded to the First City girls, then looked carefully at Nescana and, after a second, nodded again, a little stiffly. Nescana nodded back, as politely as she knew how, but she wasn't sure she liked this girl very much. Second City girls could be more stuck up than First. But it was too early to tell, and anyway, neither of them might succeed and then what would it matter?

The last girl was a slim child who couldn't have been more than twelve; her father walked with her and she kept starting to look up at him and then jerking her gaze away. She was probably also Second City, judging from her dress, which was undyed linen but better than Nescana's, embroidered at the hem with red flowers and birds and gathered at waist with a narrow red sash. She left her father at the foot of the stairs. He gave her a little push upward and she ran up, pausing halfway to turn back and wave at him. He nodded and smiled and made a little pushing motion and the girl turned around again and came the rest of the way up, last of them all to arrive at the landing.

The girl in blue nudged the one in white, who looked around at all of them, nodded to everyone in turn, and said, "My name's Erienè Lantanasca. I'm seventeen. This is my cousin Etanea Lantanasca. She's sixteen tomorrow." She didn't give their father's names or positions, which might be arrogance—*Everyone knows the Lantanasca family*—or kindness, because she must have realized Nescana was from the Third City and a lot of Third City people didn't offer their father's names when they introduced themselves to strangers. Nescana never had. Locally everyone knew who she was and who her brothers were, and outside their own neighborhood no one cared who they were.

The big Second City girl nodded to the two First City cousins. "May you celebrate your birthday in the kajuraihi novitiate! That would be a fine birthday present!" she said to Etanea, sociably enough. "It's almost my birthday too—I'll turn twenty in seventeen days. My name's Taorè Sotanai."

Everyone nodded and murmured, instantly understanding, as Nescana did, that this young woman had very nearly aged out of any possible audition. Older boys didn't have as good a chance as younger ones; everyone knew that. Nescana felt better about Taorè having that dragon pendant. She probably needed all the luck she could get.

The little girl opened her mouth and closed it again, blushing. She was obviously too shy to speak, so Nescana said to her, in her friendliest way, "I'm Nescana. I'm fifteen, so I'm the youngest except for you. What's your name?"

The girl smiled gratefully at Nescana. "Ciera," she whispered. "Ciera Serofeina. I'm twelve—almost."

"Almost twelve!" said Erienè, smiling at her. "The dragons like the younger ones; we all know that. You've the best chance of us all, perhaps." The girl blushed again and ducked her head, but she was obviously pleased. Erienè looked around at everyone and gave a little nod toward the open doors, assuming authority with the natural ease of a high-born First City daughter. "Shall we go in? It's nearly first bell already. Do you suppose anyone else is coming?"

"Who'd risk being late?" said Nescana. She waved a hand at the long strand of feathers fluttering in the breeze that had come up as the morning brightened. "If anybody does, the door's clearly marked."

"You'd think there'd be more than five of us," Taorè said, frowning.

"Who knows how many girls fall in love with the wind?" said Erienè. "Maybe not many."

"Who knows how many might long for the wind, but are already married, with a baby on their hip or one on the way?" said Nescana. Hardly anyone in Third City made it to twenty unmarried. Most married at fifteen or sixteen or seventeen. If the illness hadn't come stalking through Third City, maybe Nescana would have married. Then she wouldn't have been able to audition. She'd have missed her chance. It didn't bear thinking of. Who knew how many girls had accepted one offer or another, never imagining for a moment the kajuraihi might open up an audition for girls?

Fewer girls might marry so young after this. Who knew how many girls might put off marriage a year or three now, hoping for another chance?

Though truthfully, Nescana had never met another girl when she and Genrai had climbed up to lie on their backs and watch the clouds go past, or the stars proceed on their orderly pathways. Occasionally a boy. But never another girl. Not that she had the slightest notion whether any of those boys had been sky-mad, far less gone on to audition. Nor how many girls might have been inside stitching piecework or washing clothes or making bread, unable to snatch even a free moment here or there to dream of the winds.

They went into the tower together: the two First City girls and the two from Second City and Nescana. No more strings of feathers marked the way, but there was only one way to go from within the tower's antechamber: a stairway spiraled down from the middle of the chamber into some hidden underground room. The stairway turned five times as it descended and then opened up to a large chamber, with three walls of dressed stone and one that wasn't there at all, the floor ending in a long, high-arching aerial walkway that led, far out in the sky, to the small Island of Kotipa. The little dragon island floated in the sky, the distant end of the walkway all but lost in the distance. The high, jagged peaks of the mountains on Kotipa were wreathed with streamers of white cloud, gilded with light from the early sun.

"Oh," whispered Ciera. "Oh, look. The Island of Dragons. Are there dragons there?" The little girl went forward to the very edge of the walkway, fearless of the yawning gulf and the sea.

Nescana thought maybe there were. The clouds and mist almost seemed to conceal long coiling bodies and immense feathered wings...she could almost imagine that the curving ripple of cloud that streaked the highest peak might actually be a half-glimpsed dragon. She'd walked forward too; they all had; not quite as close to the edge as Ciera, but close.

Before she could quite decide, steps sounded behind them, crisp and confident, and they all turned quickly as Wingmaster Taimenai and Novice-master Anerii and another younger kajurai came into the chamber. The young man was the one who'd marked the tower doorway with the string of red feathers, only Nescana hadn't realized he was a kajurai until now, when she saw him better and realized his eyes were kajurai eyes.

All three of them wore black. The younger man had a single steel stud at each wrist and at the collar of his shirt, but Nescana didn't know what that might signify, though it certainly meant something. The feather braided into his hair was red, like the novice-master's. Only the wingmaster himself had a black feather.

Wingmaster Taimenai nodded to them all impartially, without showing any sign of recognizing either Nescana or—she watched particularly—the First City girls. The novice-master glowered at everyone with the same impartiality. Nescana was careful not to meet his eyes or in any way suggest that they'd met or that he'd been kind to her or that she was here only because of his kindness. She was certain Master Anerii would not welcome any familiarity from a girl who might soon be a novice, and certainly not now, when no one knew one way or the other.

"I'm Taimenai Cenfenisai," the wingmaster told them, his tone crisp and impersonal. "This is Anerii Pencara, master of novices, and Rei Kensenè, who is a kajurai of the second rank. You are welcome here and we're glad to see you. I shall be personally pleased if any or all of you succeed, and I wish you the blessings of the Gods and all good fortune." He paused. None of the girls said anything.

The wingmaster nodded slightly, which might have meant approval or just acknowledgement. He continued with the same brisk, impersonal manner. "As you may know, it's not our decision nor any decision of men that will make you kajuraihi." Half turning, he pointed out toward Kotipa. "That is the Island of the Test; the Island of Dragons. There the dragon magic that lifts all our Islands is particularly strong; the presence of dragons particularly close. If you would touch the wing of a dragon, you must cross the bridge to the Island of the Test. There you will do whatever you find to do, and become novice kajuraihi. Or else not. There is some risk to this endeavor. Occasionally a boy has been injured attempting what you will attempt today. Occasionally a boy has died. Some of the hazards you will face will be obvious when you come to them. Other perils, perhaps more to be feared, are less obvious. To succeed, you must be brave, and you must be careful, and you must perceive and yield to the will of the dragon." He paused again, then added, "Any of you may withdraw now if you wish."

Nescana glanced at Etanea, who stood to her left, and then Ciera, on her right. And beyond them, to Erienè and Taorè. None of the other girls moved. She made sure to keep her own feet still.

Wingmaster Taimenai looked at each of them, one at a time, starting with Taorè and ending with Erienè. At last he gave them all one brief nod and an even briefer smile. "The walkway spans a good distance, but not so far as it may seem from here," he told them. "You'll go one at a time, a tenth-bell between each girl and the next. Don't linger on the far side of the bridge; go on briskly. You are each meant to face your trial alone."

"But what should we *do?*" Ciera asked him.

The wingmaster gave her a small, encouraging nod. "Whatever seems good to you, child. I can tell you nothing but that. Go where you think you should go; do what you find to do. You must be finished by dusk, but the whole day stretches before you; with only five girls, you needn't risk yourselves with reckless speed. Take your time, take care, do whatever you find to do. Erienè Lantanasca, you will go first. "

They went in order of rank, which Nescana might have expected, but hadn't. Erienè took the first place with a casual assumption of right. Nescana didn't protest going last, after even little Ciera. She would only look selfish and impatient. Besides, she thought if anybody might need extra time, it would be Ciera, who was hardly half the size of big Taorè. Anyway, as the wingmaster had said, they'd all have plenty of time anyway.

There was no steadying magic on the aerial walkway that linked the two Islands, Milendri's carved balcony to the wild cliffs of Kotipa. Nescana might have expected that too—but she hadn't. She'd seen most of the other girls pause as they stepped out onto the walkway, especially Etanea, but she'd thought it was just the height and respect for the unknown trial that lay ahead and probably general nervousness. It hadn't occurred to her that it might actually be possible to fall, especially since Ciera, who'd gone last before Nescana, hadn't hesitated at all, but just skipped right out onto the walkway and darted up the curving path without the slightest sign of nervousness.

Even Nescana wasn't quite that cool-hearted about heights, and she'd been climbing around on Third City rooftops since she was a lot younger than Ciera. She was sure—almost sure—Second City girls like Ciera weren't allowed to run around on rooftops, yet the child had dashed up the walkway, so lithe and fast that she made Nescana feel timid and sensible. It was an unfamiliar feeling.

So was the fear of falling. She couldn't remember ever actually being afraid of that before. But this part of the test made sense. Obviously it made sense. Fear of heights must be a terrible thing for a kajurai. Probably dreaming of flight wasn't the same as truly putting on wings and leaping into the empty air. It made sense to test boys—and girls—who thought they wanted to fly.

She wasn't very afraid. The floating stones of the walkway were broad and level, and the gaps between them no more than twice the length of her hand. Nescana didn't let herself look down or hesitate more than a second. But she didn't run up the curve of the walkway as lightly as Ciera either. Obviously running would be bad for her dignity.

Once she was out on the walkway herself, she found the paving stones were mostly about one long stride across or two short steps, but some were bigger and some smaller. The gaps between the stones were mostly about the length of two hands, but some of the gaps were longer and some shorter, so she learned quickly to watch carefully and not let herself relax too much even after the nervousness about height and empty air and unexpected gusts of wind had faded. It seemed to take a long time to reach the top of the arc, though she knew from watching the other girls that it took just about a tenth-bell to go that far and she presumed it would take about the same amount of time to descend the far side of the walkway and reach Kotipa.

So really there was no need to hurry.

Nescana paused at the top of the curve, kneeling on the broad paving stone to gaze first back the way she'd come—the three waiting kajuraihi were visible, black against the red stone.

The white towers standing proudly at the edge of the drop caught the sunlight and compelled attention; it was a stunning view and not one for which Nescana had been prepared. She stared for a long moment. Then the depths drew her eye and she looked below the level of the balcony where the walkway had started. Carved into the Island to each side, she could now make out all kinds of other balconies and wide windows and one great archway that looked big enough for dozens of kajuraihi to come or go all at once. A great rounded shaft descended below that, one side of it visible where it had been carved out of the red stone and built out where the stone did not cooperate with the design. All along that side, narrow windows had been carved out. Gauzy draperies of many brilliant colors stirred in the morning breeze, letting in the light and keeping out some of the day's coming heat.

When you only walked aboveground, you could forget how much of Canpra had been carved into Milendri's stone. At least, Nescana could. She supposed her brothers, and anyone else who'd ever cut out or carried the discarded stone, must remember those underground chambers and passageways much better.

She looked straight down from the walkway, wondering how big a mountain of broken stone must lie down there beneath the waves, centuries of discarded fragments of stone piled up and up below Milendri...if the sea had a bottom. Maybe the stone just fell forever, through uncounted watery realms ruled by sharks and sea dragons. Mist veiled the sea now, so she could only catch glimpses of the endless waves below.

At last she turned forward toward Kotipa.

The Island of Dragons seemed much closer now; she seemed to have come much more than halfway, though that was probably an illusion. Drifting mist swirled across the walkway between Nescana and Kotipa, but she could tell that small, contorted trees grew out of the rugged stone, not only at the edge but right down on the cliff faces. The red rock was veined with white marble and with some other kind of stone, grey streaked unevenly with a brighter red. Mountains above and broken stone below; mist above and below; she could hear a Quei call somewhere distant, but she couldn't see it even when she looked.

Getting to her feet, she started forward again, more slowly now, not for fear of putting a foot wrong but just because it seemed disrespectful to run down to the Island of Dragons as though she were running to meet a friend.

The walkway came down at last, rather steeply, into a paved courtyard about as far across as Nescana might have thrown a stone. The paving stones were like the bones of Kotipa: mostly ordinary red, but some grey streaked with black and that brighter red. There was nothing in this courtyard, nothing but paving stones and a scattering of fallen leaves and grit.

All around the courtyard, steep cliffs reared up, not quite sheer, but rugged and difficult, broken sharp-edged rock offering no way out of the courtyard except for one obvious path on the far side. The path, twisting and steep, looked difficult enough, but at least there was no question which way a girl was supposed to go. Nescana had worried about that *Do what you find to do,* but this part was easy.

Or at least it was easy to decide what to do. The path was harder to manage in practice, even for a girl as tall and strong as Nescana. The first part wasn't bad, but then the path turned around a jutting bulge of stone and led almost straight up a sheer cliff. A girl's dress wasn't very suitable for something like that, and Nescana wished she'd borrowed something from Nekei, who was closest to her in height. She had worn shoes for the audition, fearing to shame her family by going barefoot. Shoes were too expensive to abandon lightly, but falling would be worse, and if she passed her audition probably the kajuraihi would provide shoes. If she failed—she refused to think she might fail. She left her shoes neatly tucked into a flattish place beside the path and climbed up the cliff face with hands and bare feet.

Where the stone had broken, the edges were often dangerously sharp. Luckily Nescana cut her palm instead of a foot, or she might have been even sorrier about abandoning her shoes. The cut wasn't serious. She'd had worse the summer she'd gutted fish in the mornings for three coppers and enough fish for herself and her whole family. She'd been ten, and her father had just become unable to work at the job he'd held all her life, so both the coins and the fish had been important; certainly worth a cut hand now and then.

This wasn't such a bad cut, and at least she didn't smell of fish. Nescana licked the blood off her palm and climbed higher, gripping the roots and branches of twisted trees to help haul herself up, even more careful of where she put her feet.

Mist drifted across the path. Sometimes she made her way through it, as though she climbed through clouds. It wasn't too hard to see where she should put her hands and feet, it wasn't as thick as the blinding fogs that occasionally rose up after the afternoon monsoon rains. She had no trouble making out the path, only sometimes when it was particularly steep and difficult she had to wonder if it really was a path or if she had possibly lost her way. But then she would come to a cliff with notches carved out for handholds, or a gap bridged with ropes twice as thick as her thumb, so she knew she was still going the right way.

She didn't much enjoy the rope bridge, even though finding it was reassuring. She edged across the rope carefully, glad again of her bare feet, and found the path relatively easy on the other side, almost level for some little distance. She paused to look back and down, trying to figure out how far she'd come, but it was impossible to judge. The mist hid almost everything.

She couldn't guess how long she'd been climbing, either. She could feel the effort of the climb in her calves and thighs and forearms, but the effort of climbing this steep path was so different from her usual work that she couldn't guess how much time had passed just from that. The mist was bright, but it seemed nowhere brighter than anywhere else. The sunlight that occasionally lanced down through the mist seemed high and strong, but the sun itself must be hidden by the bulk of the mountain. She guessed it might be around midday. Her stomach pinched when she thought of that. She wished she'd saved half a lamb pastry or, perhaps more practical, wrapped up some almonds or something in a bit of cloth and stuffed the packet in her pocket. She hadn't thought of it.

She'd been hungry before, though. Not often, not like some families, but they'd had a hungry day now and then. She knew she could go a lot farther and work a lot harder before hunger would really be a problem. She was thirsty too, though, and that was worse. Though the mist dampened the stone and made the path that much more treacherous, she hadn't passed any rivulets of water trickling down the cliffs.

Standing still and feeling sorry for herself wasn't going to help one bit. Nescana sighed and went on, carefully, not hurrying.

Then she stopped in surprise. She was almost sure she could hear voices.

She was almost sure Wingmaster Taimenai had said they were each supposed to make this climb alone. But she was *certain* she heard voices.

Well, it wouldn't be her fault if she met some of the other girls. She could hardly go around them. So she went forward, following the path.

At the base of a sharp cliff maybe five or six times her own height, where the path became a series of carved handholds and two metal stakes driven into the stone for footholds, she found Erienè and Ciera. The two girls were sitting together on the flattest part of the path, talking earnestly, Erienè in a low, calm voice and Ciera worried and excited.

Nescana had expected possibly Erienè and her cousin Etanea. Those were the two she'd have assumed might wait for each other and climb together, and since they were First City girls, she'd thought they might not have the strength or stamina to climb very fast, so it seemed reasonable she might pass them on the path. Taorè was so big and strong, Nescana had expected she would probably have a pretty easy time; and Ciera was so little and light and quick-footed that it'd been easy to imagine her flitting right up the cliffs where Nescana struggled.

But here was Ciera sitting beside Erienè instead. They both looked up when Nescana appeared. Ciera jumped to her feet, but Erienè did not.

Then Nescana saw—and felt stupid for not realizing earlier—that the First City girl was hurt. She'd hurt her foot, or ankle, or maybe both. She had that leg drawn up, and yes, now that she looked, Nescana could see how swollen and purple her ankle was even from this distance. Erienè had a stick, a twisted limb from one of the small trees that grew here and there along the path. It was hard to judge with the girl sitting and the stick lying beside her, but Nescana thought the stick looked too short to make a good crutch, and not really straight enough.

"She hurt her ankle!" Ciera said anxiously. "The rope bridge was *awful!*"

Nescana could just imagine. She walked over, nodded to Erienè, and crouched to examine her ankle. It looked even worse close up, swollen to twice the size it should have been. None of the bones looked out of place, but obviously Erienè wasn't going to be putting any weight on it anytime soon. Nescana looked up again, meeting the other girl's odd greenish eyes. "That's not good.'

"I was so stupid," Erienè said in a low voice. "I fell almost at once. I thought I could go on, I thought after all I had the whole day. But you see this cliff is impossible. *Neither* of you can help," she added to Ciera in a firm tone. "You should go on."

"She keeps *saying* that," Ciera told Nescana. "But she's made it this far, and she got across the rope bridge, and how much farther can it be? I went up and looked and the path isn't so *very* bad farther on. It's just this cliff, only she won't even *try*."

"You helped her on the bridge?"

"The wingmaster didn't *say* we couldn't help each other," Ciera said defensively. "I didn't do very much. I just carried her stick across for her. That's hardly any help at all."

"He said we were to each go alone," Erienè said, in a patient, firm tone that suggested she'd said this before, probably more than once. "You should not risk your own audition. Especially when there isn't anything you can do. If you try to help me up that cliff, you could fall yourself—and it wouldn't work anyway. You can *see* it wouldn't work. You have to put your left foot on that spike there. You can *see* that."

She was right. It did look impossible. "I can't believe you got this far," Nescana said truthfully. "Did your cousin help you? But then why leave you here?"

"I made her go on much earlier," Erienè said tiredly. She rubbed the bridge of her nose, closing her eyes briefly and leaving a streak of dust across her cheek. She somehow still managed to look elegant despite this. "I made her leave me at the place where the path narrows and curves out over that gap, you know—"

Nescana could envision exactly the place. She winced, thinking of trying that gap with just one good foot.

"I told her I wouldn't try to go on, I would wait there. But then while I was waiting, I thought, if I crawled, it would be safe enough."

Nescana would hardly have called that safe. Erienè had been lucky. She was no longer jealous of the Quei feather the First City girl wore in her hair—she'd certainly needed luck more than Nescana. "How'd you manage the place after that, where it's all sharp rock and you have to kind of pull yourself up sideways?"

The other girls nodded, knowing just the spot Nescana meant. "Taorè helped me there," Erienè admitted. "She's very strong. I didn't *ask* her to do that, but she's so strong and it only took a minute. But I told her she had to go on. She's almost twenty. If she fails this audition, she'll never have another chance. The rest of us—" she shrugged one shoulder. "Maybe they'll hold another special audition next summer, or the summer after that."

And maybe they wouldn't; maybe they'd go back to holding just one audition every three or four or five years, and Erienè and probably Etanea and maybe even Nescana would all be too old to try. And more than likely married, unless they risked turning down every offer for the chance of *maybe* a second chance to audition. Nescana might take that risk. A First or Second City girl probably wouldn't be allowed to.

"*I* could try again," Ciera pointed out, with an air of having made this argument before. "It's not such a risk for me. Anyway, the wingmaster didn't say we couldn't help each other on the path, he just said we're supposed to face our trial alone. It's not fair if you can't even face your trial at all!"

"The path is *part* of the trial—"

"I don't think it is—"

"It doesn't matter really," said Nescana. "The important part was where he said it won't be his decision that makes us kajuraihi. It's the dragons that decide in the end. The rest of it is just rules. Rules aren't important. Especially if nobody finds out you broke them."

Both the other girls looked at her, Ciera wide-eyed and impressed, Erienè nonplussed.

The First City girl answered at last, "Even if we were to decide there's no rule against helping each other on the path, even if we were to agree that we might break rules with impunity—which I don't, and can't—it would still be impossible for me to make that climb." She gestured upward, toward the cliff with the carved handholds and metal stakes.

They all followed her gesture. Nescana winced inwardly, studying that cliff. It was not so very high, but falling from anywhere near the top would probably yield worse than a badly sprained ankle.

Still. Still. Still..."This cord," she said suddenly, reaching to lay a fingertip on the green cord that wrapped around Erienè's waist. "It's silk, isn't it? Silk is strong. And green is lucky. How long is it?"

The cord was long enough, they discovered, to

reach halfway down the cliff and back up again. Twice the length would have been more convenient. But the cord was long enough to tie firmly around a firmly-rooted small tree to one side and about halfway up. Ciera climbed up like a marmoset to tie the rope in place, after Nescana showed her the right kind of knot and made her practice it because having the knot unravel would not be good.

Then Erienè stood carefully on the middle of the cord, on her good foot, and Nescana ran the cord around her shoulders to take the weight, and she and Ciera together pulled Erienè up to the middle spike and held her there while she got her hands in place and transferred her weight to the spike.

Then it was all to do again, with a different tree and, it turned out, a much more awkward and difficult job lifting because there was no good place to brace a foot at the edge of the cliff. By the generosity of the Gods, Erienè managed to hold on until they were ready for the second part, and Ciera didn't make a mistake with the knots, and Nescana's arms and back didn't give way until Erienè got a firm hold at the top and could pull herself the rest of the way up.

They all sat together afterward, panting and inspecting their new collection of bruises and scrapes and, in Nescana's case, the long welt across her hands from the thin cord. It hurt, but she could move all her fingers, so she supposed none of the little bones in her hands had actually been crushed. Vivid images of broken hands had come into her mind, there at the end.

"Ouch," Erienè said, tilting her head in sympathy. "I'm sorry."

"Just let's not do that again," Nescana said. "But we'd better get the cord back, just in case."

"Those knots are wonderful, the way they can't pull loose but you can still get them off pulling the other way." Ciera, first of them to recover, came back with the coils of silken cord in her hands and gave it to Erienè. "Your poor dress."

The First City girl looked ruefully at the stained, ripped white cloth. "Not very practical. But it made my mother happy when I said I would wear it."

"How long do you suppose we took, getting up that cliff?" wondered Nescana. It couldn't be later than the second bell of the afternoon, surely. The mist wasn't as bright, but probably high clouds had come up to cover the sun.

Still, once she said that, they all, by common consent, scrambled up and went on. The path was better now, or mostly better, or at least in comparison to rope bridges and sheer cliffs it seemed better even though it was still steep and still treacherous with broken, sharp-edged rock just where a girl might want to set her hand for balance.

Ciera ran ahead and then back, telling them that nothing too much worse lay ahead. Erienè made her way slowly, with her stick, which Ciera had brought up the cliff for her. Nescana had been right; the stick was both too short and the wrong shape, but it was better than nothing. A little better than nothing. She put her arm around Erienè's waist and that was more help than any stick. But slow. She tried not to feel too impatient with Erienè's best pace, or at least not to show how impatient she felt.

"You should go on," Erienè said at last. "You should make Ciera go on. She would listen to you, if you agreed with me. I'm too slow. What if dusk falls and none of us have come to our trial? How can we judge how much time has passed? I think it's far past midday now."

Nescana was pretty sure the other girl was right. She was tempted to agree and run up the path as fast as she could go. Which would probably lead to her own broken ankle or worse, and anyway she could not possibly run as fast as Ciera. As far as she could tell, the Second City child was just as fresh and energetic now as she had been at dawn.

"It's not that late," she said, as though she knew. "There could be another cliff."

Then Ciera darted back around the curve of the mountain and said, "It's just up ahead! We're at the top, this is nearly the top here! There's a tree! And a pool!"

The two older girls stopped where they were and looked at each other.

Then Erienè asked in a cautious tone, "Did you see Etanea? Or Taorè?"

Her eyes wide, Ciera shook her head. "No! I didn't think of that! I wonder where they could have gone. Maybe that's not the top after all. I didn't see where else the path might go, but maybe—"

"Perhaps it is the top," Erienè said. "Perhaps you will find out. Go up, Ciera. Go up and see what you find to do there." She lowered herself carefully to sit down in the middle of the path. "Nescana and I will wait," she added. "Nescana will wait a tenth-bell, and I will wait a tenth-bell after that."

That seemed fair, though Nescana had no idea how they'd judge the time with no sight of the sun. A pool sounded wonderful. She was so thirsty. But she could wait another tenth-bell. She didn't mind waiting for Ciera, who hadn't stayed to argue, but dashed away again. She sat down beside Erienè and immediately, for the first time since starting the climb, found herself worrying about what the trial might actually be.

There was no sound from above. The mist whispered past, muffling hearing as well as sight, but it was very much as though little Ciera had run ahead of them into another world. Maybe the mist was a kind of dragon magic itself. Nescana would not have been surprised. She said after some time, "You were supposed to go first."

"Now I will go last. I'm lucky I have a chance to try at all. Thank you for your help, Nescana." Erienè looked up the mountain, along the path. "I forgot to thank Ciera. My mother would be ashamed."

"You can thank her later, when we're all novices."

"Ah. Well, I shall hope for that chance."

"Anyway, she knows what she did and she knows you're grateful, and she was too excited to notice anyway. I thought she was timid, but she's a brave little thing."

"She is kind. That's better than brave, sometimes." Erienè paused. "You are kind as well, and brave."

Nescana shook her head. "I didn't crawl across the gap where the path got so narrow, or cross the rope bridge with just one foot, or trust anyone to lift me up a cliff."

"Well, you had no need to, since you were not so stupid as to sprain your ankle at nearly the beginning."

Nescana nudged the other girl's shoulder. "I hope you succeed. I hope we all succeed. Taorè and Etanea too."

"I hope we will. But it's never all the boys."

Nescana nodded. It never was. It was generally about one in five. There'd been five of them today. If only one of them made it...despite being Genrai's sister, she thought it would be Ciera, who seemed born to fly. Or Erienè, who was so determined she'd made it all this way with only a little help.

If Nescana became kajurai and any other girl also succeeded, she hoped it would be Ciera or Erienè. That probably wasn't fair to the other two, who hadn't done the least thing wrong, but she couldn't help how she felt.

"It's been a tenth-bell, I think," Erienè said softly.

"Good fortune, Nescana!"

The top of the mountain wasn't quite so close as Ciera had made it sound, but Nescana climbed the last steep slope, edged her way around an awkward place where a shelf of stone narrowed the path, and found herself half stumbling as the path abruptly ran out level before her. For a long moment she just panted, bracing her hip against one last gnarled tree, feeling as though she'd come right out upon the height of the world, as if she might reach up and touch the sky itself. The mist had cleared, or at least...mist still concealed the path when she glanced back and down, but when she looked ahead and up, the air was warm and clear and the sky above a deep and perfect blue. It was very quiet. There was no sign of Ciera. Nescana didn't even find that surprising, though she couldn't have explained where the other girl might have gone, or how.

Ahead, not far, grew a graceful white-barked tree with silvery leaves and small golden fruits about the size of Nescana's thumbnail. The tree leaned out over a pool of clear water, and Nescana thought she had never in her life seen a more welcome sight. She hoped it was all right to drink the water from that pool. She was fervently grateful Wingmaster Taimenai hadn't forbidden it. *That* would definitely have been a trial.

But when she walked slowly forward, she found a cup beside the water, so she knew she was supposed to drink from the pool.

The cup was of white stone, about as wide at the top as Nescana's palm, about twice as tall as it was wide. Nescana knelt beside the pool, filled the cup, and drank. The water was very cold, colder than any water she'd ever tasted; colder than she had ever imagined. It tasted of the winds; not the warm comfortable winds that blew around and across the city, but higher, colder, wilder winds. It chilled Nescana's tongue and made her teeth ache. She set the cup down slowly. Then, following an impulse she didn't understand, she filled the cup again and poured the water out at the base of the tree.

The white bark was smooth and oddly translucent. The leaves seemed more silvery than ever. The golden fruits that grew amid the leaves were the color of honey or pale amber. Each little fruit was perfect, as though neither insect nor bird ever came here. They were shaped like teardrops, and fragrant in a way that was somehow familiar, though whatever the fragrance reminded her of, the memory seemed lost in her childhood.

Nescana touched one of the fruits. It was warm from the sunlight, and gave slightly to the slight pressure of her fingers, and it fell softly into her hand.

So she ate it. It was not like any other fruit she'd ever tasted. It was sweet, but it tasted like the water from the pool. It tasted like the high winds: cold and crisp and wild. The seed was sharp enough to cut her tongue, but she ate that too without even thinking about it, swallowing the seed whole. The taste of blood in her mouth was strange; it tasted wild to her, and sweet, not like blood at all.

Cold seemed to spread outward through her blood; cold and a peculiar dizziness. Nescana knelt down again beside the pool, before she could fall. She filled the cup again with hands that shook, but she did not drink. She looked into the water that trembled in the cup, and it was as though she looked into the sky. A cold wind came against her face and ruffled her hair, and she tried to set the cup down before she could drop it, but she wasn't sure she succeeded. Leaning back against the slender white bole of the tree, she closed her eyes and fell up and out, up and out, vision blurring, all sense of place and position lost, falling into the wind.

She woke in an unfamiliar bed; not a pallet rolled out on the floor, but a real bed with a real feather-stuffed mattress, though the mattress wasn't very thick nor the bed very wide. The sheets were good linen; the pillow, like the mattress, stuffed with feathers. Nescana couldn't remember what this place was nor how she'd come here, but she felt only mild puzzlement, not anxiety. She felt that in a moment she would remember.

Above her bed was a window, the shutters open now to let in the soft, angled sunlight of early morning. This seemed odd, though she couldn't have said what time of day she thought it should be. To one side was a door, closed, set in a paneled wall. To the other stood two other narrow beds like her own, both made up neatly, unoccupied; and across the narrow room two more beds, also empty. Nescana felt surprised and disappointed by her solitude, but she couldn't think who she'd expected to find with her in this place. Not her brothers. Someone else.

She got out of the bed. She was wearing unfamiliar clothing; not one of her own dresses nor exactly a dress at all, but a simple beige shift gathered at the waist with a red cord. She fingered the cord curiously, wondering why it seemed to remind her of something.

Moved by some impulse, she stepped up on her bed and looked out the window.

The sun was high in a cloudless morning, sunlight pouring down across the endless sea. The sun was the same, and the sea. But everything else had changed. Nescana could see the wind. She could *see* warmer, lighter air pouring one way, above cooler denser air rushing another direction; the layer where the two winds mingled was a dazzlement of eddies and ripples.

Higher still, up at the very vault of the sky, dragons flew. Nescana could *see* them, their long coiling bodies and their long graceful necks and their great spreading wings. They were transparent as water, white as cloud, invisible as the sky itself, but she could see them. They were so high they might have been the size of sparrows, but she could *see* the winds that they both created and rode and she knew they were immense. She drew a breath of longing, her heart pounding; she spread her fingers as a bird might spread its wings, wanting to cast itself into the sky. She knew she *could* fly. She remembered everything. She knew she was kajurai.

Behind Nescana, a door opened softly, and closed just as softly. After a long moment, the sound filtered slowly through her awareness and she turned.

"Nescana," said Genrai.

Her big brother looked exactly the same as she remembered, but different. His shoulders were a little broader; he had filled out in the chest—he was less skinny overall. Genrai had always been strong; now he *looked* strong, and somehow older, even though he'd only left them this past spring. And of course his eyes were different. He had crystalline kajurai eyes now, which seemed to catch the light oddly even indoors.

Her eyes must look like that now too.

Nescana didn't speak. She crossed the narrow room and held out her hands. Her brother folded her fingers in his and smiled down at her. Not very far down. Nescana had always been tall for a girl.

"Welcome," Genrai said to her. He pressed her hands. "Welcome! Well done! I knew you'd try the moment they said they were having an audition for girls. I knew you'd have no trouble with the climb or the rest of it, but no one can guess whether the dragon's magic will root itself in anyone. I'm so proud of you."

Nescana didn't think she'd done anything to be proud of. In fact she knew she hadn't; only given the dragon magic a chance to work its way into her. She was happy. Of course she was happy. Or she would be, though none of this felt quite real yet. But at the same time she felt...bereft. She wouldn't go home again, not until she earned rank as a kajurai, but that wasn't it. She'd braced herself for that. Her brothers would be fine; she'd made sure they'd be fine; she wasn't worried about that. It wasn't the thought of her brothers that bothered her.

She said, strangely hesitant, "No one else succeeded? *None* of the other girls? Not even Ciera? I thought surely if any of us succeeded, it'd be Ciera...or Erienè. It hardly seems fair after she tried so hard! And poor Taorè, it was her last chance, she'll turn twenty in hardly more than a senneri..."

Her brother was looking at her quizzically. "You knew the other girls that well?"

Nescana only shook her head.

Genrai didn't press her. He said only, "Well, I'm sorry for it, if you'd made friends with them. Perhaps there'll be another special audition next summer; I know they wanted more than one girl. Someone's persuaded Wingmaster Taimenai and the other wingmasters it's important. I'd put a silver on the *someone* being Ceirfei. He's courting Trei's cousin—that girl mage, you know—I think he wants more girls to enter the Hidden School and some to audition for the kajuraihi, to make it easier for her. And he'd be very persuasive."

Nescana had not known anything of the sort, and didn't know who this Trei might be except apparently the cousin of the famous girl mage, but she nodded.

Genrai was going on. "Anyway, you see the wingmaster gave you a third of the novitiate sleeping hall; he'll want to fill it up if he can. Maybe some of your friends can try again, though I'm sorry for the one who'll turn twenty. That's hard."

He would know just how hard. He'd been seventeen when he'd auditioned, and known the whole time his first chance would be his last. Erienè was seventeen, hadn't she said she was seventeen? Nescana resolved to press Prince Ceirfei about a second special audition, not too many months in the future. If he had any influence at all, then the more persuasive he could be, the better.

"I'll show you the baths and you can finish waking up. I know it's confusing at first. You'll be starving—breakfast was hours ago; it's midmorning now. But I'll bring you something, all right? Novice-master Anerii says he wants to see you as soon as you're presentable. He seems bad-tempered and stern, but don't worry, he's not as harsh as he seems..."

Nescana let her brother lead her to the baths and show her the clothing that was waiting. It was boy's clothing, exactly like Genrai himself had been wearing now that she thought about it: a sleeveless gray shirt and black trousers with narrow cuffs that buttoned. Nescana hadn't thought about it, but boy's clothes did seem better suited to flight than any kind of dress. Someone had plainly realized that.

A red sash, not the silken cord that would tie up a girl's dress. Nescana ran the sash through her hands and finally pinned it on.

Finally Nescana came out to find breakfast. There was a room with a long table and a fireplace, though no fire was burning right now. Genrai wasn't there, and the room was far too large for just one girl by herself, but clutter took up all one end—feathers and thread and withies, papers and scrolls and pens and little jars of ink. Someone had left the top off one of the jars of ink, she found when she paused to look at the feathers. Just like a boy. She capped it herself, a small task that made her feel more at home.

Genrai had left food waiting for her, as he'd promised. A plate of figs, and one of small pastries, and a loaf of good bread with expensive butter. Nescana had forgotten how hungry she was, but she remembered as soon as she saw the food, and crammed the first pastry into her mouth nearly whole. It was filled with dried fruit and cream, and seemed at the moment very possibly the best thing she'd ever eaten in her life.

She paused then, thinking of a different taste. A different kind of fruit. She'd cut her tongue on the seed...but she'd swallowed it anyway. That seemed incredible now. Except she'd had to. It had tasted...it had tasted...what did it even *mean* to say that something tasted of high, cold winds and wild magic?

"There you are!" snapped Novice-master Anerii, jerking her out of her confused, and confusing, memories. The novice-master was standing in the doorway, frowning thunderously.

Nescana stood up, uncertain whether she should bow or only nod, or say *sir,* or just what.

The novice-master waved her impatiently back to the table. "Eat something, girl! You youngsters always wake up ready to fall over." He took a pastry himself, then dropped into a chair across the table and shoved the plate back toward Nescana. He said in a quieter tone, "So you see, you were right. Just you. Taimenai had to admit he was glad I'd made that private arrangement with you so you could audition. I'm thinking we should set up something more systematic for you Third City youngsters. You can't be the only one to have that kind of problem; you're just the first to stroll right in and ask Taimenai about it."

Nescana couldn't think what to say to this, but Master Anerii didn't seem to expect her to say anything. He went on briskly, "Now, there's rules for all the novices, but there're special rules for you. I thought we'd better get that clear right off. It's hard because you're the only girl, and the first one. I think I've got the basic idea worked out, but we'll see how it goes and if you find out you've got problems with rules I'm laying down here, don't just *break* them, *talk* to me, understand?"

This seemed fair. Nescana nodded cautiously.

"You're starting off behind, but Genrai and the others'll tell you the ordinary rules and get you up on all that. For you, though, you listen to me: stay to your own part of the novitiate after hours, keep out of the boys' sleeping hall completely, and keep to your own allotted hour for the baths. We discussed putting a bolt on your door, but we decided against it. You even come close to a whisper of a suspicion you might need a bolt, that's a problem and you tell me about it."

"Yes, sir," Nescana agreed at once, though she felt if Genrai hadn't been her brother, she would be pretty close to a whisper of a suspicion right now, even without meeting the other novices. She didn't say so. After all, Genrai *was* her brother.

"We've never had girls before, so I expect we'll have trouble of one sort or another and I expect we'll sort it out. All the same, the less trouble we have, the better. A couple of the boys are too young for you anyway, and it should help that Genrai's your brother, but don't you *deliberately* stir up trouble, you hear me?"

"I wouldn't!" Nescana promised. "I won't." She might have felt insulted, except she knew some girls who definitely would have done exactly what the novice-master was implying.

"They won't either, or they'll hear from me," Master Anerii told her. "If things get complicated, you let me know. However things work out, and we don't expect you to take vows like a cloistered nun and this isn't a temple, but listen to me: do *not* get pregnant while you're a novice or you'll think Milendri itself fell on you, understand?"

Nescana tried not to laugh. "No, sir."

The novice-master eyed her. "Got all that?"

"Yes, sir, I think so. The boys stay out of my sleeping area and I stay out of theirs, nobody intrudes when anybody's bathing, I don't tease the boys or start trouble and they won't bother me either; and definitely don't get pregnant."

"And *talk to me* if you run into trouble, or if the rules don't seem to fit what we need."

"Yes, sir." Nescana hesitated. But she felt she ought to say something...and she wanted to know how Master Anerii would respond. So she said after a slight pause, "I might...I might have already broken rules, sir. On Kotipa."

The novice-master gave her a curt nod. "You mean the way you and the little one, Ciera, helped Erienè Lantanasca make it up to the top? The whole lot of you helped her over one rough spot or another. I thank the Gods none of you broke your necks, the risks you took! We do keep an eye on you all, of course," he added drily at Nescana's obvious surprise.

Of course they did. The girls all ought to have guessed. Nescana said cautiously, "We weren't sure about the rules."

"The dragon magic sorts it out in the end," Master Anerii told her. "The rules make it easier for that to happen. Pity that Lantanasca girl didn't succeed; she's got grit. But an injury like that fills the mind and heart till there's not much room for magic."

"Are you going to hold another special audition? One she might—"

"That's business for the wingmasters, novice." Master Anerii's tone was unexpectedly curt. Nescana closed her mouth.

But he added, "I'll tell you, we don't much approve of novices who'd ignore someone else in trouble. Good job, and good job again for telling me. I think you're a brave, honest girl and I'm glad you made it through."

Nescana was too startled by this unexpected praise to answer, but the novice-master didn't seem to expect her to respond. He pushed his chair back and got to his feet. "Now, you know we don't allow our novices to send or receive letters, but we'll make one exception for you right up front. You write a letter—can you write?"

Nescana shook her head.

"Well, you'll learn. All right, then you'll tell me what you want to say and I'll write it, and send it off with a couple senneri's worth of coin for your brothers. They can answer so you'll know they got it. But don't expect to make all that back and forth a regular business, novice. The rules are there for a reason."

"No, sir. I mean, yes, sir."

"That's the way. Very respectful. Good girl. Very well, come on, I'll show you where to make your offering to the Gods. Water and wine are always by the altars, and a knife to draw a drop of blood. Then the letter. Then I'll turn you over to your brother and let him and the other novices show you how to sort out a pair of wings, and then this afternoon you'll learn how it feels to fly. Right?"

Nescana stood up. She was a little scared and very excited, but below and around and through those other feelings, happiness was starting to bubble up inside her. And something else, something deeper and more complicated than happiness. It felt...it felt like something that would deepen, and last, and never wear out. It felt like magic, but different.

She thought she might recognize it, from a long time ago, from when she'd been a child and both her parents had been alive. She thought perhaps it was joy.

LILA

This novelette is a quiet story that takes place in a world that might almost be ours, if our world had a little bit of inexplicable magic that emerged around the edges from time to time. Lila is not the protagonist, but she is important to the story. She is also an homage to my first dog, a Papillon, who, when he passed away from cancer ten years ago, left a surprisingly large hole in my life for a five-pound dog.

Lila is not necessarily a Papillon. I wrote her with very little description, so that she could be almost any fluffy, tiny dog. So many dogs of that description have enormous courage.

They unfolded from pebbles, first. From limestone pebbles in driveways and planters; from the quartz inclusions in river rocks, from sharp-edged bits of flint along the edge of the old quarry where the rock had long ago been broken and left lying.

They came out of the water, too. From the foam where the little waterfalls of the river dashed down the mountain, from the still pools where the deeper water lingered in shadowed eddies, from the cold green quarry lake where children swam during long summer afternoons. They were the colors of the stone and water: foam white or cloud grey or translucent green. The white ones were streaked with rust along their breasts and the undersides of their wings; the green ones dappled with shadowed grey and blue.

Sometimes they left behind fragments of shells, not quite like ordinary eggshells: delicate layers of pale stone on the outside, glistening and nacreous on the inside. Mad collected half a dozen broken shells, but the remnants were fragile, and overnight the pearlescent layer sublimed like ice kept too long frozen, leaving behind only curved layers of ordinary limestone or chirt.

The dragons were far too small to frighten anyone. They were the size of sparrows, mostly, or occasionally as large as starlings: wingspans as long as a woman's hand, whippy tails twice as long again. The children of Springdale tried to catch them in nets, but once their wings were dry they were quick as hummingbirds. Only a few of the more persistent and energetic boys caught one that way, and discovered to their disappointment that the dragons would not live through the night if kept in a jar or aquarium, no matter whether you punched holes in the lid of the jar or what you tried to feed them. Then the dead dragons would dissolve into the air like the nacreous layers of their shells, and you would be left with only a few uninteresting bits that might be bone or chips of limestone, or at best one or two curiously shaped little teeth. The scientists collected a few or paid the boys to do it, and so did the reporters, but with no better result. If there was a way to keep a dragon alive once you caught it, no one had discovered it yet.

One morning near the beginning, Lila caught one as it emerged from a limestone pebble. She brought it in through the pet door, as proud of herself as if she'd caught a mole or a mouse. The dragon was one of the little streaky white ones, pretty and delicate as a porcelain ornament, but now with its neck limp and wings trailing. Mad took it away from Lila and held it curled in the palm of her hand while the little dog danced on her hind legs and yipped to have it back.

Mad was sorry the little dragon was dead, but Lila was so pleased with herself that she didn't have the heart to say so. "You're a brave, bold hunter," Mad told the little dog. "But please consider sticking to moles in the future, yes?" And she put the dragon out of the way on a counter so she could check Lila's face and neck and legs for injuries. Lila knew all about moles and mice and hadn't been bitten since puppyhood, but dragons were as new for her as for everyone else and she might not have realized how long and agile they were. Like snakes, really. That was a disturbing thought—

"They're not poisonous," Boyd Raske said from the kitchen door, propped open now to let in the breeze. "Or at least the one that bit Tommy Kincaid wasn't."

Mad nodded to him, not at all surprised that he had dropped by, or that he'd recognized her sudden fear. Boyd Raske noticed a lot; a little too much, sometimes. And he kept track of everyone in Springdale. Particularly anybody who might be grieving or angry or thinking about getting into trouble. He'd had been making a point of wandering by Mad's house every day or so since Christmas. Since her mother's funeral, in fact. She supposed that one day he would stop coming by. When that happened, she figured, she would know she was...over it. Or at least, over it *enough*.

But she said only, "Good to know, Deputy. Tommy got bitten, did he?"

"I know. It *would* be Tommy. If that boy didn't have more lives than a cat, he'd be dead as a doornail." Boyd stepped into the kitchen and stroked Lila under the chin with the tip of one finger, smiling when the little dog wiggled in Mad's arms and licked his hand.

When she'd first met him, Mad had assumed Boyd simply spoke naturally in clichés, as politicians spoke in soundbites or preachers in sonorous exhortations. Later, she had decided he was probably doing it on purpose to amuse himself, or maybe to amuse her.

She'd been the one to start it: she'd met the new deputy at the gallery, when he'd been looking for paintings to dress up the Bateman's little house, which he was renting. Something about his expression—lack of expression—as he studied one of her paintings had led her to comment that mostly she painted clichés because clichés sold better than originality. He'd been looking at one of her portraits of Lila, and he'd nodded solemnly and answered, "Clichés are comforting. If they're the right clichés." Then he'd bought a different painting, the one of the maple branch where the leaves at the top of the painting were all the colors of autumn fire, but the ones that dipped into the shadowed pool were ambiguous, as green and translucent as the water, so that it was impossible to tell where the tree ended and the water began, impossible to tell whether the leaves were real leaves or somehow themselves shaped out of green shade and water.

Of all her paintings in the gallery at the time, that one had been Mad's favorite. She had never asked Deputy Raske what he saw in it, or where in his little house he'd hung it. And though he knew she'd painted it, he'd never said a word about it to her.

Now Mad said solemnly, "Tommy's taken so many years off his mother's life, I expect she's practically turning in her grave."

"Mrs. Kincaid is a resilient woman, fortunately. Did Lila get bitten?"

"Apparently not." Mad ran her hand once more across the little dog's feathered ears and set her on the floor. Lila immediately hurled herself at Boyd, who caught her handily when she leaped at his chest. He tucked her under his arm, petting her firmly. She looked even smaller and more elegant in his big hands, all fluff, the kind of little dog who ought to be curled on a velvet cushion with a pink rhinestone collar and painted toenails. Not that anyone who knew Lila expected her to sit inside on a velvet cushion when she could be out in the yard, digging for moles or hunting mice through the overgrown lilacs. Or catching newly hatched dragons.

Boyd crossed the room to peer thoughtfully at the dead dragon on the windowsill. "Shame," he murmured. "Pretty little things. I don't suppose you want to paint this one?"

Mad shrugged. "No. Not now." She felt uneasy and faintly annoyed, and uneasy with her own annoyance, which she knew Boyd—Deputy Raske—had done nothing to deserve.

"Figured probably not. I'll take it away, then." Boyd folded the poor crumpled thing up in his handkerchief, glancing at Mad for permission. "Unless you want to take it into town yourself? Might do you good to get out of this haunted house for an afternoon."

Mad rolled her eyes. "What are you, Tommy's age? It might be crumbling around the edges, but haunted?"

Boyd said mildly, "For you, it is." But he avoided an argument by talking to Lila instead. "Tough lady," he told the little dog. "Good job keeping the garden safe." Then he added to Mad, "Not as tough as she thinks she is, though. You might want to keep her in. Or on a leash. Poisonous or not, the little dragons do have teeth, and you've got a good many more up here than anywhere in town."

Mad shrugged. She was still annoyed, but only a little. She was fairly certain that Boyd could no more stop himself offering helpful, protective advice than he could stop breathing.

Her house, perched among and atop the limestone bluffs above Springdale, was nearer the quarry than the town and nearer the river than either: just the kind of country best suited to produce dragons, apparently. Mad had been one of the first people—maybe *the* first—to see a dragon crack open a pebble and unfold its damp wings. Not the first to report what she'd seen, though. Leave that to boys like Tommy Kincaid, or to men of unimpeachable reputation like Deputy Boyd Raske.

Mad's discretion had been only so much use. One of the reporters and two of the scientists had been very persistent; the reporter wanting to ask Mad all about her mother; the scientists wanting to walk over every inch of Mad's property, collecting samples of the rocks and earth and water. The scientists had been tolerable, actually. But it had taken Boyd to get rid of the reporter, once the woman realized who Mad was. Who her mother had been.

That was probably why Boyd had driven up from town today. Just to make sure the reporter had not come back.

"We're fine," Mad told him. "Thanks for taking care of that, though." She nodded toward the handkerchief hiding the dead little dragon. "I know they like to look at them before they start dissolving."

Boyd shrugged. "I'm going that way anyway." He turned toward the door, then turned back. "I expect I'll swing by tomorrow. Need anything?"

"No," Mad said immediately. And then, more firmly as he hesitated, "No, Deputy. I said, we're fine."

"Of course you did." Boyd stroked Lila once more, set her on the couch, touched a finger to his hat in casual salute, and was gone.

For three more weeks, the dragons were everywhere in Springdale: perching along the eaves of people's houses, chasing the bees that buzzed around the crabapple blossoms in the town square, spiraling up in alarm when the church bells rang for Sunday services.

Then, about as soon as everyone got used to them, they were gone. The first ones had emerged from pebbles and river-froth near the beginning of April. On the second of May, they gathered in flocks like blackbirds in the fall. On the fifth, they all spiraled suddenly up into a cloudless sky: the size of sparrows and then the size of bumblebees and then the size of gnats and then gone.

For a few days, everyone in Springdale expected them to return, or at least descend somewhere else, maybe miles away—maybe hundreds of miles away, like monarch butterflies or ruby-throated hummingbirds. But if they came back to the ground anywhere, it must have been somewhere without people, because no one reported it.

By the end of the next week, all the reporters were gone, even the one interested in Mad's family history, and the fickle attention of the American public had been recaptured by celebrity scandals and the sudden revelation of the new President's love child. The people of Springdale turned back to important concerns, such as the dreadful performance of the high school football team and the unseasonable weather, which was very dry and warm for so early in the year.

At the beginning of June, when everyone had practically forgotten the dragons, they started emerging again. But this time they didn't emerge from pebbles and water foam. This time, they came from deep water, from the reservoir and still pools along the bank of the river; and they came from stones in retaining walls and in foundations and walkways in the park. The stones cracked and the shells shattered and the dragons spilled out and unfolded their damp wings to dry and then flew away.

The older part of the courthouse collapsed one

morning midway through June, when nineteen dragons suddenly hatched, one after another, out of limestone blocks in the foundation. Luckily it was a Sunday, so no one was actually in the courthouse, but several people at the outdoor tables by the café had to run for shelter when the building came down.

Mad didn't see any of that, but she heard about it. Everyone heard about it. By that time, the reporters and scientists had come back, and they discussed it endlessly. The scientists tried to capture dragons, mostly without success. The dragons were in the air so fast, and no one was going to catch any of these larger dragons with a butterfly net. So the scientists collected shell fragments instead, and shards of broken stone. They timed the sublimation of the nacreous layer within the shells, which was thicker in these larger shells, but still too ephemeral to analyze properly, and tried to find patterns in where and when the dragons emerged. The reporters were even more annoying than the scientists. They gazed earnestly at the cameras and mouthed empty phrases to hide the obvious truth that they didn't know anything, that no one knew anything. Mad carried her old television out to the garden shed and never turned on her phone.

Mad might have missed the excitement at the courthouse, but she saw the dragons that emerged. She could hardly have missed them. All nineteen of them flew past her house as they rose into the heights in a single spiraling line. One after another, like ballerinas performing a choreographed dance, she thought; not much like the random flight of birds. The spiraling flight of the dragons carried them past the bluffs below her house, out over the quarry lake and back again hardly twenty feet from her back deck, up and up into the vastness of the sky. They were the size of hawks, of vultures, of eagles, some of them. Some of them were larger than that. The last, pale as an owl, was the biggest. It had wings that stretched, she was fairly sure, farther from tip to tip than she could have reached with both outstretched arms.

It turned its head as it slid by Mad's high garden and the rickety back deck; turned its head and looked at her with eyes white as frost. Then its curving path carried it away again across the quarry. Its shadow drifted across the lake like milky emerald, until, as it neared the higher bluffs to the east, it tilted its wings and slid up in the sky after its fellows, up and up, until it vanished against the hazy light.

Mad set up her largest easel in the center of the deck and began to paint a spiraling flight of white dragons against sky and green water. She blurred the land beneath, veiled it in mist as it was sometimes veiled on chilly mornings. She blurred the dragons as well, made them ambiguous, visible and invisible in the pale light, there and not there amid the shadows of high clouds...they weren't really white, not even the palest of them. Not pure white. That last one had been a pale gold two shades darker than ivory, the undersides of its wings lavender two shades lighter than wisteria flowers. Its eyes had been true white, though, casting back the sunlight like the eyes of cats or foxes cast back headlights at night...she picked up a dab of chromium white on her brush and began to suggest another dragon, larger than the rest, pale against a pale sky. Then, far below the dragons, she delicately sketched in a tumble that might be broken stone and the shards of dragon eggs.

Lila had danced and whirled and barked at the dragons as they flew past, certain to the depths of her indomitable soul that she alone was responsible for protecting the deck and the house and Mad, sure that *she*

238

was the one keeping them out of the yard and away from the hillside below. Mad smiled at her, five pounds of fluff, a handful of a dog who had never been frightened of anything in her life, all bright eyes and sharp-pricked ears and a plume of a tail. But she also looked thoughtfully at the open sky. At last she found Lila's collar and a leash.

"Just for today," she told her. "Just while I paint. I'm sure they're gone, I'm sure it's fine, but still."

Lila thought the leash was a wonderful idea. She thought it would be splendid if Mad stopped painting and did something more fun. She dashed toward the front of the house, uttering sharp little yips and dancing with excitement. *Come on! Come on! Hurry hurry hurry!* She was so confused and disappointed when Mad didn't pick up her keys and follow that in the end Mad sighed, took one last look at the dragons she'd begun to suggest in a sky that might or not might be the ordinary sky above Springdale. Then she put away her paints and brushes and went to town after all.

Everyone was talking about the courthouse, of course. "Did you hear, Mrs. James and her youngest were so close they were almost hit by falling shingles off the roof!"

Almost hit was as close as anyone had come to disaster. Someone had driven their car into a lamppost as they swerved; that was the worst of it. Of course part of the town square was cordoned off to keep people clear of the fallen rubble, away from the area where more debris might yet fall.

Naturally, boys kept ducking under the tape to grab souvenir shingles and chips of broken stone and, most coveted, bits of broken eggshell, though those were supposed to go to the scientists. Mad beckoned to Tommy when he ran up to pet Lila, and he gave her a piece of shell as big as her hand before crouching to let the little dog jump onto his knee. Lila stood up on the boy's knee, put her front feet on his chest, and licked his chin. Tommy laughed, and Mad gave him a handful of tiny biscuits and watched tolerantly as he sent Lila quickly through her repertoire—dance in a circle, jump through my arms, down! Up! Tommy was the only other person Mad would let work with Lila. Despite his well-deserved reputation for mischief, the boy had the intuition and focus to work perfectly with a quick little dog like Lila.

"I heard you got bitten," she told him.

Tommy gave a dismissive little jerk of his head. "That was ages ago. One of the little ones."

"Yep, that's what I heard. Better watch out—these aren't so little."

"Yeah! Take a finger right off, I bet!"

His enthusiasm made her laugh. She measured the curve of the shell fragment and decided the whole egg must have been about the size of a soccer ball, though probably not as round. She ran a finger across the iridescent interior. She fancied she could almost feel a faint chill as the unearthly layer of whatever-it-was sublimed into the air; almost see a faint mist rising from the shell. That was probably her imagination.

"Five hours and six minutes from hatching till it's all gone," Tommy said authoritatively. "If it's like the last piece I found. But this egg was bigger, so maybe it'll take longer. I'm going to see what happens if you spray it with hairspray, like you do to fix a pencil drawing."

Mad had taught an art class at Springdale's middle school. She'd thought Tommy had mostly noticed the hairspray as something to tease the girls with, but he must have been paying a little attention after all. She said, intrigued, "You could try it. But pencil doesn't sublime off paper the way this stuff sublimes off the rocky part of the shell..."

"I'll try it anyway! Next chance I get!" Tommy declared.

"If your mother doesn't want you taking her hairspray, you could use—"

"Madison Martin? It is Ms. Martin, isn't it?" asked someone behind her. "Can I call you Madison? Madison, can I ask you just one or two questions? How do you feel about—"

"Nobody calls you *Madison*!" Tommy said to Mad, indignantly.

Mad sighed. "Don't I wish." Turning, she raised her eyebrows pointedly at the woman who'd spoken.

It was the reporter. Of course. A pretty woman with a limpid gaze, not nearly as stupid as she looked, Mad thought. And certainly not nearly as friendly as she pretended.

"Not interested," Mad told her. Lila wiggled all over, wanting to greet the reporter; Lila promiscuously loved everyone, even reporters. Picking her up, Mad started to walk away.

But the woman darted after her, not letting her go, smiling and smiling a false, clichéd smile, pretending that they were friends, pretending that she had the *right*. "Madison! Ms. Martin! Let me just ask—"

"You're a reporter, aren't you?" Tommy asked with great interest, trotting after them. "Want to see my snake?" He brought one out of his pocket, a delicate little ringneck that curled around his fingers, and held it out toward the reporter, who shied away with a little squeak of surprise.

Mad ducked away, across the street from the ruins of the courthouse, into the gallery and out the back with a little nod for the clerk at the counter. Smart kid, Tommy Kincaid.

But after that, Mad had no wish to linger in town.

Even so, she didn't go directly back to the car; as far as Lila was concerned, no trip to town was complete without a stop at the pet store for some of those jerky-wrapped biscuits and maybe a new soft toy to destroy. Lila liked dissecting the toys, removing the squeakers and leaving synthetic cottony fluff all over the room. When Mad was too sick of herself and her life to paint, sometimes she still had enough energy to stuff the insides back into Lila's toys and sew them up. It was a job that echoed life in so many ways: destruction took so little time and repairs were so tedious and so temporary. It hardly took any time at all to rip out even the most painstaking stitches...

Lila, oblivious to Mad's darkening mood, cheerfully removed every soft toy from the lower bin in the store and scattered them all over the aisle. She attacked a horrible purple-polka-dotted elephant with particular enthusiasm. Mad sighed and tucked that one under her arm. The elephant might be hideous, but not even the cutest toy looked like much after Lila had disemboweled it. Stitching this one up with big, sloppy Frankenstein stitches might even improve it.

Then a wary look out at the street—no lurking reporters, so far as Mad could tell—and back to the car and out of town, Lila standing up in the passenger seat so she could bark out the window at every person they passed. She barked twice as enthusiastically at her buddy Romeo, the Lindstrand's handsome pit bull, who pricked his ears and hauled little Rebecca Lindstrand halfway into the street when he heard Lila.

Mad waved to Rebecca, but she didn't stop. She felt a little guilty about it. Romeo adored Lila, though she bullied him unmercifully whenever they visited, and stole all his toys except one extremely heavy ball she couldn't begin to pick up. Even that she guarded fiercely and wouldn't let Romeo near. But Rebecca was obviously on her way to the pet store herself, and letting the two dogs play was difficult if they couldn't let them off leash.

So she turned left and left again, past the church and the cemetery and out of town, and up the long road that wound its way up among the limestone bluffs and around the quarry and finally led to Mad's mother's house. The shadows were lengthening by that time, the moon a translucent sliver in the pale sky although the sun was still well above the forested hills.

The house did look a bit worn from this angle. Mad usually didn't notice; it was too familiar. But Boyd's comment must have lingered in the back of her mind, because today she somehow couldn't help but study the house as she gathered up her purchases and beckoned Lila to join her. The afternoon sun showed clearly how the black paint meant to seal the foundation was peeling, how the stain was wearing off the logs of the house in uneven blotches. The screen of the porch was torn here and there, and the porch itself sagged at one corner, though it was safe enough if you stayed to the left as you went up the stairs. Last year's leaves moldered beneath and beside the porch, and some kind of determined vine with narrow serrated leaves and poisonous-looking black berries was slowly making its way up along one windowsill as though it were trying to find a way into the house. Wasps hummed—the nest clung to the eaves, but far enough from the door that Mad had never bothered to get rid of it. Paper wasps were not very aggressive, yet the drone of their activity somehow seemed ominous today.

Taken all in all...the house did look haunted. She hadn't been able to deny that to herself, not since Boyd had made that comment. It looked like a witch's house, the kind undisguised by gingerbread and gumdrops. It looked like the kind of house where the witch would be waiting for you inside, with her great cauldron and her bottles of heart's blood and infant's tears...

"I could paint that," Mad said out loud. But, though Lila yipped cheerfully as though to agree, Mad knew she really couldn't. She would never have the courage to paint this house as it should be painted. If she tried, she would feel the house itself looking over her shoulder disapprovingly. Or her mother's ghost.

Not that the house was *actually* haunted. Mad wasn't so weak-minded that she believed in ghosts. But it wouldn't matter. If she tried to paint the house, she knew she would have to stop before she even had the basic shapes blocked in. She would have to destroy the canvas and throw out all the paints and brushes she had tried to use, get all new ones, or she wouldn't be able to paint anything at all.

Mad wasn't blind, or proud. God knew she didn't have reason to be *proud*. She knew she didn't have half her mother's fierce, brilliant talent. But she had come to understand that she had a little talent of her own, something smaller and tamer but real enough. She knew she would never, ever be able to paint this house for fear she might see, mercilessly revealed in that attempt, its soul.

A dragon whipped by overhead, pearl and smoke in the afternoon light, and Mad unclenched her hands and made herself smile at the wildly barking Lila, who was tugging at the end of the leash, *so sure* she could catch that dragon if Mad would only let her try. *Lila* had no idea of her own tininess, her fragility. *Lila* didn't doubt herself, or fear that she might be about to hurl herself into a quest that was too big for her.

And since she didn't, Mad had to protect her from her own bravery. Picking her up, Mad went up the steps—carefully, on the left side—and into the house.

But the ghost of her mother seemed everywhere all

that evening.

Oh, not literally. Of course not. But the creak of old boards sounded a bit like someone moving about upstairs, in the master bedroom as likely as not. There almost seemed an echo behind the clanging gurgle of the hot water pipes, like someone calling out: *Mad, sweetie, I need you in the studio, come up here!* Not that there were any distinguishable words to that echo. Obviously not. Mad knew perfectly well that the summons echoed only in her mind and memory.

The house wasn't haunted, obviously. The only ghosts people ever truly saw were the ones they carried with them, in their minds and their hearts and their flinching memories. The departed disappeared as soon as they were forgotten.

Mad wished she could forget her mother. Though everyone else would remember her, even then. Mad's famous mother, who had been able, it was rapturously claimed, to capture in her portraits the very essence and soul of her models.

It wasn't true. Mad's mother had found it so easy to lie with paint. So easy to show her clients only the parts of their souls that they actually wanted to see. They ate that up, the shallow, posturing Hollywood celebrities, and the politicians who thought they were important statesmen but were really only a different kind of celebrity. They loved the flattering portraits Marissa Martin had painted for them. And too many of them also loved the portraits she had painted of her little daughter: nudes of Mad at five years, and nine, and thirteen. Disturbingly eroticized portraits, which critics called *edgy* and *sophisticated* and normal people knew actually skirted far too close to depraved.

Mad hated to think how many rich men and women had one of those portraits hanging in their homes. She had no idea how many her mother had painted. She tried never to think of it.

And she never painted people. She painted beech - trees leaning over water, trees whose reflections might possibly, if you looked closely, weave their way into a reflected faerie world; and she painted peach-colored roses whose color bled imperceptibly into the sunset until you couldn't quite decide if the roses were physical flowers or perhaps made of light; and she painted maple branches whose leaves might be fire above and water below. And when she painted portraits, they were of dogs, whose souls she could tell the truth about without fear.

Maybe Boyd was right. Maybe she should leave this house, sell it, let some contractor knock it down and build something else on the site. Or just open all the windows and doors and walk away from it and let the woods and weather pull it down.

But she knew she wouldn't. She couldn't. Anywhere she went, she would carry her mother with her. She didn't know how to leave her past behind.

The second emergence of the dragons gradually tapered off toward the end of June. A few of the scientists lingered, unobtrusive, but most of the reporters had passed on to other stories after the first week or so, and the other tourists left as fewer and fewer dragons unfolded from the stone of Springdale and spiraled up into the sky.

The days became hot and slow. Families brought picnic lunches up to the bluffs, and children swam in the quarry lake. The courthouse was repaired with stone prudently brought in from a distant corner of the state where no dragons had ever been seen, and the mayor of Springdale planted a tree in the courthouse lawn to celebrate. He planted a dogwood. Mad thought it should have been something stronger. An oak. A red oak, that would live a hundred years, with leaves that would turn to fire in the fall. She painted that tree, falling leaves that might be flickers of flame and the suggestion of a great castle looming beyond it, that might be nothing but a chance jumble of broken rocks. But she wasn't particularly happy with the way the painting came out. It sold for a good price at the gallery before she could decide what she ought to have done differently.

Mad taught Lila the signal exercise from advanced obedience, and the drop-on-recall—flashy tricks that drew admiring comments when she took the little dog to the park. Lila loved showing off and being admired, and Mad liked people to pay attention to Lila because if they were admiring the little dog, that meant they weren't privately thinking about Mad and her mother and her mother's paintings.

"Smart as a whip, isn't she?" was Boyd Raske's comment when he saw Lila's drop-on-recall, which she performed, as always, with flashy brilliance. She leaped into her recall, hit the ground in a split second when Mad gave the down signal, and whipped instantly back into the recall when she got the signal. When she reached Mad, she leaped into her arms, which wasn't part of the exercise, but Mad had expected it and caught her without difficulty.

"She learned that in three days. It's a mystery how she does it. A genius with a brain the size of a walnut." Mad put Lila down so the little dog could dash to Boyd and leap into *his* arms. The deputy caught the her neatly.

Boyd held Lila up so she could kiss the tip of his nose, then tucked her under his arm and strolled over to hand her back to Mad. "Hot as blazes today."

This was more oblique than Boyd's usual advice, but Mad deciphered it without trouble. "I was just about to head over to the café to get her some water. And me some ice cream." She clipped Lila's leash to her collar and they both turned toward the east edge of the park, which gave onto the town square and the café.

Boyd watched Lila dash ahead and dart back. "She'd like ice cream too, I expect."

"And she'll get some. A dab won't hurt her. I don't even have to ask anymore; they always give her a sample cup of vanilla."

"Lucky she doesn't know what she's missing."

Mad grinned. Boyd was a rocky-road man. "You allowed to eat ice cream on duty?"

The deputy took off his hat and fanned himself with it. "On a day like today, it's all that keeps me in fighting trim." He hesitated, uncharacteristically. Then he added in an absent tone, "You know, we've got that reporter back in town. That one woman, you know."

Mad was sinkingly certain she knew exactly which reporter he meant. "Why? No dragons anymore."

"Yep, she's done with dragons, apparently. She's moved on to bigger and better things. She's doing a piece on famous people of the county. Over in Manchester, there's a guy who writes horror novels. And a woman in Barton who set some kind of hang-gliding record."

"And me. My mother's daughter." Mad tried to sound light. Unconcerned. Flippant.

"And you," Boyd said seriously, not for a moment believing Mad's light tone.

"Well, thanks for the warning. I'll set Lila on her if she annoys me."

"That should do it." Mercifully, Boyd changed the subject. "I liked that last painting of yours in the gallery."

Mad gave him a sidelong glance. "You didn't buy it."

"No. I liked it, but it wasn't quite right. I don't think it was something you really saw. Or wanted to see. I sort

248

of thought you might have had something else in your mind's eye when you painted it."

Mad stopped dead.

"Or that's what I thought when I looked at it, but what do I know? I don't know anything about art."

"No," Mad said slowly. "No. You're right." He was right, and she hadn't even realized it. Only, even now that she understood what had gone wrong with that painting of the red oak, she wasn't quite sure what image she ought to have painted instead. The oak itself...she didn't think that had been the problem. No. But she almost thought she saw, in her mind's eye, something else beyond the flaming oak: a looming shape that was neither a tumble of randomly fallen rocks nor a ruined castle. Something else. Something—

Lila yipped, then, knowing they were heading for the café and impatient for her ice cream, and Boyd made another comment about the weather, and the moment was past.

Mad never did quite figure out what the red oak painting had wanted to be. She couldn't paint after that. The blindness of her painter's eye blocked her; she couldn't see what she wanted to paint and so she couldn't paint anything. It felt to Mad like the house was laughing at her inability to sort out her own vision. She could practically hear her mother: *Painter's block is just the laziness of a minor talent, Madison. Real genius can't be blocked. Inspiration floods out of her like water through a broken dam.* And then her voice would change and she would purr, You're *my inspiration, Madison.*

Mad tried to block out the remembered voice. She got her paints out and stretched a canvas on her easel and then stood and looked at it for a while. Then she put everything away again and took Lila for a long walk in the woods instead, down the path through the woods to the quarry lake and back up the other way, along the base of the bluffs and up again, half a path and half clambering over and around jumbled rocks. She had to lift Lila over some of the rougher places, which didn't shake the little dog's confidence one bit. Lila always knew she could handle anything.

At the beginning of September, when daylong rains finally moved in and broke summer's heat and drought, dragons began to emerge once more. This time they were larger still. The smallest Mad saw was the size of a hang-glider, and the biggest looked large enough to carry off a cow. A good-sized calf, anyway.

This time, the dragons emerged from the bluffs to the north of Springdale, mostly. The limestone cliffs cracked and broke and fell and shattered, but that was better than dragons unfolding themselves from the foundation stones of homes or churches or public buildings in town. The mayor had signs placed at the campground: Danger: Falling Rocks. Mad thought anyone too stupid to figure that out on their own deserved to have rocks fall on their heads. Boys rode their bikes up to the bluffs below Mad's house, though, and dared each other to dash in and grab a fragment of shell. That was something else, and she worried about it.

"Tommy Kincaid says they can hear the cliff face start to go," Boyd reassured her when she asked him about that. He grinned at Mad's expression. "That boy got a map and stuck a lot of pins in it. He explained he's trying to figure out how to predict where and when the dragons will come out."

"He's a smart kid. Maybe he will." Mad wouldn't be surprised. "He showed you his map?"

"He hit me up for a box of colored stickpins, like cops use in movies to figure out where the bad guy is. He figured we'd have plenty at the sheriff's office."

Mad raised her eyebrows. "Well, did you?"

"Yep. I gave him a box. I didn't explain we mostly use 'em to post boring memos on the bulletin board and hardly ever to solve crimes. Naturally it's important to uphold the image of the sheriff's office."

"You're not worried he'll get himself into trouble, trying to track down these dragons?"

"Mad, to be honest, I don't think Tommy Kincaid's in as much danger as you are, in this house of yours up here on top of this cliff."

Mad stared at him. She'd never thought of that.

"I can't help but think of the way the courthouse came down," Boyd said apologetically. "I've been thinking maybe you should move to town. Just for a while. Until the dragons stop emerging. I mean, you never know. Better safe than sorry."

"I can't move to town," Mad said automatically. Then she paused, looking around. She knew it was true, but she wasn't sure why. It wasn't even truly her house. It was her *mother's* house. It wasn't as though Mad actually *liked* it. The house was too big and too old and most of all filled with too many memories. And it was a nuisance. The water pipes clanked in the summer and froze in the winter; the gutters had to be cleaned every fall and the roof patched every spring.

But it wasn't going to *stay* her mother's house, not forever. Mad was slowly making it hers. Maybe that was why she couldn't leave. Not until she'd finally found the courage to strip this house of the memories that were its ghosts. Not until she'd emptied it out and left it hollow and echoing, haunted by nothing but time and gradual decay.

They were both in the kitchen, where Mad spent most of her time. The kitchen in summer, the sunroom in winter, the back deck where she set up her easel when the weather was fine, the dining room which she had converted into a bad-weather studio by the simple expedient of giving the table and chairs and china cabinet and sideboard and all the china to Goodwill. Her bedroom was beyond the new studio, and she never went upstairs. She never needed to. She never wanted to. But someday she would go up there and clear everything out of her mother's bedroom and her mother's bath and her mother's studio. The studio would be the worst. She knew there were a good many of her mother's paintings still tucked away up there. Some of them would be childhood portraits of Mad. She didn't want to see them, knew she would not be able to resist looking at each one as she threw it on a fire. She *would* burn them. Once she gathered her nerve enough to intrude on her mother's realm.

She wouldn't give any of her mother's clothing to Goodwill. She knew that. She would burn all that, too.

"Maybe in the spring," she said out loud. "I'll do it in the spring."

"I'd rather you thought about moving now," Boyd said, not having followed Mad's train of thought. Or maybe he had, because he added, "Sometimes your past doesn't let go of you. Sometimes you have to reach back and amputate it, and I don't think it gets easier if you wait. Maybe you could at least look at apartments in town. Or houses for sale. There's a nice little place on the corner of Elm and Second, one of those new homes where the Seddon's hayfields used to be. Big yard for Lila, big windows, plenty of light for painting."

"This really isn't any of your concern, you know."

Boyd affected surprise. "I just happened to notice that for-sale sign. Thought you might be interested. This house isn't good for you. And every journey begins with a single step, you know." He considered Mad's expression and added, "But better late than never. First thing in the spring, all right?"

Mad shrugged and promised him she would think about it, without exactly specifying what she would think about. But she couldn't imagine actually leaving this house. She couldn't imagine it would ever let her go.

She was actually watching at just the right moment one day, midway through September, when a dragon, lustrous green, emerged from the quarry lake. Drops of water fell like diamonds from the tips of its wings and scattered from its lashing tail as it climbed into the sky. Its claws and its spiky mane were transparent as water, its eyes lucent as pearls. Its wingspan might have been twelve feet, or fifteen, or twenty—Mad couldn't tell. But it was easily big enough to snatch up the Lindstrand's pit bull Romeo, far less a tiny dog like Lila. Surely the dragon wouldn't actually pluck a dog right off someone's back deck, but Mad picked up Lila and held the little dog close. The dragon didn't approach them, of course. It turned and turned again, spiraling into the sky.

"They never actually attack anything," she muttered, more to herself than to Lila. This was true so far as she knew, but the words didn't sound as reassuring in her ears as she'd hoped. Perhaps she needed to hear someone else say that. Someone like Boyd Raske, who had the skill of making anything he said sound like he was handing down the word of God engraved on a stone tablet. But he would probably ask her what she thought would happen if a dragon that size emerged from the cliffs below her house, and tell her again that she should move to town. And she didn't want to argue. She put Lila down again and turned toward the kitchen door.

"Yoo hoo! Madison! Ms. Martin!" called a voice from the front of the house, familiar and unfamiliar at the same time. Lila dashed past Mad, yapping with excitement and delight at the idea of a visitor, but Mad's heart sank even before she remembered where she'd heard that voice. Then she remembered.

"Why now? Why me?" she muttered out loud.

It was the reporter, of course. By this time, Mad had learned the woman's name. It was Brittany Silverstone, or so she claimed. That sounded like a stage name to Mad; like the name chosen by a woman with more ego than taste because she imagined it would sound good when she was anchoring the evening news.

But whatever the reporter thought of herself, it didn't matter. It *wouldn't* matter. As she walked toward the front door, Mad told herself, still out loud, "This is *my* house. I can tell her to leave. If she won't go, she's trespassing, so I can *make* her leave." Since this was true, it should have sounded decisive and firm. To her own ears, it sounded...weak. Like the helpless protest of a child faced with a demanding adult.

"Ms. Silverstone, this isn't a good time," she told the woman through the screen door. But this, too, sounded weak.

"Oh, call me Brittany!" chirped the reporter, oozing overfamiliarity and nudging at the door as a hint that Mad should open it. "What an adorable little dog! I've seen you with her in town. Did you train her yourself? She's so cute!"

Mad was tempted to declare, *She bites—you'd better stay out there.* But it was too late. Brittany Silverstone had already nudged the door open and was energetically petting Lila, who was standing with her delicate little feet on the woman's knee, her beautiful plume of a tail waving.

"What a splendid place you have up here!" cried Ms. Silverstone, with blatantly overdone enthusiasm. "With that road, I bet you must get iced in practically all winter. But the view from the back must be stunning." Giving Lila one last pat, she straightened and strolled through the door and toward the back deck just as though Mad had invited her in. Lila dashed in circles around her, bouncing with delight. Mad trailed after them, stiff with resentment.

"Oh, you're painting!" The reporter had stepped out on the back deck and was gazing at the canvas propped on the easel, her hands clasped over her heart in theatrical delight.

"Trying to paint," Mad muttered, meaning to imply that Ms. Silverstone was interrupting. But the other woman affected not to hear her, and Mad couldn't quite bring herself to be openly rude.

The painting was of Lila, sitting on a blue velvet cushion, one small foot resting on a mouse-shaped toy with a little bit of stuffing peeking through a seam. The painting captured a bit of the mischief that always glinted in the little dog's eyes. But it was a trivial painting. A cute little cliché. Something to keep Mad's hands busy while she tried to sort out the blockage of imagination that was stopping her from real painting.

She knew exactly what was wrong, of course. But she couldn't figure out what true idea she might be trying to express, so she didn't know what to do to unblock her mind's eye.

"It's wonderful!" declared Ms. Silverstone. "So darling! The apple doesn't fall far from the tree, does it, Madison? Your mother must have been so proud you followed in her footsteps. Well, not *quite* in her footsteps, of course. Marissa's work was so much more *cultured* and *urbane*, but this has such *simple charm*, I'm sure you must have many *local fans."*

"Cultured," Mad repeated tonelessly. "Urbane. Is that what you'd call my mother's work?" She wanted to shout, Don't you mean *exploitative* and *perverted?*

But Ms. Silverstone leaned forward earnestly, protesting, "Oh, but *your* work recalls a *simpler time*, Madison! A simpler, more innocent time! Your work offers such a wonderful *contrast* to your mother's work! That's my idea, you see, an article featuring your sweet little puppies and fairy tales juxtaposed with your mother's sophisticated nudes. And a show, of course! I've approached a *very good* gallery, they could do *wonderful* things for your career, and let me tell you, Madison, they're *quite* interested! We all *know* your mother had paintings she never sold. She always said she kept the best for herself! You could make those available. Just think of your mother's wonderful portraits alternated with your own pretty little—"

"Get out," Mad ordered. "Get out." She no longer cared whether she was rude or offensive.

But Ms. Silverstone's expression remained unoffended. In fact, instead of offended, she looked...confused. She was still smiling, that same wide, insincere smile, as though it were the only expression she knew how to wear, but behind the smile she seemed simply blank.

Then Lila, tired of being ignored, yipped and danced and waved her plume of a tail, and Brittany Silverstone looked down at her, and in that moment her smile became real. And Mad realized, as though her mind's eye had opened, that the other woman truly did not understand why her plan was so offensive. That she honestly had no idea what the problem was with Marissa Martin's paintings. That the silly young woman actually thought she was being helpful. She simply was not very bright, and she'd been taught to believe she was being chic when she admired perversion.

Nothing Brittany Silverstone thought or believed or suggested or mistook mattered. None of it had to matter to Mad at all.

Then Lila began to bark again.

But it was different this time. There was a new note to her high-pitched little yap. It wasn't the excitement with which Lila greeted every stranger, it wasn't the delight with which she met people she knew, it wasn't the predatory let-me-at-em yap with which she demanded Mad let her out to chase a squirrel that had gotten into the yard. This was different. Louder. Lila was backing up and turning in circles and barking, barking, barking, angry and frantically defiant.

And the earth trembled.

Without a pause for conscious thought, Mad scooped Lila up in one hand, grabbed Brittany Silverstone's wrist in the other, and ran for the door, off the back deck and into the kitchen, through the studio and down the front hall, dragging the other woman with her, not listening to her confused protests, which were half drowned anyway by the force of Lila's barking. Out onto the porch and down the steps and along the rutted driveway, past her own car and Ms. Silverstone's car beyond that, with Lila twisting to get free and barking fearless challenge at the house behind them, on another twenty feet, and twenty feet more...and the young reporter jerked herself free and cried like an offended child, "Hey! What's the big idea?"

Mad stopped, panting with terror and exertion, glad to use both hands to keep Lila safe, not caring a whole lot what Ms. Silverstone did. They were far enough away. She thought they were. Probably.

She could hardly believe the younger woman hadn't figured out what was happening. But then, she'd already realized Ms. Silverstone wasn't very bright. Certainly nothing like as sharp and sensitive and perceptive as Lila.

Behind them, the house...swayed. It actually swayed. Mad could see the patched roof actually *tilt*, one end dropping at least a foot, and then another foot. Loose shingles skidded and fell. The tip of a young pine near the house whipped back and forth, and the whole house started to slide toward the cliff.

Behind them, there was the crunch of car tires on the gravel driveway, and Tommy's young voice cried, "Mad! You're okay!"

It was Boyd Raske, who pulled his car over to the side of the driveway and got out, one hand firmly keeping Tommy Kincaid at his side rather than letting the boy dash forward. He was pale, and grimmer than Mad have ever seen him. "A little farther back," he told Mad and Ms. Silverstone, not a suggestion.

Mad moved to join them, shakily, walking quickly but not running. She didn't dare run in case she dropped Lila. Ms. Silverstone didn't follow at once: she was staring—gaping really—at the slowly toppling house. By this time, it was practically on its side, leaning way out over empty space. Mad couldn't imagine trying to claw her way out of disaster, if she'd still been in the house now.

It wasn't just the house, either. The whole cliff edge was going, and she suspected her car and the reporter's car were going to go as well. The whole cliff was breaking, stone cracking like gunshots and the ripping groan and crash of wood as trees fell. Even Ms. Silverstone was backing away at last.

"It was Lila," Mad said. Her tone sounded amazingly calm in her own ears. "I was so distracted by—by other things, if she hadn't barked, I don't know if I would have understood. Not in time." The little dog was quiet now, trembling in Mad's grasp. Though even after all that, she was trembling, Mad could tell, more with excitement than fear.

"For me it was Tommy," Boyd told her. "I didn't like the thought of you up here, but without Tommy's stickpins, I wouldn't have known a dragon was likely to come out right below your house, or when. And even so, I would have been too late."

"You're exactly on time," Mad told him. She stood with Boyd and Tommy as the house slipped at last irrevocably over the shattering edge of the cliff and disappeared, carrying with it all Mad's memories and all the echoing ghosts of her mother.

And the dragon rose.

It was enormous. The size of an airplane. Larger. The size of a roc, that could lift an elephant in each taloned foot. Its long elegant head and graceful snakelike neck broadened to muscular shoulders and vast wings, gold banded with sapphire, that seemed to blot out half the world. Its neck and body and long whippy tail were a rich iridescent color, like a golden pearl streaked with carnelian. Its eyes, each larger in diameter than Mad could have reached with both outstretched arms, were black as the starless sky.

But though it passed so close that the wind of its wings nearly made Mad take a step back, it didn't see them, or didn't care. The sheer indifference in its gaze did make her flinch and step back, but Boyd put an arm around Mad to steady her. She leaned against his side, staring up at the dragon that was climbing into the sky.

In Mad's arms, Lila barked defiance, perfectly certain she was the one driving the dragon away. She was surely too small for a dragon to notice, surely too sensible to run too close to the newly broken edge of the cliff, but Mad was careful not to let her go.

Then the dragon was gone into the heights. It had seemed to move slowly, but it was gone. And so was Mad's mother's house, and a big chunk of the surrounding bluffs. Mad looked around, feeling unreal, as though she might be dreaming. Behind her, the ordinary world, everything just the same as always. Before her, the gravel driveway ran out onto a new raw edge of the earth, and beyond that only sky.

"Mad! You didn't save *anything!*" Tommy said,

sounding awed. "*Everything's* gone!"

"All the rest of your mother's paintings!" cried Ms. Silverstone, seeming to realize this for the first time.

The corners of Boyd's eyes crinkled with a hidden smile. "Every journey begins with a single step," he declared sententiously. "Or so they say. But I kind of think Ms. Martin was about ready to take that step."

Mad looked at Tommy, and then at Ms. Silverstone, and then at Boyd, and finally at Lila, still cradled safely in her arms. "I saved the only thing that mattered in that house," she said at last. "Deputy Raske's right. If the rest is gone, that's all right. Let it go. Let it all be past and gone."

"But where will you *live?*" Tommy asked, a bit plaintive. "I mean, that was your *house.*"

"I'll find a different house. A new house, just built. A house without any past at all. I hear there's a nice one on Elm."

"Well, as long as there's a good yard for Lila," Tommy said authoritatively, and looked puzzled when Mad laughed.

Mad painted her mother's house broken at the foot of the bluffs. She painted the rubble, all splintered wood and broken stone, uprooted trees and shattered windows, surrounded by flaming oaks above and ice-green water below. High above the cliffs, the sky was commanded by the sapphire-and-pearl dragon. The unkind past lying in ruins below the wings of the unknown future, for of course no one knew whether there might yet be more dragons, or whether the ones that had already emerged might return. But the dragon in the painting did not seem interested in anything below.

The dragon drew the eye, of course. It was meant to draw the eye. But if one looked particularly closely at the wreckage below the bluffs, one might see a painting, upside down so whatever image it had held was invisible. Its frame was broken, and a twisted spike had torn through the canvas. In front of this, poised triumphantly atop the broken rubble, stood a tiny dog, five pounds of fluff and courage, not only proudly defending all her territory against enormous dragons, but completely unimpressed by lingering ghosts.

Mad had had offers for this piece, including, surprising her, one from Brittany Silverstone, and one from the gallery Ms. Silverstone had gotten interested in Marissa Martin's daughter. But she knew she wouldn't sell it. She was going to hang it herself, in this new house. Somewhere she could see it, and be reminded that the past could after all be torn down and left behind, as a dragon left behind the stone in which it had incubated; and that a sufficiently indomitable spirit could face any challenge, however outsized, with glad confidence.

"You should hang it over your couch in the living room," Boyd said from the garden gate. He already knew she meant to keep this painting, although Mad hadn't said so and he hadn't asked.

He'd dropped by, as he did, just keeping an eye on Mad, almost the way he kept an eye on anyone else in town. But not quite. Just as he would let her pour him a cup of coffee almost but not quite as he would accept a fresh-baked cookie from Mrs. Kincaid.

Lila raced over from the far side of the yard, where she'd been hunting dragonflies, and leaped confidently into Boyd's arms. He caught her without fuss and told her what a fine fierce hunter she was, and smiled at Mad when he found her studying him.

"Maybe I'd like to paint you with her," she told him.

He didn't say, *But you never paint anyone's portrait*. He only said, "I think—or I hope—that I might like to see myself through your eyes, Maddie Rose."

Mad thought he might. She hoped he might. She thought she might like to see herself through his eyes, too. She didn't ask how he'd known her middle name, or why he'd suddenly decided to call her by it. She thought she might be willing to be called by a new name, now. She thought she might be willing at last to let him show her the world he saw.

THE KIEBA

The final version of The Mountain of Kept Memory *differs
quite a bit from the first draft. Originally Erest was a main character.
Then he got cut and Gulien took over Erest's role, with considerable
revision of the plot to make that work.* Mountain *wound up a tighter,
better novel for the revision, but the change did leave me with an
orphaned character and the first part of his story.*

*Luckily the Kieba has been around for a really long time, more
than long enough for many small-scale human dramas to play out
around her and around her mountain. I moved Erest's story to an
earlier time, so this novella takes place several generations before
the events of* The Mountain of Kept Memory, *just a few years after
the first few families settled at the foot of the Kieba's mountain.*

The day his little brother Kevi was stolen was the
same day Erest climbed over the Kieba's wall for the
second time in his life.

The first time he had climbed that wall, he had
hardly known what he was doing. That had been ten
years ago, almost. Erest had been only nearly five. His
father Big Tomren and his mother Elina, and his older
brother and sister, and his father's brother Uncle Toras
and his mother's brother Uncle Gilad and both their
wives and three older cousins—they had all made their
way to the bend of the river below the Kieba's mountain
that spring, to build homes and barns, plow land for

golden drylands wheat and deep purple amaranth, fence pastures for goats and three milch cows and a bull, plant cottonwoods and willows and tough, hardy apples along the river, and make a new home for themselves.

The river had brought them, of course; the river that meant there was no need for the hard, dangerous work of sinking a well. It was a good river, neither very wide nor very deep, but reliable even after several years of drought. Farms stretched all along the length of that river, except here, close by the foot of the Kieba's mountain, where people were afraid to settle. When Erest's family came there, they had to go two full days' travel past the next-nearest farm. It was hard, building without neighbors. But they weren't afraid. Or maybe some of them might have been a little bit afraid. But Erest's father said unfailing water was a kind of liquid courage that would last longer than the kind that came from a few too many mugs of beer.

Erest hadn't understood the joke, not then. But he knew it was a joke, because his father, Big Tomren, didn't need to build up his courage with either water or beer. His father was already the bravest man in the world; that was why he wasn't scared of the Kieba. Erest and his brother and his sister and their cousins weren't scared at all, either. Little Tomren and Taria and Aris and Cam and Riana were just as wildly excited as Erest to live at the very base of the Kieba's mountain, right outside her wall—and disappointed that they never saw the Kieba herself, not once. Not when the first small, cramped house went up, nor when the goats were turned loose in the first pasture, nor even when their mother left hopeful little gifts of wheat rolls or molasses cakes on top of the Kieba's wall.

The gifts were always gone in the morning. Little Tomren would run out to check before breakfast and then run back to tell the others. It never occurred to

Erest, not until years later, that a fox or crow or one of the small drylands deer might have eaten the bread.

That summer, when Erest had been just about to turn five, he had been an unpredictable little boy with more energy than a puppy and more curiosity than any ten kittens—or so his mother, Elina, always said when she was telling a rare guest that baby story.

All Erest's life, his mother told that story to almost every traveler who passed a night at their farm. Guests always wanted to know all about the Kieba. The story embarrassed Erest every time. His mother always laughed when she said the part about energy and curiosity, but she meant it all the same. "Too brave for his own good, and far too adventurous," she would say fondly, smiling at Erest. "From the time he could toddle, Erest always wanted to go farther than anyone else, and he was too little to know he might get into trouble. All my sons are fearless. It's hard on a woman to have fearless sons."

Though it embarrassed him, before the accident Erest had liked it when his mother told travelers that story. His mother left out the scarier, more difficult parts. She made it all about Erest's childish bravery and adventurousness, so the story always made him feel brave and adventurous. Now...now it was different.

After the accident, everything was different. His mother still told that story. Now Erest hated it. But he couldn't let his mother see he hated the story, because it would hurt her—and hurt Kevi too. Especially Kevi. Right after the accident, Erest had *wanted* to make his little brother feel bad. He was ashamed of that now. So he made himself pretend not to hate that baby story about courage and adventure.

Usually few travelers came by Erest's family's farm. Going around by Little Caras instead of straight east added many days of travel to anybody's journey, but going the long way also let travelers avoid passing close to the Kieba's mountain. The people of Carastind might be proud that the Kieba made her home in their country, but even so most travelers went by the other road, the one that cut far south from the great city of Caras, ran through the drylands to Little Caras in the curve of its oxbow lake, and then circled north and east again until it came at last to Kamee, hard against the river, sixty miles east of the farm. From Kamee the road led away to the whole world: to Estenda, on the other side of the highlands, and then on and on, to Illian and far Markand. Erest had looked at his older brother's maps, so he knew how it was.

But the spring after the accident, it seemed that one traveler after another took the shorter way and stopped at the farm because it was the best place for miles and miles. If Erest's mother thought a traveler or a party of travelers looked respectable, she would let them roll out their blankets in the fragrant hay barn and feed them supper, and if they wanted to hear about the Kieba, which they always did, she always liked to tell that baby story about Erest.

When he'd been little, Erest had always thought it was too bad they always wanted to talk about the Kieba instead of their own adventures. The Kieba never did anything anyway. Or she did lots of things, no doubt, all kinds of secret magic that kept the world safe from plague and disaster. But she always did it up there on her mountain, so there was nothing anybody could *see*. But travelers didn't want to talk about themselves. They always wanted to know what it was like to live in the shadow of the Kieba's mountain. They clearly thought they were brave to spend a night on the farmstead. Erest had never quite understood why people were afraid of the Kieba, but he supposed growing up in the shadow of her mountain and believing she accepted gifts of bread and cakes made it hard to be nervous of her. Most people weren't so used to knowing she was right there, practically a neighbor. But they always wanted to hear all about her, and so Erest's mother always told that story about Erest climbing over her wall.

Now that Erest knew he would spend his *whole life* watching other people come and hearing their stories and then watching the dust that rose over the road as they went on their way... now he knew he would never, ever go anywhere himself...he didn't want to hear about anybody else's adventures any more than he wanted to hear about his own.

Erest knew, he had always known, that his mother had hoped he would stay on the farmstead, wed a sensible girl and bring her here, build an addition onto the main house, raise wheat and amaranth and cattle and goats, have children of his own that would grow up and build homes in their turn on this sprawling farmstead along the river, in the shadow of the Kieba's mountain. His father had hoped a son of his would stay on the farmstead; he had hoped that Erest would name a son of his own Tomren again; that there would be men of that name here in this farmstead in fifty years, and a hundred, and two hundred. A man wanted to build something that would outlive him.

Erest had wanted all those things too, except first he had wanted to see at least some of the world. The city of Caras—he wanted to see that. Or maybe he wanted to go farther, the other way, east, venture out of Carastind, travel through Illian or Markand. How wonderful that would be! And then he could come back and tell his mother...and everyone ...all the stories about those far places. He'd have those memories for all the rest of his life, even if he never went more than a day or two from the farmstead again.

Now he knew he would never travel anywhere. Worse than that, he would never even be able to put in the kind of day's work a man should, never wed a girl. For the past year or more, Erest had looked forward to seeing the miller's daughter Liss when he helped take grain to the mill. But he hadn't seen Liss since the accident. He never wanted to see her again. What girl could like a man with only half a left foot? What kind of *man* could Erest ever be, when he would never be able to manage a man's work, but would have to stay inside, helping his mother and sisters and girl cousins with easy chores that could be done sitting down?

Erest had thought one day he would have been proud to name a son Tomren. That would never happen now. Nothing at all would ever happen. The only adventure Erest would *ever* be able to look back on was the time when he was five, and climbed over the Kieba's wall.

Erest had been supposed to collect eggs from the hen yard, which was his task then. It was a task for little children, for the hen yard was near the house and all the hiding places where the hens laid their eggs were low, close to the ground, mostly near the roosts that lined the covered end of the yard. Erest was supposed to feed the hens and the strutting red-feathered rooster. Then he was supposed to find the eggs and bring them to the kitchen, and then check the withy fence that kept the hens in their yard and the dryland foxes and the little tawny desert cats out. He was supposed to weave more withies into the fence if he found any weak places, and make sure the pans of water under the shaded roosts were clean and full.

That was a lot for a child who was just five. Erest did not mind searching out the eggs, although he had to carry a switch to keep the rooster and the mean black hen away from his bare legs. He didn't mind washing and filling the heavy pans of water: that was an important task in the drylands. Checking the fence was also important, because if a fox got into the hen yard, it might kill all the hens and that would be a disaster for the whole family. But creeping along the fence, looking for any place a fox or little drylands cat could get in, was awful. It was boring and uncomfortable and he had to pay attention the whole time because there always *were* places where more withies ought to be woven into the latticework, and then that work was also boring and uncomfortable.

It was just natural that a boy would feel he deserved a chance to do something fun after all that. He had searched out the eggs, twelve of them, enough for griddlecakes for everyone tomorrow as well as soda bread today. It was a good thought: griddlecakes made with milk and fine-ground wheat flour instead of amaranth porridge cooked with water. Erest liked porridge, especially with molasses, but griddlecakes with butter and honey were better.

A boy who'd found as many as twelve eggs deserved a chance to go look for adventure, especially on a perfect summer morning when the sun was not yet killing hot. The small kitchen garden was planted, but the seeds had gone in late and the plants were small. There was nothing to harvest. The weeds hadn't had a chance to start crowding the good plants yet, so that was all right. He might have gone to watch his brother finish milking the goats, but that wouldn't be very interesting and anyway, if he did, Little Tomren would probably find something else for him to do. And his cousins were worse; they would definitely want him to help with their chores.

Besides, Erest was *allowed* to go down to the river after finishing with the hens. He was *allowed* to climb the big cottonwoods and look for wood duck eggs, or splash in the shallows and catch frogs, as long as he also watered the little seedling trees.

So it only seemed fair he might go the other way, through the pasture, and just *look* at the Kieba's wall. That was the best adventure he could think of, because if you climbed up to the top you could sit on the edge of the wall and look over. Maybe you'd see something special: one of the falcons or foxes that wasn't really a falcon or a fox, but one of the Kieba's servants. Maybe you'd even see the Kieba herself. Little Tomren claimed he'd seen her: walking high up on the slopes of her mountain. He said you could see right away she'd been a goddess once, long ago, at the beginning of the world, but he wouldn't explain how you could tell.

Little Tomren made things up sometimes. But Erest believed with all his heart that Little Tom truly had climbed to the top of the wall and glimpsed the Kieba. He wanted to do the same; he wanted to do more; he longed to show his brother he was brave too.

Erest had set the basket of eggs carefully aside in the shade outside the kitchen door where his sisters or mother would look for it. Then he ran down to the river, but instead of turning to follow it upstream, away from the farmstead, he turned the other way and followed it right through the just-finished back pasture. Luckily the bull, lying in the shade of the cottonwoods, did not notice him. Erest went quietly through that part of the pasture, careful as a fox, because he was very brave but he did not want to risk the bull coming to see who he was and why he was in the pasture. He was not a mean bull, but he was a bull and not an animal for a little boy to tease. But Erest was careful and quiet, or else the bull was lazy and not inclined to investigate a small trespasser.

Then Erest came to the Kieba's wall.

It was not a wall meant to stop people from getting onto the Kieba's mountain. It was only shoulder high for a grown man, which meant hardly above elbow-high on a man as big as Erest's father, though of course the top was far above Erest's head. Still, the wall was meant only to mark out the boundary of the Kieba's land so that people would know not to trespass. The stones were rough, providing easy handholds, and the top of the wall was flat and smooth so a boy could easily climb up and sit there on the wall and see the Kieba's mountain, or look the other way, far over the flat drylands.

Only on that day, following the curve of the wall, Erest had stumbled upon a place where the winter weather or the violent spring storms had cracked one of the big stones straight through. That stone had fallen, and then some of the flat red rocks laid across the top of the wall had fallen as well. The miniature rockslide had left an irresistible gap for any boy who'd bravely made his way through the pasture and past the bull. Erest knew, with the perfect surety of a very young child, that no one in the entire world could possibly have turned his back on a gap like that one. Just a step and another step and he could pull himself up and stand right in the narrow gap, with the Kieba's forbidden mountain *right there*, so near Erest could reach down and touch the gritty soil without even stepping through the broken place in the wall. So of course he had to do it, and then when the warm red earth did not open up to swallow him whole, how could he possibly resist the impulse to step right through and stand just for a moment on the Kieba's forbidden mountain?

Of course he had to do that, just so he could tell Little Tomren he had.

"How a baby that age could get all that way and then keep right on going up the mountain, one little foot after another!" That was what his mother always said later, when she told that story. "But that's Erest. Even when he was so little, once he started out on a journey, he would never turn back halfway." Erest had been wearing a blue shirt that day ten years ago. The dye had streaked, that was why his mother had gotten the shirt cheap, but it was a good bright blue, like a flake off the sky. That was how she had spotted him, already high up on the mountain's shoulder.

At that point in the story, travelers would always turn to stare out the kitchen window at the Kieba's mountain. It was the only mountain in all of Carastind. It wasn't a great grand mountain, the kind travelers said raked into the sky in southern Markand. The Kieba's mountain was rounded at the top, and lumpy where it trailed off into a series of bumps on the western side. Like the surrounding land, it was all red sandstone and dry sun-bleached grasses, with here and there stunted scrub oaks and pines. But it was mountain enough to stand out starkly from the farm's pastures, from the fields of golden drylands wheat and purple amaranth and the flat desert beyond.

And, of course, the Kieba's mountain had her wall all the way around it, miles and miles of wall, which made it different from every other mountain in the world. The wall was because the Kieba lived at the top and she liked her privacy. Anybody, no matter whether they came from a town hardly more than a day's travel from the mountain or from far Caras, knew better than to climb it and intrude on the Kieba's privacy.

Erest had meant to step right back into the gap, and through it, returning quickly to the safety of the farmstead's side of the wall. Only he went just a little way up the mountain first, just a few steps, so he could look for an interesting stone or something else he could show Little Tom to prove he'd come up onto the Kieba's mountain. He'd found a good one, a broken pebble almost as big as his fist, plain on the outside but glinting with purple crystals on the inside. He'd pounced on that, crowing with delight because his brother would have to believe him now.

Then he'd run back to the gap, but when he'd started to go back through it, he'd discovered the bull had heaved himself to his feet and was ambling slowly toward the wall.

Erest understood immediately that there was no possible way for even a very small boy to sneak through the gap and across the pasture now. But the gap was much too narrow for the bull to come through after him. Obviously the way to stay safe would be to follow the wall around to the edge of the pasture and then climb over it there, once he was out of the bull's way. The Kieba shouldn't mind—he was sure she wouldn't mind. Nearly sure. He would just stay right by the wall, which was nearly like never having crossed it at all.

Except he found after he'd gone just a little way that the wall was actually smoother and less easy to climb on the inner side.

So he thought he would find a scrub oak near the wall and climb that. Except then he didn't see any tree growing close to the wall.

Then when he'd stopped to think what might be better to do, he'd happened to look up the mountain and he'd found a big dark-eyed hare sitting up on its hind legs and watching him, ears attentive, not more than a short stone's throw away. A thrill went up his spine: maybe that hare might be one of the Kieba's servants and not a real hare at all. Of course he had to try to approach the hare, any boy would have to speak to it and see if it would answer. So he'd started up the mountain instead.

The Kieba's forbidden mountain! Even years later, Erest wondered how anybody could expect a boy to stay away from that his whole life, and never mind all that about curiosity and cats. There were hundreds of stories about the Kieba, so many you could tell a story every day for a whole year and still have tales left untold. She had once been a goddess, and then when all the other gods and goddesses had fallen and died, she had outlived them all. She wasn't a goddess anymore—Erest didn't understand that part, but that was what people said. The Kieba was no longer a goddess, but she was still immortal and still commanded the powers of the dead gods. All the ordinary kings of the world listened to her and obeyed her commands, not just because she was so powerful but because she made cures for all the plagues that beset the world. Without the Kieba, the whole world would wither and die.

The Kieba ruled a thousand servants in the form of hawks and wolves and foxes and hares. She ruled other servants too, that had far stranger and more terrifying forms. That was what Little Tom always said when he told one of those stories. He always said it in a special impressive tone: *servants of strange and terrifying forms*. Erest had only the vaguest ideas about what those forms might be. He imagined shadowy things with lots of teeth, or maybe shining creatures of mist and light. Either way, he knew the Kieba saw everything and she could do anything.

Anybody would have been curious. Anyone would have wanted to look at the hare, find out if it was truly a hare or something else, something mysterious and important. Of course Erest had forgotten all the stories about trespassers. He struck up the mountain directly toward the hare. Then naturally he had followed it when it dropped to all fours and lolloped slowly away around the curve of the mountain's shoulder. What else could a boy do, when the hare looked back when he stopped? The morning sun caught in its liquid eyes so they glinted blood-red. The hare *wanted* him to follow it. Erest was sure it wanted him to follow it. Or he told himself he was sure of that. He followed the hare, scuffing his toes through the gritty soil and scrambling over tilted slabs of red stone, holding the pebble with the crystals inside tight in his fist.

Then he had looked up and found the Kieba herself watching him from a shelf of broken stone.

She had hardly been any distance from him then, and she was clearly watching him, so there was no question of slipping away unnoticed. Only he had not realized at first that she was the Kieba. She hadn't looked a bit like a goddess, nor even like a woman who had once been a goddess. He'd thought the Kieba would have the head of a hawk or the slit-pupiled eyes of a cat or maybe wide shining wings like a dragonfly. Her hands didn't have six fingers or claws instead of fingernails; her skin wasn't furred or feathered or anything but ordinary skin. She didn't look a *bit* like a goddess. She just looked like a normal person. She wasn't even any taller than Erest's mother, and she might have been about the same age, so maybe she was old, but she didn't look ancient or immortal. But even though she gazed at Erest, her expression was distant. Remote. Like she was thinking about other things that were much more important than a boy who'd ventured to her side of the wall. That made her seem strange even though she didn't have fur or wings or the head of a hawk.

Erest asked, *"Are* you the Kieba?" Then he said quickly, since she must be, "I'm not trespassing! I just wanted to look at the hare. Anyway, the wall was broken."

The Kieba smiled at this and put out a hand to him,

looking suddenly so ordinary that Erest forgot his momentary fear and came forward. "Broken, is it?" said the Kieba. "Yes, I see. Of course a brave child would come through the breach. What is your name?"

Erest was taken a little aback. It hadn't occurred to him that she might not know him, because didn't she know everything? But then she said, "You are Tomren's second son, yes? Erest is your name. You are how old? Five?" So she did know him after all.

Erest nodded, then reconsidered because he knew better than to lie to the Kieba. "*Almost* five. Soon. In summer, when the dragonflies come over the pastures, I'll be five then. My mother will make a cake and put a dragonfly on it, a purple one, with burnt sugar wings—if I ask her, she will. She made a cake with honey and pears and put a bee on it for Little Tom, but dragonflies are better than bees." He thought for a second and then added, because at five he wasn't above trying to bribe a goddess, "I'll bring you a piece of my cake if you like. I'll bring it through the gap in your wall." When she smiled, he added heroically, "The piece with the dragonfly and the sugar wings. That's the best part."

"You like dragonflies, do you?" The Kieba was clearly amused.

"I like the sugar," Erest said candidly. "I like the way it crunches and the way it sticks in my teeth." He showed her the pebble he'd found that was plain outside and filled with purple crystals on the inside. "The crystals are colored like a dragonfly, see?"

Then he turned, startled, as his father arrived.

Erest's father, Tomren, was a big, broad man with shoulders like one of the plow horses and immensely strong calloused hands and a deep, deep voice that had slammed down like a quiet but powerful hammerblow when Erest started to explain to him that this was the

276

Kieba.

"Erest," he said in a strange, hard, flat tone. "Son. Be quiet."

Then he strode forward, set one big hand on Erest's shoulder, dropped heavily to his knees, and said to the Kieba, "Forgive my son's trespass, Kieba. He is only a child. He doesn't know your law. Not yet. It's not his fault we—*I*, I didn't teach him well enough. I promise you, he will know better after this."

Until then Erest had thought the Kieba was nice but not much like a goddess. He was shocked speechless when he saw how his big, unshakable father was afraid of her.

"Indeed, I don't hold babies to account when they flout my law," the Kieba said to Big Tomren. "I hold their parents to account for that." Her tone had been distant, but friendly enough when she spoke to Erest. But her voice was different when she spoke to his father. She didn't sound friendly now. She sounded like stone, like her own mountain. Erest gripped his hollow pebble in both his hands and tried to figure out what she meant, but he hadn't understood, not then.

"That's right. That's just," Big Tomren agreed immediately. His deep voice was not suited to any swift tumble of words, but now he spoke quickly, as though he wanted to get the words out before the Kieba could decide what to do. He said, "I know there's a price to pay. I'll pay it. But let me take my son down, give him to his mother. Then I'll come back. I swear I will come back. I'll put you to no trouble. But let me take the boy to his mother first."

The Kieba just looked at Erest's father for a long moment. Tomren stared back at her, waiting. Erest didn't understand what any of it meant. But he understood *something*, because he hadn't tried to shake off his father's hand, even though his father's grip was tight enough to hurt. He would have bruises on his arm by evening, but he didn't protest. He didn't even wiggle. By then he was scared enough that he didn't dare move, far less interrupt.

At last the Kieba said, "You bid fair to become a good neighbor, Tomren. You and all your family. I don't mind your farm here. I like to look down at the home you are creating here. I like to see your happiness and industry. I will be pleased to see your family prosper. Take your son back across the wall. Teach him to respect my boundaries. That will satisfy me." Then she looked back at Erest. "That's called a geode, that hollow rock," she told him. "The crystals are amethysts. Keep it, if you like. Some people think geodes are lucky. Perhaps that one will bring you luck. You'll need luck if you go on as you've begun." Then she turned and walked away, up the mountain.

Erest remembered later how he felt, standing on the slope of the mountain, clenching the geode in his hand, watching the Kieba walk away. Somehow, that was the moment he really believed that she was a goddess. Or had been, once.

Guests always found the part about the lucky geode reassuring, for some reason. Not just the part where the Kieba said she liked Tomren's farm and liked having his family living at the foot of her mountain, but the part about the geode. They always wanted to see it. Erest always liked showing his geode to them.

Or he had liked that, before the accident.

Erest's father had carried him down the mountain. He had not explained very much about the Kieba. He would never have told any of the more brutal stories to a child of five. Erest had heard all those stories later. His father had only explained that people who went up the Kieba's mountain never came back down.

That had been enough. Erest had understood all at once that his father had expected to be one of those people who went up the mountain and didn't come down again. He had been shocked again when he finally understood that, shocked to tears. He was grateful his mother never put *that* in the stories, even if he had been only five. She also left out the part where Tomren stood by sternly while Erest carried stone after stone to repair the gap in the wall. Big stones, big enough that a child could only lift them with a struggle; and when there weren't enough loose ones on the right side of the wall, Erest's father had made his son carry the rocks from the surrounding countryside through the pasture one at a time. It had taken all that day and most of the next, and by the end Erest had been too exhausted to cry, even though the stones had rubbed blisters on his hands.

That story was a good one the way Erest's mother told it. The memory was...not entirely a good one if Erest thought about it too much and remembered it too well. But that story and those memories were why Erest climbed across the Kieba's wall the second time.

Erest knew he had to cross the wall after he realized, after everyone finally realized, that Kevi was gone and that he hadn't just strayed down to the river to get out of his chores.

After everyone realized why their most recent guest must have left so hurriedly before dawn, Erest knew he had to go up onto the mountain to find the Kieba.

So after Erest's father and Uncle Gilad and Uncle Toras and Aris and Cam, and Taria's husband Lucos and Riana's husband Chad and Chad's second cousin Merek saddled all the plow horses and the mules, and took every axe and heavy hammer they owned, and rode as fast as they could to try to catch up with the man who had taken Kevi, Erest, who was nearly fifteen and by all rights would have ridden with them except for his crippled foot, stood silently by with his mother and sister and the other women and watched the dust that followed them east and north along the road.

Then he made his way instead across the far pasture and scrambled up and over the Kieba's wall for the second time in his life.

It was a lot harder, now, to put one foot after another. This past spring Erest would have run across the pasture without thinking, or even noticing. Now it seemed to stretch out forever. He put one foot in front of the other: one step and then the scraping *thump* of his crutch. The crutch wasn't quite long enough anymore; it had been too short for a month or more now. He'd grown, but he hadn't wanted to say anything about it or ask Uncle Gilad, who was the best of them all with wood, to make him a new crutch. He'd even thought he could get by without a crutch, now. But by the time he was halfway across the pasture, he was really glad he hadn't been too proud to bring it. And then, when he clambered painfully across the Kieba's wall and started up the steep slope of the mountain, even more glad.

He'd left his geode with its hidden amethysts on Kevi's bed, trusting his brother *would* come home to find it there. He'd thought of bringing it with him, but then he'd decided he had to leave the geode for his brother. Kevi needed luck more than Erest did, now. Besides, how else was Kevi ever going to believe that Erest had really and truly forgiven him for the accident? Especially when Erest *had* blamed him for so long, and still did, a little. He tried not to. He was pretty sure he shouldn't. So he left the geode for Kevi, even though he missed its familiar weight in his pocket.

The only important thing he carried with him were memories. Memories of the Kieba saying, *I like to see your happiness and industry. I will be pleased to see your family prosper.* And, *Some people think geodes are lucky.* And then, after the accident, the memory of how she'd sent dozens of jet-and-citrine wasps to sting away the pain and stop the creeping infection.

She'd done that much for Erest. Surely she would do something for Kevi, when he was in even worse trouble.

The mountainside seemed a whole lot steeper than he remembered. There was no path. It wasn't like anybody was *supposed* to cross the wall and go up the mountain. Erest seemed to have come a long way already. When he looked back, he couldn't see the wall—only the rolling slope of the mountain and, seeming far below, the neat-bordered fields of wheat. Past those, the tawny grasses and red grit of the drylands reached out all the way to the horizon where the sun rested on the edge of the world. If he did not find the Kieba soon, it would be dark, and then what? His crippled foot ached steadily, and sometimes, when he put it down wrong, jolted with savage fire. Every time he passed a convenient rock, he wanted to stop and rest. He set his teeth and kept on.

There were birds here: little russet-capped sparrows flitting among the sparse grasses, and tiny finches with purple-streaked throats. It was so quiet on the mountain that Erest could hear the faint sound of their wings when the little birds fluttered up and the rustle of the grasses where they landed. The stories agreed that birds were the Kieba's eyes, but surely not little ones like those?

Some of the stories claimed that the Kieba might cut off a foot that had touched the ground on her side of the wall. Erest didn't know who had told him that one: one of his brothers, maybe, or one of the boys in Teree, the town where they went to have their grain ground at the mill. Lots of people believed it. He never had. Now he wondered if it could be true. It would be sort of funny if it were true.

Other stories were more interesting, but also sometimes more frightening. One he'd heard only this past spring claimed that the Kieba might imprison a man who dared spend the night on her mountain, that she could open up the stone so that he would fall into the everlasting darkness beneath the mountain and be trapped there forever. The story claimed that if you sat on her wall at midnight, you could hear the cries of men imprisoned below the earth. The sons of the miller in Teree had asked Erest if that were true, so he had snuck out of his bed for three nights in a row and listened. He hadn't heard anything except the high voices of bats and the shriek of an owl, but the next month he'd told the boys he had heard faint screams because the story was so much better that way. He found himself listening again now, though, even though it wasn't dusk yet and not even the bats were out.

Liss, the miller's pretty daughter, had shuddered at his description of the faint underground screaming. Erest thought of that now, of how she had pretended to believe him so that she could also pretend to be frightened and he could act brave. He was almost sure she'd been pretending, even though she'd sounded really sincere when she'd sworn she would never go anywhere near the Kieba's mountain. Her brothers, Oren and Kemris, had begged to go home with Erest and listen all night, but their mother wouldn't let them visit Tomren's farm even though all the boys swore they wouldn't set foot on the wrong side of the wall. That had suited Erest because, after all, he'd made it up about the screams.

At the time, he hadn't minded frightening Liss. Or letting her pretend to be frightened. He'd thought he would see her next month too, and the month after that. There would be plenty of time to coax her to visit and coax her mother to allow it. Her brothers could have escorted her, his own mother could have met her; everything would have been just perfect. He was sure his mother would have liked Liss. He was sure Liss would have learned not to be afraid of the Kieba, except a little bit so Erest and the other boys could show her how brave they all were.

But then, after the accident, he had never gone back to Teree at all.

Liss actually had come to the farm for a few days, though, with her mother, right after the accident, to help Erest's mother. Erest had almost no memory of that. That had been after his foot...what was left of his foot...had gotten infected. He didn't remember much about that part, not until after the Kieba's wasps had stung away the infection, and then the wasps had frightened Liss and her mother, Kevi had explained later, and they'd gone back to Teree before Erest even knew they were there.

Which had been stupid. The Kieba had sent those wasps to help. It didn't make any sense to be scared of them. His mother had said, *They don't like to be reminded the Kieba is right here.* Which was also silly, because thinking of that should have made them feel better, safer, as long as they stayed on the right side of the wall.

He was sure Liss hadn't been frightened. Her mother was nice, but scared of everything.

There were just so many stories, and some of them were a little bit scary if you believed them. One said the Kieba might turn trespassers into foxes or cats or crows or owls, and another that she might cut them to pieces and feed them to the animals that were her servants and pets, and yet another that she would flay them alive and use their skins to give her creatures human shape so they could walk unseen among men. By now Erest had heard *all* the stories. He'd made plenty up himself, to see how much he could get the boys in Teree to believe, so he knew they weren't all true. But some of them might be true. *He* hadn't made up that one about the everlastingly dark cells underneath the mountain. Maybe that story was true.

And this time, unlike when he'd been a baby, Erest didn't even see a hare to show him the way. He couldn't help but wonder whether maybe the Kieba might be a lot less tolerant of a boy who was nearly fifteen trespassing on the wrong side of her wall than she had been of a child not even five...

Above him, the Kieba said, "Well, young Erest. I admit I am surprised."

Erest was surprised, too. He jumped, and of course his weight came down wrong, and he nearly fell. He clung to his crutch with both hands, sweating with pain and clenching his teeth, unable to speak. He'd had a whole speech prepared, and now he forgot it. He'd meant to say—he'd meant—well, he wasn't sure, but he knew he looked clumsy and stupid. He could feel himself turning red.

The Kieba stood on a ledge above him, the shadows from the higher slopes stretching out long around her. She looked just as he remembered her. In his memory, she looked old. But he had been only five, after all, and he saw now that the Kieba wasn't old at all, even though she looked exactly the same. She had a smooth unlined face and skin that had never been weathered by sun and wind. She wasn't as tall as he remembered. He thought that if the Kieba were standing next to him on level ground, she might actually be shorter than he was. He would have thought a goddess would be taller. Even a woman who had once been a goddess. Even if that had been a long time ago.

"Well?" said the Kieba.

Erest tried to decide if she sounded offended, and thought she didn't. Not exactly *offended*. But she didn't sound exactly friendly either. He said quickly, "It's Kevi. I mean, a man took Kevi. He pretended to be a—a merchant or a trader or something, but then he *stole* him."

The Kieba tilted her head, not seeming much alarmed. "This man broke my law at the very foot of my mountain? This seems unlikely."

Erest had never considered the possibility that she might not believe him. He stared at her, trying to decide if she *actually* didn't believe him or if it just sounded that way. "I know," he said. "I mean, I wouldn't think so either, except maybe he wasn't from Carastind. He said he was from Estenda. Maybe people from Estenda, I mean, they're so far away, maybe they don't know you like we do..." his voice trailed off at the skeptical lift of the Kieba's eyebrows.

"Estenda lies under my eye. I assure you, its people know me," said the Kieba. "Kevi is your younger brother, yes? But not so many years younger. A boy, but not a child. An adventurous boy. Perhaps he wished to go with this man. Perhaps he wished to go out into the broad world—"

"No!" Erest protested, and faltered, realizing he had interrupted her. But she did not seem angry. She only watched him patiently, waiting for him to explain. He went on more carefully. "They take children Kevi's age. Child-thieves, I mean. They steal children who are old enough to travel fast, but not old enough to get away. They say they aren't breaking your law, they say they aren't slaves, those children. They make them sign something, and they pay them, but only a little, not enough to buy themselves free—"

The Kieba held up one hand, silencing his clumsy explanation. But she only asked, "How do you know this, Erest?"

He hesitated, not knowing how to answer this because everyone knew about child-thieves. Everybody knew child-thieving was rare, but not as rare now as it had been ten or twenty years ago. "I—everyone knows. Even on a trip to little Teree, anybody younger than sixteen or seventeen, my father won't let us to go anywhere alone. Not even me, I mean when I could go that far, and I'll be fifteen this summer."

"Everyone knows this."

Her tone was so flat, Erest couldn't tell whether she believed him or not. "My father says children stolen in Carastind are sold on to merchants in Estenda, and then on to Illian or Markand, and the people who should stop it take bribes and look the other way. My mother...she wanted to ask you..." She had wanted to ask the Kieba why she allowed this trade in children, but Erest's father wouldn't hear of her taking such a risk and so in the end she had not gone up the mountain to seek the Kieba.

And now Kevi...Erest truly didn't want to think about what might happen to his little brother. He wished his mother had gone to ask the Kieba her question. But he wasn't sure he should admit that she had wanted to trespass on the Kieba's mountain. Except maybe he wanted even less to admit that his father had stopped her. He looked into the Kieba's bland, unreadable face and couldn't tell whether she was angry, or with whom.

No one in Erest's family had thought they needed to worry for themselves. Child-thievery was something that happened in towns, not outlying farms, and certainly not so close to the Kieba's mountain.

And now Kevi was gone.

The man from the city had seemed so pleasant, and much too well-to-do to need to steal anything. He'd worn an impractical white shirt with fancy white buttons and finely fitted breeches of doeskin. He had boots that laced up the side and a really nice horse. Why would a man like that need to steal a child he happened across along his way?

Not even Erest's mother, who was usually good at judging people, had suspected that this polite well-to-do man could be a thief. Worse: a child-thief. How should she have guessed, how should any of them have guessed someone so nasty would come along this unpeopled road, or dare pass so close to the Kieba's mountain? Or that a man like that would look like anyone else, that he'd be *able* to put on so friendly a show or speak so nicely?

The traveler had bowed to Elina, his hand over his heart, as though he bowed to farm wives every day. He'd been riding fast all day, he said, and he was delighted to find a pleasant homestead here in the middle of the drylands. He would be happy to pay silver for a comfortable room and a good dinner and grain for his horse.

Erest's mother had wondered aloud, as she sent her family hurrying to make a room ready and fetch cream from the cold cellar and apple preserves from the pantry, why such a man might be in so great a hurry that he rode fast all day, and alone. Plainly he was at the very least a wealthy man, maybe even a minor noble. He obviously ought to travel with servants and guards and perhaps even his own pavilion, so that he need not ask shelter of ordinary folk. But she had not demanded answers of the man himself.

No doubt she asked herself later why she had not questioned the man more strictly.

It wouldn't have mattered. He would have lied, of course. Erest knew better than anyone how skilled and smooth a liar he was.

Their guest had been perfectly willing to talk

casually with Erest and Kevi when they went out to take care of his horse, and Erest hadn't noticed anything suspicious about him. He hadn't *looked* for anything suspicious. He'd just thought their guest friendly and good-humored, surprisingly unassuming for a rich man. Mostly Erest had admired his horse. This was a dark bay mare, almost black, with dappled flanks and a pretty head, clean legs and a deep chest and plenty of slope to her shoulder. Erest had admired Little Tom's gelding the last time his brother had visited, but this mare was better.

She'd been working hard in the heat and took some time to walk down. Erest would have liked to walk her, but of course he couldn't; Kevi got to do that. But when she was cool, Erest leaned his crutch against the stable wall and helped brush her. She was well-mannered as well as beautiful and let him steady himself with a hand against her hip as he rubbed the sweat marks off her back. When he was finished, Erest patted her neck and gave her a piece of dried apple. He wished he had a horse like her, not that a farm had much use for pretty horses. He couldn't see a mare like this hitched to a plow. Though he thought if he did own her, he'd be more careful not to let her risk overheating.

The man thanked Kevi for walking his horse cool and stood by chatting in a friendly way while Erest cleaned her up and Kevi brought down hay and grain for her.

He gave his name as Cherest Aren. He said he was a merchant from Estenda and claimed to trade in glass and unpolished jewels from Carastind, and also in dyes and alum from Illian, and silk and fine cloisonné from Markand. Erest had believed him—maybe that was all even true, just not the whole truth. But he thought now that it had been a great bundle of lies. Except the part about being from Estenda. That part, Erest thought had probably been true. Everyone knew that the Estendan merchant-princes had never forgiven Carastind for breaking away from Estendan control, and then they resented Carastind again because the Kieba lived there and not in Estenda. He could believe a wealthy Estendan might try to skirt the edges of her law.

But at the time, neither he nor Kevi had seen any reason not to believe every word, nor had either of them worried about the man being Estendan.

"You should meet Little Tom!" exclaimed Kevi. "Our brother. He trades in gems and dyes too. And wheat, but that's boring compared to gems and things, except he says wheat is reliable and important. He brought us this wonderful clockwork toy from Markand last time he visited—a bird that hops and sings, I'll show you when we go in, it's much better than wheat. He works for a merchant in Caras, but he travels sometimes, just like you. You don't know him? Tomren is his name, really."

Aren laughed indulgently. "There are so many merchants in Caras! I don't know your brother, but good for him. Trade can be an exciting life for a decisive man of keen judgment and good taste. He's right, you know: wheat is a more reliable basis for trade than gemstones. Men can live without gems, but everyone needs bread. But I admit I favor silk above all other goods. I'm on my way to Markand now, to see about a silk orchard that isn't yielding as it should."

"A silk orchard," repeated Kevi, obviously trying to figure this out. He straightened up from brushing the dust off the mare's legs, his expression deeply skeptical. "Silk doesn't grow on *trees*!"

"Ah, but it does, in a way! You grow trees, and worms eat the leaves and make the silk."

"Worms!" Kevi looked impressed. "Is that true? Are they big ones? I wish I could see them! Someday I *will* see them." He was clearly trying to imagine worms that made silk. "Someday I'll go to Markand and see the silk orchards. I'll go to Illian, too—"

Erest had said nothing, and Kevi had suddenly realized that of course *Erest* would never get to go to Markand or anywhere else exciting—and remembered it was his fault. The younger boy fell abruptly silent.

"I've no doubt someday you'll travel the world, a bright, brave boy like you," Aren said cheerfully, missing the awkwardness of the pause. "No, the worms aren't very big at all, but they're special. They're caterpillars, really. Boys your age climb the trees to pick the youngest, most tender leaves where the moths lay their eggs. Silk farmers bring the eggs indoors to hatch and those boys have to pick a lot more leaves to feed the worms as they grow. It's a job for the bravest boys, because the trees are so tall."

"*I'd* climb them!" declared Kevi, lured out of his self-consciousness by this image. "If I was in Markand, I'd climb them all the time! I'm not scared of heights. Maybe someday I *will* go to Markand."

Erest had pretended to be so busy checking the mare's feet that he wasn't listening at all, but he couldn't help darting a quick, angry glance at his brother at that last declaration.

"I can see you wouldn't be afraid," said the man lightly, looking Kevi up and down. "You have the build for climbing, and you're neat with your hands."

In his memory, Erest could see the avaricious look in the man's eyes and hear the speculation in his tone. If Erest had been paying attention to anything but his own anger and the effort of hiding it, he might have noticed those signs at the time. But he hadn't noticed anything, hadn't suspected anything. Not until it was too late.

"Anyway," Cherest Aren had added, "I'm sure any boy who lives way out here, away from everything, on a lonely farm like this one, isn't scared of much.

Especially with a haunted mountain right next to you."

Erest could see that Kevi wanted to say, "It's not *haunted*." He wanted to say that himself, but it would be rude to correct a guest. He said instead, "There's nothing to worry about. We stay on our side of the wall—"

"Mostly," said Kevi, slyly.

"And the Kieba stays on her mountain," Erest finished, giving his brother a look because there was hardly any story he wanted to hear less, anymore. Kevi ducked his head and said instead, to Aren, "Are you hungry? Supper will be ready soon."

"Wonderful!" said the man, and led the way out of the barn just as though he owned it and the boys were hired servants. Kevi ran after him. Erest followed more slowly, careful of his foot and awkward with the crutch, even after so many weeks. He wasn't exactly offended at Aren's superior air. The man was rich, after all. Though it did seem a little strange that he would be traveling alone if he were rich and used to servants. But it never crossed Erest's mind that the man might be lying about anything. About *everything*. He had wondered if maybe Aren might say he was looking for an adventurous boy to take on as an apprentice. He would bitterly resent Kevi being chosen for some wonderful apprenticeship, but he wouldn't exactly blame his brother for going. Or for coming back with wonderful stories about all kinds of adventures in Markand silk orchards.

He would *try* not to blame him.

Dinner was special. Erest's mother and sisters and the other women had baked pies with beef and beets and parsnips, and cooked crayfish in cream, and made loaves of soda bread with wheat flour and flat cakes with amaranth flour, and baked apple pies with more of the cream poured through holes in the top crust while they were still hot from the oven. Erest's father and the other men came in from seeing the farm settled for the night, stamping the dust off their boots and full of compliments about Cherest Aren's bay mare, which they'd paused to admire on their way in.

Tomren came closest to suspecting Aren. Not generally untrusting, Erest's father nevertheless wondered how a man with a horse of that quality came to be traveling so hard and lonely. "For she's a pretty thing," he declared in his deep, heavy voice. "Good legs on her, and a good, deep chest, but she's not the sort I'd expect to see way out here in the drylands. More suitable for riding out in the city, I'd think. I guess you must be in a hurry to get on about your business, for she came in fair blown. I saw how long it took my boy to walk her cool."

Erest looked at his father quickly, for despite Tomren's mild tone, there might have been a criticism in those words for the mare's hard use, and he recognized that he, too, had been uneasy about their guest's handling of her. Only he hadn't let himself say anything, or even think about it.

"Ah, well, she loves to run," answered their guest, smiling and unoffended. "That suited me today, for it's true I like to leave the dust behind me when I travel. It's also true I was grateful for your son relieving me of the chore of walking her down. He's good with all the stock, I'm sure."

"He is," granted Tomren. "All my sons know their way around the stock."

Kevi ducked his head and pretended to be much absorbed by the beef and parsnips to hide his pleasure in the compliment. Erest looked away, because these days the best he could do was handle the chores with the hens and some of the milking.

Cherest Aren turned his smile on Kevi, who now exclaimed, "He's going all the way to Markand! He has a silk orchard there. Did you know silk comes from *worms?* It's true!"

"It is," his father agreed. "Or so I've heard, though linen's a good deal more practical for folk like us." He nodded to Aren. "Not much need for men like you to work with linen, I expect. Silk's different, I guess. Those worms are touchy, maybe, seeing you're in such a hurry to get on your way. Even so, if you don't mind advice from a plain man, you might want to take tomorrow's journey at an easier pace. No matter her love of speed, I expect you'll find that mare's willing to ease up, and would be the better for a gentler journey than I think she's had today."

Erest was embarrassed that his father would put his opinion forward like that, but also uneasily glad that he had, for the mare's sake. He was also relieved their important guest only laughed and agreed easily, with no trace of offense.

He took a few pieces of dried apple to the mare after dinner, and pieces for the plow horses and mules too so they wouldn't feel hard done by. The mare was resting quietly, he was glad to see, with no sign that she'd taken the least harm from her fast pace. He fed her a few more apple slices, patted her neck again, and went to bed uncertain about what he thought of Cherest Aren, who was so friendly and interesting, but didn't necessarily seem kind or thoughtful.

Erest dreamed all night about riding that bay mare along roads that ran out forever, always approaching the high walls of a distant city but never reaching the gate. Then the dream changed, so that he rode instead through orchards of tall trees. Clouds of moths fluttered among the leaves, and silk in every color streamed from the branches. His heart lifted to see the bright silk, and to feel the light flex and give of the mare beneath him, and he knew there was no end to the orchard and he was glad of it.

He flinched later, remembering that stupid dream. Because, of course, when he woke early the next morning, Cherest Aren was already gone, and so was Kevi.

When Kevi didn't turn up at dawn to see to the milch goats and pick out the stalls in the stable, Erest was annoyed. He was even more annoyed by the time he finished all the stalls and filled the water buckets by himself, taking twice as long as anyone else because he had to carry just one bucket at a time. But all morning, he just assumed his younger brother had gone out early to talk to nice, friendly Cherest Aren before their guest went on his way. He assumed Kevi had given in to the urge to run alongside the mare for a bit when Aren rode out of the farmstead, and then that he had gone on down to the river, skipping out on his chores so he could daydream about Markand and climbing trees to pick leaves for the silk worms. It was infuriating because at eleven Kevi was old enough to know better, but Erest just planned to make his brother do all the evening chores to make up for it.

Only when Kevi didn't turn up for the noon meal did Erest start to wonder. But even then no one else seemed inclined to worry. Aunt Laria, Uncle Gilad's wife, only said tartly that if Kevi wanted to dawdle by the river all day, he needn't think she'd let him steal so much as a slice of soda bread before supper and serve him right if he perished of hunger beforehand. The men didn't even know he was missing; they'd gone off early to repair the stone walls that fenced the farther pastures, taking leftover meat pastries with them, with no plans to come back much before sundown.

But Erest, who was supposed to see to the kitchen garden first thing after the noon meal, left the garden after pouring a token bucket or two of water over the melons and then made his clumsy way down to the river. He was faster now than he had been when the crutch was new to him; he knew how to balance and swing himself along, and the path was smooth enough.

He meant to smack Kevi and yell at him for leaving all his work for everyone else; he meant to drag his brother back bodily if necessary. He could do it with one arm and still manage the crutch. Kevi wasn't big for eleven, and Erest's arms and shoulders and back were strong from having to take so much of his weight for months.

He didn't admit to himself he was worried until he checked all the best crayfish holes, and the deep pool where the big cottonwood had a rope you could swing out on and fall, splashing, into the cool water.

He couldn't find Kevi anywhere.

All those wasted hours, resentful and annoyed as he dealt with the chores and then resentful and annoyed as he searched up and down the river. And all the time...Erest felt sick every minute that it took to make his way back up to the main house, thinking about where his little brother might have really been all that time. Carried away by a man who had turned out to be nothing like he seemed, every hoofbeat taking him farther away from his home and his family. Aren would take Kevi to Markand, no doubt, where he would climb a lot of trees whether he was afraid or not. Unless the man sold him to someone worse than a silk farmer.

He was surprised, when he reached the house, to find that his mother believed him at once. She rang the bell to summon the men almost before Erest had finished his confused explanations and accusations. He understood later that his mother had begun to wonder already, probably even sooner than he had himself. That she had heard his stumbling account of searching along the river with terror but without surprise.

His father, summoned so hastily, had said nothing at all. He had only listened to his wife's quick, sharp, "I think that man took our boy," and nodded once. A single glance had sent the other grown men running to ready the horses and mules, and they were out of the farmstead's yard and hidden in a rising cloud of dust while the echo of those words still seemed to ring in Erest's ears.

Erest hadn't insisted on going with the men. He had thought of it. He had wanted to. But all the way back from the river, all the time while waiting for the men to come in answer to the bell, he had already been thinking *They'll never catch up.* He'd been thinking, *Someone has to go find the Kieba.* And he had known already who that had to be.

He was the one to whom she had given the geode with its bright amethysts. He had spoken to her once, and she hadn't been angry, or hadn't seemed angry.

And if she was angry this time...well, if she *was* angry, Erest was the one with a crippled foot. The one whose life had already been taken away. If someone had to pay a price for disturbing the Kieba, who else would be a better choice?

Someone had to go. Someone had to do it. If Cerest Aren was truly a child-thief, if the Kieba wouldn't help, then Kevi would never come back. Erest's family would never be able to catch up to Aren, not with him mounted on that fine mare and all of them on farm horses and mules. They would *never know* what had happened to Kevi. It was too terrible to think about.

Erest was certain the Kieba would help. She *had* to help.

But he could not tell, now that he actually faced her, whether her view of the disaster was at all the same as his own.

The Kieba tilted her head thoughtfully. She did seem willing to listen, though her expression was cool rather than friendly. Erest said fast, "The man took Kevi this morning or maybe late last night, and my father and everybody went after them, only the man got away hours and hours before we figured it out, and he has a fast horse and all we have is plow horses and mules. They won't catch them, they can't, not on heavy horses like ours, so the man will get to Estenda and then he'll sell my brother, and we can't stop him."

The Kieba still said nothing. She might have been thinking about anything, maybe about something else that had nothing to do with Kevi or the child-thief. Erest hesitated. Then he said cautiously, "You could—"

"Yes," said the Kieba, her tone thoughtful.

"I mean," said Erest, "I know about the wall now. I know your law." He stopped, his mouth suddenly dry. He had not expected to be afraid. He hadn't been afraid when he'd realized he had to come here and tell the Kieba and get her to help. Now, face to face with her, and with her sounding so distant and hardly interested, he *was* afraid. He swallowed hard.

The Kieba said nothing to help him. Her expression was abstracted, as though she were thinking of other things.

Erest tried to sound as steady and brave as his father that other time. "I know there's a price, sometimes. Usually. I know that now. If there's a price to pay, then I'll pay it." He added in a rush, "I'm no good anyway, not with this foot. Kevi's more use than me and he's only eleven. And he may be a brat, but he doesn't deserve to be dragged off and *sold* someplace, and you *said* you like to see my family happy, you *said* that, and everybody knows slavery's against your law—"

"Yes," said the Kieba again. "I am already

searching."

"You are?" Erest's voice squeaked embarrassingly. He went hot.

"Yes," said the Kieba patiently. She studied Erest. "You came here expecting that you might have to pay my price for your trespass. You came to me because your injury makes you useless, do I understand correctly? You determined that your brother is worth more to your family than you, and so you came to find me. Sit. Show me your foot." She nodded toward a nearby flattish rock.

Erest stared at her. Then he hobbled to the rock, lowered himself carefully down on it, crooked his left foot over his right knee, and carefully unpinned the cloth in which he wrapped his foot now that it was impossible either to wear shoes or go barefoot. The shape of his foot became clear as the cloth came away. He had to force himself not to look away from the part that was left. He pretended that the foot he was looking at was just an object, neither ugly nor even very interesting.

From beside his big toe straight across to the opposite side of his heel, his foot was just missing. The scar along that side of his foot was raised and smooth and shiny and, at the moment, bright pink with overuse.

The Kieba considered the foot, and then shifted her gaze back to Erest's face. "I cannot restore the missing part. It was an unfortunate wound. But you have forgiven your brother for it, I see, though the injury has rendered you so useless to your family."

"I try not to let him see..."

"The scar? Or that it hurts you? Or that you feel you have become useless? Either way or all together, it's kind of you to hide your distress. Especially from the one who dealt the blow."

Erest didn't admit that at first he'd gone out of his way to make his brother feel guilty. He had been so angry, and he hadn't even been able to make himself look at his foot. He'd kept thinking the accident with the ax was just a dream, that it hadn't really happened, or at least not to him. That ugly thing wasn't *his* foot. *He* wasn't crippled.

Then Kevi had tried to run away. Erest was the only one who knew that. He'd caught his brother wrapping up half a loaf of bread and a change of clothes, and he'd realized...not that he'd gone too far, exactly. More that he'd just been wrong.

He said, "It wasn't his fault. It really wasn't. We were both fooling around. I should have known better—I did know better. I was so stupid. Playing around with an ax!"

The helpless, horrified fury of it came back; the bitter rage of learning just how crippled he was and what that would mean, and of knowing it was his fault as much as anybody's. He rubbed a hand hard across his mouth and managed to add, "Thank you for sending your wasps, Kieba. They helped." They had helped a lot. They had taken away some of the pain and all of the infection.

It hadn't been enough. He was still crippled. But he didn't say that.

"Mm." The Kieba didn't seem to really be paying attention. "Of course, you are trying to bear too much weight on it, without proper support. And it is still healing. And the nerves and bones...hmm." There was no pity in her tone. More an abstracted thoughtfulness. She put out her other hand and a rod of iron and crystal fell out of the air and into her hand.

It was about as thick as Erest's thumb, twice as long as his hand, made of twisted black iron with twin threads of black crystal running around it from one end to the other. From the way the Kieba held it, it must be heavy; heavier than it looked.

The Kieba traced a fingertip down the line of the crystal, from one end of the rod to the other and back again. Then she bent, grasped Erest's heel firmly and drew the tip of the rod quickly across the edge of the mostly-healed wound. She did it again. The scar grew less pink, and the ache eased.

"There," said the Kieba, straightening and carelessly tossing the crystalline rod back into the air, where it vanished. "That should be somewhat improved."

Erest wanted to ask whether her kindness meant she wouldn't after all demand a price for his trespass. But somehow he felt it would be wrong to ask anything like that. He said instead, "Thank you. Thank you very much, Kieba. It's much better. But Kevi—"

"Yes."

"They won't catch them. You can find them. I know you can. Only no one else would ask you. Not fast enough, anyway. Not until it might be too late even for you." He took a deep breath. Then looking her in the face, he added, "I'm not a baby now. I'm almost fifteen. I know all the stories and I guess maybe some of them are true. If there's a price, I will pay it. If it's my life for my brother's, that's—" he hesitated because no matter how bad his foot was, he couldn't make himself say *That's all right*. He said at last, remembering what his father had said, "That's just. If you save Kevi."

"Do you say so?" said the Kieba, but a little absently, as though most of her attention was on something else. Then she said, "This child-thief will have known your family would pursue him. He will have ridden fast for the border." Her mouth twisted a little in an expression Erest could not read, and she added, "Once he is a day's ride away, you are correct, your family would never come up with him. Even if your father did not turn back, as I expect he would not. Once this thief crosses into Estenda, he believes you will have no recourse at all."

Erest nodded dumbly.

"I am your recourse. You need not fear for your brother."

She sounded so certain. Erest believed her immediately.

"I have been recently too much occupied with other matters, perhaps. I was not aware...you say this has become a common practice, this theft of children?"

Erest didn't know what to say. He was afraid to say *yes* in case the Kieba took his answer as an accusation. He didn't want to say *no* in case she thought it wasn't a problem worth pursuing. He said at last, "If it happens at all, isn't that too often?"

"Yes," said the Kieba, in a thoughtful tone. "Yes. I think you are right. I think I need not have much patience with these persons who steal children. Better if someone had informed me of the practice. I have become too remote from ordinary folk, perhaps. I think...well, we shall see. Ah, now, there we are."

Erest stared at her. She sounded exactly like someone who had found something she'd mislaid, but surely that was too fast...

"And the thief, indeed," murmured the Kieba. Her gaze had drifted away from Erest; she gazed vaguely at the air a foot to his left. "Farther from this place than I expected. They have indeed been traveling swiftly today."

"But—" said Erest.

The Kieba blinked, and looked back at him. "All is well. One of my servants has found your brother: one of my little owls, swift and keen-sighted in the darkest night. My owls are neither the greatest nor the most impressive of my servants, but this one will prove adequate to its task. You wish to see?" She gestured, and a large circular slab of soapy-looking black crystal appeared, standing upright in the air.

Erest stared. Then he grabbed his crutch and scrambled up to look more closely. The crystal wasn't really stone, because its surface rippled heavily when the Kieba touched it, like a liquid that was much thicker than water but thinner than molasses. The black surface clouded as though she had breathed on it, and then cleared. Only now it wasn't like stone at all; it was like looking through a window of smoky glass, and suddenly they were looking out across a flat campsite near the river.

The sun was low in the west, the river blazing like fire in its light. Big cottonwoods leaned out over the water. The mare was tethered under the trees, her saddle lying on the ground not far from her hooves. Her head was low; she had worked hard all day and she was tired. Erest was sure Aren had not cared for her as carefully as he ought, and then was ashamed for worrying about the mare when all his attention should have been on his brother.

He could see his brother perfectly plainly. A little flame blazed within a circle of stones, a small frying pan set over the stones to heat. Erest could hear the crackle of the fire and the wind in the cottonwood leaves; when the mare shifted her weight and blew, he heard that, too. Kevi sat on an upended log by the fire, huddling down into himself. He wasn't crying. That seemed good. But he was sitting very still. Too still. Kevi never sat so still.

The danger to Kevi seemed so much more real and immediate now that Erest could see him, see how frightened his brother was. He wanted to ask the Kieba if she was *sure* she could protect his brother, but he was afraid to offend her. Besides, he was afraid of speaking out loud, in case his voice should carry to that other place, that campsite, and Cherest Aren should hear him.

"A farsight mirror, made of the living crystal of the mountain," murmured the Kieba. "You may speak, if you wish. It is my mirror, not theirs. They cannot see or hear us."

"Oh," said Erest, trying not to sound too amazed. "Kevi—he *is* safe? Can you—can you *reach* through your mirror?"

"One can only listen and observe. But your brother is safe. I promise you."

Erest nodded, believing her.

Cherest Aren, if that were truly his name, was just coming back to the fire with his arms filled with wood gathered below the cottonwoods. Even now, after riding fast all day, he looked almost as polished as when he'd come down the road from the city and asked so politely whether they might have a room to let out for travelers. But now, even though he still looked well-to-do and civilized and everything, he didn't look at all *nice*. He stood on the other side of the fire, smiling at Kevi. It was not a kind smile. It was the sort of smile that suggested Aren knew how upset and scared Kevi was, and knew that he had caused this misery, and didn't care.

"It's not so bad," Aren said. His tone was light and cool and faintly mocking. "The man I have in mind for you isn't a bad sort, you know. He sells boys on to Markand merchants. They treat indentured boys well in Markand. Maybe you'll enjoy your new life. Some boys do, I expect."

Kevi didn't look up, but he rubbed the back of his hand across his face, so Erest knew he was crying, or maybe trying not to cry.

"My advice to you is, learn to smile. People like a cheerful boy. You'll likely go to a better situation if you smile."

Kevi stubbornly refused to look up. He certainly made no attempt to smile or look cheerful.

"Ah well," said Aren, his tone was still lightly mocking, yet not without an appalling kind of sympathy. "Never mind. You'll have days and weeks to learn to put on a smile. But try to take my advice, boy. It'll go better for you in the end."

Kevi spat into the fire, which sizzled and leaped up.

Erest leaned forward, tense, as Aren frowned. He was afraid his brother's abductor might become angry, except the Kieba had said Kevi was safe. If she said so, surely it was true.

A little owl, tawny wings flashing silently, darted through the gathering dusk. It called, a sharp *te-whit, te-whit*, as it flew. Aren's bay mare jerked back and tossed her head uneasily, her ears flicking back and then forward. The owl flew fast in a circle and dropped to perch on a cottonwood branch above Kevi's head.

"There we are," murmured the Kieba. "So you see that your brother is safe."

Erest stared at her, incredulous. "It's so small—"

"It's not what it seems. Other servants of mine will follow, but the owl is enough. Watch."

The owl was tiny. But if the Kieba was satisfied, Erest knew—hoped—believed that it must be fiercer than seemed possible.

Cherest Aren had glanced at the owl in surprise when it had flown into the light of the fire, but seemed to have no suspicion it might be anything out of the ordinary. Kevi gulped and rubbed his hand across his face and got to his feet as though he somehow guessed it carried the Kieba's mark and her attention; as though he guessed it was her servant and hoped it might hold a promise of safety. Maybe he did guess it. He'd grown up hearing that story about Erest and the Kieba. Maybe he'd guessed, before anyone else, that Erest might go to the Kieba. Maybe he'd hoped all this long day that the Kieba would reach out her hand to stop Aren.

Even if Kevi hadn't guessed it from the first second, Erest thought his brother ought to figure it out pretty fast. The owl certainly wasn't acting like an ordinary owl. It cried again, wings half spread, bobbing its head aggressively at Cherest Aren. Then it launched itself into the air, flew in a circle, and came down fast, straight at the man.

Aren jerked back with a startled cry, snatched up a burning stick from the fire, and struck out at it. But the owl dodged and swooped, and suddenly Aren shouted and dropped the stick, blood springing crimson on his hand. The owl caught up the stick before it could fall to the ground. That stick should have been too big for the little owl to carry and the flames, streaming back as it flew, almost engulfed it, but it didn't seem to mind either the weight or the fire. It flew in a circle again, gathering speed, flames trailing behind it like the tail streaming out behind a spring comet. This was too much for the mare, which had already been uneasy. She reared up, broke her tether, and galloped away into the drylands. Erest exclaimed, and Cherest Aren shouted after her, but the owl darted at his face, threatening him now with fire as well as sharp talons, driving him backward, his arms over his face.

The owl dropped the burning stick into the fire and flew back to Kevi. Erest's brother put out an arm, maybe meaning to ward it off, but the owl landed on the boy's wrist, delicately, careful of its talons. Kevi slowly lowered his arm, staring at it, and the owl drew itself up to its full diminutive height and said *te-whit* to him, but very softly.

Cherest Aren cursed, staring. Then he visibly gathered his nerve, seized up the pan from its place over the fire, and stalked forward.

Erest leaned forward, half reaching toward the Kieba's mirror and then flinching away before his hand fell on its surface, afraid he might somehow disrupt her magic. "Doesn't he know it's your owl?" he asked, desperate for reassurance.

"He is a fool, perhaps," murmured the Kieba. "He would do better to run. Though flight would avail him nothing. Do not fear. The owl alone would be enough, but another of my servants will arrive very soon. Ah, yes. There."

A stag had stepped delicately out from among the shadows cast by the cottonwoods. It was one of the ordinary blacktailed deer, but bigger than any deer Erest had ever seen. Its head was black, its long neck dappled with silver, its shoulders bronze, its legs as black as its head. Its antlers gleamed with firelight, streaked with light red as blood; the last light of the sun pooled in its eyes and turned them to fire. It took a step forward and then another, setting each small hoof down with precise deliberation. One step and another, turning its beautiful long head to gaze across the fire at Cherest Aren.

The man backed up, his mouth open, stunned. The owl was forgotten. The frying pan fell from his hand, clattering on the rocky earth. The stag made no sound at all, but lowered its antlers, the tines glittering sharp as knives. Muscles rippled in its haunches as it gathered itself.

Aren dodged sideways before it could charge, running for the cottonwoods—that was a good idea, the best he could do, though Erest bet he wished he'd tied his horse better. He laughed out loud—he couldn't help himself—at the man's frantic scramble to get up into one of the trees before the stag reached him. The Kieba smiled slightly.

"But how do you make them do that?" Erest asked her. "The owl, and the stag? Even if they *are* servants of yours?"

"It is not an owl," said the Kieba, her tone a little

absent. "Nor is that truly a stag. They are made in those forms so that they may go freely to and fro in the world." She had been gazing at the events unfolding in her magic window, but now glanced at Erest. "You are satisfied that your brother is safe?"

Erest looked quickly back at the mirror.

Kevi was still standing by the fire. He seemed stunned, blank. His gaze was on the stag, which was now stepping softly around the cottonwood tree in which Cherest Aren had taken shelter, placing each small hoof carefully, tossing its head and snorting. There was good grass along the river, but the stag did not seem interested in grazing. It looked like it would be perfectly happy to wait all night for Aren to venture out of the tree.

But Kevi did not look like he felt safe. He looked uncertain and frightened.

Then the little owl nibbled his hair and murmured *te-whit* in his ear, and at last Kevi smiled. A little shakily, but he smiled. He stroked the owl's breast, streaked tawny gold and buff, and the owl fluffed up its feathers and then smoothed them down again, blinking its golden eyes.

"So he is quite safe. He will meet your father on the road," the Kieba said, in a tone of mild satisfaction.

"He can't go far....He's only eleven, and you can see he's tired already ..."

"Indeed."

The Kieba said nothing more, but the stag tossed its head once more beneath the cottonwood tree. Firelight slid across the smooth, sharp tines of its antlers until they looked like metal, edges sharp as the blade of an ax.

Then it turned, light on its hooves for all its muscular strength, and came back toward Kevi, leaving Aren in his tree as though the man were of so little account it had already forgotten him. The stag minced delicately around the fire and, just as Kevi began to back away, knelt and then lay down, turning its head to gaze at the boy in clear invitation. Or maybe in command. When Kevi still hesitated, the little owl flew suddenly from his arm, flicked around in a quick circle, and perched instead in the crown of those spreading antlers.

Kevi laughed. He straightened his shoulders and nodded, as though coming to a decision, and came forward to hold out his hand to the stag. It snuffled his fingers, and Kevi patted its neck as though it were a horse, rested his palm for a moment on its withers, and then scrambled up to sit on its back.

The stag rose to its feet with a swift rocking lunge, but obviously with a care for the boy on its back. Kevi pressed his hands against its neck, gripped with his legs, and didn't fall off. He straightened carefully once the stag was standing, then seemed to decide he was all right, and patted the stag. It snorted, flicking its enormous ears.

Then it walked out of the firelight and into the darkness, the owl riding in its antlers and Kevi on its back. Erest thought none of them were going to look back, except at the last moment, his brother turned his head and stared back at the man in the tree just for a second or two. He didn't laugh or point or call out. Only that one look, an unexpectedly solemn expression on his young face. Then he turned his face forward again, and he and the stag and the owl all vanished into the dark.

But the view of the campsite was still clear, and Erest made a wordless sound of protest as Cherest Aren slipped boldly from the cottonwood, took one step after boy and stag and owl, turned, and ran instead after his horse. Erest turned urgently to the Kieba, pointing. "He might—the mare—he might find her. He could still get away. Would you let him go? After what he tried to do?"

The Kieba tilted her head, unsmiling. "Calm yourself. Watch."

Erest turned back to the mirror in time to see one gray shadow and then another slip through the campsite and disappear into the dark, following Aren's trail. Smoke gray dappled with charcoal, long and lithe-bodied, they were cats—but much larger than farm cats. Larger, even, than the stock dogs that worked the cattle. Erest had not had any idea cats could be so large, but he guessed that Cherest Aren would not enjoy being their prey.

A tree would not save him a second time. Cats could climb.

"They won't harm the mare, though?" he asked, without quite realizing beforehand that he meant to protest that idea. Those cats were clearly large enough to hunt a horse, if they found one trailing its tether far from the protection of stable walls. "It's not her fault that man took Kevi—" he added, and broke off, because that sounded stupid even to him. But it was *true* and he said again, not confident but sure he was right, "Nothing is her fault. She doesn't deserve to be hunted by giant cats. She's already tired. She could run herself to death just for fear of them, and it's not *fair*."

The Kieba regarded him without noticeable annoyance. "Shall I send a less frightening servant of mine to bring that mare to a place where she will be safe and comfortable?"

Erest hadn't expected this offer, and for an instant was too startled to answer. Then, embarrassed, he caught hold of his wits. "Yes! Please, Kieba. If it's not too much trouble—if you don't mind. Thank you!"

She nodded gravely. "I think it will prove very little trouble. Perhaps I may have use for a mare of that quality myself. Do not trouble your mind for the beast. She will come safely through the night and the day that follows. My servants will not harry her; they will hunt only this thief of children. I will send another, kinder servant to guide her gently where she should go."

Erest let out a breath he hadn't realized he'd been holding. "Thank you," he said again.

She nodded back, somber, and touched the black stone of her window. Its surface rippled as the image faded. She made the crystal mirror vanish again with a casual gesture and asked Erest, "You are satisfied that your brother is safe?"

"Yes," agreed Erest. "Of course." He only then realized why she might have asked. His life for his brother's—and Kevi was safe. He stared at her, unable to move or look away. He didn't believe she would put him to death—he didn't believe she would imprison him in a lightless prison deep within her mountain—he definitely didn't believe she would turn him into a deer or a cat. But he was afraid anyway. He was afraid of all those things, even though he didn't believe any of it would happen. His insides all clenched tight.

Erest hadn't realized until that moment that he was scared—really scared. As soon as he realized it, he was deeply ashamed. He had promised he would pay her price—he had come here knowing he might have to pay it. The Kieba had done her part: she'd found Kevi, and gotten him away from the man who had stolen him, and now she was bringing him back to his family. She had even agreed to send a servant after the mare! After all that, only a coward would try to get out of paying her price. But he *was* a coward. He hadn't known that about himself until this moment.

He pretended as hard as he could that he was actually brave. After a moment, he managed to say, "Yes, he's safe. So if—" but he couldn't say the rest of it. He shut his eyes in shame.

"Your mother has come after you," the Kieba told him.

Erest's eyes flew open. "No," he said. He stared at

her. "Kieba—my mother—you won't—it wouldn't be right—"

"No," said the Kieba. "Do not fear for her. Your mother is quite safe. She may come up, and I will speak with her. You may speak with her as well."

Erest swallowed. He was almost sure the Kieba meant, *So you can tell her goodbye*, but he was afraid to ask. He didn't want to know for sure.

Erest's mother had come, just as the Kieba had said. She had crossed the wall and climbed up the slopes of the mountain in the dusk. The moon, already visible, was nearly full. Now the Kieba set all the stone of the mountain alight as well, with a soft white glow very like the moonlight. Erest's mother had been walking fast, almost running. She missed her step when the unexpected light bloomed around her, but caught the branch of a twisted oak to steady herself. She saw them then: the Kieba first, then Erest near her. She straightened, staring at the Kieba, wordless. Erest wanted to go to her, but he didn't dare. He balanced on his good foot, gripped his crutch hard, and didn't move.

His mother stood for a moment, and then came the rest of the way more slowly and stood facing the Kieba, her face still.

"Elina," the Kieba said gently, "Your young Kevi is safe. He is under my eye and within my hand. All who went out after him are safe: even now I watch over them. Soon your son will come to his father. They will camp where they are tonight, for their animals will be spent and all of them will need rest. But they will come back to you tomorrow. Nothing will harm them. The man who stole your son is within my hand. I have several questions I wish to ask him. He will not escape my attention, I promise you."

Erest's mother understood at once what the Kieba

311

hadn't promised. She said, "Thank you, Kieba. I am so grateful. Truly. But, if you will permit me to ask—is *Erest* safe?"

"Erest is no longer a child. He knew well enough he broke my law to cross the wall. You know it, too."

Erest's mother gazed at the Kieba, but not in surprise, Erest thought. It was the way she might have stared at a winter storm racing across the drylands: knowing calves would be lost in the flash floods and the winter wheat ruined under the pounding hail, but also knowing that storms are part of winter and nothing you can do will turn them. She said, a little disjointedly, "Kevi—when that man—I should have come to you myself—"

"Yes," said the Kieba. "If you or Tomren had come to me, I would have reached out my hand to take up Kevi and asked no price at all."

Erest stared at her, stunned. He opened his mouth and closed it again, unable to think of anything to say. Or it was more like he thought of a thousand things to say all at once, but then couldn't get any of those things clear enough to actually say it.

His mother looked just the way Erest felt. She shook her head, slowly, as though she was trying to make herself believe she'd heard it wrong, that the Kieba had actually said something else. She started to speak, but stopped, exactly as Erest had.

"You, I will send home, however," the Kieba said to Elina. She was smiling a little, but her expression was impossible to read. "Lest all the women of your steading follow, seeking you and having no fear of me. And then the children in their turn, and at last, no doubt, the dogs."

Erest's mother's lips tightened as the Kieba spoke. She stood straight, lifted her chin, and said, "We owe you so much, and now I have to ask you for so much more. But it's unkind of you to mock me."

The Kieba did not stop smiling, but her smile changed somehow, becoming more human, or at least more familiar. She walked forward to take Erest's mother's hands. She said, but gently this time "I am not mocking you, Elina. I am humbled by your bravery. When I saw Erest had come up the mountain, I thought you would come as well. I am even pleased you have come seeking your son."

This took Erest's mother thoroughly by surprise. He saw all at once that she was almost in tears. She started to speak, hesitated, and then said, with a quiet dignity he had somehow not expected, "But you are not pleased Erest came to seek you for his brother's sake?"

"Oh, he has pleased me as well," answered the Kieba. Letting go of Elina's hands, she turned to look at Erest. "I asked whether you would be willing to trade your life for your brother's," she reminded him. "You said you would."

Erest wanted to fling himself down at her feet and beg to be allowed to go home, but somehow he couldn't, with his mother watching. He straightened his shoulders and said, "Yes. I said I would pay your price. I will." He sounded stiff even to himself, but he couldn't help that.

"Yes," said the Kieba. She turned her head, gazed out at the wide moonswept reaches of the drylands. She said quietly, almost to herself but not really, "I seldom take human servants. I seldom see much need for them. Nothing important evades my eye or my hand...unless, from time to time, I cease to pay attention. Then all manner of wickedness may slip by. This practice of child-theft should have come to my attention. But I had allowed myself to become too remote. I did not notice it." She turned back to Erest and spoke gravely. "Sometimes, when my attention turns too far from human concerns, I find human servants useful. They may go here and there among the peoples of the world, watching and listening and carrying always their own independent point of view. They may bear me word of troubles too small and trivial for me to otherwise notice."

Erest did not know what to say. It was obvious what the Kieba meant, but it seemed incredible. He couldn't even imagine what kinds of things a servant of hers would need to know, but he was sure he didn't know any of them. And his foot—he started to say, *But I'm crippled.* But he stopped himself. He didn't want to sound stupid—she hadn't actually *said*—

The Kieba tilted her head, watching him. "There are more plagues now than for many years; there is a great deal that must command my attention. I am much engaged with that work. Yet I do not wish to become entirely inattentive to the affairs of ordinary folk. But a servant of mine must be willing to step aside from his home and go out into the world, wherever I may choose to send him. He need not renounce his family—not to offer me the sort of service I wish from you. He may come and go from his family's home. But when I call him, he must leave those he loves and go where I bid, about such tasks as I may set."

"But—" said Erest, and stopped.

"Your injury need not trouble you. I think you will find that time and appropriate treatment will carry the healing forward farther than you now imagine, and the proper sort of boot will compensate for the remaining difficulty. Nor need you expect to walk out upon the road when I send you here or there. I will supply a suitable mount. I imagine that mare may prove her worth."

Now Erest couldn't speak for a different reason. This was all too much to readily grasp.

"A servant of mine must be brave, and clever enough, and he must have a good heart. It is a hard thing to lay on a man. Easier, in some ways, for a boy who is not quite fifteen. No doubt many boys in the world would do. But I think you will do well."

Erest still didn't know what to say. He looked helplessly to his mother.

She moved a step closer to him, but she looked only at the Kieba.

But the Kieba still spoke to Erest. "Some of the things I will ask of you will be hard. There would be many years during which you would dwell in one kingdom or another, learning the tenor of life in that place, discovering whether customs had arisen that contravene my law, whether there might be any matter of which I should be informed. But always you would come back. It would not be the life your mother's son might have expected to lead. But I think that life might not displease you."

"But—" said Erest. He looked quickly at his mother and then back at the Kieba. "You—are you sure? I mean, I hardly know... well, anything, except about milking cows and planting and ordinary things like that—"

"You will learn," said the Kieba. "You were curious enough to cross my wall when you were a child, and brave enough to cross it again now in answer to your brother's need. I would not suggest this course for you if I believed you were not fit."

Again, Erest looked at his mother.

This time she came to him quickly. She started to brush the hair back out of his face, but then drew back. "You're so young," she said, but wistfully. "But of all my children, you're...you never...even more than Little Tom, even more than Kevi, you always want to run ahead, and you never turn back. I thought I would...I never wanted...but I don't want to hold you back, Erest." She turned to the Kieba. "But I'm sure there's risk—"

"There is risk in everything," the Kieba said gently.

"A fall in the river, a bone caught in the throat, a stranger who is less friendly than he seems. It is not safe to live. No one who lives fails to die."

Erest's mother nodded wistfully. "Well, but from what you say, he wouldn't leave us forever? He would come back sometimes?"

"His life would belong to me and not to you, nor to himself. Still, it is not my intention nor my wish to leave your family bereft," the Kieba said, still gently. "Even I cannot know with certainty what the future holds. But, Elina, children grow up, and often they leave you. That is the nature of children. You know that. I think Erest would do well in the service I require. But there are other boys. Shall I choose another?"

"No!" said Erest. The idea of a new life, a different life where he would go everywhere and see everything...a life where his foot would be, if not exactly healed, at least better...a life where he would be *useful*...he wanted that. He was astonished at how much he wanted it. He looked anxiously at his mother, not knowing how to say any of this. But he thought she might understand. He hoped she would.

"I will take your son because he has put himself into my hand and because he will be useful to me and because he wishes it for himself," the Kieba said to his mother. "But, Elina, in days to come, don't fear me. You need not. For you and for your family, the wall is merely a marker: you should respect it, but you need not fear to cross it. If a child climbs the wall, anyone may come and fetch him. Or if there is trouble of a serious kind, if you need me, then any of your family may come up the mountain."

"Oh," said Elina. Erest could see that his mother wasn't sure whether this promise was a bribe or a payment or a gift, but she straightened a little, as though she had been carrying a weight and now it had been lifted. She looked at Erest and then back at the Kieba. She said at last, "I hope we will never have the need to impose on your generosity again. But we are very grateful."

"Yes," said the Kieba. "It is a liberty I had not thought to allow. I'm sure you will teach your children to be respectful and not to intrude without need. But as I told Tomren, I'm pleased to see your family flourish." She said all this without emphasis, and added in the same tone, to Erest, "Come. It isn't far." Then she walked away, out of the brilliant moonlight and into the jagged shadows of the mountain.

Erest swung his crutch around and followed her. He only looked back once. His mother was standing in the silvery light, gazing after him. She half lifted one hand, not quite a wave, and he did the same, and then turned again to follow the Kieba and didn't look back again.

ENDNOTES

I hope you enjoyed these stories! If you'd like to see more of any world or character—more than I've shown you in the novels and stories out so far—let me know. I'll keep requests in mind the next time I put together a collection.

If you enjoyed this or any other book of mine, I'd appreciate it if you would leave a review at **Goodreads** or **Amazon** or any other site you prefer.

ALSO BY

PRAISE FOR RACHEL NEUMEIER'S BOOKS

THE CITY IN THE LAKE

"It's the poetic, shimmering language and fascinating unfolding of worlds that elevates this engrossing story beyond its formula...Fans of Sharon Shinn's books will find a similar celebration of the natural world—from the dense darkness of a forest to the 'crystalline music' of the stars—in this vividly imagined debut."—Booklist, starred review.

"Oh my God, I was so not prepared for how awesome this book is. Prose, setting, story, characters, everything is top notch and I too loved this book."—Ana Grilo, the Book Smugglers.

THE FLOATING ISLANDS

An ALA Best Fiction for Young Adults selection
A Junior Library Guild selection
A Kirkus best-of-2011 selection

"Intelligent, richly detailed fantasy featuring two young cousins battered by losses, personal passions, and larger events...The author delineates complex characters, geographies and societies alike with a dab hand, deftly weaves them all—along with dragons of several sorts, mouthwatering kitchen talk, flashes of humor, and a late-blooming romance—into a suspenseful plot and delivers an outstanding tale that is self-contained but full of promise for sequels."— Kirkus Reviews, starred review.

HOUSE OF SHADOWS

"I loved *House of Shadows*. The characters, writing, and magic captivated me, but there was a lot to love in the details as well—the dragon, the cats who were characters in their own right, female characters with different situations and types of inner strength, and just a little bit of romance."—Kristen at Fantasy Book Café.

THE GRIFFIN MAGE TRILOGY

"The Griffin Mage Trilogy is recommended to anyone who enjoys a fantasy story that focuses on vivid storytelling with more emphasis on interaction instead of bold fighting."—Jasper de Joode, Fantasy Book Review.

"A theme running throughout the trilogy is the importance of trusting people with the freedom to make their own decisions, even if you may not like the result. The plot of *Lord of the Changing Winds* is full of difficult moral choices, so if you like your fantasy to be subtle and complex, this could be the trilogy for you."—Geraldine at Fantasy Reads.

THE KEEPER OF THE MIST

"Reminiscent of classic YA fantasy in the vein of *Howl's Moving Castle* and old-school Robin McKinley, *The Keeper of the Mist* is utterly, unequivocally awesome."—Thea James, The Book Smugglers.

THE WHITE ROAD OF THE MOON

"A richly rewarding stand-alone story evoking far more color than its titular tint might suggest."—Kirkus, starred review.

"An imaginative, slow-building YA fantasy... Neumeier [chooses to focus on] bonds of friendship and respect between the characters rather than romance. It's a refreshing change of pace from the pervasive romance-oriented young adult fantasies. ... reminded me distinctly of Robin McKinley's style."—Fantasy Literature blog.

WINTER OF ICE AND IRON

"Neumeier's writing has a spare, haunting quality...Best of all are her characters ... they work together beautifully, and their romance has a number of interesting and unconventional complications. The character's hook; the writing holds. It's comfort food, but more satisfying than most."—NK Jemisin, NYT book review.

"There's very little I can say that can even do any sort of justice to the wonderfully intricate story, the characters that get under your skin, and the intrigue seeping through the pages. ... You need to take your time with this, to become immersed, in this slow-burning fantasy that will reward you if you devote your time to it." —Utopia State of Mind blog.

ACKNOWLEDGMENTS

Elaine Thompson was kind enough to critique these stories; my brother Craig Neumeier also provided a critique. Michael and Linda Schiffer and Hanneke Nieuwenhuijzen read through the final manuscript and caught a few more inconsistencies and questionable details, plus (as always) a truly startling number of typos. Thank you all!

Robert Massey came up with the title for this collection, which was inspired by a Lord Dunsany collection called *Beyond the Fields We Know*. Thanks, Robert! Much appreciated! It's a great title, and as we all know, *titles are hard.*

Made in the USA
Middletown, DE
08 September 2018